After Hours

Jenny Oldfield was born in Yorkshire in 1949 and studied English at university. She has had stories published in magazines such as *Bella*, *Woman & Home* and *Cosmopolitan*, and has written crime novels, and books for young adults. She lives in Ilkley with her two children.

JENNY OLDFIELD

After Hours

❖

PAN BOOKS

First published in paperback 1996 by Pan Books
and simultaneously in hardback by Macmillan

imprints of Macmillan General Books
25 Eccleston Place, London SW1W 9NF
and Basingstoke

Associated companies throughout the world

ISBN 0-330-34187-1

3 5 7 9 8 6 4 2

A CIP catalogue record for this book is available from
the British Library

Typeset by CentraCet Limited, Cambridge
Printed and bound in Great Britain by
Cox and Wyman Ltd, Reading, Berkshire

For the Holmes family of Beckwithshaw

PART ONE

For better, for worse

CHAPTER ONE

November 1923

The great Wurlitzer rose into the auditorium as Sadie Parsons settled into her plush velvet seat. Richie Palmer had brought her along to the Picturedrome as a special treat. The organ came into view with a cascade of rich notes which rang out through the vast cinema. Overhead, the projection light flickered, cigarette smoke mingled with dancing motes of dust. Onscreen, the titles came up for the cartoon shorts.

'Hurrah, it's Felix!' someone in front stood up and yelled in a raw voice of recognition. An animated drawing of a cheeky cat strutted across the screen, while the organist played his 'Keep on Walking' signature tune. The front row went wild.

'Sit down!' another voice called from further back. 'And take off yer hat!'

The enthusiastic boy in the wide flat cap subsided into his seat, then subtitles appeared with a moving ball of light which bounced from word to word in time with the music. A thousand people sang as Felix the Cat danced the Braziliane.

Wreathed in smiles, Sadie joined in. It was Saturday night in a miserable November. The year of 1923 was grinding to a close amid more food shortages and strikes in London's East End. Victory in the Great War seemed hollow to the maimed men bearing placards who still trudged the streets of Southwark looking in vain for work. But here, in the fabulous new Picturedrome, singing along with Felix, they could forget their woes.

Richie shifted closer to Sadie and slid his arm along the back of her seat. She shot him a quick, shy glance, but his square, handsome face gave nothing away. He sat silent, chin up, smoking his cigarette, while the Wurlitzer sank into the floor amid a sea of coloured lights.

The audience clapped and stamped, impatiently calling out for the main picture to begin.

'Get a move on, why don't you?'

'Ta-ra-ra-boom-de-ay!'

'The bleeding thing's broke down!'

The boys in the front row stood on their seats and jeered. The magic square of light from the projection room stayed obstinately blank.

'Give us our money back, or else!'

'Fat chance!'

Seats clattered on their hinges, the boys shook their fists at the screen. Calls of 'Sit down, for Gawd's sake,' came from further back. 'And take off your bleeding hats!'

'What's the betting them little pests talk all the way through the picture?' Sadie whispered to Richie. She'd made all the running so far this evening, though it had been his suggestion to come and see the new Valentino film. He was hard to weigh up; scowling through his cigarette smoke, but with his strong arm quietly resting along her shoulders. She pursed her lips and concentrated on the screen instead.

More titles appeared at last. A woman sat down at the piano to one side of the screen and played rousing introductory music. Valentino's flashing eyes peered down from beneath an exotic turban. Sadie sat transfixed.

But the antics onscreen which so fascinated her scarcely held Richie's attention. He'd got what he wanted, just sitting here alongside his boss's sister; he'd got her to say yes after months of being put off. Close to, her dark hair escaping in wavy strands from under her close-fitting crimson hat, her heavily lashed eyes and full mouth were all that mattered. Light, reflected from the screen, flickered on her pale, triangular face; real, living and warm, sitting close to him in the darkened cinema.

Tension onscreen mounted. The pianist thumped out her set-piece struggle music. Sadie held her breath. Valentino vanished amid swirls of tent canvas and clouds of sand. The pianist played heartrending music, tears brimmed, Sadie dabbed them away before the houselights came on.

Richie sat forward and ground his cigarette into the floor. He stood up and hitched his jacket square on his shoulders, hardly glancing behind to check that Sadie could keep up as he made his way through the crowd towards the Exit. She fixed her eye on him, hatless, and head and shoulders taller than most. 'Nuisance!' she said to herself. She wrapped her warm coat around her, tucked her bag under her arm and wove her way up the aisle. Walter wouldn't have treated her this way, she knew. She began to regret accepting Richie's invitation. He couldn't even be bothered to escort her out of the cinema like a gentleman.

All ravishing, romantic thoughts flickered out with the last whirrings from the projector. Real life was a chain of trouble and daily problems; like her brother-in-law, Maurice Leigh, who was the manager of the picture house and who now stood talking to Richie in the foyer.

Sadie pulled up short, looking for an escape. But Maurice spotted her and beckoned her over. 'How's my favourite little sister?' he greeted her. 'Beautiful as ever, I see.'

5

Maurice stooped to give Sadie a peck on the cheek. Dark and dapper in his fashionable suit, Maurice was all smiles. He was genuinely fond of Sadie. 'You know Richie Palmer, don't you? He works at the taxi depot for—'

'Leave off, pal. She's with me.' Richie stepped forward and spoke abruptly. He took Sadie's arm.

Maurice cleared his throat and kept control of his expression. What would Jess say about her kid sister flirting with the mechanic when he went home and told her, he wondered. Though the smile stayed steady, his voice caught him out. 'Did you enjoy the picture?' he asked.

Sadie nodded, hot with embarrassment. 'Smashing, except for them little hooligans in the front row.'

Maurice's smile tightened. His eyes flicked from Sadie to Richie and back again. 'Don't worry, sis. By this time next year them front-row pests will be back-row Romeos, and you won't get a peep out of them.'

'But there'll be hundreds more of the little blighters to take their place.' She laughed. She held her head up; she had a right to a night out when she felt like it. Walter Davidson, her official beau, was always busy down at the depot. She stared defiantly at her brother-in-law.

Maurice laughed back. 'They pay to get in, don't they?'

'And the rest of us! We don't chuck away hard earned cash to hear their kissing noises in all the best bits, or them yelling "Oo-er!" and sucking their lips at every end and turn.' She and Richie followed Maurice towards the grand exit.

The manager turned, hands in pockets. 'You're getting past it, Sadie.' Still his eyes narrowed when he glanced at her companion, but he held out a cigarette and a light to him.

'Cheek.' She pulled her hat over her forehead and tucked back the stray curls, ready for the cold night air. She waited while the two men discussed this and that: a good result for the Palace, a new refinement in car engine design. Though he seemed to have hopped the wag for much of his school life, Richie was car-mad. He knew all there was to know, even about the most up-to-date models. So Walter and Rob had been glad to offer him steady work taking care of their two Morris Oxford taxicabs. They'd seen him strip down an engine, spread pistons, gaskets, casings, nuts and bolts all over the floor, and have it put back together in working order before the day was out. But he was a bad timekeeper. They talked often about having to lay him off. The threat hung over him, ready to enforce the next time he put a foot wrong.

At last Richie nodded goodnight to Maurice and led Sadie out into the street.

'Say hello to Walter from me,' Maurice called after her. He stood, hands in pockets, still watching the two of them like a hawk. 'If you run into him before I do, that is.'

She gave him a curt nod. At twenty-five years old, she reckoned she didn't need to ask Maurice's or anyone else's permission over whom she chose to go out with. Before the war, maybe, when she was younger and things were different. Frances, her eldest sister, lived at home with them at the Duke in those days, and she'd kept Sadie well in line. But not now. She stepped out confidently, arm-in-arm with Richie Palmer, high heels tapping along the dark pavement, a shapely leg showing beneath the tube skirt of her dark red coat.

Behind the bar at the Duke, Annie Parsons called last orders. She made a show of sweeping the empties off the bar and carrying them down to Ernie at the sink. 'Don't none of them take a blind bit of notice,' she grumbled.

'Look at them all sitting there without moving a muscle. They got bleeding cloth ears, all of them!'

Ernie nodded and grinned. He enjoyed this nightly ritual; his stepmother yelling out last orders, only to be ignored, his pa, Duke Parsons, happily serving pints of best bitter, Annie grumbling behind his back.

'Now, don't go on, Annie.' Duke leaned his elbows on the bar, gold watch-chain swinging forward from his broad chest. 'It's a Saturday night, ain't it?'

'And it'll be the same on Sunday, Monday and blooming Tuesday night!' Annie breathed hard on a glass and polished it to perfection. 'According to you, Wilf Parsons, there's no such thing as licensing laws. Oh, no, it's all "Drink up, Jim, and have one on the house!" with you.' She reached on tiptoe to put the glass on its shelf above the bar.

'We just gotta be thankful we can plod along,' Duke growled back. It was the same reply as always. 'No one's flush with money down the court these days.'

'Play me a different tune, Duke.' Annie shook her head and wiped on. They'd been married almost ten years now, and the patter was always the same.

'Well, who am I to deny them a drink when they've cash in their pockets to buy one?'

Ernie nodded at this too, and plunged more glasses into the sudsy water. Year in, year out, the routine reassured him and bound him safe in the arms of his large family. Gradually the terror of being accused of Daisy O'Hagan's murder had receded into the darkest recesses of his simple mind. He knew what he knew; he was innocent, he washed glasses, Duke and Annie would look after him.

'How about a sing-song, our Amy?' Arthur Ogden, a permanent fixture at the bar, called out to his daughter.

Amy had rolled up at the Duke for the evening with

some of her pals from the living-in quarters at Dickins and Jones, where she worked as a shop assistant. They'd signed themselves out, all five of them, writing down the Duke as their destination; East End girls glad of a good night out. They jumped at the chance to sing along to a tune on the old pianola.

'Let's have that Scottish one, "I love a lassie"!' Ruby Thornton sprang to her feet and made a beeline for the stack of pianola rolls. '"A bonnie, bonnie lassie!"' she trilled above the hubbub of glasses, striking a bold figure with her dyed blonde hair cut daringly short.

Amy's mother, Dolly, got there first and ferreted around in the cardboard box containing the rolls of perforated paper. 'It's here somewhere. I don't mind singing along to that one myself.'

'More like "One of the ruins that Oliver Cromwell knocked about a bit",' Arthur muttered to Bertie Hill. He didn't expect a reply. Hill was a miserable blighter, unpopular due to the fact that he'd recently bought up Eden House, the old tenement block at the bottom of the court where the O'Hagan family still lived. A new landlord was always treated with suspicion: he could start thinking about turning out tenants and razing the whole lot to the ground, like they did down Meredith Court last year. 'Did you hear they found two baby skellingtons buried in one of them cellars?' Arthur said out of the blue. 'Never put a name to them neither. Said they could have lain there mouldering for twenty years and nobody knew a thing!'

Charlie Ogden, standing at his father's side after an evening on duty at the Gem, gave the old man's drinking arm a nudge. 'Lay off, Pa, for God's sake.' Life was gloomy enough. 'He's had one over the eight,' he explained to the landlord.

Bertie Hill smiled his tight, humourless smile and drank up. He rapped his empty glass down on the bartop, picked up his trilby hat and prepared to go home. 'Time for my beauty sleep.' He smirked. He'd taken a back room in his own tenement to tide him over. The story went that he'd been a copper, up on the other side of the water, who was thrown out of the force for being crooked; a rumour seized on by Dolly and some of the market women. 'He looks like a copper,' they agreed. 'And he smells like one. Carbolic soap, and the stuff they use to scrub the station up Union Street.'

Few people said goodnight to Hill's burly, sandy-haired figure as he made his way through the etched and bevelled glass doors of the Duke of Wellington public house.

They carried on with their sing-song, which was in full swing by the time Richie Palmer came along Duke Street arm-in-arm with Sadie. Bertie Hill tipped his hat to them both as he turned and disappeared down the court.

'My poor feet!' Sadie hesitated fifty yards down the street and sighed. They'd walked all the way from the Picture-drome and it was almost midnight. The strains of 'Stop yer tickling, Jock!' and the shrieks of the women easily reached them as she stooped to examine the splashes on her pale cream stockings.

The walk home had been mostly silent, with Sadie still half-cross, half-guilty that she'd agreed to come out with Richie in the first place. She thought of faithful Walter stuck behind a telephone in the taxi office. At last, as they'd come down by the side of the giant Town Hall, she'd been driven to sarcasm. 'My, ain't you the chatterbox!' She'd tugged at Richie's arm to signal that they should cross the road. It was cold, the damp had seeped through the thin leather soles of her shoes, and she was downright miserable.

At first he hadn't responded, only shoving his hands deeper into his pockets and trapping her arm against his side. 'Well, if it's small-talk you want,' he said, hurrying her up the kerb, ducking down an alley towards Union Street.

'Small-talk, any talk.' She frowned. 'Anything would do. Like, why you asked me to walk out in the first place.'

He stopped suddenly. 'Like, why you said yes,' he countered. He stood looking down at her, the mist settling in his straight, dark hair.

'Because I wanted to see the picture,' she said awkwardly. When he spoke, she noticed that he slurred his words together slightly.

'You could do that any time.' He looked down at the pavement as they turned from each other and began to walk on.

'Then it was because you asked me, I expect.' She went a step or two ahead.

'You could've said no, like you always did before.' He followed Sadie's slight, small figure, warmly wrapped in soft red cloth. The hat made a bell shape on her head.

'And don't I wish I did say no!' She turned exasperated. 'You ain't been very friendly to me, Richie, and I don't know why!'

'What's friendly?' He came up close, took her by the elbow.

'Talking. Telling me about yourself.'

He shrugged. 'What's to tell?' The shadowy alley where they stood was full of scuttling, whispering sounds. Footsteps echoed along the main street. 'Talk,' he said, shrugging again. 'Hot air.'

Sadie found herself staring up into his face. His eyes gleamed, then he turned away, though he still held her arm in its tight grip. In profile, his forehead jutted over a long, straight nose. His top lip had a slight upward tilt, his jaw was set strong and firm. She raised one gloved fingertip to his lips.

He bent and kissed her. Her hat fell backwards from her head and the glossy halo of wavy hair came free. Her lips, soft and warm, opened slightly.

She felt the dampness of his hair, the hard smoothness of his collar. She was in his arms and she was kissing him.

Then he eased back and stooped to pick up her hat, brushing puddle-water from its velvety surface with his coatsleeve. 'Don't put it back on,' he said as he handed it to her, 'I like to see your hair.'

The compliment took her by surprise as much as her own sudden desire to kiss Richie Palmer on the lips. 'That's more than Pa did when I first came home with it all chopped off.' She stuffed her hat into her bag, trying to lighten the mood. 'Pa's got old-fashioned ideas, especially about women's hairstyles. He said he'd divorce Annie if she ever came home with her hair looking like mine! And I don't know what else.'

Richie put his arm around her shoulder. He felt the light sweep of the offending haircut against his wrist. 'I like it.' He almost smiled as they walked on up the alley. Their silence was easier, though a question still hovered as they saw Bertie Hill raise his hat to them and heard the raucous music drift towards them from the pub.

'And will you go with me again?' Richie stopped and drew her into the shelter of Henshaws' doorway, out of the cold rain that had begun to fall.

Sadie shook her head. 'I don't know, Richie. Maybe I ought not?' She looked away, catching her own reflection in the eating-house window.

'Why?' the low, slow voice insisted.

'What will Walter think? Or Rob, for that matter. You could lose your job over something like this.'

His mouth twitched down into a grimace. 'It ain't my job you're fretting over.'

She frowned and tried to sidestep him back on to the street. 'Maybe. Maybe not. But I am bothered by us walking out together again, Richie, and that's a fact. I wish you wouldn't ask me right now.'

He leaned against the door, rattling it with his shoulder, letting her step by. 'Well, then, I expect you'll let me know when I can ask again. Send me a telegram. Call me on the telephone.'

'Don't be like that.'

'Then don't you.'

They walked the last few yards down Duke Street in another kind of silence. At the brightly lit double door she paused to look up at him, but Richie turned and walked across the street without looking back. She didn't even know where he lived; not one thing about him. Yet she'd kissed him on the lips. She darted inside the pub, a hot flush of guilt on her cheeks.

CHAPTER TWO

'This allotment will set me up good and proper,' Arthur Ogden declared as Sadie came in. Annie stood behind the bar patiently paying attention. 'You just see if it don't!'

'Good for you, Arthur.' Annie went on wiping glasses. She waved at Sadie. 'Hello there. Bleeding long pictures they show up at that Picturedome place!'

'Picturedrome.' Sadie rolled the second 'r'.

'And come again tomorrow. We was worried about you, girl.'

'Well, there's no need.' She drifted into the emptying room, perched on a stool and placed her bag and gloves on the bar. 'Here I am, safe and sound.'

Arthur, listening in, returned Charlie's earlier nudge with a vengeance. 'Look lively, son, and buy the girl a drink. Can't you see she looks done in?'

Charlie dug into his pocket and ordered Sadie a glass of port wine.

Duke obliged. 'You never walked back, did you?' he asked his youngest girl as he pushed the glass along towards her. 'Who was you with? Them typewriter pals from work?'

'That's right.' Sadie nodded. She sipped her drink to avoid meeting Duke's eye.

'And what's the matter, couldn't you get Walter to send

out a taxicab to pick you all up?' Charlie interrupted. 'That's a bit tight of him, ain't it?'

Sadie gave her old boyfriend a scornful look and turned to Arthur. 'What was that you was saying about an allotment?' she prompted.

Charlie's brows went up as he pulled at his own pint glass. 'Them typewriters ain't wearing trousers and trilby hats by any chance?' he muttered.

Again Sadie ignored him. 'Go on, Arthur, tell us about your cabbage patch.'

'Hallotment,' Arthur announced, very grand. 'Down the side of the railway embankment on Meredith Court.' The words rolled inside his mouth and slipped over his tongue. He drew descriptive pictures in the air with his free hand, while the other stayed clamped around his empty glass. 'It's going to make me a man of substance, I can tell you. That little patch of land is going to bring pride *h*and prosperity to the Hogden family!'

'Pride and what?' Amy breezed up to say goodnight. 'Leave off, Pa, and say goodnight. Time I was off.'

'Shame!' Dolly squeezed Amy's arm as her daughter made a sour face. Though Amy fretted about having to live in at the Regent Street shop, Dolly knew she liked her life in the West End better than the office life Dolly had once planned for her. She didn't waste much sympathy on Amy's grumbles as she watched her, Ruby and the rest out of the door. Then she turned back to Sadie. 'Arthur ain't boring you with tales of his giant Brussel sprouts, I hope?'

Sadie laughed, feeling her balance return, her heartbeat slow back to normal after the confusing episode with Richie Palmer.

Little Arthur bridled and drew himself up. 'No I ain't! You just wait, Dolly Ogden, till them rows of carrots come up perfect, and all them beautiful onions and cabbages. When I've sold them on the market at a tidy profit, you'll be laughing on the other side of your face!'

Dolly's smile was as good-humoured as ever. 'You ain't never held the right end of a spade in your life, old man. And you don't know a dandelion from a dockleaf. No, it's another of them flash-in-the-pans, if you ask me.' She eased her husband's grip from the empty glass and stood him upright, then pointed him in the direction of the door. 'And we all know who'll be down there digging and weeding, don't we?' she said to Sadie with a wink. 'And that man's name ain't Arthur Ogden.'

'Nor Charlie neither,' her son warned. 'You won't catch me dirtying my hands for a few frostbitten turnips.' He drank to the dregs, then put down his glass.

'I never thought it was,' Dolly called cheerfully. She shepherded Arthur through the front hallway on to the dismal street.

There was the round of goodnights, scraping chairs, swinging doors before the bar eventually emptied, leaving Duke to lock up behind his regulars. Annie laid clean towels over the row of shiny new pump handles, then she dimmed the gaslights. It was already the early hours of Sunday morning.

'Bye bye, Sadie,' Charlie said. He stayed to the very last, still curious about her flushed face and evasive manner when she first came in. He looked a slight, sensitive type in his Prince of Wales tweed jacket, with his light brown hair brushed across his forehead from a side parting. His face was still fresh, smooth, even slightly womanish. He regarded his long-lost sweetheart from under furrowed brows. 'I hope you ain't doing nothing I wouldn't do?'

Sadie flicked her hair behind one ear, pouting back at him. 'I'd go help Dolly get your pa home safe if I was you, Charlie.'

She outstared him easily, and he went off down the court with the usual Saturday night feeling that his own life stood still as the rest of the world hurried on by. Twenty-six, still unattached, still working for Maurice Leigh in the chain of cinemas he managed, but going nowhere fast. His work hours were unsocial, his teenaged dreams of bursting upon the world of cinema with wondrous improvements had so far come to nothing. He'd talked to Maurice about the chances of improving synchronization between sound and vision on the new talkies by incorporating the soundtrack on to the edge of the cellulose film by a series of patterned dots, like on a pianola roll. Maurice had listened approvingly, nodded his head, considered it carefully. Then he'd told him that as far as he could judge, there wasn't the demand for it as yet. 'They flock to *see* Negri and Pickford, not to *hear* them talk,' he'd advised. 'Hold your horses. Work at it, Charlie; it's a bright idea. But bide your time.'

That was in the very early days, in his first flush of enthusiasm. Now, however, Charlie was in a rut, and he knew it. He'd chucked his chances over his scholarship for grammar school by throwing in his lot with the moving pictures game. At the same time, nearly ten years ago, he'd chucked his chances with Sadie Parsons. Sadie was considered the smartest, most admired girl around, and didn't Charlie know it.

'What's eating you?' Dolly asked as he crossed the threshold of his terraced home down Paradise Court. He'd slammed the door behind him. She sighed. 'No, don't tell me, I don't want to know. Just lend a hand up these stairs with your pa, for God's sake, and don't stand there looking like a wet weekend.'

It was Rob Parsons' last job of the evening to pick up his sister, Hettie, from the Mission on Bear Lane; a favour he did every Saturday night, when Southwark's streets were full of helpless, hopeless drunks who'd turned up too late to get a bed with the Army. They curled up instead in the tunnelled walkways that ran under the railway line, or lurched out of alleyways in blind, aimless pairs.

He pulled up outside the new redbrick Mission with its arched windows; worn out, easing his artificial leg into a less painful position, wanting his own bed. He watched a woman with a small child stagger unsteadily in the direction of his idling cab. He saw his sister emerge and come down the steps, leaned over and opened the passenger door. 'Hop in, Ett, I'm freezing to death out here.'

She stepped on to the running-board, then collapsed exhausted into the leather seat. 'Sorry!' She loosened the stiff ties to her dark blue bonnet and sighed.

Rob eased the Bullnose into gear and edged away from the pavement, too late to avoid the woman with her outstretched hand. He dipped into his pocket, found two coins and flung them to her through the window. Hettie had closed her eyes and sunk her head against the seat. The woman, hair loose, scrawny-armed, backed into the mist with her child. The car rolled off down the road, heading for home,

'Had a hard night?' Rob glanced at his sister. This work for the Army, on top of the dress business she'd set up with Jess, was wearing Hettie out. She sat pale and still beside him.

'The usual. How about you?' She opened one eye and rolled it towards him. 'You ain't exactly a bundle of laughs yourself.' She studied his slight frown, the jaw set tight. 'Ain't nothing wrong, is there?' It didn't take much to see that Rob had something on his mind.

'Nothing I can't put right.' Rob steered through the empty streets, long since rid of their tram and bus traffic. In the fog, the old acetylene lamps on his car scarcely penetrated the gloom. 'Electric headlamps,' he muttered, changing the subject. 'That's the up-and-coming thing, Ett. Electric. Powered by a battery that starts up the engine and works a windscreen-wiper too.' He turned at long last into the home stretch of Duke Street.

'Never! Did you go over Ealing way tonight?' Hettie enquired. She knew that her brother often picked up their brother-in-law and took him home to his posh new neighbourhood after work. She pulled herself out of her own exhaustion and tried to make pleasant conversation.

'I picked Maurice up from the Picturedrome and drove him over.'

'And did you see Jess?'

He shook his head. 'I never stopped off. There was another job waiting.'

'You've been busy, then?'

'Pretty much. Could be better.' They drew up outside the Duke. Hettie prepared to get out.

But she turned back and touched his elbow. 'Rob,' she began.

'What? Get a move on, Ett. Let me drive this old girl down the depot. I need some kip.'

'I know. But Rob, something happened tonight. I can't get it off my mind.' She looked out of the cab window at the lights dimming inside the pub.

19

'Down the Mission?' Rob knew she never made a fuss unless it was something serious. He studied her for a moment, finding himself wishing that she would ease up, get out of that drab Salvation Army uniform that looked like it came out of the Ark, and be more like the old, carefree Hettie, pre-Daisy O'Hagan, pre-Ernie's trial. She used to dance and sing her way through life then.

'Yes.' She shook her head. 'Don't mind me, it's probably nothing.' She pushed down on the door-handle. 'It's just we gave a bed to a newcomer tonight. In pretty bad shape. I ain't never set eyes on him before.'

'And?' Robert prompted.

'He was rambling on a bit, drunk, of course. It felt like trouble, that's all.' She began to regret giving voice to her worry.

'Trouble? Who for?'

'For Annie and Duke.' But she opened the door and scrambled out. 'Look, forget it, Rob. Pretend I ain't never mentioned it, OK?'

He blew out his cheeks and shrugged. He guessed it was something about the old man's habit of serving after hours. Rob sometimes got a bit hot under the collar about that himself, thinking that one of these days it could get them into trouble. They were tightening up the licensing laws again. He'd even heard they planned to put a full stop to alcohol altogether in America. But he nodded at Hettie. 'As you were, Ett. My lips are sealed.'

She leaned in and nodded. 'Thanks, Rob. I expect it'll all blow over. The poor old geezer'll have sobered up by morning. He'll be on the move again. Sorry I brought it up.'

Rob watched her slip quietly down the court, by the side of the pub to the back entrance. She'd brushed it off, whatever it was, but he made a mental note to warn Duke to be careful about who he served after hours.

Now he had his own bone to pick with Sadie; something he hadn't wanted to mention to Hettie until he'd had it out with their wayward kid sister. He turned the car back on to Duke Street, recalling his little chat with Maurice earlier that night. The railway arches at the top of the street loomed into view. He'd park the Bullnose and lock her up for the night. Then he'd hurry back on foot.

Maybe Sadie would still be up, having a cup of cocoa with Hettie before they both went off to bed. He pocketed a list of scribbled messages left on the table by Walter, then went out and bolted and padlocked the big wooden doors. 'Davidson and Parsons', it said on a newly painted sign, 'Taximeter Cabs for Hire'.

He went off down the street, shoulders hunched, cap pulled well down, a familiar late-night sight limping home to the Duke.

CHAPTER THREE

Jess heard the click of the front-door lock. Maurice was home from work. She looked up from the paper pattern she had carefully laid on to the silky silver-grey fabric on the front-room table, under the glow of the standard lamp. First he would steal upstairs to look in on sleeping Grace and little Maurice, then he'd come back down to tell her about his day. Taking three pins from her mouth, she tucked them neatly into the pattern to secure the cloth beneath. Then she glanced into the mirror over the mantelpiece. Strands of hair had worked free of the loose bun at the nape of her neck. She tucked them back into position and straightened her blouse into the waistband of her skirt.

Maurice took the stairs two at a time. Along the landing, he spotted Grace's bedroom door standing open. When he peeped inside, it was as he'd suspected; that little monkey, Mo, had decamped from his own room further down the corridor and come to snuggle up beside his big sister. Their two dark heads lay together against the white pillow, round-cheeked and peaceful, their breathing light, almost silent. He tiptoed across the carpet, turned down the blanket on Mo's side, and, careful not to wake him or Grace, he took the boy in his arms and carried him to his own bed. He smoothed the pillow, stroked his farehead, then bent to kiss his son's soft cheek.

At the sound of his return downstairs, Jess came to the hallway. She greeted him with a smile and an embrace, noticing the usual smoky, damp smell of his overcoat and the shadows around his eyes. He was working too hard. She took his coat and hung it on the hallstand.

'Mo's been on his travels again,' he mentioned as he took off his jacket and unbuttoned his waistcoat. 'Sometimes I think he gets there in his sleep.' Maurice hitched up his shirtsleeves and followed Jess into the dining-room.

'Did you take him back?' Through in the kitchen, Jess put the kettle to boil on the gas stove. It was a point of difference between them; she liked to leave the two children snuggled together, but Maurice insisted that Mo should get used to waking in his own bed, now that he was six and going to school.

'Yes. But don't worry, he's still fast asleep.' He wandered into the kitchen for a cosier chat. The sight of Jess, reaching for cups from the pantry cupboard, her slim waist shown off by the tight-fitting skirt, pleased him. His arms encircled her from behind and he kissed her neck.

She returned his embrace with a light kiss on the cheek, then went to stir milk and sugar into the cocoa, waiting for the kettle to boil.

Maurice leaned against the cupboard watching her. 'What've you been up to while the cat's been away?'

'Not playing, if that's what you think. Sewing.' She glanced up. 'I've an order to finish for Monday.'

'And can't Hettie do it?' He didn't like to think of Jess always working, making clothes for the well-to-do women of their new neighbourhood. He felt it could damage their name here in Ealing; people always found a way of looking down on others. As an East End Jew he knew this all too well.

'Hettie's at the Mission on a Saturday night, you know that.'

And because he was feeling edgy about the dressmaking business which Jess and Hettie ran from a small shop on the High Street, he grumbled on. 'Sadie came up to the Picturedrome tonight,' he said.

'Yes?' Jess handed him the cocoa, still smiling. 'To see the great screen lover with her pals, I expect?'

Maurice didn't answer directly. 'She was wearing that red outfit you made for her. You can't hardly miss her.'

Jess laughed. 'Don't she look a picture?' She enjoyed the way Sadie chose to look these days. As a young and single woman, she could get away with the new short skirts, the dark eye make-up and lip rouge.

Maurice grunted. 'I expect Richie Palmer thinks so too.' He wandered off into the sitting-room, moved a newspaper from a low table and sat with his feet propped up, head back, trying to wind down.

'Richie Palmer?' Jess had to call through from the kitchen. 'What's he got to do with it?'

'That's what I thought. But that's who she was with tonight. Richie Palmer from Rob and Walt's place.' He predicted to himself the effect this piece of news would have.

Jess came through, hands on hips. 'Maurice, you ain't kidding me?'

He shook his head. 'You could've knocked me down with a feather. What's she see in him, for God's sake?' They knew Richie only as the surly mechanic at the taxi depot; hardly a likely candidate for Sadie's attention, even if she

24

wasn't already walking out with one of the bosses from there.

Jess frowned and shrugged. 'It's her business. And I expect they was just friendly, that's all. You know how much Walter has to work these days. You can't blame Sadie for going out and enjoying herself.'

Maurice applied this to his own situation. The idea of Jess going out and enjoying herself, as she called it, touched a raw nerve. 'Some would.' He bent forward to pick up the newspaper. 'Like your pa, for instance.'

Jess went and crouched by his chair, one hand on his shoulder. 'Oh, Maurice, don't go telling tales on Sadie! Pa's got enough to cope with.'

He glanced at her over the newspaper and curbed his next remark. Instead he said, 'Why don't *you* have a quiet word with Sadie, then? Explain how it looks to other people when she goes two-timing Walter for some shady character like Richie Palmer.'

Jess breathed out sharply and stood up. 'Maybe Sadie don't care how it looks to other people.'

'Then she should, tell her.' Maurice closed the subject. 'It says here the Welsh miners are on strike again for more pay.' He pointed to a headline. 'It's back to the old hunger marches, it seems like.'

Jess looked at the photograph of coal-blackened faces beneath worn-out caps; a ragged procession of half-starved men. 'Quite right too. They deserve a decent living,' she said hotly.

'But not strike for it. Look what happens to the whole blooming country if they go on strike, what with winter coming up.'

Jess turned away. 'There's no talking to you, Maurice.'

25

She went out into the polished hallway, automatically pausing to listen to any sound from the bedrooms. All was quiet, so she slipped into the front room to take up her sewing. Half an hour later, she heard her husband close the sitting-room door and go quietly upstairs. Then she switched on the radio, turning the loudspeaker volume low, listening as she cut and tacked the silvery cloth to news of hardship in the Welsh valleys; children working in the pits while her own two slept soundly in their beds.

'Come to bed, Duke,' Annie said. She stretched across the hearth and tapped his hand. 'You look done in.' The fire flickered low in the grate, Hettie and Sadie were both safely back home.

'You go,' he told her. 'I'll hang on here. I want a word with Rob. I don't expect he'll be long.'

'Hm.' She was unconvinced but, nag as she might, she knew the old man would never get himself off to bed before all the others were in. Old habits died hard. 'Rob can look after himself, you know.' She rose stiffly from her seat, ready to go through.

'Better than most, I reckon.' In spite of the loss of one leg during wartime action, Rob managed to keep himself fit and active. It hadn't stopped him from learning to drive either; a goal he'd set his heart on as soon as the war was finished. If people said, 'No, you can't do it,' to Robert, you could bet your life he'd prove them wrong. So he'd worked, saved and borrowed the money to set up this taxicab business with Walter Davidson, down at the old carter's yard. They were making a go of it too, though both their cars were past their best and cost them plenty in repairs. Duke was proud of Rob. He'd settled down and got over the bitterness of what had happened to him in the trenches. 'That's him now,' he told Annie. He heard the bolt being shot across the back door.

She stooped to kiss his cheek. 'Chin up.' She thought he looked a bit down tonight. 'It'll all seem different in the morning.' His old face seemed sunken. After all, he was going on seventy and still putting in a long day's work.

Duke sighed.

'Look here, business ain't that bad. We get by.'

He nodded. 'Don't mind me, Annie. You go off, get some sleep, and I'll ask Rob to take us out in that contraption of his to see Jess and the littl'uns.'

Annie's face lit up. 'When?'

'Tomorrow.'

'Oh, Duke, that sounds nice!' She loved visiting the posh house that Maurice had set Jess up in, with its lawned front garden and fancy leaded windows. Grace and little Mo would tumble over themselves to answer the doorbell. Jess would give the warmest of welcomes.

'Consider it done,' he said, as she disappeared happily off to bed. He rose to greet his son and offer him a nightcap before he dimmed the last lamp.

But Rob, flinging his cap on to a chair, looked round, disappointed to find Duke alone, sitting up in the small hours. 'Where's Sadie?' he demanded.

'Gone to bed. Why?' The old man went to fetch the whisky bottle from the cupboard. He recognized the tone of voice, registered trouble brewing. 'Sit down, have a drink, son. You look as if you could do with one.'

Rob swilled the whisky round his glass, then knocked it back. The stump of his leg hurt where it was strapped tightly to the artificial limb, and the daylong effort of changing gear with it had taken it out of him. 'You'll never guess what Sadie's been up to now!'

'Hush. Ain't no need to yell, Rob. Whatever it is, can't it wait till morning?'

'No, it bleeding well can't.' Robert's anger boiled over. 'She's only two-timing Walter, that's all. She's a rotten little flirt, Pa, and she don't deserve a decent bloke like him.'

Duke sighed over the inevitable row between his hot-headed son and his youngest daughter. 'Two-timing, you say? Mind you, they ain't exactly engaged,' he reminded Rob. His own whisky hit the back of his throat and trickled down.

'As good as. Look, Pa, you don't mess about when you got someone steady. You gotta tell her.'

'In the morning,' Duke agreed. 'We'll get the full picture off her, then we'll see.' He blamed himself if Sadie was turning flighty. He'd spoiled her in the past, let her have too much of her own way. He didn't hear the bedroom door click, or see the white figure advance down the landing. 'If she is pulling the wool over Walter's eyes, we'll have to sit down and talk to her then.'

Rob, with his own back to the door, wasn't satisfied. 'Walter's my best pal, Pa. I've known him all these years and he ain't never said or done a rotten thing to no one. She can't just come along and make a fool of him!'

'Keep your voice down,' Duke warned. But then he turned to see Sadie herself standing there, almost as pale as her long cotton nightdress. He retreated to the fireplace, seeing that it had gone past remedy. Sadie and Rob would go at it hammer and tongs; they'd wake the whole street before they'd finished.

'Who's making a fool of who?' Sadie trembled as Rob

whipped round to face her. She held herself steady by holding on to the door-handle. 'And who's been telling you fibs, Robert Parsons?'

Rob snorted. 'Oh, so Maurice is a liar now, is he?'

'Maurice?' Her heart sank and her voice went faint. Events slotted together: her brother-in-law had opened his big mouth as soon as ever Rob had picked him up to take him home to Ealing. Soon everyone would know about her and Richie Palmer.

'Yes, Maurice! That shut you up, didn't it? He saw you in the back row with that hooligan. As if you didn't know!'

'We wasn't in the back row,' she protested, a red flush creeping up her neck.

'No, but you was *with* him, you admit that much?' He went and faced her, daring her to deny it.

'So what?' Up went her chin. 'What's it to you?'

'Oh, nothing,' Rob sneered. 'You're only my sister. Walter's only my best pal and business partner.'

'And what do you think?' she asked hotly. 'You don't think I'm cheating him, do you?'

'What am I supposed to think?'

'Now, hold your horses, you two.' Duke stepped in between the flashing looks and raised, accusatory voices. 'I don't know what's going on here, but this ain't the time or the place for it, I do know that.' He could see Annie advancing down the landing, a shawl covering her night-dress, her hair in a long braid over one shoulder.

Robert laughed and backed off to pour himself another drink. His own face was patchy and flushed. 'Oh, I get it,' he said sarcastically. 'You arranged everything with Walter beforehand. He gave permission for you to go spooning with Richie Palmer?'

Duke's brow wrinkled. He switched his gaze to Sadie.

'We wasn't spooning! And I was going to tell him just as soon as I got the chance!' she insisted.

'Oh, you was going to tell him,' he mimicked. 'Well, that makes everything swell, 'cos if *you* don't, I will!'

Sadie felt Annie appear at her shoulder and turned to grab her in heartfelt appeal. 'Oh, Annie, ask Rob not to! If he tells Walter, it'll hurt him. I gotta talk to him myself in my own way. I *will* tell him, I promise!'

'Steady on.' Annie led a shaking Sadie by the wrist and sat her down by the fire in Duke's own chair. 'And you steady on too, Rob. Give the girl a chance to tell her side. We gotta hear the whole thing and give ourselves time to calm down.' She put an arm around Sadie's shoulder. 'Don't take on, girl. You only went to the pictures with Richie Palmer, I take it? So far as I know, it ain't a hanging offence.'

In the face of Annie's kindness, Sadie dissolved into tears. 'But I never meant it to get out, Annie. I knew it'd hurt Walter if he found out. Only I wanted to see the picture, and Walter's so busy, and it's a Saturday night, and—'

'Strike a light!' Rob said roughly. He paced across the patterned carpet.

'I didn't mean no harm!' Sadie crumpled into Annie's arms once more.

Annie glanced up at Duke. 'You ain't fifteen no more, girl. You're a growed woman. You can walk out with more than one young man if you like, you're welcome. And there ain't no law against it.' She held up a hand to stem Rob's noisy protests. 'Only, I do think you oughta clear it with Walter first.'

Sadie sniffed and pulled herself together. Her dark hair fell as a curtain to shade her face. 'I ain't never going to see

Richie no more,' she vowed. 'It ain't even as if he's nice to talk to.'

In the background, Rob snorted.

'But you'll still tell Walter what you done?' Annie checked.

Overwhelmed by family pressure, and her own swelling sense of guilt, Sadie gave her promise. Rob heaped more insults on to Richie's head, calling him a no-good drifter who'd end up on the scrap-cart before too long. She watched as Annie calmed Rob down, and saw her efforts to cheer Duke up, before she dried her own eyes on a handkerchief and slid off to bed.

In her own room, Sadie found Hettie sitting in the wicker chair, her long hair flowing over her shoulders.

'It was only a little fling,' Sadie insisted quietly, defiance stiffening her stance once more. 'I weren't never going to see him no more!'

'I know. I heard.' Hettie looked her full in the face. 'Walter's the best there is, surely you know that?'

'I do, I do! No need to rub it in, Ett!' Sadie rolled back her sheets and stumbled into bed. She pulled the covers tight under her chin. 'I could kill that Maurice,' she muttered. 'Landing me in this fine mess!'

Hettie shook her head. 'I don't know about him landing you in it, but did you notice Pa?' she asked anxiously across the darkened room. 'I been worried about him lately, Sadie. I don't suppose you saw how he took it all?'

But Sadie, exhausted, was already falling asleep.

Jess worked quickly and expertly, running up seams on the machine, watching with satisfaction as the dress took shape. The trimming would be a wide band of glass beads

31

handsewn around the hem and plunging neckline. A sash would tie tight around the hips to show off the straight shape that all the customers preferred these days.

She thought back to the time when she and Hettie had rustled up an outfit ready for her to go with Maurice to the Town Hall Christmas dance. That had been the beginning of it all for her; the escape from drudgery and the stigma of Grace's illegitimate birth. That tight bodice and clinched waist seemed to belong to a different world. How long was it, for instance, since she and Maurice had been out dancing? Before they came to the new Ealing house that faced on to the Common? Before Mo was born? Well, staid, well-to-do women didn't dance along to the new whispering baritones, or cavort to the Charleston. What would people think?

She used one of Maurice's phrases to laugh at her own silliness, then snipped a thread and held the dress up for inspection. Not going straight up to bed with him had been her small act of defiance after their scratchy conversation about Sadie. Now that was lost in a sea of reminiscence, as she delved deep into their marriage.

There was no doubt about his success as the forward-looking manager of the biggest cinema chain in the city, and it had given them a lot of what other people could never dream of having. They'd moved away from their East End roots, and up in the world. With careful planning, they were able to instal a telephone, and gradually buy the new, streamlined furniture that was replacing the carved mahogany style of her childhood. Soon Maurice would start looking for a Morris Cowley motor car; not brand-new, but still dearer and more stylish than the Model T, as far as small cars went. Jess tilted her head from side to side as she re-ran word for word the endless conversations about whether they could afford to buy and run a car, and if so, what type? And how much? And petrol at one and six a gallon.

The biggest problem for Jess in all this, setting aside the wrench of having to move away from family and friends, was a growing feeling that Maurice's ambitions were all well and good, but that he gave no room for Jess's own dreams to take root and grow. They basked in the sunshine of his success, his good business sense and eye for fads in the fast-moving picture trade, which kept his cinema chain well ahead of all East End rivals. But her own poor little business, dressmaking with Hettie, was overshadowed and neglected. She even felt that Maurice would uproot it if he could, and throw it away like a useless weed. He never said so in so many words. But then he never praised her efforts either, and sometimes suggested that Grace and Mo might prefer it if she gave up the work. 'It's not as if we need the money,' he told her, in a spirit of husbandly generosity. 'I earn enough, and I don't like the idea of you working your fingers to the bone. It's like the old sweated labour.'

'That's all you know,' she challenged. 'Our little shop is in a good spot on the High Street. We're getting to be very fashionable with a certain class of lady round here.' They'd graduated long ago from the repairs and alterations of their humble beginnings above the Duke.

'The trouble is, wives round here don't go out to work much.' Maurice's dark brows had furrowed. 'It ain't Paradise Court!'

'I know it ain't!' She'd looked at him long and hard. 'What about Hettie?' she said finally. 'Don't I owe it to her to keep on?'

So he'd let the matter drop, and she often stayed up late at night, after the children had gone to bed, making up orders for chiffon party dresses and crêpe-de-Chine visiting outfits. During the day, she would enjoy her time with Hettie in their chic little shop. She took pleasure in the cut and quality of their tailormade clothes.

'You know it's two o'clock in the morning?' Maurice's voice interrupted her train of thought. He peered round the door, sounding subdued, seeing her still sitting there in the pool of light.

Immediately she felt contrite. 'Can't you sleep?' she asked as she stood up and came halfway to meet him.

'No.' He'd come down dressed in pyjamas. 'Was it my fault?'

'What?' She glanced at his ruffled hair, his tired face. 'No, it's mine. I should've realized.' She could never sleep when Maurice stayed up late either. She went and put her arms around his neck. 'You should've let me know before now.'

He kissed her. 'I knew you were busy.'

Stroking his cheeks she whispered, 'Not too busy,' and felt his arms tighten around her.

'You'll come now?' he murmured. Their passion, undimmed by the years, rekindled easily. His arms pressed her to him. She leaned back to unpin her hair and let it fall loose to her waist. Tilting sideways, he kissed her neck, then led her from the room.

The light burned all night long. In the morning, Maurice came downstairs and turned it off before he opened the curtains and went through into the kitchen to make tea for Jess and take glasses of fresh milk up to Grace and Mo.

CHAPTER FOUR

November faded into a raw, dripping December, accompanied by rain and fog. They were short, cold days, harbouring a continuing fear of hunger in the docklands. Still, the East Enders found things to be cheerful about, whistling the old wartime songs in the streets, standing in long, damp queues to watch Crystal Palace rout the northern opposition, then emulating their heroes during Sunday matches in their local park.

On the second Saturday of the month, Palace were to meet up with arch-rivals Derby County. Walter Davidson and Rob gave themselves a rare afternoon off from taxi work, leaving Richie in charge of the depot. Tension between the three of them had slackened off during the weeks since Sadie's heart-to-heart with Walter, when she confessed the mistake she'd made in going to the picture-house with Richie. She told him she hadn't realized how it might look; she hadn't meant any harm and she was truly sorry. She didn't mention the kiss.

Walter had kept both her small hands in his during the confession. He said he understood how much she liked to go to the pictures, and he didn't blame her for taking a night out. He was sorry he couldn't leave work to take her more often himself, only they were still building up the business, getting known beyond Duke Street, down Union Street and Bear Lane. It was wrong of him to neglect her, he knew. There was really nothing for him to forgive.

After this, Sadie felt worse. For a start, she might have welcomed a small show of jealousy on Walter's part; there was her female pride at stake. Second, her confession had only been partial, to save Walter's feelings, she told herself. But she'd deliberately missed out the tumult in her heart when she kissed the silent, infuriating Richie Palmer. From now on she must keep out of his way, as a safeguard to her own peace of mind. Her stolen night out with him would be the one and only.

Duke and Annie approved when they saw her and Walter back together. Walter was part of the scenery; steady as they came, loyal and true, a big support to Rob when he first came home wounded.

Walter's own war had been spent as a motor-bike dispatch rider around Ypres. It had kept him out of the thick of things on the front line, but he stored many terrible memories which he would forever keep to himself. His belief in the justice of the Allied cause had kept him going through thick and thin. Later, he'd trained as one of the first drivers of the new military tanks, and was in the last push of the autumn of 1918. He came home a hero to a country exhausted by war, unable to offer him a means of keeping body and soul together. So he and Rob resorted to their boyhood dream of setting up by themselves. They took casual employment on the docks and markets, working like navvies to scrape money together. Over the years, their meagre savings of one pound a week rose to thirty shillings, or on a good week, thirty-five. Still, their target seemed miles off.

Help came along for the pair of them at last in the

unlikely shape of Mrs Edith Cooper. She heard of their struggle to start up from one of the girl assistants in her husband's drapery store. Mrs Cooper held a soft spot for Robert; he'd come to talk kindly to her on the death in action of her only son, Teddy. She'd seen in Robert all the maimed and wounded victims of the war, the wasted youth, the terrible price of victory. This dainty, fastidious woman, an East Ender herself in the days before her husband's success, had once more requested Rob to visit her at home. She offered him a loan of £200 to be paid back according to a set plan at a low rate of interest. She wished him well, shook his hand and stood at her window, shielded by a long net curtain, watching him to the gate. Rob went with his head high, eagerly in spite of the impediment of his leg. Tears stood in her eyes. Her husband, Jack, sneered and told her she'd be lucky if she ever got back a penny of her investment. 'Throwing good money down the drain,' he complained. 'And times are this bad.'

Cock-a-hoop, Rob and Walter sat up late debating whether to spend their cash total of £350, £150 of which they'd saved for themselves over a three-year period, on one brand-new Morris Cowley with its revolutionary American engine, or on two older, used Bullnose Morrises. They'd gone for the latter; two cars meant twice as much business when there were two of them able to do the driving. They found premises to rent at the old carter's yard under the railway bridge, installed a telephone and put up their nameplate. For two years now they'd struggled to repay their loan and to make ends meet. Each month, with a gleam in her eye, Edith Cooper unsealed the brown envelope and held up the five-pound note to show her disbelieving husband.

It was a rare Saturday when they decided to take time

off, but the Derby County game was a needle match and the whole of Southwark would be making a mass exodus to the Palace ground in Sydenham. When they spotted Tommy O'Hagan trudging along Duke Street through the pouring rain, water rolling from the brim of his trilby hat, they pulled up to offer a lift. The car, notorious for its poor road-holding, skidded to a halt.

Tommy quickly gestured to his companion to hop in too, and the pair of them slid gratefully into the back seat. Glancing in his mirror, Rob saw that the uninvited guest was Bertie Hill, the unpopular new landlord of the O'Hagan tenement block. Tommy, keeping an eye open for the main chance as usual, had obviously thought it wise to keep well in with the man. He sniffed and shook his hat on to the floor. 'Blimey, Rob, ain't we glad to see you.'

But Hill was the sort to put a dampener on the conversation with his snide remarks. He would assume familiarity where there was none, and managed to put Rob's back up the moment he stepped on the running-board. 'Whoa, Dobbin!' he cried as the cab slewed sideways into the pavement. 'Ain't you got no control over the old girl?'

'About as much as you've got over your mouth, I'd say,' Rob replied. He slapped on a grin from the outside without meaning it, before he pushed the car into gear and set off at breakneck speed. 'Mind you, I have to admit the brakes ain't so hot,' he remarked, deliberately swerving wide of the giant tramcar which bore down upon them.

Bertie Hill took a damp Woodbine out of his breast pocket, lit it and inhaled deeply. 'Now, a Daimler,' he said slow and easy, 'there's a beauty of a car, if you ask me.'

'I was in a Daimler once,' Tommy told them. 'She went like a bird, all the way down to Southend and back. Next thing I knew, the geezer what drove it was cooling his heels up the station at Union Street. Turns out this Lefty Harris had nicked the Daimler from Earl Somebody-or-other. Tries to lay it on me. I says I can't even drive the bleeding thing, so how the hell can I nick it? In the end, they had to let me go.'

Walter and Rob enjoyed the story. Tommy had a way of dissolving tension. He was always in a scrape from wheeling and dealing on the market, always one step ahead, but at the same time a strong family man who took home much of what he earned to his ma and pa. He kept just enough to socialize and get by. He had been the mainstay of the O'Hagans after Daisy's tragic death, reckoning he'd no time for the birds or for settling down.

'Hey, Tommy, there's just one thing wrong with that,' Rob protested. 'You can drive almost as good as me!'

'But the coppers don't know that, do they? They take me out and put me behind the wheel of one of their Model Ts. I looks it all about like this, and takes hold of the handbrake. "Is this to turn the engine, or what?" I ask. And I let it go and we freewheel down the hill until the copper grabs hold of the wheel and slams the handbrake back on. "Just wait till I get my hands on that Lefty Harris!" he squeaks. He's gone as white as a sheet. They give Lefty six months in the Scrubs, no messing.'

'And *did* you nick the Daimler?' Walter leaned back to listen to Tommy's reply. Rob had begun to edge the car into a side street not far from the ground.

Tommy looked at him, all wide-eyed innocence. 'You know me, Walt!'

'That's why I'm asking, Tommy, believe me!' Walter winked, and the subject was closed.

Rob parked the car. The four of them pulled their hats down and joined the trudge up the street towards the turnstiles.

Sadie stared down at the rain-sodden street. 'Look at them poor blighters,' she said to Hettie. Two women, shawls over their heads, pulled a sack half-full of coal along the pavement. 'I bet they've been picking by the railway.'

From the comfort of their living-room above the pub, Hettie and Sadie watched the women drag the sack. 'A land fit for heroes,' Hettie remarked, sinking into the shadow of Giant Despair. With an effort she shook herself free. 'I dunno, Sadie, there's a lot of work to do before we can afford to rest.' Picking up her bonnet and fixing it on her head, Hettie got ready for her long, busy shift at the Mission.

'Anyone'd think you can do it all single-handed, the way you work yourself to the bone, Ett.' Sadie thought her sister looked worn out. 'Them women struggling down there ain't your fault, you know. You shouldn't take on.'

Hettie tied the bow smartly under her chin. 'They ain't my fault, but they are my sisters, Sadie, as sure as you are, and I can't let my sisters suffer in silence. We all gotta work and pray, and ask God to forgive our sins, until we reach the Heavenly gate.'

'And I suppose I gotta watch *you* suffer in silence?' Sadie refused to let the point drop. She knew that Hettie worked herself to the point of collapse on behalf of the poor down-and-outs.

'I ain't suffering,' Hettie protested. 'I'm doing God's work.'

She looked so pained and surprised that Sadie regretted

40

her sharp tone and went up to her. 'I know you are,' she said gently. 'And I'm just a horrible sinner, getting at you when I know you're a hundred times better than me!'

Hettie smiled. 'Who's counting?'

'I am. I'm a wicked woman, and don't I know it!'

'How? How are you wicked?' Hettie linked arms and fondly stroked Sadie's wavy hair.

'Pa thinks I am. The other day he asked Frances not to bring me no more lip-rouge from her chemist's shop because it ain't ladylike.' Poor Sadie had been kept under strict control since her escapade with Richie.

'And what did Frances say?'

'She told Pa not to be so old-hat. All the girls wear lip rouge these days.'

'See.' Hettie smiled. 'Frances has her head screwed on.' Of the four sisters, Frances was the one they looked up to. Even Duke stood in awe of her since she'd married Billy Wray, the widowed ex-newspaper vendor, and gone to live with him above the Workers' Education place in Commercial Street. 'You ain't wicked just because you wear a touch of make-up. Same as the women who come into our shop; they ain't terrible vain things just because they want a dress to look nice in.'

'But you don't know the half of it,' Sadie told her. Her one serious transgression, the luxurious, forbidden kiss was beginning to worm its way out of her conscience.

'I know one thing.' Hettie glanced at the clock on the mantelpiece. 'I'm gonna miss my tram if I don't get a move on.' She gave Sadie a quick smile. 'Why not come to church with me and Ernie tomorrow?' Her hand was already on the doorknob.

Sadie half-nodded and smiled. 'I'll think about it.'

But as soon as Hettie vanished downstairs, Sadie's

41

brooding mood returned. Feeling the urge to shake herself free of it and make herself useful, in a pale shadow of Hettie's own missionary zeal, she decided to heat some soup and nip down to the depot with it. Rob and Walter would be glad of a warm lining to their stomachs on an afternoon like this. Quickly she set the pan to boil on the range. She put on her broad-brimmed grey hat to keep off the rain, and slipped into a matching wrap-around coat. Then she set the pan inside a linen teatowel at the base of her shopping-basket, tied the towel in a knot to secure the top of the pan, and set off on her errand.

Puddles barred her way when she reached the cinder-strewn yard where Rob and Walter garaged their two cars. One of the Bullnoses stood safe inside, under the brick arch of the massive railway bridge. The other was missing; presumably out on a job. Carefully she picked her way across the yard, trying to shield her basket from the worst of the rain. 'Rob?' she called as she peered inside towards the corner office. There was no sign of life. 'Walter?' Cautiously she stepped inside.

Richie Palmer eased himself from under the stationary car and stood up. He'd recognized the voice and the ankles, and thought for a moment that if he stayed put, Sadie might well conclude there was no one there and turn right around. But he'd look a fool if she spotted him hiding, spanner in hand. So he got up to face her, watched her spin round at the clink of metal as he rapped the spanner on to the ground. This was a meeting he could well do without.

'Where's Rob?' Sadie felt her throat go dry.

'At the match. They both are.'

'Oh.' This possibility had never occurred to her. She was

irritated; even her good deeds turned against her. Richie was the last person she'd planned to bump into. 'Are you sure? They never take a Saturday off.'

'It's Derby County.'

She tilted her head back. 'I brought them some soup.'

Her remark hung in the air. Richie looked steadily at Sadie, aware of how she'd avoided him since their night out together. It was clear that she wished the ground would swallow her. 'I'll tell them you dropped by,' he said.

'Oh no!' Even being here, alone with Richie, would upset Rob if he found out. He'd think she'd planned it. 'No, never mind. I'd best be off.'

He didn't respond, wiping his hands on a rag slung from a hook on the wall. Then she felt ashamed of treating him so badly, and angry that this was how others arranged her life for her. Why shouldn't she talk to him? Talk was only talk. 'Shall I leave you this soup?' she offered.

He wished she'd make up her mind; either he was below notice, or he wasn't. When he'd taken her out to the picture palace, she'd proved in one unguarded moment that she found him attractive. Then she'd gone and cut him dead. Now she was being friendly all over again. Cat and mouse. He stared silently at her.

His gaze succeeded in unnerving her. 'It was Rob, really,' she explained. 'He went mad at me for walking out with you.'

'Were we walking out? I thought we went to see a picture.'

She nodded and turned away, resenting being teased.

'I ain't good enough, I don't suppose?' Richie stood in her way.

'It ain't that. Rob don't care about that. But it's Walter he's thinking of. Walter's his pal!'

43

'And does Walter own you? What about you? What do you think?' He kept his distance, but didn't offer to shift.

''Course not. Only, I owe it to him. Oh, I don't know!' She backed off. 'It's best left alone.'

'Is that what you think?'

His look, his slow voice hooked her like a fish on a line. 'Yes, it's what I think!' She felt the rain slanting against her back as she stepped outside.

'And is it what you feel?'

'It's the same thing, ain't it?' With a sudden change of mind, she rushed forward and thrust the basket into his arms. 'Don't ask me!' she cried.

'You said that before.' He caught her by the elbow. 'Remember?'

The shock of his touch ran through her. She felt herself tremble, then she struggled to get free.

He let her pull away and stand upright, but he'd brushed his face close to hers, smelt the rose of her soap or perfume. 'I'll move on, then,' he said abruptly. He decided in an instant. 'It ain't no good hanging round here waiting for this whole thing to blow up in my face. Your Rob's got a temper. I'll go; you won't have to worry no more.'

'No!' Once more she let herself down, gave herself away. 'I mean to say, there's no need. You're wanted here to work on the cars.'

Richie looked away. 'You'd best get out of here. They'll be back soon.' The match would be over. He had several messages from customers to hand over to his bosses when they returned. 'You can have a lift if you want.'

'No.' She darted out into the heavy downpour, careless of the huge, dirty puddles. 'I can walk, thanks.' And she ran off, her thoughts as ragged and confused as ever.

Richie deposited her basket on the desk, squatted down,

44

took hold of the front bumper of the old Bullnose and swung himself from view once more.

Palace had lost two-nothing. The home crowd had sung 'Abide with Me' right through to the dying seconds, to no avail. Bertie Hill blamed the muddy conditions, Walter said that County were the best side on the day. Rob coughed the engine back into life as the other three flung open the doors and piled into the car. He swung his disappointment into the violent turning of the starter-handle, but he'd forgotten to retard the engine. The motor caught fire and turned at full speed, kicking back the handle, nearly taking his thumb with it. Rob cursed and climbed into the driver's seat. They drove in subdued silence; only after they'd drowned their sorrows in a pint or two of best bitter would they be able to take their defeat philosophically. The inside of the car smelt of wet worsted and stale cigarette smoke. The windows steamed up, the old car refused to grip the wet road.

'Thanks for the lift, pal,' Tommy said. Rob had stopped to drop Bertie and him off at the Duke. 'Another day, another dollar, as they say.' He shrugged and slammed the door shut.

'You been watching too many American pictures,' Walter warned. But he knew Rob was anxious to get back to the depot. The rain would mean plenty of taxi business tonight; people didn't like standing in a queue for the tram, getting soaked on their night out.

But halfway down Meredith Court, the Morris started churning out steam from under the bonnet. The plugs had overheated and the car was losing water fast. 'Bleeding thing!' Rob cried, mouthing curses as Walter scrambled in the boot for the emergency canvas bucket. He filled it at a nearby standpipe while Rob lifted the bonnet and eased the cap off the radiator. Minutes ticked by. Richie would already have booked them in for jobs, expecting them back by now.

Walter shook his head. 'This old girl's on her last legs, you know that?' His face was serious as he refilled the radiator. 'She ain't reliable no more.'

Rob sighed. He leaned against the door biting his thumbnail. 'Got a spare three hundred and forty-one quid on you, pal?'

Walter gave a hollow laugh. He felt in his pockets. 'Well, it just so happens . . . no!' He slammed down the bonnet and chucked the canvas bucket into the boot. 'Things are a bit tight right now.' He turned the starter-handle while Rob advanced the engine. They'd lost a good fifteen minutes waiting for it to cool.

'*We beat 'em on the Marne*,' Rob growled, swinging the car back into the slow crawl of traffic. He chanted the old war song with savage irony.

> '*We beat 'em on the Aisne.*
> *We gave them hell at Neuve Chapelle . . .*'

He blew his horn furiously at a cyclist who had wobbled out from behind a crowded omnibus.

> '*And here we are again!*'

'Steady on, Rob!' Walter warned. He made a grab for a hand-hold as the car swerved to one side. 'Ain't a thing we can do about it.' He resigned himself to getting Richie to strip down the engine of the old car one more time.

'Maybe. Maybe not.' Rob's brain was a riot of ideas,

some feasible, some not. They could sell both Morrises and buy one new Cowley. They could team up with another outfit, cut down on overheads, start saving all over again. They could borrow more money. 'Maybe not!' he repeated, careering through puddles with a hot hiss of steam. He pulled to a halt outside the depot, leaped out and slammed the door as he went inside.

Walter jumped into the serviced car still parked inside the garage. Richie handed him an address, saying the woman had already rung up twice to ask where he was. Rob started up the engine, Walter put his foot down and was on his way. Rob went into the office to check the next job on the list.

'What the bleeding hell's this?' he asked, shoving a basket to one side. He glowered at the scrawled messages.

Richie frowned. He stood in his shirt-sleeves, a wide leather belt buckled carelessly round his waist, his collarless shirt open at the neck. 'Sadie brought it in,' he answered. His choice had been to get rid of the basket and avoid awkward questions, or to leave it on view. Some stubbornness in him had chosen the second option. Now he stood looking steadily at Rob as the information sank in.

Rob, never one to ask questions, pounced on the one unacceptable fact. 'She never came down here?'

'She did.' Richie took his jacket from a peg behind the door.

'By herself?'

He nodded.

Rob kicked a chair to one side and slammed the office door shut. Its glass panels rattled. His eyes widened, his fists clenched as he pinned Richie into one corner. 'Now listen, Palmer, you leave that girl alone, you hear me? You lay one finger on her and I'll break your neck!' He faced his strong, able-bodied opponent head on, without a scrap of fear. Even when Richie unfastened his belt and swung its brass buckle out in front, wrapping the leather strap around his wrist for a firmer grasp, Rob refused to back off. 'Come on, then! Come on! What you waiting for?' He crouched low and made a beckoning motion.

'You don't want a fight,' Richie warned him, low and menacing. 'Ain't nothing worth fighting over.'

Further enraged, Rob swung at him. Richie dodged sideways, escaping from the corner. He was three or four inches taller than Rob, younger, fitter.

'I'm telling you, lay off my sister. She ain't interested, get it? She don't want nothing to do with a hooligan like you!' Rob spat with ineffectual rage. He swung again, once more missing his target.

'You'd better ask her that.' Richie put the desk between himself and his boss. He never even raised his voice.

To Richie, things had suddenly changed. Five minutes ago he'd been prepared to vanish, without wages, without explanation! He'd take his cap and jacket off the hook and never show up again. This thing with Sadie was too complicated. Since he never knew which way she'd jump, he felt the whole affair was out of his control, and he was uneasy. Besides, whenever he saw her, his urge to hold her and the memory of kissing her that once resurfaced and threw him further off balance. He didn't like that feeling one bit.

Now it was different; Robert had come charging in with orders, with the idea that he could lord it over Richie and rule his life. Richie had never been able to bear being told what to do. Brought up by Barnardo's, he'd learnt to follow his own instincts to survive. He took the children's home for what it gave him – food and shelter – but he hated the rules and Christian browbeating that went with them. He left there when he was ten years old. His teenaged years on the streets had toughened him up and taught him never to trust. Then two years of army service had fuelled his obsession with car engines. He gleaned information and experience from working on supply lorries that travelled between the Belgian coast and the front line. Like many uneducated men, the war had at least given him a trade. Otherwise, it only served to reinforce his rebellious spirit.

He had one sergeant-major who treated him like dirt; Richie got the worst billets, the most dangerous tasks in a battle of wills to see if he would crack. But it came to a bad end. The sergeant-major had sent Richie over the top on reconnaissance once too often. He and the other men had stayed put in the trench until they heard a hail of enemy fire. But the sergeant left his own strategic retreat a second too late. A shell had landed in the trench over Richie's head, leaving the sergeant-major hanging on the old barbed wire. Later, Richie would sing that wartime favourite with vicious enjoyment.

Rob wore a dark moustache, just like that sergeant-major. His upright bearing gave him a military air. He was the type who never showed a soft side. His temper was always ready to flare and he didn't like to be crossed.

'Look, I ain't gonna take none of your cheek, you bleeding idiot.' Rob jumped down Richie's throat. 'Sadie's spoken for. Why can't you get that into your thick head?' He got ready for his third lunge, this time raising the heavy brass phone, holding it like a club. The wire wrenched from its socket and dangled uselessly.

Over his head, beyond the glass partition, Richie spotted the rapid approach of Rob's eldest sister, Frances. He lowered the belt and unwound it from his fist. Instinctively

Rob dropped his own guard. 'You heard me,' he warned. 'You leave her alone.'

Richie turned away and took his jacket without a reply. But the set of his shoulders spoke defiance. 'Try and make me,' he suggested. It was in the angle of his cap, in his curt nod at Frances as she came in. He loped off across the cinder yard.

Frances Wray, as she now was, had spoken earlier on the phone to Hettie. She'd set off for the Duke as soon as she could, hoping to catch her sister before she left for the Mission. Hettie's tone had been uncharacteristically down-beat. Though she'd been quick to deny that anything was amiss, Frances had decided to leave work and pay her a visit.

Since Rob's depot was on her way and it was raining hard, Frances thought she might ask Rob for a rare favour and catch a lift to the Duke. Now she shook out her black umbrella and closed it, glad to find someone in. 'Cheer up, it might never happen,' she told Rob. His face was like thunder.

'It already did.'

Frances glanced after the retreating figure of Richie Palmer. 'Well, anyhow, run me up home to the Duke, there's a good chap. I need to see Hettie and I'm afraid I've left it late.' Frances sighed. 'Why do customers always have to come in at the last minute? You'd think they'd show more consideration. Don't they know we have our own lives to lead?' She'd been mixing pastes and making up pills until well after five o'clock.

'No, didn't you know?' Rob tilted his chin up and fixed his tie straight. He was beginning to recover from his

50

argument with Richie. 'You ain't a human being. You're a machine for peddling pills and potions, that's all.'

'Ta very much, Rob.' By now they'd climbed into his cab and backed out of the yard on to the dark street. Frances sat quietly in the passenger seat, listening to the swish of the tyres through the puddles. In her feather-trimmed hat and fawn, tailored outfit, she looked quietly respectable as always. 'Ett didn't sound her usual self,' she commented, separated from the familiar sights of Duke Street by the steamy windscreen. 'She ain't mentioned nothing to you, has she, Rob?'

He came to a halt outside the pub. 'There was something, but she didn't say what. I think she's got a lot on her mind. She won't even say nothing to George, though, so there's no use asking me.'

George Mann, also a pal of Rob's, stayed quietly in the background of Hettie's life, and he had become part of the Parsons family. He'd taken Joxer's place as cellarman at the Duke, after Joxer had uprooted and drifted off on his silent, lonely way. George had been glad of a job during the lean period after the war. Duke said he owed him a steady place after he'd snatched Rob from certain death on the battlefield; it was George who'd lifted the wounded soldier on to his back and staggered with him to safety. 'He'll stick like glue,' Annie warned. She knew the type; strong and silent, pretty much alone in the world, fond of his home comforts, and quickly falling for Hettie.

Her heart and soul were with the Army, however, and at first she gave him little encouragement. Then, almost passively, she began to accept his persistent attention. Duke had acknowledged Annie's point of view. But, 'He'll do for me,' he said, 'now that Joxer's slung his hook.' For more than three years George had grafted and quietly impressed.

'And she won't say nothing to Sadie?' Frances enquired, still wondering about Hettie's troubles. She prepared to brave the wet street.

Rob tossed his head.

'I take it that's a "no"?'

He followed her into the rain. They shifted as quick as they could into the front porch. 'Sadie ain't listening to no one at present,' he said in disgust.

Frances braced herself and pushed open the door. Annie, busy at the bar, waved noisily. Duke looked up, pleased by the rare visit from his eldest daughter. She was thirty-nine, with a sensible marriage under her belt and a good job at Boots, and he felt proud of her if a little distant. He still didn't hold with her opinions, which were too modern for his taste, though since women had got the vote, he'd noticed she'd quietened down a good deal. Still, there was something aloof about her; she meant well, put her husband and family at the top of her list of priorities, but she lacked the common touch. 'One look from her would freeze a man's beer in its pint pot,' was Arthur Ogden's way of putting it.

Frances went upstairs ahead of Rob, only pausing to shake the rain from her jacket and hang it up. From the landing she heard the telephone ring, and Sadie's voice as she answered it. Something made her hesitate.

'Ett, is that you?' she heard Sadie ask. 'Calm down, Ett. Don't get worked up. It ain't like you ... Yes, I can hear. But are you sure? ... Yes, I think I heard Frances come upstairs just now. Hang on a tick, Ett. Don't go away. I'll go get Frances for you.'

Slowly Frances turned the handle and went in. She looked at Sadie's pale, shocked face, saw her standing holding the telephone mouthpiece out towards her. She went and took it from her.

'Oh, Frances!' Sadie cried. 'Ett's here, and she's in a fix. She's at the Mission and she says Willie Wiggin has just turned up!'

'Annie's old husband?' Frances held the phone to her ear in disbelief. Everyone in the court knew the story of how Annie had been deserted by Wiggin, who'd gone off to sea and eventually been declared missing, presumed dead. Ett's voice sobbed along the wire, while Sadie made a grab for her arm, pleading over Ett's incoherent tears. 'Tell her there's some mistake, Frances! Tell her it's just some mad old drunk. It can't be Wiggin. It can't be!'

CHAPTER FIVE

By the time Frances and Sadie arrived at the Bear Lane Mission, Hettie had managed to calm down. She was standing at a long trestle-table doling out soup and bread, quakerish in her navy-blue uniform. She looked tense, but under control. Her two sisters signalled they would wait by the refectory door until the soup queue was served. Hettie nodded and wielded the big metal ladle, though the smell of potato and mutton from the steaming pot was as much as she could stomach. Doggedly she worked on, dealing kindly with the row of shuffling, dejected tramps.

'Oh my God!' Sadie breathed. It was her first view inside the Mission, and it struck her as a picture of hell. The refectory was a long, bare room with arching roof beams and high, narrow windows. Tables were set out in rows along the length of the room, and hunched shapes huddled over their meagre rations.

These men, segregated from the women and children, were clothed in rags. They sat to eat, wrapped in old trenchcoats tied around with sacking, padded out with newspapers. Bundles of rags perched on the benches beside them; they were reluctant to be parted from one scrap of their belongings. Their feet, under the bare wooden table, were shod in old, misshapen boots, stuffed with paper that was worn to a waterlogged pulp. Many were caked in mud. They scoured their empty enamelled bowls with crusts or dirty fingers, chewing with toothless gums. Their faces were caved in by poverty; unshaven, shadowy, suspicious.

'They're the lucky ones,' Frances reminded her sister. 'At least they got a bed for the night.'

Sadie looked on in horror, her gaze flicking from one face to the next, praying that this wasn't the man claiming to be Wiggin; or the next, or the next.

At last Hettie finished her work, wiped her hands on a linen towel and came across the hall. She was composed, pausing when an inmate stuck out his hand to accost her and accuse her loudly of some uncommitted crime. 'It's a crying shame!' the old man shouted. 'So it is. It's a shame, and I want something done about it!'

Hettie bent to soothe him, promised that everything would be all right if he took his empty bowl to the hatch and picked up his bed ticket for a good night's sleep. She patted his hand until he released her and she could go on her way. She woke another man, fast asleep at the table, and helped him to his feet, not flinching at the sight of a livid, distorting burn that scarred one side of his face.

Sadie came forward almost in tears. To her, Hettie was an angel. She could solve everything, find a way through for these hopeless cases. She would be able to dissolve away this small problem over Wiggin. 'Hello, Ett.' Sadie gave her a brave smile, aware that Frances had come up quietly beside her.

'We came as quick as we could,' Frances said. 'Where is he? Do you want us to try and get some sense out of him?'

Hettie nodded. She led the way out of the refectory,

down a long cream and brown corridor towards the men's sleeping quarters. The dormitories, well aired, with rows of bunks to either side, were a step up from the old workhouses, but offered few luxuries. A warm blanket, a promise of breakfast in return for a chore successfully carried out, was what persuaded the homeless to stay on after their spartan suppers. Included in the bargain was a dose of hymn-singing and allelujahs, which most considered a price worth paying in return for refuge from the elements.

Hettie turned right, up a narrow flight of stone stairs. 'The thing is, he keeps coming back regular as clockwork, every Saturday night.' She spoke quietly over her shoulder to her two sisters. 'First off, I hoped it'd be just the once. They drift off and we never slap eyes on them again, some of them. But he came back the next week, I think it was the last Saturday in November, and I hoped to goodness he'd change the tune and stop going on about this woman called Annie. It was a load of rubbish mostly, but it put the wind up me.'

Frances listened carefully. The upper storey of the Mission contained more men's dormitories. Glancing to either side, she could see barrack-like rooms, each of which gave beds to thirty or forty men. 'Just "Annie"? Is that all?' She grasped at a straw. After all, there were hundreds of Annies round here, lots of room for Hettie to have jumped to the wrong conclusion.

'At first, yes. I had to help him to bed, he was so drunk. He moaned the name "Annie" over and over, then it was "Paradise Court". He held on to my arm. He told me he'd left his Annie down the court and gone away to sea. But now he'd come back to find her.' Hettie stopped and turned helplessly. 'I prayed hard, Fran. And God forgive me, I prayed for him to go away and never come back! I was glad when he went the next morning, poor old sinner. And I can't tell you how much I dreaded seeing him come through them doors again!'

'But he's here now?' A deadening feeling had seeped into Frances that the old tramp's story might indeed be true, and that here was someone who could turn up out of the blue after twenty-odd years and set their lives in turmoil. Her voice flattened out into a monotone, jerking between her narrowed lips.

Hettie breathed in sharply. 'I was in Reception earlier on, helping the major with admissions. The major calls out names and issues blankets, I write down the name and give each man a number for his bed ticket. "Wiggin," the major says. It comes over loud and clear, the first time I've heard it. My hand can hardly write it down for shaking. I look up and see he's back right enough. And now I've got his last name and a face to put it to.'

'So you telephoned us? It's all right, Ett, you did the right thing. We'll help you sort this out if we can.' Frances managed to control her fears and take charge. 'Show us where he is and let's see what we can do.'

'It's Annie and Pa I'm worried about,' Hettie whispered, leading the way into a dormitory. 'Whatever'll we do, Fran?'

Frances gave her a brief shake of the head. The three women went in at last, and two of them being in civvies attracted a certain amount of attention. Eyes swivelled in their direction from the bunks and from groups of men huddled by radiators. 'Oo-er!' came the old-fashioned call from shrivelled, cracked lips. A cackle went up, fuelled by Sadie's obvious blushes. Then a lone baritone voice struck up into the sudden silence.

'You are the honey, honeysuckle, I am the bee,
I'd like to sip the honey from those red lips, you see . . .'

Sadie shuddered and forced herself to walk on.

'This ain't the place for the ladies to kip,' another, rougher voice called out. 'You missed your way, I think!' His laugh turned into a hoarse cough.

'Ain't we the lucky ones?' someone else cried. 'Good tommy in our bellies and fine lady visitors!' His wild eyes stayed riveted on Sadie's fashionable short skirt.

'Nah!' His companion from the bunk above cut in. 'They ain't no fine ladies. They're soul-snatchers, just like the rest!' He sneered and spat on to the floor, before rolling over and pulling the blanket over his head.

Hettie, used to the name-calling, went right down the central aisle, reading off the number on the end of each bed. But when she came to the one supposedly occupied by the man who called himself Wiggin – number 407 – she came to a sudden halt.

'Is this it?' Frances had followed close on her heels. She stared at the empty bed, the blanket thrown to one side.

'Where is he?' Sadie panicked more at the idea that the man was lost than at the previously dreaded idea of having to confront him. He might drift back on to the streets, find his way down to Paradise Court before they could check his story.

'You looking for the old Jack Tar?' The man with the decent baritone voice jumped up from his bottom bunk and approached them. He was among the most sober and alert of the men, ready for a good mystery. 'He jumped ship.' He smiled, eyeing the three women in a lively way. 'You should've seen him. He was punching the air and shadow-boxing like the devil. Then he stands up on the edge of the bedstead. Blimey, I thought he was a goner. He topples forward and crashes down, then he rolls over and makes for that door on his hands and knees. Gone. Man overboard.' He winked at Sadie. 'I don't like these soul-snatchers and their jingle-jangle music no more than the next man. But I reckon I have to put up with it unless I want another wet night under the arches. That's the way it is. But not that old bag of bones. I reckon he came to just enough to see where he'd landed up, and the idea of all that song and prayer at five in the morning was too much for him. So he hopped the wag. And who can blame him?' He glanced from Sadie to Frances, then to Hettie, trying to make her rise to his bait.

Sadie had to back off from the reek of the man's breath, while Frances went to look through the far door leading into another dimly lit corridor. 'You mean he went this way?' she asked.

The sober man, standing upright, with his hands casually in his trouser pockets, nodded.

'How long since?' Hettie spoke sternly.

'Five minutes.' The man's cocky smile faded.

'Where does this lead?' Frances asked Hettie. The three of them had made their way from the bleak dormitory on to the darkened landing.

'Down some back stairs to the refectory,' Hettie reported. The cackle of catcalls and insults had begun again as the men's insolent cheerleader recovered his nerve and set up his tune of 'Honeysuckle' once more.

Sadie shut the door behind her. 'Let's be quick,' she said. 'Maybe we can catch him up.' She darted down the stairs; it was vital to get hold of this old tramp before he could spread his wild story.

But down in the refectory, an adjutant stood on a raised

platform, praying for the batch of souls who'd just partaken of the skilly and hard rolls. Fifty or sixty men bowed their heads, more likely in sleep than prayer, as the Army preacher began his speech of salvation: 'Poor as you are, hungry and ragged as you are, be sure that you will feast in Paradise. No matter how you starve and suffer here, you will rest one day at God's heavenly feet. Pray with us, dear brothers, that the path may not be long and weary, that we may feast on His Host and pray for His forgiveness . . .'

Anxiously, Sadie, Frances and Hettie scanned the rows of bowed heads. At last Hettie had to admit that she recognized none of the captive audience. 'No,' she signalled, retreating from the hall.

'Where's he got to?' Sadie frowned. She looked all about.

'What'll we do now?' Frances was the one to think ahead. They must talk face to face with the man before they could frame a real plan of action.

'My bet is he won't get far,' Hettie told them. 'He ain't strong. I don't see how his legs could carry him all the way up to the court, even if he could find his way at this time of night.' They stood in the churchlike entrance, looking out at the pale faces pressed against the window; the men who'd arrived too late for shelter. 'Leastways, he ain't managed it up till now.'

Sadie nodded in relief, but Frances shook her head impatiently. 'We're jumping way ahead of ourselves,' she told them. 'We're supposing things before we know they're true. How do we know for sure this *is* Annie's old husband? He's given Hettie a load of gibberish, he's got a couple of names right. But who's to say he is who he claims he is? No, we gotta take this one step at a time.'

Hettie frowned. 'You ain't heard him, Frances.'

'Exactly. I could kick myself. We missed him by five minutes. But you say he shows up here every Saturday?'

'Now the weather's turned bad, yes.'

Frances took a deep breath. 'Right, here's what we'll do. We'll wait a week. Then we'll come back early in the evening and talk to him.' She quietened Sadie's protest. 'A week ain't long to wait after all these years. We don't say nothing before then. Not a word.'

'But maybe we should warn Annie?' Hettie had had more time to consider this option. 'If it was me, I think I'd want to be the first to know, not the last.'

Frances knitted her brows. 'I don't know, Ett. What difference does a week make, like I say?'

'And what about poor Annie? She'd be like a cat on hot bricks.' Sadie imagined how their stepmother would feel. 'Not knowing if it really is Wiggin or not. That don't seem right.'

So Hettie gave in. She saw that it was two to one, and she trusted Frances's judgement most of all. 'Next Saturday, then,' she agreed.

Frances and Sadie pulled on their gloves and tucked their collars up around their chins. They kissed Hettie on the cheek and she waved them goodbye, watching them brave the army of lost souls who had been locked out. Then she went back to her calling.

CHAPTER SIX

Now every tramp in the streets of Southwark seemed to pose a threat to the happiness and security of the Parsons family. Hettie's description of 'Wiggin' as just over five feet tall, thin, bent by age, undermined by drink, a tiny, shambling figure of a man, could be taken to include many of the more hopeless cases taking shelter under the railway arches, staggering out to beg for a few small coins.

More than once that week, gazing through the window of her chemist's shop, beyond the bright purple, blue and red carboys on display there, Frances had cause to start and wonder. An old tramp would thrust his nose up to the window, tattered grey coat hanging wide, his body wrapped in woollen rags, his trousers shiny with grease and many sizes too big. Or she would be behind her counter, sorting loofahs and sponges to size before pricing them, when she would glance up at another of these fearful sights; rheumy-eyed, skin lined and engrained with dirt, holding out a skinny hand for a dose of black draught to help ease his permanent hangover. Once, a man so scared her on her evening route home, as he lurched out of a derelict shop doorway and crumpled into a heap at her feet, that she rushed on and fled upstairs to the comfortable flat she shared with Billy. There she poured out the whole story of 'Willie Wiggin'.

Billy Wray was startled by the state his wife was in. He promised whatever help he could. They'd been married for six years, following a decent period of mourning for his first wife, Ada, and he was still devoted to Frances. Like most of the rest of the world, he put her on a pedestal, admiring her cleverness, her interest in good causes, always respecting her opinion. For her part, Frances trusted Billy with her life, often went to him for advice, and gave wholehearted support to the workers' publications which Billy edited and composited from a back room of the Institute. He was a self-taught printer, having given over his newspaper stall on Duke Street to young Tommy O'Hagan, and he put his painstakingly acquired skill to work in support of the many new unions for shop and factory workers which were springing up in the East End. Now in his late forties, he had mellowed into a sinewy, spare-framed man; his fair hair had turned grey and thinned at the temples, but he was still very upright and smart.

He greeted Frances's distressing tale with concern, then shook his head. 'Ain't no getting away from it, it sounds like bad news,' he told her as he brought a cup of tea from the kitchen and got her to put her feet up by the fire. 'It's turned you into a bag of nerves for a start.' Personally he thought it unlikely that fate would push this very same tramp into a ragged heap at Frances's feet. He heard from her that a police car had pulled up at the kerbside when they spotted her in trouble, and hauled in the vagrant for a breach of the peace. This had upset his sensitive wife all the more.

Frances sipped the tea. 'That ain't the point though, Billy. The point is Annie and Pa. What'll this do to them if it turns out to be true? If this really is Wiggin come back after all these years?'

He sat opposite her, leaning both elbows on his knees. 'Don't you think you owe it to Annie to let her know as soon as possible?' he asked softly.

She stared back, bit her lip and sighed. 'Not yet, Billy. Not when it's coming up to Christmas and all. Let's wait until Saturday and we can see what's what.'

Saturday the 20th was when things would come to a head. Frances kept in close touch with Hettie by phone. On the Friday she took another call from the pub. It was eight-thirty on a cold, clear night. Hettie asked if she and George Mann could pay them a visit.

They arrived at the Institute within the half-hour. Billy shook George's hand and showed them both up to the tasteful modern room which Frances had made into a home suitable for the respectable, childless couple they were. A valve radio stood on a sleek, veneered sideboard, with a pair of headphones hung neatly to one side. The pictures on the walls were light, modern watercolours in ash frames which Billy had made himself. The rows of books on the alcove shelves were to do with social issues such as education and family planning, or else slightly controversial modern novels, many by women.

Frances made their visitors feel at home. Billy offered to send down to the local pub for beer, but George shook his head. It seemed matters were too serious.

'What is it, Ett?' Frances stood up and took off her steel-rimmed glasses which she'd lately taken to for reading. Her own hair was greying at the temples, but it was cut into a good, shoulder-length bob which gave her an up-to-date air. 'It's Wiggin again, ain't it?' She dreaded the next day and their planned return to the Mission.

Hettie nodded. She nudged George's arm. 'It's bad this time, ain't it?'

The cellarman hung his head and studied the backs of his own broad hands, placed squarely on his widespread knees. All eyes were on him and he wished it otherwise. Reaching up to ease his necktie, he coughed. 'I'm afraid it is.'

'Well?' Frances's anxiety broke through in a schoolmistressy prompt.

'I bumped into him,' George said apologetically. 'Without intending to, you understand.'

Frances felt the stuffing go out of her. She leaned forward in her own chair. 'Oh, George, no! What happened? Tell us, quick!'

'It was earlier today,' George began. He felt his colour rise. Frances scared the living daylights out of him, if the truth be known. 'I heard the dray roll up for a delivery, and I went out to meet it.' He stared at the fawn, flowered wallpaper for inspiration. Hettie nudged him again. 'Well, there I was lifting the barrels off the cart, and I'd just stopped for a chat with Harry Monk, the carter. We call him Harry the Priest on account of his name . . . and anyhow, we're chatting ten to the dozen, then I turn to roll the first barrel down the slope. But instead I bump into this old heap of rag and bones. He was standing in the road, waving and going on something shocking.'

'What was he saying?' Frances gasped. It seemed as if the old runaway had found his way to the court after all.

George breathed out through his long, straight nose. 'Not a lot. Just a name. Annie's name. He kept shouting it over and over.'

'And did she hear?'

'No. I reckon she was out down the market.'

'Let's be thankful for small mercies,' Frances breathed, composing herself by folding her hands in her lap. 'What do you think, Ett? Does it seem like Willie Wiggin to you?'

Hettie nodded. 'George told me the second I got back home from the shop. Then I rang you. 'Course, George here didn't have a clue who the old man was, and when he tells me, he's all of a puzzle about it.'

George came back in. 'I was thinking, what's the old sod want, shouting for Annie like that? I'm hoping Duke don't come out and hear. It wouldn't look too good, you know. So Harry and me, we hoiked him up on to the old dray cart and laid him out comfy under one of the horse blankets. He was asleep as soon as his head touched the boards.'

'Drunken stupor, more like.' Frances failed to muster any charitable feelings towards the old tramp, but then her gaze dropped under Hettie's reproachful stare. 'So what happened next, George?'

'Harry said he'd take him right on up the Mission for me. He has to pass that way anyhow.' He turned to Hettie. 'I knew you and your pals could fix him up, and I knew Harry had only to drop off another four barrels before he makes his way back to the brewery. So I says yes, that's the best thing for him, and that's the last I saw of the old chap. As far as I know, the Mission's where he ended up.'

Billy broke the silence that followed. 'Like I said, it's a bad business. It was a narrow squeak, only saved by George's quick thinking. What if Annie *had* been in this afternoon? Or what if Duke had heard the row and come out to investigate? What if Duke had been the one to spot him?'

Both Frances and Hettie froze at the very idea. So far,

their plan had been to keep the tramp away from Annie until the case was proved either way. But the effect on Duke had also preyed on everyone's minds.

Billy continued. He stood, arms behind his back, back to the fire, offering his best advice. 'Look, you plan to visit the old man tomorrow, don't you? Well, my idea is that you should talk to Annie *before* you go, give her the chance to come along with you. It's *her* old man, when all's said and done.'

'*May be* her *ex*-old man!' Frances protested.

'No, if it is him, then there's no ex about it. That's a knot you can't untie for love nor money. If I was a betting man, I'd lay money on it,' Billy said quietly. 'How come he found his way back to the Duke otherwise?'

'Coincidence,' Frances suggested. 'And where's he been all these years?' She still felt it was impossible; like a man rising from the grave. She sprang to her feet and began to pace the floor. 'And if so, even if it is him, what right's he got to come back now and upset everything?'

'What's "right" got to do with it?' Billy shook his head. But his wife looked stricken, so he went and put an arm around her shoulder. 'Don't take on. Let's wait and see.'

George waited a decent interval for Frances to recover. 'I think the same as Billy,' he told Hettie. 'Annie's gotta be in on this. I can't look her in the eye no more, knowing what's brewing behind her back!'

Hettie's eyes filled with tears. 'You're a good man, George, and you're right. We gotta tell Annie!'

'Tomorrow,' Frances insisted. 'Let them have one more night's peace together. We'll tell her tomorrow!'

*

Sadie had planned a full day before the dreaded visit. She spent Friday evening at Jess's house, stopped over, got up at six when the household was still fast asleep, then made herself breakfast of boiled egg and toast. She changed into her work blouse and dark blue skirt, brightened up her outfit with the red hat and coat, then hurried out to the Underground.

She sat all morning at her desk in Swan and Edgar's office, checking through bills and typing out invoices. For once, as long as time flew by, she didn't mind working on a Saturday morning. That afternoon, she would stop off at Duke Street market to buy small Christmas gifts for the family; a new striped tie for Ernie, a box of Ashes of Roses face powder for Jess. That was if the family managed to celebrate Christmas this year. Fear of what lay ahead if this really did turn out to be Annie's husband made her shudder and pull her coat close. She clocked out of the building at twelve sharp, and set off down the cold street.

'Hey, missie, what do you call this?' her supervisor, Eric Turnbull, called after her. He came rushing out in his pinstripe waistcoat and shirt-sleeves, his glasses perched on his forehead, hissing at her with his affected lisp. 'You don't call this a letter to a valued customer, I hope?' He came and thrust a piece of paper under her nose.

Sadie wrinkled it and stepped smartly back. 'Is something wrong, Mr Turnbull?' She was afraid she'd been genuinely caught out; her concentration had been poor all morning and the shiny typewriter keys had swum before her eyes.

'Wrong? That's putting it mildly, I'm afraid, Miss Parsons.' He stabbed at the paper with his forefinger. 'Look, here's a capital F! Who ever heard of a capital F for "faithfully"? And this here, this is a comma where there should be a full stop. And here, a full stop where we all know we need a comma!' He looked aghast. 'Where did you go to school, may I ask?'

Sadie sighed. 'I'm sorry, Mr Turnbull. I've got a lot on my mind.'

Turnbull, who saw his job as a balanced combination of bullying and humiliation, was about to continue his tirade, when Sadie's ears picked up the familiar hooter call of one of Rob's taxis. Her spirits lifted at once. She hadn't expected a lift and supposed that it was either Rob or Walter turning up to do her a favour. 'I'm sorry, Mr Turnbull, I gotta go. That's my taxi!' She fled across the pavement. 'I'll put it right first thing on Monday morning. I already clocked out, you see!'

'Taxi?' The supervisor choked on the word. He watched Sadie step on to the running-board. Even he, in his elevated position, had to catch a bus home. How could Sadie afford to take a cab?

Sadie had collapsed with a loud sigh of relief into the front seat before she realized that the driver was neither Rob nor Walter, as she expected, but Richie Palmer. Immediately she stiffened and sat up straight. But it was too late. Richie rejoined the flow of traffic, his hands firm on the wheel, his chin jutting forward.

'Surprise,' he said quietly. 'Walter sent me out on a test run. I just put a new patch on the radiator.' He tapped the dashboard. 'She runs like a dream, touch wood.'

'How did you know I was at work?' Sadie challenged. She still felt glad about getting one up on Turnbull, and she looked at her rescuer with a bright smile. She perched crosslegged on the leather seat, her hand on the armrest.

'A little bird told me,' he said. In fact, he'd overheard Walter discussing it with Rob. When they'd sent him out in the car, he'd seized the golden opportunity to meet her out of work with both hands, knowing that she would finish at midday.

She laughed. 'Thanks anyway. You got me out of a tight spot back there.' She wouldn't have put it past the small-minded Turnbull to have dragged her back to retype the dratted letter then and there.

'Pay me back if you like.' Richie took up the joking tone. He was showing off with his driving, nipping in and out between omnibuses and lorries.

'How's that?' She noticed him take a detour down towards the Embankment, but she didn't object. Their speed on the wide road thrilled her. Walter always drove well within the twenty miles per hour speed limit.

'Come along and see the new Chaplin picture.'

She shot him a look. 'You got a cheek!'

He shrugged. 'You can say no. It's a free country.' He shot on to Blackfriars Bridge and over the river.

Sadie looked down at the immense stretch of steel-grey water. Coal barges chugged upriver to feed the power-stations, a small cargo ship crossed their wake and headed out to sea. 'So it is,' she agreed. 'I can say yes. I can say no.'

'Which is it to be?' Richie overtook a trail of slow cars behind an old horsedrawn dray. ''Cos I'm sick of hanging around.'

Sadie remembered their last conversation at the depot and her tone altered. 'I thought you said you was moving on?' she reminded him.

'Something came up.' He glanced at her, held her gaze. 'Is it yes or no?'

'The new Chaplin, you say?' She knew that details of the invitation were a diversion. Yet she couldn't muster the courage for a direct reply.

'Tonight,' he put in quickly.

'Oh, no, I can't. Not tonight.' The visit to Hettie's Mission was firmly fixed. She noticed the flicker of a small muscle on the side of his jaw.

'Rightio.' He swung left, thin-lipped, avoiding her eyes.

'But maybe I could sometime next week!' She rushed into it after all. This was the last offer she'd get from Richie Palmer. He wouldn't stand being put off once again.

His eyelids flickered. 'Monday?' he suggested.

She nodded. 'But not the Picturedrome this time. Let's go somewhere new.'

'You choose,' he agreed. His voice, laconic as ever, betrayed none of the triumph he felt.

'Meet me out of work at six.' It was all fixed, for better or worse. Minutes later, he pulled up at the end of Duke Street and dropped her off to do her shopping in the market.

When Sadie finally arrived home with her basketful of Christmas novelties, she found the pub already crowded with men celebrating a home win, or else trying to escape the pre-Christmas frenzy of shopping for turkey and tree. Ernie and Duke, all hands to the pump, worked to slake their customers' thirst. George had been called on to lend a hand. He was serving beer to a couple of men she'd never seen before; apparently friends of Bertie Hill, who stood in close conversation with them. At present, there was no sign of Annie.

With her basket over her arm, and her feet touching the ground for perhaps the first time since her decisive taxi ride, Sadie ran upstairs. She had about an hour to get ready before she, Hettie and Frances went off to the Mission. She

71

burst into the living-room, totally unprepared for what greeted her.

Annie sat in her own chair by the fire, staring into its glowing depths. Frances stood uneasily to one side, twisting her wedding ring around her finger. Hettie was over by the window, as if trying to melt away to nothing.

'You ain't gone and told her?' Sadie cried. She rushed forward to hug an unresponsive Annie. 'You ain't never gone and told her! Look what you done!' She hugged the slight, stiff frame. Annie was the only mother Sadie had ever known, and she could see how much they'd hurt her by dropping this terrible bombshell. Annie bowed her head on to Sadie's shoulder.

'We had to, Sadie. It was for the best,' Hettie told her. 'Don't think it was easy, for God's sake.'

'But we ain't sure. We don't know nothing for sure!'

Frances lifted one hand to her mouth. 'He was here, Sadie. He was outside the Duke yesterday afternoon, only thank God Annie was out.'

Sadie drew a deep breath. She rested a cheek against Annie's fine grey hair. 'Look, we ain't sure, Annie. Chin up. You never know.'

Annie spoke for the first time. 'It's him all right. I can feel it in my bones.' She managed to straighten up and sit with her shoulders back. 'I should've known it was too good to last.' She looked round the room, from the sewing box on the table to the clock on the mantelpiece, to Duke's empty chair.

'Don't say that!' Sadie wanted to cling to her shred of hope. 'We'll go and find out all we can for you, Annie. You just gotta stay here and hope and pray.'

But Annie, who'd never shirked anything in her life, would meet trouble full on. That's the way she would have

72

it; not to be caught unawares by a misplaced concern for her welfare. 'Frances and Ett done right telling me, girl. And there ain't no way I can let you three take my trouble on your young shoulders.' She stood up. 'If anyone's staying here, it's Frances and you, Sadie. I'll go along with Ett and put everyone's minds at rest.'

Hettie came obediently forward.

'You sure, Annie? You sure you're up to this?' Frances saw the determination on her stepmother's face. 'It ain't nice down at the Mission. Why not stick to our first plan? Let us go and talk to him.'

But Annie shook her head. 'You can do one thing for me, though.' She looked from Frances to Sadie. 'You two can go down and fetch Duke for me. And one of you can stay and cover for him in the bar.'

This time it was Hettie who objected. 'Annie, can't it wait? It'll only upset him something dreadful.' The thought of Duke in distress pushed her to the brink. 'Wait till we know for sure.'

But Annie stood firm. 'Just go down and fetch him, there's a good girl,' she told Sadie. 'If old Wiggin is back in the picture, I gotta tell him now. Whatever happens, we ain't got no secrets between us, Duke and me.'

CHAPTER SEVEN

Duke steadied himself by holding on to the banister rail. He took an age to climb the stairs. It was the first time in their nine years together that Annie had called him away from serving behind the bar on a Saturday night.

'She ain't ill?' He looked up at Frances, feeling his heart pound, grasping the rail.

Frances shook her head. 'She wants you to go see her in your room, Pa. She's got something to tell you.'

The muscles in his chest contracted, he took two or three short breaths and carried on his way. 'Ain't no need to drag me up at this hour, is there?' he grumbled. 'Don't she know it's our busiest time?' He tried to trick himself into believing that this was a trivial problem, not worth abandoning routine over.

Frances saw his hand shake as he turned the handle to their bedroom door. She retreated into the living-room to wait with Hettie.

Annie sat on the double bed. She raised her head as she heard Duke come in. It was painful to her to see the misery of apprehension in his eyes. 'Come and sit down over here, Duke.' She patted the white counterpane and smoothed a place where he should sit.

'You ain't ill?' he said again.

Annie took his hand. 'Fit as a fiddle.' He was shaking. She must get this over with. 'No, but I got bad news. Are you ready for this, old son?'

Rob? Jess? The little ones, Grace and Mo? Their names sprang to mind. He imagined harm or danger to each one in turn. 'It ain't little Grace?' he said. His darling, his first grandchild.

Quickly Annie shook her head. 'No, it ain't nothing like that. It's us. Now, you gotta hear me out, Duke, then we can see what to do.' She cupped his hand in both hers and drew it close to her, shutting her eyes and rocking gently as she told him the news. 'Something, or I should say some-one, has turned up. Now it might be something or nothing, we don't know yet; I gotta go with Hettie to find out. What it is, Duke, we think Willie's showed up again down at the Mission. Leastways, he says he's my old man, and I reckon I ought to go and find out.'

Duke sat quiet. No one was dying. No one was hurt. He was grateful for that. The actual news caught him stone-cold. 'That's a winder, that is.' He sighed.

'I had to tell you.' Annie stroked his lined cheek. 'Poor Ett, and the others, they was in agony, but you and me gotta deal with it. What do you say?'

He nodded. 'What do you think, Annie, is it him?' His voice stuck in his throat. He had to recollect where he was by concentrating on Annie's silver brush and comb set on the dressing-table. He caught sight of his and Annie's reflection in the mirror.

She sighed. 'Something tells me it is, yes.'

Duke's head sank to his chest. Beside him, Annie seemed small as a child, her eyes bright with tears, her chin up.

'If it is him, we'll have to think what to do,' she urged.

The room seemed clouded, nothing would stay still even

75

for a second. 'Give me time.' He nodded, he made a supreme effort to raise his head and got to his feet. 'Off you go with Ett, Annie.' He raised her up too. 'She'll look after you and make sure you come to no harm. I'll still be here when you get back.'

She didn't want to let go of his hand. ''Course you will, silly old sod!' Annie brushed away her tears. 'Where else would you be? Now, just you get down them stairs in the bar where you belong!' She dabbed her eyes with the corner of her apron and went to the wardrobe to fetch her boots.

To Hettie, the streets had rarely seemed so mean and cold. Rob had volunteered to run her and Annie to the Mission. Just as well; a freezing mist shrouded the shopfronts and dwelling places, the streetlamps failed to pierce the gloom.

'Turn left here.' Hettie leaned forward to tap Rob's shoulder. 'You just missed Bear Lane. What you playing at?'

He swore and took the next left, then left again. 'Can't see a bleeding thing,' he complained. He checked in his overhead mirror, caught sight of Annie sitting ramrod-straight on the back seat, her black coat buttoned up, a wide-brimmed grey hat shading her face. 'Everything all right back there?' he asked.

Annie nodded. 'Blooming lovely. Keep your eyes on the road, young Robert. Ain't no use us having an accident right this minute, is there?'

Rob grinned. 'That's the spirit, Annie.'

'Hm.' She took a deep breath as the taxi drew up outside the Salvation Army hostel. 'Ready?' she asked Hettie.

'Ready as I'll ever be.' Remarking on how well her stepmother was managing, Hettie got out of the car and held out her arm.

Annie climbed out, then paused to thank Rob.

'Ain't nothing. Good luck!' He gave her a worried smile.

'We'll need it. Ain't no point you hanging round here, though. Gawd knows how long it'll take, and you need to get off and earn some pennies.' She turned and stared up the forbidding stone steps. Then she took Hettie's arm again and marched straight up them. 'Don't mess about now, Ett,' she warned. 'Or I might just turn tail and run!'

Hettie took her swiftly past the huddled queues, straight through the entrance hall to the major's office. There Annie was greeted by the firm handshake of a tall, upright woman with long grey hair tied back in a plain bun, her blue uniform crisp and smart with its maroon epaulettes and brass buttons.

'Major Hall, this is my stepmother, Annie . . . Parsons.' Hettie hesitated over the second name. 'She's come to see Wiggin, one of our admissions. He's in the sick bay.'

The woman checked down a list pinned on a notice-board. 'Ah yes, we admitted him yesterday afternoon. We had to bring the doctor in. Yes, yes, of course.' She came out from behind her wide desk. 'Thank you for coming, Mrs Parsons.'

'I'm only doing my duty,' came Annie's stolid reply. She wondered whether the major knew about the strange circumstance behind her visit.

Major Hall nodded. Behind her spectacles her grey eyes shone frank and clear. 'Not without a struggle, I imagine,' she said kindly.

Annie grunted. 'How is he?'

The major glanced at Hettie. 'Don't expect too much,' she warned them. 'The doctor recommended rest, but he said recovery would be slow, if at all.' She waited for them to take this in. 'The drink has undermined him, I'm afraid. He's an old man, and he's not strong.'

'Will he know me?' Frown marks creased Annie's forehead. She clutched her black umbrella close to her chest.

'Why not go up now and see?' Major Hall suggested. There was a businesslike quality in little Annie that she'd taken to at once. 'Remember, God is with you.' She smiled. 'A rod and staff, a comfort still.'

'Hm,' Annie said again. 'I need something along those lines, and that's a fact!'

Hettie glanced at the major's raised eyebrows as Annie turned and marched out of the office. 'Good luck!' Major Hall nodded, thinking that Annie was the type of soldier they could do with in their ranks.

The Mission's sick-bay was less crowded than the main part of the building, and staffed by nurses in starched white uniforms. The inmates, stripped of their filthy rags, lay in clean white beds, many awake and staring at the high, arched ceiling. Some were moaning and calling out for help. Annie's determination met another test. She hated illness and decay; they made her afraid, then angry. She hated hospitals and doctors and the idea of not being able to look after yourself. It was a fate she herself intended to avoid at all costs.

'You still feeling all right?' Hettie sensed her hesitation at the door.

Annie sniffed. The strong, sharp smell of disinfectant was overwhelming. The soft shoes of the nurses squeaked over the polished tiled floor. 'Just tell me where he is,' she managed to gasp. 'There's a good girl.'

'Third bed on the right.' Hettie pointed. 'I'll come with

you if you like.' She had to overcome her own growing fear to make the offer. This could be a turning point for the whole family. She thought of Duke busy behind the bar.

But Annie patted her elbow. 'You wait here. Third on the right, you say?' She saw that the man in the bed was awake as she advanced slowly down the aisle towards him.

It was the wreck of a human being; a shrunken, demented old man who writhed to escape from his sheets, who fought the air with his fists and cried out at invisible enemies. He was foul-mouthed and frightening.

Annie took a final step forward. She drew a chair from under the bedside table and sat close to the bed. 'Willie?' she said quietly.

The man continued to beat the air, sitting upright at the sound of her voice. She saw his face. There was no flesh, just skin and bone. The mouth opened in an awful curse; it was toothless, a gaping, slavering black hole. The skin was covered in sores, the head shaved. The red-rimmed, swollen eyes could scarcely open. He tore at his sheets with twisted hands.

Annie looked at him in terror. 'Willie?'

The mouth issued another thick, incoherent curse. The face turned again in her direction, but the eyes stared straight through her. It was Wiggin.

She put out a hand to touch the cold claw that tried to beat her off. 'Willie, it's me, Annie.'

He pulled away. The name seemed to mean something to him at least. 'Annie! Annie!' he roared, like a man just home from the pub and demanding his supper. 'I'm back, Annie! Annie! Annie!'

She shuddered. 'It's me, Willie. I'm here.' She tried to restrain the fighting hands.

More terrible curses, a violent coughing fit, a struggle to be free. 'Wiggin, sir! 02753!' He lay back at last and gasped the number, hands held to attention at his sides. His head jerked upwards and back.

'Willie, it's Annie.' She withdrew her hand, spoke as if to a feverish child.

He stared back without recognition. 'You ain't Annie!' he accused vehemently. He wrenched his head from the pillow and tried to sit up. 'I ain't never seen you before! Annie! Annie!' The screams rose in pitch, then his body convulsed and he fell back. A nurse came and put her arm around Annie's shoulder.

Annie looked up broken-hearted as Hettie rushed to help. 'He don't know me, but it's him all right.'

Annie and Duke decided on a family gathering. Sunday would be a good day to bring over Jess, Maurice and the kids from Ealing. Frances would come along to the Duke with Billy; they would meet up in the afternoon, once everyone had had time to come to terms with the shocking news of Wiggin's reappearance.

On his wife's return from the Mission, Duke had gone straight upstairs to hear the worst. He was prepared for it and took it without flinching. 'No, don't tell me.' He sat down heavily in the wicker chair. 'I can see it in your face, Annie. It *is* Wiggin, ain't it?'

Annie sat on the bed, white and drawn, her hat lying across her lap. 'He's in a bad way, Duke. They reckon he might not pull through.'

'And if he does,' Duke said slowly, 'we're in a fix, ain't we?'

'Two husbands is one too many for me, you mean to

say?' Annie looked up, grasping at the shreds of her old fierce and lively self, shaking a fist at fate.

'For any woman living, I should think. Well, Annie?'

She stood up to embrace him. 'Two like you, Duke, would do me any day.'

'Try telling that to the vicar.' Gently Duke let her go. 'It looks like we ain't married no more, don't it?'

Annie's dark eyes blazed. 'We're married, Duke. They can say what they like, ain't nothing can alter how I feel about that!'

The last nine years had been the best of her life. Marriage to Duke Parsons had brought double helpings of happiness that she'd never dreamed of before. He was a stubborn, proud, old-fashioned type of husband; breadwinner, decision-maker, grumbler, worrier. A generous-hearted, stalwart friend. It wasn't as if they never had a cross word, and Annie gave as good as she got. But they believed in each other, that was the thing. Neither had had a moment's doubt since they'd reached that altar and promised, 'For better, for worse.'

'The law says different,' Duke pointed out. 'You know how I feel, Annie, and I know what you're going through, believe me. But we got to try and keep a clear head here. For a start, what's going to happen to Wiggin now?'

'He's staying put. He ain't going nowhere, not for a week or two.'

'But he can't stay at Ett's Mission for ever.'

'No. I already thought of that. That side of it ain't so much of a problem. I still got a bit put by from the old market-stall days, and I can dip into that and find a place for the poor old sod to stay. I'll pay his rent for a bit.'

Duke's frown deepened. 'You're sure you can manage that?'

She nodded. 'Call it my rainy day money. And if this ain't a rainy day, I don't know what is.'

He saw her mind was made up and began to follow her line of reasoning. 'It'd be somewhere nice and handy, I take it?'

'I thought of the tenement down the court. Joe O'Hagan was just saying this new landlord has kicked a lot out for being late with the rent. There's plenty of rooms free. Willie could take one on the ground floor with no steps.'

'That's the ticket,' Duke agreed, though his heart was sinking. 'You think he can get by?'

Annie recalled the wrecked piece of humanity she'd just encountered. 'No, Duke. I'll have to look after him.' She looked him straight in the eye.

He lifted his hand to stroke her hair. 'I know, Annie,' he said sorrowfully. He cleared his throat, rising to the challenge of her selflessness. 'I been thinking about it. We gotta do the right thing, and I'm saying to you now, love you like I do, and will do to my dying day, I gotta tell you you're free. You ain't under no obligation to stay on at the Duke, see.'

'Free?' Annie repeated the word like a death sentence. 'You ain't sending me on my way, Duke?'

His voice broke down. 'Never in this world, Annie darling. Only, we gotta do what's right.'

Annie went and clung to him. 'I'm trying. But this is hard. I'd cut off my right hand for this never to have happened!'

'But it has.'

They talked long into the night, growing calmer, trying to look ahead into the future. The first thing they wanted to do next morning was to include everyone else in what had taken place. They asked Hettie to break the news to

Jess, while Sadie explained to Ernie that Duke and Annie had hit a problem they wanted to share with the family. Everyone was coming to Sunday tea.

Ernie nodded and went and got his best collar from the top drawer. He polished his boots and paid special attention to his teeth and hair. It was Ernie's wide, simple smile that greeted Mo and Grace that afternoon as they leaped upstairs.

'Now you all know this ain't the sort of Christmas get-together we had in mind,' Duke began. They'd arrived in Sunday best, as smart a bunch as he could wish to greet; the two men in their tight-fitting suits with wide lapels, the girls beautifully kitted out, thanks to Jess and Hettie's skill with the needle. His grandchildren were shiny clean in white collars and socks. 'No need to say why not, worse luck,' he went on. He looked down at Annie, who sat in her own fireside chair, turning her head this way and that with birdlike precision, her face glad as little Mo scrambled on to her knee.

Duke stood next to her, back to the fire, with the others gathered round, sitting or standing, and Rob leaning against the mantelpiece in his usual self-assured pose. 'Annie's asked me to start doing the talking,' he said. 'She wants you to know she ain't thrilled by Wiggin turning up out of the blue. But he's a sick man, and Annie wants to look after him.'

Frances leaned across and murmured to Billy. Jess warned Maurice to hear Duke out.

'Now, we all know her too well to try and change her mind. So she's been down the court this morning to have a word with Bertie Hill about renting a room.'

'How sick?' Maurice asked, in spite of his wife's warning. It was where everyone's thoughts were tending.

'Pretty bad,' Duke confirmed. 'But if he does pull through, Annie wants to have the room ready and waiting.'

'Even after what he's done to you?' Again Maurice was the one to give vent to a common feeling. 'This is the one what left you in the cart, remember? Not so much as a by-your-leave, according to Jess here.' He recalled the details of Annie's story; how Wiggin had taken off during one of his regular trips to sea. He'd told Annie he'd be away for two or three weeks. Weeks turned into months and months into years, and not a penny, not a word did he send. She wore out his old boots, tramping up and down the court, scrimping and saving to get by, building up a life for herself by running her haberdashery stall on Duke Street market. She'd been abandoned, but she refused to let it beat her. Only after years of silent struggle did she give Wiggin up for dead and set her sights on the widowed landlord at the Duke. When Duke had eventually proposed marriage, Annie had her runaway husband officially declared missing at sea, presumed dead; only to having him turn up again now, doing his Ancient Mariner act.

Now Annie felt it was her turn to speak. She touched Duke's hand. 'It ain't that simple, Maurice. Yes, he left me in the lurch, I don't say he didn't. But it depends how you look at things. According to the law, and Duke and I have talked this one through, Willie and me is still married.'

Sadie looked at Frances in alarm. Rob stood up and moved restlessly round to the back of the group, out of his father's gaze. The others stared wide-eyed or frowned at their own feet.

'But according to Ett, he don't even know who you are!'

Frances intervened. 'How can you still consider yourself married to him?'

Annie ploughed on. 'It's not me. It's the law, Frances. Ask Billy, he'll tell you the same thing as me. Anyhow, I ain't that hard-hearted. I gotta find the poor bloke a roof over his head, whatever he done. You all see that, don't you?' She pleaded for their understanding. 'Duke seen it straight off!'

Jess came up and took Mo gently from her, stooping to kiss her cheek. 'Poor Annie,' she said. She carried the boy back to her own chair.

'Thanks, Jess.' Annie sniffed into her handkerchief. 'And your pa has told me he won't hold me to vows that ain't legal no more. He says I can go.' Her voice trembled, her hands shook, a solitary figure in her big fireside chair.

'Not to Wiggin!' Sadie's outrage broke through.

Ernie heard Annie's last words with dawning dread. Slowly the picture of how things might change formed inside his head. He wandered out on to the landing and sat at the head of the stairs, frowning at the wall.

Annie shook her head. 'No, I ain't never going back with him. There's no law says I have to be his wife again, as far as I know; only the one saying I can't be your pa's no more.'

'More's the pity.' Frances looked up at Billy. She knew what Annie and Duke must have gone through to reach this decision.

'Pity is right,' Annie said. 'Anyhow, the plan is, I'll move my bits and pieces out of here this evening, back down the court to my old house.' She moved swiftly on. 'I'll need a hand from you, Rob, to carry my trunk in your cab. And I'll need plenty of elbow grease to get the old place shipshape again. Where's Ernie? Grace, sweetheart, you run and find him and ask if he'll sort out the rats in the cellar like he used to.'

Her enforced cheerfulness drove Hettie to tears. She'd prayed all morning in church for this not to happen; Annie having to move out, down to her dusty, deserted house in the corner of Paradise Court.

'Don't take on, Ett. Ain't nobody died yet, is there?' Annie couldn't bear it if good, strong Hettie broke down. She spotted Ernie drift back into the room, gazing uncertainly from her to his pa. 'Listen here, Ern!' Annie went and seized him by the hand. 'I ain't going far. Ask your pa; he says it's for the best. And I can carry on working behind the bar. So cheer up, things ain't as bad as they look!'

She repeated her own advice to herself later that evening when she sat down at her own lonely fireside, amid the smells of carbolic soap and lavender polish, with only the silver-framed portrait photograph of Duke smiling down at her from the mantelpiece.

CHAPTER EIGHT

The women of Paradise Court approached the Christmas of 1923 with a mixture of dread and determination. This was the time when finding presents for the children and a bit of extra meat for the table became a pressing burden to people already working through the night to exist, taking in washing or going out to clean in hotels and restaurants. Those who could bring home leftover bread and a knuckle of boiled bacon considered themselves lucky. The others took in still more outwork. Katie O'Hagan, for instance, sat the little ones around the kitchen table with cardboard and paste, where she supervised the making of matchboxes. She was set on buying their mother, Mary, something special for Christmas out of the one penny per hour which made up each child's average earnings.

Some of the men tried hard too to make this a time of seasonable enjoyment. But many were demoralized by chronic unemployment in the docks, and they took refuge in the pubs, often staying till well after midnight. Joe O'Hagan, his health failing, struggled to keep on his porter's job at Jack Cooper's drapery store, but nevertheless was one of the Duke's regulars, along with the unemployed Arthur Ogden. On the Monday of Christmas week, he came in with twelve shillings worth of hard-earned tips, laid it on the counter and demanded a supply of drink to keep him going through the festive season.

Annie looked at him tartly from behind the bar. 'What'll it be, Joe?' To her mind, a man wasn't a proper man unless he could regulate his drinking and put his family before his own need to block out harsh reality.

'The usual.' Joe sighed and rolled his cap to fit in the pocket of his worn jacket. 'Times are bad, make no mistake,' he told Arthur in his flat, sad voice. 'A man in work is a lucky man, believe me.' Over the years, Joe's hangdog look had increased; he stooped under the weight of his responsibilities, his pale, thin face was lined as tissue-paper, and his wide mouth had turned down in a permanent scowl.

Annie noticed his hand shake as he raised his glass to his lips.

'Go easy,' Duke warned Annie under his breath. 'Make sure he can get home in one piece.'

'I'll see him on his way,' she promised. Under the brand-new arrangement of Annie living at the bottom of the court, she could easily walk Joe home to Eden House.

Dolly Ogden's sharp ears picked this up. Tingling with curiosity, she leaned over the bar for a confidential chat. 'You made a nice job of them front windows of yours, Annie. I seen you out there yesterday afternoon with your leather and bucket. Shining like a new pin, they are now.' She nodded her approval.

Annie sniffed. She intended to give nothing away.

'Took me aback a bit, I can tell you.' Dolly creaked still closer, her old-fashioned stays straining against the bar-top, Like many of the older women, she stuck to the clinched and corseted look of her own youth. She derided the new, flat-chested style, showed off her cleavage and hid her girth behind strong laces and whalebone. 'I never thought in a month of Sundays that I'd be seeing you move back in down the court!'

'I seen you on your doorstep, Dolly.' Annie went on steadily serving. 'I never seen you offering to lend a hand though.'

'I never liked to butt in, Annie.'

'Since when?' Annie put money in the till. 'Pull the other one!'

'Anyhow, I seen Rob and Ernie helping to carry your stuff down. Charlie was working, otherwise he'd've lent a hand.'

'But not me with my bad back,' Arthur put in. 'Can't lift nothing heavy these days. It goes without a by-your-leave, and there I am, laid flat out. I have to go steady on the allotment, else I'll put it out good and proper.'

'But it don't stop you lifting a pint glass,' Dolly observed. She felt cheerful; the pub's shiny mirrors and fancy windows took her out of herself, the company and a fine old gossip did her good. 'Annie, you and Duke must have had a ding-dong battle for you to pack up your stuff and move out!'

'No.' Annie clamped her mouth tight shut. She swept empty glasses from the bar and took them to the sink.

'You can't fool me, Annie Parsons! It don't make no sense otherwise.'

'It don't to you, Dolly. But it do to Duke and me.'

'It ain't natural, Annie. A man and wife can't live in separate houses. I mean to say, Arthur here snores something shocking, but I ain't kicked him out of bed yet and we been married twenty-eight years.' She sighed; Arthur's snoring was one of the crosses she had to bear.

Annie knew it would only be a matter of time before the news broke. She spotted the sturdy figure of Bertie Hill come through the doors; she must tackle him about renting a room for Willie. Then the whole world and his wife would know. She shook her head at Dolly. 'Wait and see,' she advised. 'And don't go bothering Duke about it. You'll find out soon enough, and when you do, I don't want you poking your nose into what ain't none of your business, you hear me, Dolly?' She fixed her to the spot with the ferocity of her stare.

'Me?' Dolly attempted outrage, but she knew Annie meant business; no tittle-tattle. 'Don't take on, I'll mind my Ps and Qs,' she promised. Then she shook her head. 'It don't seem right to me.' She thought Duke looked worried and worn out, and she could tell Annie was only putting a brave face on things. 'It don't seem right at all.'

On the same Monday before Christmas, Sadie had to perform her own version of 'doing the right thing'. She went to work, and after Turnbull's public dressing-down over the badly typed letter, she'd put her head down and got through more than her fair share of work.

She sat at a long desk with three other typewriters, all women. They were all under thirty, nicely dressed, their nimble fingers flashing across the black and silver keyboards, sitting upright at their tapping machines. The work may have been repetitive, and Turnbull's standards ridiculously high, but it was clean work, and they had the sense of belonging to the modern age, free of the slave labour of factory and domestic work.

Turnbull's bark was nasty, but it was worse than his bite. In fact, the chief clerk held uneasily on to his own job; the women had proved themselves to be fast and efficient office workers, and he knew that his era of pen and paper and handwritten ledger books had passed for ever. He was a tall, thin man with grey hair that grew low on his brow but was combed straight back in a thick, greased pelt. He wore a grey moustache and thick glasses. At home he had a wife ill with tuberculosis, and three grown-up, unmarried daughters.

When lunch-break finally came, Sadie made her excuses to the other girls and slipped out to the depot to see Walter. She hoped to find him alone; Rob had mentioned a business appointment and Richie had been given a day off. But she knew she had only half an hour to break her news. Her stomach felt tight and fluttery as she half ran down Meredith Court, across the cinder yard into the gloomy garage.

Walter looked up from the desk with a smile. The sight of Sadie was enough to raise his spirits as he pored over the lists of figures which Rob had left for him to study. She came towards the office, stepping neatly between lathes and hoists, looking anxiously towards him. His smile faded as he came to meet her. He altered his expression and prepared himself for a serious talk.

Sadie had known Walter for most of her life. He'd been a pal of Rob's at school, then he'd worked at Coopers' and stood by the family all through Ernie's trial, before following Rob off to war. Unlike her brother, Walter had survived unscathed and come home to take up the old dream of running a taxicab business. The Army had helped build up his physique. His tall frame had filled out and he wore his wavy brown hair short and neat. He spoke little about life in the trenches and he even hid his disappointment with King and Country when they failed to offer him a decent means of making his living. He saw other young East Enders, more prepared to skirt wide of the law than he was, rising in the world through dubious trading on the docks or on the markets. Others got themselves a training in trades he didn't understand or care for; hotel work in the West End, or making new-fangled electrical equipment in the great new factories that sprang up wherever they demolished the old blocks of flats.

Walter lacked the ambition of a Maurice Leigh, but he was steady and determined. Over Sadie he was downright dogged. This was the woman he set his heart on, once she'd outgrown her schoolgirl crush on Charlie Ogden. She had spirit and good looks, and the war had brought Walter enough self-esteem to suppose he could win her if he set his mind to it. He knew he was braver and more steadfast than other men, thought that even if it was a deficiency within him that had let him go over the top into enemy fire without hesitation, then this was the same quality that made him reliable and loyal. He had patience. He would save towards the taxicab dream, and he would be there for Sadie, to take her dancing or to her favourite pastime, the picture-house.

In time this had won her over. She knew other men who were flashier, funnier, more charming, but not one paid her the same level of attention as Walter. He admired her looks, her decision to better herself by taking typing classes at night-school, the ease with which she held down her job at Swan and Edgar. As far as Walter was concerned, she could do no wrong. To be quietly adored was not the fate of every girl she knew, so for two or three years Sadie had counted her blessings and basked in Walter's affection.

Now she knew that what she had come to say must hurt him. 'Walter, I got something to say.' She took off her hat and sat down at the desk.

'I heard about Annie and Duke. Rob told me.' He hoped this was it; that Sadie had slipped out of work to tell him her troubles at home. But it didn't seem to be that. She could hardly bear to look him in the eye.

'It ain't that, Walter.' Sadie sat twisting the fingers of her gloves together. 'Though it's bad enough, believe me. No, this is about you and me.' She paused. How could she say that she meant to break off?

But this intimation was enough. Walter got up and turned his back for a second. Then he faced her. 'You don't want us to go on no more?'

Hearing him speak it out loud was a shock. She felt her safe world go crash. But that was just it; it was too safe going out with Walter. She was twenty-five years old and she'd seen so little of the world, done so little for herself. People were bound to think that going out with Richie Palmer was no substitute for Walter Davidson, who ran his own set-up and adored her through and through, as anyone could see. Richie was footloose; a moody type who might take off one day, never to be seen again. But he'd kindled her desire, an uncomfortable flame that let her know she was alive and desirable herself. She'd never felt that with Walter. She knew he respected and admired her, but he'd never treated her with true passion. She shook her head. 'I don't think I do, Walter.'

He longed for her to deny it. He wanted her to vanish from the room. He'd raise his head again, and there she would be, dashing across the yard towards him during her lunch-break, a smile on her face. They'd talk of this and that. He'd kiss her soft mouth. 'What happened?'

'Nothing happened, Walter.' She hoped to get away without telling the whole truth.

'Yes it did. You found someone else?'

She nodded once, then changed her mind. 'No, not

exactly. Only, I find I . . . *want* someone else. I ain't got him yet. I ain't cheated on you, Walt!'

'But it's Richie Palmer,' he said quietly. Her silence confirmed it. He thought it through. 'He ain't good enough for you, Sadie.'

'You *would* say that.' She felt a spurt of defiance burst through her guilt.

'But he ain't. He's a drifter. And have you thought what Rob will say now?'

She was angry. 'What's it matter what Rob says? Or anyone else? What matters is what you say, Walt! I ain't heard about that, have I?' She stood up to face him.

'What difference would it make?' He felt defeat settle on him. He wouldn't make a fool of himself by fighting. Pride held him up. 'I ain't going to beg you not to do it, Sadie. I ain't that kind. You know how I feel about you.' Against his judgement, he reached out to put his arms around her. For a second, her head rested against his shoulder. When she raised it, her eyes were full of tears.

'I'm sorry, Walter. I truly am.' She seemed to recognize and feel his distress. When a strong man was hurt, her tenderness overflowed. Yet she was the one to hurt him. In confusion, she pulled herself free.

He breathed a deep sigh. 'I ain't gonna say nothing to Rob,' he told her. In his own mind this wasn't completely altruistic; the affair would grow out of proportion if Rob found out, and there'd be less chance of things blowing over and of his getting back to normal with Sadie.

'Thanks.' She grasped his hands. 'I'll tell them at home in my own time. And you won't take it out on Richie neither? It ain't his fault.'

This was harder to promise, but Walter quickly saw wisdom here too. 'His job's here as long as he wants it,' he

94

said. 'As long as he keeps to time. And I'm here too, Sadie, waiting for you. You'll think of that sometimes?'

The tears flooded over as she nodded once and headed for the door. She was convinced now that she'd done the wrong thing. 'I must be mad,' she said through her tears. 'Letting go of you, Walt.' He took a step towards her, she met him eye to eye, then turned away. 'I gotta go now!' she whispered.

She sat red-eyed at her desk all afternoon, convincing herself that she would call it off with Richie. She would creep back to Walter and eat humble-pie, say what a terrible mistake she'd almost made, ask him to go on as if nothing had happened. Yet she knew again, as the black hand of the clock ticked towards six o'clock, that Richie would be out there waiting after work, and that something strong in her would welcome the sight of him, that her good resolution would dissolve away, and that she would fling herself into their evening out together regardless.

Monday, Tuesday and Wednesday crawled by for Annie and Duke. Bertie Hill had cast the pub landlord an odd glance when the request came from Annie for a room in the tenement, but his rule was never to ask questions where money was concerned. 'Tired of serving after hours?' he quipped. He took the first month's rent in advance and counted it out on to the bar. 'Can't say I blame you neither.'

'It ain't for me.' Annie faced him without blinking.

He looked up. 'Oh, well, ain't none of my business.' His face had an insolent half-smile.

She resented his attitude. 'That's right, it ain't,' she snapped.

'It's room number five, down the back,' he told her.

She knew those odd numbers on the ground floor; they faced on to ash-pits and rubbish heaps stacked up against the factory wall. Their windows overlooked sooty bricks, the filthy yard bred disease and harboured rats. Her stomach turned. 'Ain't you got nothing facing out front?' she demanded.

His small, mean eyes blinked, he shook his head. 'A view costs extra. Besides, ain't none of them for rent right now.'

Annie knew quite well that Bertie Hill was lying. He shoved up the rents and stuck tenants wherever he pleased. It was useless to argue.

'Take it or leave it.' He shrugged.

She nodded. 'I'll send Ernie down for the key later on.'

That was Tuesday. On the morning of Christmas Eve, Wiggin walked half-naked out of the Mission sick-bay, down the main corridor, demanding his clothes. Major Hall telephoned Annie to warn her he was on the move. 'He's not really fit to go,' she told her. 'But he insists. I thought you would want to know.'

'I'll come and fetch him,' Annie promised. 'What kind of Christmas present do they call this?' she grumbled to George Mann, who was shifting new barrels into position in the cellar. 'Tell Duke for me, will you? He's out buying last-minute things. Tell him I have to go fetch Willie.'

She flew out into Duke Street, her coat still unbuttoned, running to catch the tram that would take her down Bear Lane and noticing with sharp irony that for once the day was fine and clear. She reached the Mission just in time to see the huddled shape of her old husband come stumbling down the broad front steps, elbows up, fending off all offers of help from two Salvation Army officers. She rushed up and seized his arm.

'Hush, Willie! . . . There's gratitude for you!' She tried

to quieten him, apologizing to the people who'd saved his life. 'I'll take you back now. I found a room down Paradise Court, I made it nice and clean for you. Come on, now.' She struggled against his shoves and curses.

'He won't take in much of what you tell him,' the Army man advised. He didn't envy Annie the task of getting Wiggin home.

Annie grunted. 'He still don't know me, do he?' She stood trying to attract his attention. 'Willie, behave! It's me, Annie!'

Again the name clicked deep inside his memory. He investigated her features for a few seconds, then he pulled away.

'Now, it ain't that bad,' she joked grimly. 'I ain't changed that much, have I?'

'Wiggin, 02753, sir!' he told her. 'See that big one in the uniform there?' He hissed and pointed to the Army man on the steps. 'He ain't what he seems!' With a mysterious gesture, he beckoned Annie down the street.

'What's he mean by this number lark?' Annie wanted to know.

The woman Army officer came down quickly to speak with her. 'We think it's a prison number,' she said quietly. 'He don't hardly know where he is most of the time.'

Annie shook herself straight. 'Prison?' She looked at Wiggin through narrowed eyes. 'No wonder you never came home, you old scoundrel!'

'Try to keep him off the drink,' the young woman advised.

'That's like saying, try to keep the rain from falling,' Annie retorted. 'You hear that, Willie? You've to stay on the wagon!' She set off, remonstrating with him all the way down the street, deciding not to risk taking a tram back to

Duke Street. Though the Army had cleaned up his clothes and the stench was certainly less, they couldn't clean up Wiggin's language for him. He shuffled along, foul-mouthed as before, shouting at invisible devils that tormented him and hovered just out of reach.

Duke and Annie decided to make the best of Christmas that year, for the sake of their customers, and for little Grace and Mo. With Wiggin holed up in Eden House, Duke gave strict orders that he must not be served in the pub, telling Annie that her old husband was in such a poor state that he would never have the strength to stagger further than the end of the court in search of the liquor that was killing him.

But Wiggin on the trail of drink was a cunning animal. He collared a lad on the street and sent him up the pawn shop with the ex-army greatcoat which the Mission had donated as their last act of charity towards him. With sixpence from the coat, Wiggin gave one penny to the lad and ordered him to spend the other five on gin and to bring the bottle back down the court. After that was gone, he would have to beg and steal his way towards the next drink. He had no pride, felt no gratitude, possessed no intention in life, save that of oblivion.

Annie found him on Christmas morning, dead drunk on the stone floor.

In the afternoon, Jess and Maurice came with the children, and there were presents, music and games. Ernie had his new tie from Sadie. He gave Grace a parcel of chocolate wrapped in silver and purple, and Mo a painted wooden soldier. No one spoke of family troubles. Maurice and Rob talked business, while Billy asked Ernie about his longtime job with Henshaw's. 'Mr Henshaw ain't there no more,' Ernie told him sadly. 'He passed away. But Mrs Henshaw says she needs me more than ever. She wouldn't know how to get by without me!'

Duke overheard and winked at Frances. 'Cheer up, girl. Have a drop of sherry,' he insisted. 'Come on, Frances, it's time you let your hair down for once.'

She tried for his sake. But she didn't relax until Annie came in, and she saw her father and her stepmother smile at one another and go on as before. If they could cope, then surely to goodness she could too.

Jess and Hettie gossiped with Sadie, the three of them heads together at the table loaded with cold ham pie and sandwiches. They sat under swathes of holly and mistletoe, talking shop and fashion, discussing the merits of various face powders and the desirability of the recent trend among women to take up smoking.

'It's only what the men do,' Sadie protested. 'You see it in all the films these days.'

'Yes, and I don't like it,' Jess put in, playing the respectable lady and mother. 'It makes them look . . . fast.' She drew the line at her own shorter skirts.

'I don't know. I like the look of them silver holders.' Hettie sprang her opinion on them. 'Not that I'd take up smoking cigarettes myself, but I don't object to them that do.'

For a time, it seemed a normal Christmas afternoon. It was only when Annie stepped out to check on Wiggin that the heart went out of their quiet celebrations and they were reminded of the problems which the new year held in store.

Rob was the first in the family to tackle trouble head on. He didn't like the way Christmas slowed London down, taking people off the streets and business out of his pockets. He would grumble about it to his occasional girlfriend, Amy Ogden, who was home for a few days, staying at her mother's place.

Amy had many boyfriends, none of them steady. She called it moving with the times. Quite the career woman, with ambitions to become supervisor of the hat department at Dickins and Jones, she was one who didn't hesitate to hitch up her skirts when fashion dictated, or to lounge elegantly against a doorpost, cigarette-holder in hand, playing the vamp. She wore long strings of false pearls and shiny rayon stockings. She curled her fair hair with the new Marcel wave, and though she worked hard at reducing her weight to suit the new, boyish styles, she never succeeded in slimming down her curves. Rob advised her not to bother. 'It ain't natural,' he told her. 'Anyhow, I like you just the way you are.'

Amy enjoyed flirting with Rob. It came naturally. She could make him laugh with her sly imitations of the narrow-voiced, la-di-da customers she dealt with in the shop. She did the accent well and made herself cross-eyed with the effort of looking down her nose. They both enjoyed sending up the middle classes; the flappers, the bright young things.

'You're only jealous,' he taunted. ''Cos you ain't got what they got.'

'What's that?' Amy blew smoke from between her red lips. She'd teased Rob for being all dressed up when she'd dropped in at the pub to arrange an evening out with him. It was tea-time one Monday early in January.

'Cash,' came the swift reply. 'The pound in your pocket to buy one of them nice new hats.'

'Says who?' Amy countered airily. 'Anyhow, Rob, how about a night at the pictures with your best girl?' She changed the subject, wondering why he was already dressed up in his suit.

'Maybe. I got something to do first.'

'Something more important than taking me to see this new Greta Garbo picture they're all on about?'

'Much more. I gotta see a man about a dog.'

'Come again?' Amy showed she was put out. She went into a sulk over her cigarette.

'A woman about a loan, if you must know.' Rob picked up his trilby hat and his walking stick. He'd arranged to visit Mrs Cooper personally to pay the last instalment of his loan. He thought it would be wise to wish her Happy New Year in person.

Amy frowned. A woman? 'Best of bleeding luck,' she said to his back as he swung through the doors.

Rob's appointment was for five o'clock. He used the lift up to the office and arrived on the dot, catching the eye of the shopgirls, who knew him of old. But today he wanted to impress with his businesslike attitude, so he resisted the temptation to stop and chat. Injury hadn't diminished his darkly handsome appearance. His square face was clean-shaven except for the moustache, and his shoulders were still broad and straight. He brushed his short dark hair to one side, took pride in himself, but avoided close involve-ment with women. He didn't want pity, neither did he want to be anyone's second-best. For who would put up with an injured husband if they could find an able-bodied one?

As the lift door clicked and slid open, Rob stepped out on to the carpeted landing. He saw that Cooper's office door was open and Mrs Cooper herself stood there uncer-tainly, waiting for him to arrive. She was a slight figure in a purple-grey outfit, with lace and a gold brooch at her throat.

Rob followed her into the office and drew out a long brown envelope from his inside breast-pocket. He handed it across the desk. As she opened it, fifteen pounds in single pound notes fluttered out. 'But this is too much!' she declared. 'Are you sure you can afford all this at once?'

He nodded and they fell to pleasantries for a while; the cold, clear snap of weather, the cost of living. Then Rob cleared his throat. As for business, he said, he had great plans for the future. 'My partner Walter and me, we want to go in for a more modern type of car, a Morris Cowley.'

Edith Cooper listened politely. Since the war and the loss of her only son, Teddy, she'd faded and pined. She was thinner, much older-looking, greyer, more subdued. Not a day went by without her thinking what might have been if she hadn't insisted on Teddy joining up. He might not have been killed in that plane crash; there might have been grandchildren, a future, a family to cushion her old age. She found herself drifting off as Rob carried on explaining the benefits of replacing the old cars with brand-new ones.

'As you know, I'm a good risk. I pay my debts on time. Never been late with an instalment,' he reminded her.

'No, never,' she agreed. She rested her thin arms along the padded armrests of the swivel chair. In the background, the whir and ping of change machines racing along their taut wire tracks punctuated their conversation.

'So I would like to set out another proposition.' Rob came to the crux of the matter. 'If you could see your way to advancing us another two hundred pounds, we would pay it back at a more favourable rate of interest than before, and use the money to invest in a new motor car. I've worked out the figures and set them down here, if you'd like to take a look.' Rob knew how to behave with Mrs Cooper; impeccably polite, direct. That way she would go on trusting him.

Edith frowned. She gazed down at the gold watch hanging as a pendant around her neck. She realized that her husband was due back from the cotton suppliers at any time now; it had been her idea to fix Rob's appointment so that she would have the satisfaction of seeing her husband's face when he realized that her 'bad risk' had paid off. But there was no way he would permit her to make another loan.

'We must expand to survive, you see,' Rob said. 'Each year the competition gets stiffer. I can see which way the wind blows; before too long all the old carters' yards will be shut down and the heavy stuff will go on motor lorries. That's something for the future, of course.'

She nodded once. 'You want to borrow another two hundred pounds?'

'Yes.' Rob sat forward in his chair. 'I won't let you down, Mrs Cooper.'

But she had faded back into her chair. 'I'm afraid it's impossible,' she said. Her hand tapped the chair arm, she glanced out of the window, heard the lift bell jangle below.

'How's that?' Rob had convinced himself of success. He'd worked out the figures to make absolute sense.

'Oh, it's not that it wouldn't be a good investment.' She shook her head and raised a pale, thin hand to reassure him. 'No, I'm quite sure that what you say is very fair, and I wish I could help, I really do!' She looked at him in mute appeal.

Rob quickly caught on. He saw how much his proposal had embarrassed her. He glanced at the oldish fixtures and fittings around the place; out of date now and slightly down-at-heel. It dawned on him; Coopers' was struggling, just like everywhere else. It had hit hard times since the coming of the massive new West End stores, it had grown shabby and unfashionable. And he'd never even noticed.

He stood up at once. 'I'm sorry, Mrs Cooper. I'm sorry the investment don't seem a sound one to you.' He was gentlemanly enough to spare her further embarrassment. Amid his own crashing disappointment, he wanted to ease Edith Cooper's position.

She nodded and stood up to shake his hand once more. 'Thank you, Robert,' she said quietly. 'And I wish you luck.'

He went out, walking tall, knowing in his heart that it was more than luck they needed to keep the taxi business afloat. He pretended not to catch sight of Jack Cooper's florid, overweight figure coming into the store as he left.

'What did Parsons want?' Cooper snapped suspiciously at his wife as soon as he reached the office.

'He came to pay the last instalment of his loan,' she told him calmly.

Cooper grunted. His features were sunken into folds of flesh, his eyelids drooped. 'Well, you needn't think it'll make any difference,' he told her. 'We'll get no more cotton or rayon yarn from Hazlitts'. No supplies without payment first; that's the form these days.'

Edith rose from her chair in alarm. 'What'll we do without the yarn, Jack?'

He sneered at her. 'What'll we do without the yarn? Close down Hosiery, of course!' He would have to lay off ten women, and that would only be the start.

CHAPTER NINE

'And what will all them women do for work now?' Jess frowned as she paused to rethread the needle of her sewing-machine. Hettie had come into the shop one morning in mid-May and told her the bad news. Coopers' were laying off still more of their workforce. This time it was the hatmakers and some of the sales assistants in the shoe department, following on the heels of the hosiery workers laid off at the start of the year.

According to Hettie, they'd held off till spring to see if trade picked up, but the displays in the big plate-glass windows had failed to attract enough customers into the drapery store. Among those with money to spend, the talk was all of Selfridges in the West End, and Woolworths, whose proud boast of 'Nothing Over Sixpence' brought in the crowds.

Hettie sat in the sunny window seat, putting finishing touches to a peacock-blue dress. Their workroom was at the back of the shop, overlooking a long garden which at this time of year was white with blossom; a world away from Coopers' attic sweatshops. 'A job's a job,' Hettie agreed. She thought of poor Dora Kennedy, who'd been in that hatters for donkey's years, suddenly out of work. At fifty or so, she was likely to be on the scrapheap for good.

'It don't seem right.' Jess resumed her sewing. The steady whir of the machine had a calming effect. 'If you ask me, Ett, Coopers' is on its last legs. I don't think they can stagger on much longer.' If the store closed down, it would leave a big gap in Duke Street; an employer of that size, even one as tight-fisted and autocratic as Jack Cooper, would be sorely missed.

'Rob told me that was the way it looked just after Christmas. He wanted to set up some business with Edith Cooper, but she had to turn him down flat. She weren't able to help.' Hettie's needle flew in and out of the soft rayon silk.

'No, now him and Walter have to get by with them two old cabs instead of buying new motorcars. Rob says they ain't reliable no more. They're on their last legs and all.' Jess sighed.

Not for the first time, the sisters counted their blessings in landing this little shop in Ealing High Street. They'd established a niche in the market as a high-class ladies' dressmaker's specializing in finely tailored, hand-finished articles made to a customer's own specifications. This way they could follow the latest fashion whims. Since the opening of King Tut's tomb earlier that year, it had been all things Egyptian. Now their ladies wanted tight-fitting, square-necked shifts with bold designs in turquoise and gold. They dressed their window accordingly with a fan of peacock feathers, lapis-lazuli necklaces and gold cloth to capture the mood of the Pharaoh's tomb. Jess was the one with the eye for design, Hettie the skilled seamstress who checked every detail.

Generally their customers called by appointment, and the shop space presented a quiet, exclusive air. The long glass counter displayed one or two expensive hats, a pair of kidskin shoes, good-quality accessories. The shelves were stacked with bolts of shiny cloth, the walls hung with Jess's design sketches and photographs from fashion magazines. They had a developing reputation for good work combined with flair, and were reckoned ladylike in their dealings with customers, and very fair in the prices charged.

'What do you think of the set of this sleeve?' Hettie held up the blue dress for examination. It was part of a large, rushed order for a lady planning a spring wardrobe to take with her on a cruise ship holiday. She'd heard of the Parsons sisters by word of mouth and descended on them with a flurry of ideas and requirements.

Jess cast a critical eye over the garment. 'I think we need to take a bit more fullness out of here.' She pointed to tiny gathers around the shoulder arch. 'That line over the top should be smooth as we can make it, and all the interest comes in the trim down the front of the bodice, here.'

They were so busy discussing details that they overlooked Maurice, who'd come in the back way. It was half past two, and he'd called in on his way to work.

Their absorption in their task irritated him. He had a strong and childish notion that sewing up a piece of cloth was more important to Jess than him or anything else these days. What on earth could she find so fascinating about the set of a sleeve? He threw his hat on to the window seat and turned to look up the garden, hands in pockets.

'I hope you remembered, you gotta take Mo to the doctor after school,' he said without preliminaries. They thought he might have a slight ear infection, and Frances had suggested they go and get it looked at.

Jess checked herself, hearing the impatience in his voice. Hettie withdrew into the shop to busy herself there. 'Hello, Maurice! Fancy seeing you! Ain't this a nice surprise!' Jess went up to him and teased him, brushing some white petals off his dark suit. She offered her husband a kiss on the cheek. ''Course I remembered. What do you think I am?'

He smiled self-consciously. 'Sorry, Jess, I never meant to snap. Will you ring me and tell me what the doctor says?'

'The minute we get home,' she promised.

'And can you fetch that book from the library for me? The one on aeroplanes I want to read.' Maurice had his usual subconscious reaction; the more Jess's involvement in the shop seemed to take her away from her role of house-wife, the more small errands he found for her to do.

Again Jess had to bite her lip. 'If I get the time,' she told him, then regretted saying even this.

Maurice went tight-lipped. She'd proved the point he was trying to make; running the shop got in the way of smooth family life. But he wouldn't argue about it now. 'I'd best be off. I'll be back just after midnight.' He picked up his trilby and brushed the pile all one way with the back of his sleeve. Returning her kiss, he strode out into the garden, up the side alley to his beloved Morris, bought that February, brand-new after all, gleaming by the kerbside. He jumped into it and glided off down the High Street.

'Don't say nothing!' Jess warned Hettie, as her sister looked to see if the coast was clear.

'Would I?' Hettie said sweetly. 'You know me, Jess. I never interfere!'

Jess laughed, then sighed. 'Maurice sees things one way, and I see them another, that's all.' They worked in silence. 'He's got his dreams, see, and there ain't much room inside his head for other people's.'

Hettie considered this and nodded.

'And he does love them kids. He thinks the world of them.' The sewing-machine whirred, stopped, restarted.

'And just think, Ett, he picked me up when I was down. He took me on when Grace was tiny, and there's many wouldn't, not with a baby hanging round my neck.'

'I ain't arguing,' Hettie repeated. 'Only, you was down but not out, remember! You was coping. You was more than coping!' She thought how Jess had come home to the Duke, pregnant and abandoned, how she'd held up her head and helped the family through the awful time of Daisy O'Hagan's murder and Ernie's trial. She'd been the backbone, the strength of the family, fighting every inch of the way. 'No need to feel so grateful to him, Jess. I should think Maurice was over the moon when he found you.'

Jess blushed and laughed. 'He was,' she admitted. 'And so was I.'

'Well then.'

They continued working quietly. Only, all that seemed so long ago; a different lifetime, two other people. Jess sat there, afraid of the gap opening up between her and her husband, unsure of how to deal with it. 'If only he didn't work so late,' she put in. 'There ain't no time to talk.'

Hettie nodded. 'But he does, and that's that. A job's a job, remember, and Maurice is working his way right to the top.'

She should be proud. She had a dozen reasons to be grateful. Jess snipped and tied and oversewed, willing herself to accept things as they were, thinking of the life that lay ahead for her two children; a nice house, proper schooling, summer holidays and lovely things to wear.

For Rob, the improvement in the weather as summer approached was sometimes enough to lift his spirits. They hadn't managed to scrape together the money to buy new cabs; so what? Richie Palmer worked to keep the two old Bullnoses on the road, and they could get by for a bit longer. He was thinking this as he pulled in one afternoon in late May at the new petrol pump outside Powells' ironmongers on Duke Street. He got out and lounged against the car in the spring sunshine, watching the young lad, Jimmie, work the petrol up the gauge by turning the pump-handle in big, energetic circles. Eight turns of the handle for one full gallon. Rob checked carefully. 'Don't you go short-changing me,' he warned. 'I ain't one of your toffs who can afford to take under the gallon, you know. Top it right up.' He knew the boy's trick of flipping the pointer over the gallon mark with a quick flick of his finger.

The lad shrugged. 'Who, me, mister?' He was all fair-haired, blue-eyed innocence. He finished turning the pump, then drew a wash-leather from the back pocket of his overalls. He set to work on the windscreen, whistling as he wiped.

'All right, all right, no need to make a meal of it!' Rob cuffed the back of Jimmie's head and tossed a penny for him to catch.

The boy grinned. He'd secretly flicked the gauge, *and* earned a penny tip. He was well on his way to another night out at the picture-house.

Rob climbed back into the car, easing his leg sideways. Up and down Duke Street, taxicabs were on the lookout for passengers. Suddenly his mood swung the other way. 'This game ain't worth the candle,' he told himself as he joined the flow. 'Leastways, it's getting that bleeding way, unless Walter and me come up with something new.' The truth was, money problems kept him working from dawn until well after midnight, then kept him awake at night. For months he'd set his nose to the grindstone and not noticed much of what went on around him. Any time he took off work, he drove up the West End and took Amy out. This was getting by by the skin of his teeth, he realized. Still, it was no worse than for anyone else, except perhaps lucky sods like Maurice.

Think of Annie. She had to come up the court each day, call in on Wiggin to sort out his food, his coal, his cooking. Then she would carry on up to the Duke to work behind the bar. Just who was married to who was the cause of much comment in the pub, after Dolly Ogden had first put two and two together and identified Annie's old husband, Wiggin.

'No wonder Annie's moved out!' she declared to an astonished Arthur. 'When you think about it, her and Duke, they've been living in sin!' She laughed uproariously.

Arthur sniffed. 'No they ain't, you silly cow. They tied the knot in good faith, didn't they? Just because Wiggin turns up out of the blue shouldn't mean she gets turfed out of here, does it?' He spoke in a loud voice, above the hum of voices in the pub. Duke overheard and moved away.

'Hush!' Dolly hissed. 'You'll get us chucked out if you're not careful!'

Rob was looking daggers at them. 'It ain't funny,' he warned.

'No, it ain't,' Dolly agreed, overtaken by decency. She coloured up. 'No offence, Rob. Only you gotta admit, it *is* a turn-up for the book!'

After a time Rob had got used to the gossip and learned to ignore it. Opinion was strongly on the side of Annie and Duke continuing to live together as a married couple. Only Mary O'Hagan told her daughter, Katie, that she could understand their dilemma. They would hear Wiggin crashing into things and fighting his invisible devils in the room below, and they would admit that as long as he was alive and kicking, there was not much that Duke and Annie could do. Tommy overheard and put in his two ha'porth. 'I don't know about *alive* and kicking,' he said with a sour look. 'But the sooner he kicks the bucket, the better.'

Mary said a quick Hail Mary an her son's behalf. But Tommy said it was a common opinion. 'The old scoundrel ain't worth wasting your breath on,' he insisted.

Because of work and worry, Rob didn't spend too much time trying to work out his family's problems. If the present arrangement between Annie and Duke held up, that was enough. Who could expect a trouble-free life these days? He had noticed that things had cooled off between Walter and Sadie, but it drew no comment. Again, that was their business, so long as Sadie behaved herself, and he had no evidence that she wasn't.

Deep in thought, Rob swung the car down Meredith Court, its tank newly full. There, at the fringe of his vision, standing on the pavement outside the Lamb and Flag, were two figures, a man and a woman. They'd just come out of the pub and paused to kiss goodbye before heading their separate ways. Rob had passed well down the street before it clicked; that was Sadie in her new cream-coloured jacket and skirt, and she was with Richie Palmer. He flashed a look in his mirror. They were gone.

Thumping the steering-wheel with the heel of his hand, Rob pressed on. He slammed on the brakes in the depot yard and hauled himself out of the car. Tact wasn't part of his make-up; he'd go in and let Walter know the score, and they could have it out with Richie when he next showed up.

Walter saw that something was eating Rob as soon as he put the telephone on its hook and looked up.

'I just seen Sadie with Palmer!' Rob came in and slammed the office door. 'And they was more than just good friends, I can tell you!'

Walter steadied himself by placing his palms flat on the desk. 'I know, Rob. No need to shout.'

It stopped him dead in his tracks. 'You know? What the bleeding hell's going on round here?'

'Me and Sadie's broken off, in case you hadn't noticed.'

Rob grunted. If two people broke off, it was up to them. 'It ain't because of Palmer, is it?'

'Maybe.' Walter had watched Sadie fling herself into the affair. He'd read the signs; secretive telephone calls to the garage during her lunch-break, Richie sprucing himself up to go out on a night. You didn't have to be a genius to see that Sadie and Richie had hit it off.

Wrong-footed, Rob let loose his rage against the mechanic. 'Slimy customer, he is. Stealing another man's girl from under his nose. Well, he's got it coming to him now!' His fist came down on the desk. The telephone jumped on its hook.

'Steady on, pal.' Walter wasn't sure how much of this he could take.

'I bet he's cock-a-hoop, he is!' Rob imagined the tales Richie would spread among his friends of how he'd broken up a beautiful friendship and shown his bosses up for what they were: one man who couldn't keep his girl, and another whose sister was a cheap little flirt. 'Well, not for long. 'Cos the minute he steps foot in here, he'll find himself out of a job and in that bleeding dole queue. Then let's see how fascinating he is to the women!'

Walter stood up and shook his head. 'No, Rob, you ain't gonna sack him. I promised.'

Again Rob needed a second to get the measure of this.

'Promised? Promised who?' He leaned forward on the desk, elbows locked, arms braced.

'Sadie,' Walter explained. 'I said I wouldn't take things out on Richie.'

'And you never said nothing to me?' Rob felt a fool. All this had gone on behind his back. 'Don't I have a say in it? Palmer's ruining a girl's good name, and that girl happens to be my kid sister!'

'I ain't standing up for what he's done, Rob.' Walter felt he was in a hopeless position. 'And maybe I would like to clock him one, to tell you the truth. But I can't.' He reached for his hat and opened the door. 'Anyhow, I got a fare to pick up over the water,' he said. 'Now don't do nothing stupid, Rob. Take it easy.' He paused a moment longer. 'What you gonna do now?'

Rob turned away in disgust. 'Knock his bleeding head off,' he muttered. 'If he shows his face in here.'

'No, you ain't,' Walter insisted.

'All right, I ain't.' Rob limped to a shelf behind the desk to pull out a black ledger. 'I'm gonna do some paperwork, that's what I'm gonna do.' He thumped the book down on the desk.

Walter breathed a sigh of relief. 'I thought you mentioned Amy might drop by?'

'Maybe.'

'Well, why don't you two head off to the picture-house soon as I get back? I'll hold the fort here.'

'Maybe,' Rob said again. He stuck his head into the lists of figures, refusing to look up as Walter choked the engine into life and headed off to collect his fare.

*

Amy Ogden signed out of her crib at Dickins and Jones with the information that she was heading down to home turf on her night off.

'Cheerio!' Sammy Hutchinson called from his top-floor dormitory where all the male assistants stayed. He saw her step smartly into the narrow alleyway as he hung his work shirt out to dry.

Amy stopped to wave. 'I know, Sammy, "Don't do nothing I wouldn't do!"' It was their refrain whenever they spotted one another going out on the town. 'Would I?' She blew a kiss then ran on to the street, heading for the Oxford Circus tube and all points south.

In the railway carriage, she took her little mirror from her clutch-bag and checked her lashes and lips, happy with an arrangement of beads and feathers forming a circlet around her newly blonde hair. She would knock Rob dead tonight, if he did but know it. She'd get him to take her out in the car, maybe downriver into the countryside. 'It's a nice night,' she said to herself as she mounted the stairs into the warm evening light, under hoardings advertising Pears' Soap and Nestlé's Milk. Nothing could dent her mood; not even the usual sights of ragged children clustered in doorways and grim-faced women shuffling down from the railway embankment with an armful of potatoes or some half-rotten cabbage leaves.

'Nice night,' she repeated to Rob as she waltzed into his narrow office in a strong swirl of lily-of-the-valley perfume and face powder.

'Is it?' He glanced up, his face a picture of peevish displeasure.

Amy laughed out loud. 'It was till I came in here!' She seized the black ledger he was poring over and slammed it shut. 'Robert Parsons, get your hat. You're gonna take me for a drive!' she announced.

'Am I?' He smoothed his moustache and frowned up at her. 'And who'll run this show while we're off hobnobbing?'

'Walter will. Won't you, Walter?' Amy's voice wheedled as she heard Walter Davidson come into the office.

'I already told Rob I would.' He hung his hat back an its peg.

'Oh, come on, Rob, it ain't as if it's a weekend or nothing!' Amy was unashamed as she perched on his knee and slung her arms around his neck.

He swung her back on to her feet. 'All right, hold your horses while I hand on these messages to Walter. Go and wait in the car.'

She grinned. 'That's the ticket' She was pleased with her persuasive powers as she went out to sit and wait. Rob always came round, no matter how grumpy he was at the start. She slid into the passenger seat and anticipated their evening out: a drive out of the city, a drink in a country pub before they found a nice quiet lovers' lane, some woodland spot where Rob would spread a blanket on the ground in the moonlight, among the primroses. It would be almost romantic, almost like it was in the pictures.

'You ain't going out tonight, then?' Hettie asked Sadie. It was unusual enough for her to comment on.

Sadie shook her head. She'd just met up with Richie for a quick drink after work, but this was her evening in for washing her hair and curling up with a good book. There'd been precious few lately, since she'd got caught up in the storm of emotions connected with Richie Palmer.

'Put the flags out,' Hettie said, caustic for once. 'It's

about time you stopped to let your feet touch the ground.' Although the whole family knew that things had cooled between her and Walter, Sadie had not confided her new state of affairs to anyone. She grew tense when the subject was mentioned, and more secretive as the weeks went by.

'Don't go on, Ett,' she said, affecting concentration. But the words on the page blurred. Although Hettie let it go and drifted downstairs to help in the pub, Sadie's own thoughts were enough to make the print swim before her eyes.

The simple fact was, she couldn't get Richie Palmer out of her mind. He was locked in there, a secret she dare not share because she didn't want to admit the strength of her feelings for him.

Richie took her out three or four times a week, usually well away from Duke Street. Still poor in the word department, he never said he loved her, but actions spoke louder than words. He wanted to be with her, touching, kissing, walking close by her side. She'd grown used to his face: the heavily lidded eyes, the straight nose, the full mouth. It was like a contour map she could trace inside her own head and conjure up to catch herself out while she sat typing, or reading, as now. The sound of his voice ordering a drink would echo in her mind, and she would look up, surprised to find herself at home or at work. His image filled her dreams, not pleasantly as a romantic hero, but as an obsession she couldn't move away from, sentenced to go wherever he went, though he might not even acknowledge she was there.

'Fool!' she told herself. She would have to get up to look in the mirror and talk straight at her reflection. 'What's happening to you? What has happened to your life?' But any resolution to distance herself from Richie melted away as soon as they met. He would clasp her hand, walk her along, claim her.

The trouble was, she read things into his silences, even if she suspected they were the wrong things; her romantic heart leading her to false conclusions, she lacked a guide to put her straight. Her sisters would never understand. Theirs would be a paler version of Rob's antipathy to Richie, and they would side with Walter, her old flame.

She told herself versions of Richie's life story, half making it up, snatching at fragments that he himself let slip. He'd always been alone; she knew that much. He'd built a shell around himself, fooling people with a hard, tough exterior. But really he was easily hurt. He was proud, despite his poor beginnings, with the pride of an animal strong enough to protect his own territory; in this case, his heart.

Sadie would gaze into his face before she kissed it. It seemed to her that even his words had to fight to escape through clenched teeth in case they betrayed him. She got used to his low, indistinct voice. It was one of the things she loved best.

Her evening at home had turned as always into the fascinating study of the workings of Richie Palmer's mind, when she heard footsteps on the stairs. She recognized Rob's tread and a lighter step, probably a woman's. Before she had time to close her book and slip away, Amy Ogden had opened the door and entered the room laughing.

'Oh no you don't!' Amy swept in. 'No sneaking off, Sadie Parsons. Put that kettle on and make us a cup of cocoa while we put our feet up. We been out driving, and we need a nightcap before Rob drives me back to the barracks!' She pretended to give a smart salute. 'I ain't signed out for the whole night, so I gotta get back.'

Something about the way Sadie put down her book, a

small, superior smile perhaps, irritated Rob. Sadie needn't get on her high horse about Amy; she was no better than anyone else round here when it came to it.

While Sadie put the kettle to boil and Amy chatted on, Rob decided to knock his sister off her perch, as he called it. 'Ain't the Duke good enough for you no more, then?' he dropped in, stretching his chin over her shoulder, pretending to sniff the cocoa.

'What you on about now?' She shrugged him off, hoping that he wasn't planning to annoy her, totally unsuspecting.

'It's the Lamb and Flag now, I take it?'

The spoon froze in mid-air. Sadie couldn't frame a reply, remembering that she'd been in the Lamb with Richie earlier that evening. What had Rob seen? Was her secret out? Eventually she stammered something about popping in with a friend.

'O-ho!' Amy spotted gossip. 'She's got a guilty conscience, I'd say, Rob. Just look at her, she's red as a beetroot!'

'Shut up, Amy!' Sadie threw the spoon on to the table. She turned to confront her brother. 'Come out with it, say what you want to say!'

Amy pretended to retreat behind a magazine, her mouth puckered, eyebrows raised. She kept her ears wide open: it promised to build up into something she wouldn't miss for the world.

'I'll say what I gotta say tomorrow morning down the depot, when Richie Palmer comes in.' Rob met her gaze. His voice had fallen to a low, deliberate pitch.

The sound of Richie's name opened the floodgates of Sadie's panic. 'No, Rob! That ain't fair, you leave him out of this!'

'I'd leave him out if he'd leave you out.' Rob intended

119

to see this argument through. He forgot all about Amy sitting there, ears flapping, as he launched into Sadie for letting down the family's name. 'He ain't nothing but a grease monkey, and you know it!'

'Keep this between you and me, Rob. You ain't got no right to talk about Richie that way!'

'No, but I got the right to tell him to move on all right, and that's what I plan to do first thing tomorrow morning.'

Amy's eyes shone. She turned back to Sadie, awaiting her next move.

Sadie took a deep breath. 'You do that, Rob Parsons, you give Richie the sack for no good reason, and that's the last you'll see of me round here!' She began to shout and flounce towards the landing.

'Tell the whole bleeding street, why don't you?' He sneered as he took out a cigarette and lit it.

'I mean it. You get rid of Richie and I go too. 'Cos you make me sick, that's why, with your bullying and throwing your weight around. Who do you think you are, telling me what to do, lording it over everyone like you do, when you're really just as bad. No, you're worse! We all know what you get up to in the back of that taxi, and it ain't nice!' Sadie shot a glance at Amy, who turned to her magazine to hide her own blushes. 'So don't think you can go on about other people and get away with it yourself, you bleeding hypocrite!' The rush of words left Sadie shaking. Her throat felt constricted, there were hot tears in her eyes.

Slowly Amy clapped into the silence. 'Hurrah!' she drawled. 'You tell him, girl.' To her credit, she recognized a good show when she saw one and didn't take Sadie's insulting implications personally.

Rob shrugged. He blew a funnel of smoke towards the

ceiling. 'It don't make no difference,' he pointed out. 'Go ahead, bawl away all you like, Sadie. But tomorrow morning, first thing, I go down that garage and I give Richie Palmer his marching orders.'

CHAPTER TEN

It was a desperate Sadie who tried to intervene between her brother and her lover the following morning. She waited at the entrance to the taxi depot, a grey woollen jacket slung around her shoulders, gazing up the length of Meredith Court, not caring who saw her watching out for Richie in the morning light.

Walter Davidson came into work at six-thirty from his lodgings further up Duke Street. He guessed at once what the matter was.

Sadie ran up to him. 'Oh, Walter, thank God you're here! You gotta stop Rob. He's got it in for Richie now, unless you can do something to stop him!' Her pretty face was screwed up in an agony of fury and despair. She hadn't had a wink of sleep, anxious to beat Rob down to the yard, slipping out of the house before anyone else was up, to stand waiting in the cold dawn.

Walter swung open the gates and walked ahead towards the office. He flung his newspaper on to the desk and hung up his hat, considering his next move. 'I ain't told Rob nothing about you two,' he assured her. Being near Sadie still had the power to disturb his even temperament. He had to turn to one side to busy himself with opening bills and letters.

'I know you ain't. The problem is, he seen us!' Time was running out. Any moment, either Rob or Richie would be coming into work. 'And now he says he'll show Richie the door, but it ain't his fault, and we ain't even doing nothing wrong. I came clean with you, Walter. You gotta tell Rob that.'

Walter sighed. 'It won't make no difference.' He'd spotted Richie sloping in across the yard. Rob himself wouldn't be far behind. 'You know Rob.'

Sadie choked and slumped down at the desk. 'It ain't fair,' she sobbed, head in hands.

'Listen, the best thing is for me to break it to Richie and give him his wages before Rob gets here,' Walter decided. 'Then it's up to him if he wants to have it out with Rob. If he's got any sense, though, he'll take the money and hop it.'

Sadie knew he wouldn't. She couldn't imagine Richie running away from a fight.

Richie had come into work as usual, collar up, shoulders hunched down Meredith Court. But when he spotted Sadie in the office talking to Walter, looking upset, it only took him a second to work things out. He stared warily at them both, then glanced over his shoulder to see if Rob was following him in.

The moment Sadie looked up and saw him, she reached a further level of panic. Common sense fled as she dashed out to meet him, desperate to warn him so he would be ready to face Rob. Rob mustn't get it all his own way.

But there was no time to explain. Rob's uneven footsteps crunched across the cinder track, he turned the corner into the yard. Richie pushed Sadie to one side, telling Walter to take care of her. He stood, feet wide apart, facing Rob.

'Right, Palmer, you know what this is about! Take your

nasty face out of here, and don't never show it no more!' Rob was fired up by the scene that confronted him, Sadie crying, begging Walter, of all people for help. He acted without hesitation, his dark eyes narrowed in an angry frown.

Richie gestured again to Sadie to stay out of it as she tried to break free of Walter. He faced Rob with a cool stare. 'Don't worry, I'm on my way,' he drawled. 'You can stick your job, Parsons. I'm sick of it anyhow.'

Rob, who had been building up for a straight fight, was caught off guard. 'Go on, get out!' He punched out the words, still expecting resistance from Richie, who, after all, was big and strong enough to give him trouble.

The mechanic turned down the corners of his mouth, shot Rob a pitying look from head to crippled toe, and turned his back. Rob lunged clumsily. Sadie wrenched free of Walter and caught hold of her brother, pulling him back by the sleeve. She saw Richie hesitate as Rob swung round to push her off, but he walked on, head high, away from the depot.

'Right, Rob Parsons, that's it!' Sadie was screaming at the top of her voice. 'You just wait!' Her helpless threats echoed under the dark roof arch. 'You just wait and see!' She ran out across the yard, up Meredith Court, too late to spot where Richie had headed off to. Weeping tears of angry frustration, she made her way home.

'What are you up to at this time, girl?' Duke came along the corridor to investigate the noises in Sadie's room. It was still early, not half past seven. He was only just up and dressed.

'I'm packing my bag, Pa, what's it look like?' Sadie could hardly see through her tears. She flung underthings from a drawer into a canvas bag, hands shaking, her stomach in knots.

'It's Rob, ain't it?' Duke knew there'd been a row the night before. Annie said so, and warned him it looked serious. Rob and Sadie were at each other's throats again, she said, and with their tempers, things could turn nasty. So Duke was expecting more trouble.

Now Sadie blurted out Rob's crime of sacking Richie. She was still beside herself, crying and trembling.

'And what's it to you?' Duke asked slowly. These days Sadie never confided in him. He prepared for a shock.

'Richie and me's walking out, Pa! That's why Rob done it.'

'Because of Walter?' It began to make sense. Rob's loyalty to his friend would override everything else.

'But Walter knew,' she insisted. 'I ain't done nothing behind his back, not since the first time.'

He looked at her shaking and crying. She was a slender, pale, dark-haired young woman, still a girl to him. Hettie wouldn't go and make a fuss like this, he thought; nor Jess, nor Frances, not over a lover's tiff. 'Pull yourself together, girl,' he said sternly. 'No need to go on.'

But she turned on him. 'Go on, Pa, take his side! You and Rob won't never understand.' She flung more clothes into the bag, tears dripping off the end of her nose. 'Ain't no use talking to you!'

'I never said I was on Rob's side.'

'You don't have to say it. Well, you won't have to watch me "going on" no more, as you call it, 'cos I'm leaving! And good riddance, says you!'

'I never said that neither.' Duke tried to steady his voice. It looked like Sadie was serious. 'Just hold on, Sadie. Where you off to, for God's sake?'

Her eyes flashed as she weighed the impact of her reply. 'To Richie's!' she said, swinging the bag off the bed, reaching for her coat and hat.

'Never.' Duke sat down heavily on the edge of the bed. He blew out through his cheeks.

But Sadie swept on down the stairs. Hettie came out of her room, still in her night things, just in time to catch a glimpse of the bag Sadie carried, before the door slammed in the hallway below. 'Pa?' Hettie peered into her sister's room, saw Duke sitting bewildered.

'Sadie's gone,' he reported.

'Where to?' Hettie came and put an arm around him.

'To Richie Palmer, she says.' He shook his head. 'Now why, Ett? Why would she do that?'

Hettie scrambled the facts together; *this* was the secret Sadie had been keeping to herself all through the spring!

'Why's she leaving us for Richie Palmer?' Duke repeated.

Hettie comforted him. 'I expect she loves him,' she murmured. 'That must be it, mustn't it?'

Sadie's morning was spent tramping the streets of Mile End looking for Richie's lodging-house. She had only a rough idea of where he lived, and had to stop to ask many times. At last, just before midday, she arrived at an old tenement block in Hope Street. This was it. She went in under the arched brick entrance and up some dirty stone stairs until she came to number twenty-five, knocked on the door and waited amid sounds of children name-calling down in the alley, heavy drays carting sacks of flour to the biscuit factory down the street, and the smells of stale cooking and fumes from cars below. When she realized she would get no reply, she sat down heavily on her canvas bag to wait.

A woman passing by on the balcony stopped to peer in at her. 'Have you tried his work?' she asked, not unfriendly. 'You'll find him down Southwark way, I think.'

Wearily Sadie nodded. 'I know where he works, thanks. He ain't there, though.'

The woman, who wore a square of coarse brown cloth tied around her head and a shapeless dress, whose muddy coloured skirt had come apart from the bodice in places, stood and summed up Sadie's plight. 'You his girl?' She seemed taken aback by the younger woman's smart cream outfit and stylish appearance.

Again Sadie nodded. 'You ain't seen him this morning, then?'

'I ain't seen him all week,' the woman replied. 'You never know with him. I sometimes think what's the use of having him as a neighbour, as a matter of fact. I never hardly see him.'

The words sank heavily on to Sadie's shoulders as the woman went on her way. She'd never asked Richie about his life in the tenement, and he'd never volunteered any information. According to the woman, it seemed a rootless, detached sort of life. With time to kill, exhausted after the morning's crisis, Sadie sat wondering what she'd let herself in for. After all, she'd left home and landed on Richie's doorstep without even letting him know. At last, round about four in the afternoon, she heard footsteps come up the stairs.

Richie turned on to the landing and saw Sadie waiting there. He held his key in one hand, stone-cold sober despite a day-long binge at the pub to help him block out the morning's events. He stared at the bag lying at her feet, then without saying a word he unlocked the door to his rooms and stepped inside.

Sadie lingered on the doorstep. Should she follow him in after all? This was a big move an her part and she waited to see how he would react. But Richie lifted her bag in silence, as if everything was understood and settled in that moment when he'd turned the corner and seen her there, smoothing down her jacket, putting one hand up to her dark hair. He led her in and closed the door behind her.

There was one room for living in, with a window facing out on to the landing, overlooking the busy street. It had a sink, a table and one wooden chair. The other, darker room to the side of the block was for sleeping. Richie had a piece of faded red cloth pinned permanently across the narrow window, a mattress on the floor, and one coat hook on the back of the door. He watched Sadie's face as she took a quick look around.

'Not much, is it?' he said.

'It ain't.' She marvelled how he could live like this, wandering back into the living-room and peering out of the window into the street.

'You can change your mind.' His hunched shoulders and lowered head suggested he didn't care if she did. Inside, he wanted to lock the door, throw away the key, keep her here for ever.

'I can.' Her own head went up. She flicked her hair out of her face and stood squarely facing him.

'So will you stay?' He gestured to her bag on the bare floorboards. 'That's what you got planned, ain't it?'

'Are you asking me?' she challenged. 'Do you want me to?'

He leaned back against the crumbling wall and turned his head away. 'Don't play games with me, Sadie. I ain't in the mood.'

Suddenly serious, she went up to him and put her arms around his neck. 'I'm here, ain't I? It took me all morning to find the place, for God's sake!' She kissed him on the lips.

He responded, held her close. 'Stay, then.'

There was only the present as they embraced once more; no thought of the future or the consequences of what they were doing. They had a place to themselves, however poor. Sadie had made the break from home.

She and Richie made love for the first time, shy and tender. There were tears, which he kissed away. Then he kissed her neck and shoulders. If they thought they could beat him, they were mistaken. He had her now, in spite of them. He would love and care for her for ever.

May days lengthened into early June. Sadie left the tenement rooms in Mile End each morning, and travelled by tube to her job at Swan and Edgar. Richie took casual work wherever he could get it. Since neither wanted to accept help from Sadie's family, they cleaned and painted the two rooms themselves. Sadie's first purchases were another chair, some bedlinen and a tablecloth. Eventually she wrote to Hettie, telling her where she was, but saying she would prefer not to come over to the Duke to visit until Rob saw fit to apologize to Richie.

'Never in a month of Sundays,' Duke said sadly.

Hettie put the letter on the table with a shake of her head. 'Let's wait and see, Pa. Leastways, we know she's safe and well.' Sadie sounded happy. There was no disguising her enthusiasm as she wrote about her new set-up with Richie.

Duke didn't like it, but Sadie was twenty-five years old and he had to get on with his own life as best he could. Summer nights brought more people out on to the streets to gossip and watch the children play. Some of them drifted into the pub for a drink before they went to bed. Trade improved slightly, though much of it went on late at night, well after hours, to Annie's disgust. 'What can I do?' Duke shrugged. 'We gotta earn a crust.' When the doors of the pub finally closed, he fretted after Sadie. And the truth was, he'd rather have the place alive and full of people, than close early and sit at his hearth without Annie.

One rule he did intend to stick to was his ban on Willie Wiggin. 'Ain't no one here will give him a single drop to drink!' he told Annie, and she would nod in satisfaction when she saw him keeping his promise. She was trying to dry the old drunk out, and largely succeeding. Though his liver was ruined, the doctor said he might not get rapidly worse as long as they kept him away from the drink. She kept her eagle eye on him, and gave orders to the tenement children to run no more errands for the lodger in number five.

But Wiggin sober was as much of a problem as Wiggin drunk. He turned to argument, accusing the O'Hagans of deliberately driving rats into his room, claiming that Annie came in to steal his money when he lay asleep, trudging up to the post office and claiming dole that he wasn't owed. He was impossible to handle, mean and vicious, and still cunning in pursuit of drink.

On the first Saturday afternoon in June, Wiggin was seen making his way along Duke Street towards the public park.

Katie O'Hagan, who ran Annie's old haberdashery stall with
all her predecessor's verve for business, spotted him wandering back an hour or so later, obviously the worse for wear.
She passed the word along, 'Tell Annie, Wiggin is off the
wagon!' She saw it'd be a miracle if he didn't get run over
by a bus, the silly old sod. Katie wound five yards of white
ric-rac braid on to a scrap of card, took threepence in
payment and craned across the stall to watch Wiggin's
progress. When she saw his shambling figure stagger to a
halt at the corner of the court, then drift crabwise towards
the door of the Duke, she thought direct action was called
for. 'Watch my pitch!' she yelled at Nora Brady on her
nearby fish stall. Then she skipped down the busy street,
eager to warn Annie personally.

She found her wending through the crowd from the
other direction, her basket full of fruit and veg, taking her
time and chatting in the evening sun. Annie turned to
Katie's call, but her smile vanished when she saw the girl's
pointed little face looking serious and she heard the latest
news. Quickly she went towards the pub, just too late to
stop a confrontation between Duke and Wiggin.

'I said, a pint of best bitter!' Wiggin had to cling to the
bar to make his demand. His head lolled from side to side,
he had trouble shaping the words. He stood there unshaven,
shouting his order.

Duke raised the wooden flap and came out from behind
the bar. He took Wiggin by the elbow, feeling many eyes
on them as he steered Annie's old husband towards the
door.

Arthur Ogden watched, then grunted into his glass. Joe
O'Hagan wiped his mouth with his sleeve. They couldn't
help but make a comparison between the two men; Duke
still sturdily built, wearing a crisp striped shirt under his

131

dark waistcoat, vigour in his grasp. Wiggin, on the other hand, had never been much of a figure, even in his youth, and was now shrunken, bent and unkempt, his mind permanently fuddled by drink.

'Come on now, Willie, let's get you safely back home.' Duke never raised his voice an these occasions. In fact, he managed to suggest he was doing a man a favour by refusing to serve him. Even with Wiggin he was considerate, steering him out on to the street.

'You take your hands off me, filthy swine!' Wiggin roared. He exploded into a writhing mass of fists and elbows. He kicked, he staggered, he spat and thumped. 'I know you, Wilf Parsons! A man just has to come in for a little drink and you throw him out! Yes, I know you!'

Taken by surprise, Duke hesitated. Maybe Wiggin wasn't as far gone as they imagined. Annie still said he didn't know her, ranting and raving at her each time she went in to cook and clean. 'You know me, do you, Willie?' Duke turned him round to face him and stood him up straight.

Wiggin came out with a barrage of obscenities that made some of the nearby women shriek in mock horror. Rob left off talking to Tommy O'Hagan at his news stall to come to Duke's assistance. If necessary, they'd lift Wiggin clean off his feet and cart him down the court between them.

'That's the way, Willie. Easy does it.' Duke managed to swivel him in the right direction again. 'Just get one thing clear, will you? You won't get served a single drop in my pub, understand? Shouting and carrying on don't make no difference. Just don't come back and try it on no more.' He was only sorry he'd not got rid of the old nuisance a minute or two sooner, as Annie came towards them, a worried frown on her face.

Wiggin put his fists up again. 'Oh, you serve those you

like, no bother! I seen you. Same old Duke Parsons, serving
right through the night. I seen your light. It always shines,
long after closing time. Ha!' He raised a gnarled finger and
pointed an inch away from Duke's face.

'Shut up!' Annie stepped in to take over from Duke. She
grabbed Willie's elbow and shoved him on down the
pavement. 'You just shut your noise, you hear!' God knew
who was listening as he ranted on. 'I told you lots of times,'
she muttered to Duke, 'if someone like Willie blabs, we're
done for!'

Wiggin roared on down Paradise Court. 'We all know
you ain't no angel, Wilf Parsons!' Children laughed, women
backed away, seeing in Wiggin the terrible shape of things
to come, unless their old men cut down drastically on the
drinking. 'We know about you, Parsons! Refuse a man a
drink at tea-time, and serve your pals right through the
night!'

Annie bundled him down the street and into the tenement. She slammed the door behind them, worried to death
about the after-hours serving. It just took one man, one
enemy, to ruin Duke for good.

Back in the bar, the crowd of weekend drinkers closed
over Wiggin's interruption as if it had never happened. Only
one or two paused to comment. Tommy O'Hagan turned
to Bertie Hill and expressed his usual opinion that Wiggin
was a man who'd outlived his usefulness. He was sick of
hearing him clattering about in the room below theirs, and
thought it a shame that the old wreck should come between
Annie and Duke, who'd never done anyone any harm. Now
he was even issuing drunken threats. 'He belongs in the
knacker's yard if you ask me,' Tommy said.

Hill raised his glass but said nothing.

Rob came in and leaned on the bar, winking at Ernie to

bring him a pint. 'I'll knock his block off before too long,' he promised. 'He ain't fit for nothing, and that's a fact.'

'People ain't animals. You can't cart them off to the knacker's yard, however much you feel like it.' Hill's tone was infuriatingly reasonable. 'It ain't right.'

'Oh, ain't it?' Rob replied. And, 'Oh, can't I? Well, we'll just have to see about that.' He admitted that he'd cheerfully strangle Wiggin if he thought it would solve anything. He swallowed down his beer in a couple of gulps and went on his way.

'Joke!' Tommy reminded Hill, recalling the landlord's old police background and noticing his dark look. 'Don't take no notice of Rob.'

Hill shrugged and drank on in silence. The waters closed over the event.

'Funny thing, that,' Arthur remarked to Dolly when she called in later that evening. 'Did you know, Duke had to chuck Wiggin out?'

Dolly gave a short laugh. 'That's life.' She pondered the situation with an ironic smile.

'Funny, though, when you think about it.' Arthur saw that Annie had popped back to help behind the bar as usual. No one could have told from looking at her and old Duke what the pair of them must be going through. They handled it well, considering.

Two weeks later, Tommy and Rob had cause to tackle the subject over again.

If there'd been any warning, any suggestion that Wiggin could do real damage, Rob said, they'd have done things differently. 'Only no one except Annie took him serious, see?' He was just coming to terms with events. The letter from the magistrates' court had arrived that morning, 20 June. 'It hit Pa like a bombshell,' Rob went on. 'And I still feel a bit shaky myself.'

'Are you sure Wiggin's your man?' Tommy could just make out from the official wording on the letter Rob had handed him that the coppers planned to drop down hard on poor old Duke. He made out the words 'summons', 'investigation', 'evidence'. There was no doubt, they were on to him with a vengeance.

'You heard him. He might be a useless old drunk, but he knows enough to give us a real headache round here. God knows what Pa can do about it now.'

Tommy shoved the letter back to Rob and leaned both elbows on the bar. George Mann had taken over the serving, with Ernie there as usual to help with the clearing away. There was no sign of either Duke or Annie. Regulars dropped in every now and then for a quick word of commiseration, but they drifted off again when they found Duke was missing. 'It's hit him pretty hard,' Dolly said to Charlie, who came in on his way to the Gem. 'I ain't never known him to leave the bar to George on a Friday night.'

'*Someone* gave the game away,' Rob was still insisting. 'And who's the first one that comes to mind?'

'Wiggin,' Charlie admitted. He didn't like to see the Parsonses in more trouble over this. 'What'll happen now, Rob? What does the summons mean exactly?'

But Rob was taken up by his own train of thought. 'You show me a pub in the whole of the East End that don't serve after hours!' He clenched his fist and smacked it down on the bar. 'We're forever getting warnings from the coppers and sticking them on the fire. Pa couldn't make ends meet if he stuck to licensing hours, for God's sake!'

Tommy, standing nearby, saw the light at last. He gave a faint whistle. 'Bleeding hell, Rob. You mean to say your old man could lose his licence over this?'

It took Duke himself several hours for this realization to sink in. While Rob and his friends fretted in the bar, he sat upstairs with Annie, motionless in his chair by the empty fireside. Hettie would soon be back from the dress shop. He'd have to explain all over again.

'Try looking on the bright side,' Annie begged. 'What if they can't prove nothing? Who'd take Wiggin's word in a court of law?'

'We can't be sure it was him.' Unlike Rob, Duke didn't want to jump to conclusions.

'No, but let's say Wiggin's word don't prove reliable, according to the magistrate . . .'

Duke shook his head. 'The police don't get up a summons without checking their facts,' he insisted. 'I reckon they already sent their men in for evidence. Someone we don't know. You seen anyone, Annie?'

She searched her memory. 'I can't think of no one, Duke.' She tried to build up his hopes because she knew the pub meant everything to him now. He'd already given up his marriage, Sadie had gone off with Richie Palmer, and now it was his home on the line! She couldn't go down the court, leaving him to despair.

'How long have I been here, Annie?'

'Thirty-five years. I remember it, Duke. Jess was just a little baby.'

'Well, I'm too old to change my ways now,' he sighed. 'What is it they reckon? Three score and ten years? I had my fair share, when you look at it that way.'

'Ain't nothing wrong with you!' she snapped. 'You'll go on for years yet!' She raised herself and walked to the window, looking out at the market traders packing up for the day. 'How long before we have to go to court exactly?'

'Two weeks.'

'Fourteen days to get something done,' she promised.

But Duke got up to join her. 'Ain't you forgetting something, Annie?'

She turned to look up at him.

'They caught me redhanded, remember?'

She threw her arms around his neck and held him tight. She willed him to fight back. She cursed Wiggin and their own carelessness.

Annie and Duke looked down together on the barrow boys trundling carts over the cobbles. They saw two of the youngest O'Hagan girls ducking in the gutter for bruised apples. A pianola tune drifted through the open window below, churning out a Viennese waltz above the hum of street life. She glanced up at his lined features, saw that his eyes were moist. She couldn't bear it if he lost everything because of Wiggin; wife, home, occupation all gone.

PART TWO

Suspicion

CHAPTER ELEVEN

June 1924

The whole of Paradise Court was up in arms when they heard what Wiggin had done.

'You know what this means, don't you?' Arthur Ogden sat on an upturned orange-box among the rows of young cabbages and leeks on his allotment.

Dolly, bent double over the tender plants, gave a short reply. 'Yes, it means no more drinking after hours. And a bleeding good thing too!' She stood up to roll back her sleeves and fix her hair.

'You don't mean that. Think about it, if Duke does get chucked out over this and a new man comes in, and that new man happens to be a stickler for the rules, what then?' Arthur groaned at the prospect of many early nights ahead.

'It'll do you no end of good,' his wife insisted. She eased her back after her labours. It was a fine summer's evening. Swallows darted overhead, an old black tomcat sat blinking on the fence, while in the background a train shuttled by. Dolly wiped her face with her apron. 'No, it ain't you I'm bothered about, Arthur. It's old Duke. What the bleeding hell's he gonna do if they take away his licence?'

There was no answer to this. Arthur sat silently brooding.

'I mean to say, it's the same as uprooting one of them cabbages and chucking it on the compost.' Dolly jabbed with her trowel. 'If he goes, what's left for him except the scrapheap?' The idea of the old man minus his pub was unimaginable. 'It's his life, Arthur, you gotta admit.' She sighed and bent slowly to begin weeding once more.

'Maybe Annie will take him back?' Arthur sat, arms folded, contemplating the ripple of pink clouds in the eggshell sky.

Dolly shook her head. 'Never in a month of Sundays. There's Wiggin standing in the way. Don't ask me why, but Annie still sees herself as married to the old sod. She has old-fashioned views on the subject.'

Arthur changed tack. 'Well, then, he could go to live with one of his stuck-up, bleeding daughters.' He gathered phlegm, coughed and spat. 'That Frances, or that Jess.'

'Jess ain't stuck-up.' Dolly pointedly ignored his reference to Frances. 'Anyhow, that ain't the point. The thing is, what's an old man like him to do when they take away both his home and his job? Come to that, what's Rob and Ernie and Hettie gonna do?' She dug savagely at a dandelion root, heaving it free in a shower of earth. She flung it into a nearby barrow.

'Like I said, it ain't good news.' Arthur stood up. Talk of problems at the pub had helped him to work up a thirst.

'You can say that again. It's like an axe over their heads, and there ain't nothing they can do.' Dolly hacked away at another root.

'I think I'll just pop along there and see how he is,' Arthur said. 'I expect he'll need cheering up.' He took his cap from his pocket, unrolled it and put it on.

'Have one for me!' Dolly watched him go, meandering up Meredith Court past the blank windows of Coopers' Drapery Stores. That was the other big news of the week: Jack Cooper had closed down and thrown eighty-five

workers on the dole. On Monday the bailiffs had moved in
and cleared the place. Not that she wasted an ounce of pity
on the shop owner. He'd been a pig in his time, and Dolly
herself had rowed with him on Amy's behalf. The son,
Teddy, had behaved badly towards Amy, and Jack Cooper,
quite wrongly in her opinion, had stood by him. That was
all water under the bridge: Teddy Cooper was just one
more dead hero, and Amy had got on in life in spite of the
setback. Still, Dolly wasn't sad to see the shop go under.
Something better would come in its place. Meanwhile,
though, half of Duke Street was out of work.

When Arthur arrived at the Duke, he found Tommy
O'Hagan standing his pa a drink, and soon muscled in on
the act. Tommy was good for a pint these days. He earned
a pretty penny on his stalls, selling daily newspapers on one,
and a range of brushes, paints and varnishes, pastes and
wallpapers on a new stall on the corner of Duke Street and
Union Street. Soon he planned to open a little shop and call
it The Home Decorator. Arthur admired his get-up-and-
go.

Joe O'Hagan stood at the bar, his baleful eye fixed on
Duke. Even as he picked up his glass and sipped the froth,
he kept the landlord in his sights. 'It happens to the best of
us!' he announced, apropos of nothing.

'What does, Pa?' Tommy pushed back his hat and drank
a long draught of cool beer.

'Getting the push. I've had it all my life, and it ain't
pleasant, believe me.' Joe's Irish accent seemed to give his
bleak words a musical edge. 'I've had the push so many
times I lost count. The railways, the canals, they given me
the push when I was a young man. I was a fine figure in
them days.' He tugged at the dark brown liquid, pulling it
down his scrawny throat in gulps. 'The bottle factory, and

the cardboard box factory and the cabinet makers, they given me the push in my time. And now Jack Cooper.' He followed Duke's activities behind the bar, inviting him to come over and share the misery of being put out of work. With the closure of Coopers', Joe had lost his part-time portering job. 'Who'll take me on now?' he complained.

Duke came across at last. 'What's that, Joe? You ain't moaning, are you?' He winked at Tommy.

'He is, and he's giving us a earache.' Tommy had had a lifetime of his father's grumbling while his mother, Mary, struggled on.

'What, you ain't sixty yet, are you, Joe? There's plenty of life in the old dog yet!' Duke stacked glasses ready for the evening trade.

The worn-out little Irishman gave a hollow laugh. 'Tell that to them as pays the wages.' And he began another long, self-pitying lament.

But Tommy cut him off. 'Stow it, Pa. Duke don't want to hear it. Things ain't exactly rosy for him neither.'

Duke sniffed. 'You can say that again.'

Arthur remembered the reason he'd called in. 'How's things, Duke?' he asked in a tone of deep commiseration.

'They been better, thanks, Arthur.' It was four days since the police summons had landed on his mat. Duke managed business as usual, but only just, as he felt the clock ticking towards his court appearance on the fourth of July.

'Any news of who dropped you in it?' Arthur's nose for gossip was almost as sharp as Dolly's.

'Nothing definite.'

'It was Wiggin,' Joe said with finality. 'Everyone knows it was him. We hear him, day in, day out, cursing and swearing and calling you all the names under the sun, Duke. He's the one, you can bet your life.'

'Ain't none of us will have nothing to do with him,' Arthur assured Duke. 'We sent him to Coventry the day it happened. Ain't no one said a word to him since.'

'Much good may that do.' Tommy polished off his pint and pulled his hat down on to his forehead. 'No, what we need is for someone to finish him off good and proper. Bang goes your witness, bang goes your case!'

'Now, now, less of that!' Duke shook his head.

'I was only trying to look on the bright side.' Tommy's wide grey eyes opened still further. He gave a wink and sauntered out through the swing-door.

'Take no notice,' Joe advised. 'With a bit of luck, Wiggin will drink himself to death before you get to court, Duke.'

'He'd best get a move on,' Arthur pointed out. 'He's only got just over a week.'

Duke went and pulled a pint for a new customer. He told George to tap a fresh barrel, then gave Ernie the first of his evening chores. 'Put fresh sawdust in them spittoons, and sweep around a bit, there's a good lad. Let's have the place spick and span.' He himself checked the gas mantles. With a grunt of satisfaction he rang up fourpence on the till. They were good and ready. He pulled out his watch; it was half past seven on Tuesday, 24 June.

While Duke stuck to business as usual, the rest of the family racked their brains over what to do. Though the taxi work kept Rob busy as ever, he made a special journey over to Maurice's house one night, soon after the bad news had come. It was late. There were few lights on along the tree-lined streets as Rob pulled up and rang the bell.

Jess came to the door to let him in. The strain of worrying over Duke told in her pale face and serious expression. She kissed her brother's cheek, took his hat and led him into the kitchen, where Maurice sat at the table in his shirt-sleeves, looking dog-tired after a long day at work.

'What do you reckon?' Rob pulled out a chair and joined him, sighing deeply. 'It don't look good, do it?'

Maurice tilted his head sideways, his sharp features half in shadow. 'Licensing laws are pretty straightforward, to tell you the truth. If you're caught breaking them, you land in the cart good and proper.' Jess had spilled out the facts to him as soon as Hettie had rung her on the previous Friday night. As far as he could see, Duke had dropped himself right in it.

'Don't say that,' Jess put in, quiet but tense. She handed Rob a small glass of whisky. 'Rob ain't come all this way just to hear that. We know Pa's in the cart. What we have to do is work out a way of getting him out.'

Maurice nodded. He, too, realized how much his father-in-law *was* the pub, and the pub was Duke. 'Right, let's think. First off, who owns the licence?' he asked Rob.

'The brewery. Pa's a tenant and he's a bleeding good one. The best there is. They know him. There's never been a scrap of trouble in more than thirty years!' Rob grew hot in Duke's defence.

'Till now.' Maurice went briskly on. 'The chances are, the brewery won't want no trouble over it themselves. They'll let Duke take the blame, never mind the profits he's put their way, and they'll just sit by till it's all blown over.'

'Oh!' Jess frowned. 'Typical, ain't it? Not a bit of trouble for thirty-five years! Then, soon as Pa steps out of line, they drop him!' She was close to tears. Why couldn't Maurice be a bit more positive?

'There *is* one thing.' Maurice worked things through. 'The brewery will want to stay out of it, right? They'll let

Duke go to court next week and lose his licence. Then they'll issue a new licence to someone else, a new landlord, and get him into the Duke as quick as ever they can.'

Jess put both hands to her ears. 'Oh, Maurice, don't!'

'No, hang on a minute. They won't like it one little bit. It gives them a problem, see, if they have to get a new man. But if we could find a way of helping them out of their difficulty; if we can find a new landlord for them before it comes to court, I think they'd jump at the chance!'

'Find the brewery a new landlord?' Rob echoed. 'Either I'm dim, Maurice, or you're round the bend, pal.' He stood up in disgust.

'No, listen. 'Course, we don't want just any old landlord.' Maurice spread his hands flat on the table. 'Look, say Duke is bound to lose his licence on the fourth? It's what they call a foregone conclusion. Well, we have to get to the brewery before then and say there's no need to go as far as court. Duke agrees to give up the tenancy.'

Jess jumped up and turned away.

'No.' Rob stopped her from leaving. 'I think I'm with you, Maurice. If the brewery can keep their noses clean, they might listen to what we have to say. But it depends on the name we come up with for the new landlord, don't it? Someone who'll let Duke stay on, someone who wants to take on the licence in name only, but let Pa run things same as always?'

Maurice nodded, his face broke into a smile. 'What do you think?'

'Good one!' Rob saw it straight away. 'You ain't thinking of volunteering for the job, are you, Maurice?'

Jess sat down again, listening hard. She turned her head from her brother to her husband and back.

Maurice shook his head. 'I got enough on my plate.

Anyhow, I wouldn't go down too well with the brewery. My face don't fit,' he said wryly. In the East End, immigrant Jews weren't considered good landlord material. 'And the name ain't right. No, I was thinking more of you, Rob old son. You're on the spot, see. You know the ropes. If you ask me, you're a good bet to put up to the brewery. What do you say?'

Rob smacked his palm on to the table. 'Bleeding brilliant!' He beamed at Jess. 'Sis, you're married to a flipping genius!'

Maurice, too, was pleased with himself. 'I'll set up a time to go and see them. You and me, Rob, we'll go along together. Let's see what they got to say.'

'What will you tell Pa?' Jess asked.

'What do you think?' Rob looked back at her for advice.

'Don't tell him nothing yet,' she decided. 'It'd be cruel to raise his hopes before we pull it off.'

Maurice nodded. 'Wear your best suit,' he said as he showed Rob to the door. 'I'll telephone you tomorrow.' They shook hands. 'Let's try to keep it in the family and keep everyone happy.' But he lowered his voice for a word of caution. 'Don't bank on nothing yet, Rob. We're doing our best, but we got an uphill struggle to keep Duke where he belongs.'

He went inside to help Jess clear away for the night. She was warm towards him as they got into bed, and she lay close, resting inside the crook of his arm, one hand on his chest.

'Better now?' he asked gently.

She nodded. 'It don't seem right. How can life be so cruel to Pa? He ain't done nothing to deserve it.'

'No, he ain't.' Maurice kissed her hair.

'And how can *I* be happy with Pa in trouble?'

He held her tight. He would ring up and try to pull a few strings with the brewery, he would do what he could. He liked it better when Jess relied on him and turned to him for help. He kissed her warm face and lips, remembering how it was in the early days; the trust between them, the unbroken passion and tenderness.

'And how are *you* bearing up?' Dolly leaned across the bar to grasp Annie's hand. It was Saturday evening and the usual singalong hadn't picked up, so Dolly gave up her vocal efforts to come and have a chat with her beleaguered old friend.

'Better since you stopped making that horrible din.' Annie wasn't about to succumb to Dolly's sentimental overture. 'Dame Nellie Melba you definitely ain't!'

A couple of young lads standing nearby in their cheap suits and trilby hats caught on. They laughed, then squawked in imitation of Dolly's operatic rendering of 'Sister Susie'. 'More like Vesta Tilley,' one scoffed, referring to Dolly's deep voice. 'Only she ain't wearing no trousers!'

'Very funny.' Dolly did her best to ignore them and turned back to Annie. 'I was saying to Charlie earlier on, ain't it a shame Wiggin had to show up when he did? He set the cat among the pigeons all right.' Dolly was dressed up for her night out in a white lace collar and a bottle-green dress of crushed velvet, whose ample skirt took up much room at the bar. She leaned closer to Annie. 'I think you're a saint to put up with it like you do. I'm a churchgoer myself, but I admit, I wouldn't give him house-room if he showed up on my doorstep and I was you.'

'Well, he didn't, and you ain't.' Still Annie was reluctant to be drawn into Dolly's gossip trap. She had too much on her mind as it was.

Undeterred, Dolly went full steam ahead. 'Especially after what he done to you, Annie!' She tutted in all directions, hoping to enlist sympathy for Annie's cause. But all she succeeded in doing was catching Frances Wray's cool gaze. Frances had been tea-time visiting and was just on her way out. She'd popped into the bar to say goodbye to Annie.

Dolly Ogden wasn't fond of Frances. 'I say she ain't natural!' she would hold forth to Arthur on many occasions. Between them the couple had set up a small campaign against the best educated of the Parsons girls, ever since her support for the window smashers way back before the war. 'It ain't nice for a woman to join marches and behave the way she does.' And when she left the pub to go off and marry Billy Wray, it was their opinion that the street was better off without her snooty face poking its nose in everywhere. Dolly felt Frances's disapproving gaze fall on her now, and it provoked her. 'I was just telling Annie, Frances, I wouldn't give Wiggin house-room. Not after what he went and did!'

Frances didn't respond at first, but when Dolly bustled across, all green velvet and lavender-water, to accost her face to face, she turned and sighed. 'What's that, Dolly?'

'I'm only saying what every single soul in this court says!' She rose up and defended herself. 'Wiggin ruined everything for Annie, we all know that. I'm just expressing my sympathy, that's all!' Two or three drinks had made Dolly indiscreet and raised the volume of her voice.

'And I'm sure she's grateful.' Frances noticed that Annie had made herself scarce. She tried to make her own excuses and leave.

But Dolly seized her wrist. 'Look here, Frances, the people round here, we care about Annie and your pa, so don't think we don't!'

Aware of several girls from the market sitting nearby, all ears, Frances tried to pull away. 'I know it,' she said quietly, trying to unwrap Dolly's fingers.

'Well, we want to know how you can stand by and let it happen.' Dolly's temper suddenly lit up. Frances Wray was a cold fish all right.

'We're not just standing by, Dolly. But what can we do?' At last Frances freed herself. She felt knocked back by Dolly's burst of anger, but separate from it. It was nothing to do with anything that she, Frances, had said or done.

'You can try getting them two back together for a start!' the older woman's voice fell into a stage-whisper. 'Don't you see how miserable it is for them?'

Frances blushed self-consciously, feeling all eyes on them. 'Hush, Dolly. Anyhow, this ain't none of your business,' she said abruptly.

This was lighting the blue touchpaper as far as Dolly was concerned. 'Ain't none of my business?' Her voice shot up several decibels once more. She turned to address their audience. 'Ain't I known Duke since he first came here?' she demanded. 'Ain't I known Annie even longer than that? And Lady High-and-Mighty here has the cheek to say it ain't none of my business!'

'I never meant it like that.' Frances felt herself go red. 'I'm sorry, Dolly.'

Dolly ignored her. 'I've known Annie, girl and woman, and it breaks my heart to see what Wiggin's done to her.' Real tears came to her eyes.

'I said I was sorry.' It was Frances's turn to take Dolly by the wrist and lead her to a quiet chair. 'Calm down. Just sit quiet a bit and tell me what you think we should do.' She looked nervously over her shoulder in case Annie or her pa showed up in the bar.

It took a few seconds for Dolly's sobs to subside. 'I ain't made of stone,' she protested.

'No more am I,' Frances said quietly.

Dolly looked up at last.

'We're all going through it, believe me. Ernie, for a start. He's beginning to panic.' Frances herself stayed awake at night, failing to find a solution to any of their problems.

'You want to get Annie and Duke back together?'

'I'd give an arm and a leg to help. But Annie won't listen. She says the law's the law, and the law says she ain't married to Pa no more!'

'And you've given her a talking to?' Dolly was sniffing and coming round from her outburst.

''Course I have. We all have. She won't shift. And Pa agrees with her, bless him.' Frances sat upright, her pale colouring highlighting her delicate features, her bobbed hair swept straight back from her high forehead.

'But have you got her to think straight?' Dolly became more secretive and urgent as she leaned across. 'You know, about how her and Wiggin got together in the first place?'

Frances was puzzled. 'How do you mean?'

Dolly stared back. 'You mean, you don't know? She ain't told you?' It had never occurred to her that the family didn't know the full story, that Annie had kept it quiet.

'Ain't told me what, for God's sake? What are you on about, Dolly?' Frances was exasperated by the big eyes and exaggerated whispers. 'Tell me straight, was there something fishy?'

'Why not ask her?' For once Dolly's lips were sealed.

'How can I if I don't know what you're on about?' Frances battled to stay calm. The pub had filled up. Duke was behind the bar now, but as yet there was no sign of Annie.

'We was sworn to secrecy,' Dolly declared. 'All them years ago. I ain't saying another word.' She gathered her dignity and stood up. 'Like you said, Frances, it ain't none of my business.'

'Dolly!' Frances sprang up to restrain her.

'All right then.' Swiftly Dolly changed her mind and whispered in Frances's ear. 'Annie was just a girl, mind. She weren't a Southwark girl born and bred. Her family was over in Hoxton, I think. Anyhow, when she came to live in the court she was already hitched up with Wiggin. We never took to them, not at first. Things was said behind their backs and Wiggin treated her bad from the start.'

Frances sat Dolly down and forced herself to be patient. She was totally in the dark about this.

'We took to Annie all right when he was away at sea. She kept things nice and clean and she never went on about her other half. She never told us nothing about herself neither; she was close on that score. Only, the story went around that Wiggin weren't her first husband, that she'd been married before.'

Frances shook her head in disbelief. 'How could she? She ain't never said nothing to us.'

'She wouldn't.' Dolly's stare held secret significance.

'Why not?'

''Cos the story was she'd been married to a man called Kearney. He married her when she was sixteen and he was no better than Wiggin turned out to be second time around. They lived like rats in a cellar in Hoxton, and he used to knock her about, and one day when he was short of money

153

for a drink, he took Annie along to the market, met up with his old pal, Wiggin, and he sold her! They said Wiggin bought her for twenty-seven shillings, which was a tidy sum in them days.'

Frances gasped. 'Oh my God, it ain't true!'

'Calm down, I ain't said there's been a murder or nothing.' To Dolly, it was one of the things that went on in the old poverty-stricken days. A bargain would be struck, the second marriage would even be given the respectability of a forged certificate.

'But why didn't she tell us?'

'It ain't something to blow your horn over, is it?'

'But don't she see what it'd mean?' Frances began to get over her shock.

Dolly shook her head. 'No, she don't. I ain't that clear myself. All I know is, it went on, and a lot of women got trapped that way. It ain't very nice, but there it is.'

'And what happened to Kearney?' Things could be even worse in one sense, if Dolly's version of events was true.

'I haven't a clue. You'd better ask her that. Choose your time, Frances, and get her to tell it all. You're the one can do it if anyone can. And you're the one who can sort out this mess for her.'

Frances took a deep breath. 'This needs thinking through.'

Dolly smoothed her skirt and bodice. 'I'd do more than think about it if I was you. And don't take too long about it.' She gazed across at Duke's sturdy figure; as much a fixture round here as the bar itself or the bevelled, fancy mirrors. 'Let's get Duke and Annie back together,' she insisted. 'It'd be a start at any rate.'

*

While Frances hesitated over how best to approach Annie on the delicate topic of her marriage to Wiggin, Sadie put in a brief appearance at the Duke.

She chose a time when she knew Rob would be absent, preferring to avoid him, but anxious to call in to see how Duke, Hettie and Ernie were bearing up. First she spoke to Hettie on the phone. 'Will Pa want to see me?' she asked. ''Cos I can stay away if he'd rather. I don't want to cause no more trouble.'

'Pa ain't mad at you, Sadie,' Hettie assured her. 'He just wishes you and Rob could make things up.'

'Well, we can't, Ett. Not after what he did to Richie.' This was a firm new principle in Sadie's life, that she wouldn't talk to Rob again so long as he refused to apologize for what he'd done.

'Come over anyway. Rob's out seeing someone. Pa's resting.' It was the Monday of the week of the court case, and stalemate. They waited and worried in a kind of limbo. 'Come and help cheer him up,' Hettie said.

Sadie arrived looking as neat and pretty as ever. There was colour in her cheeks and a liveliness about her as she embraced Hettie and Ernie at the top of the stairs, then went into the living-room to see Duke.

'Surprise, Pa!' She stepped forward, holding out her arms, still half afraid of a lukewarm reception.

Duke held her for a second or two before he let go, then he looked her up and down. 'My, but you're like your ma,' he said quietly. 'Didn't I always say you was like Pattie? Now, Ett, put the kettle on while Sadie makes herself at home. Sit down here and put your feet up and tell me all your news.'

Sadie felt swamped by a rush of emotions. Where she thought she'd feel defensive over Richie and angry with

Rob, keeping a distance from her old life because of it, she found now that she was overwhelmed with homesickness. She'd settled in with Richie in his Mile End tenement, and she was deeply in love with him, but she saw now what it was to have her heart pulled in more than one direction. Duke was old, she realized. He put on a brave front, but he was old and hurting badly. He was tired and sad, and she wanted to help. 'How are you coping, Pa?' She took a cup of tea from Hettie and set it down in the hearth.

'Bearing up.' He eased himself back into his chair.

'And have you got any plans?'

'Not yet. Let's see what happens on Friday first.'

Hettie explained that if the magistrates ruled against them, they would be given a short time to make other arrangements.

'But does it mean you'll have to move away from Duke Street?' Sadie glanced at the familiar objects; the clock on the mantelpiece, a pair of matching Chinese vases with a blue design.

'Let's wait and see,' Duke insisted. 'Listen, girl, I ain't gonna think about it till Friday, and that's that. Just tell us how you're getting along. How's work? How's your young man?'

'I'm fine, Pa. Work's the same.' She blushed. 'Richie's fine too. He looks after me, so no need to worry on that score.' The young lovers were still in the honeymoon period of fulfilling one another's wishes, being there when needed, bringing home little presents of cufflinks and brooches. Their two rooms now looked bright and cheerful. Sadie had imprinted her presence in the shape of new white curtains, proper plates and cups, a pole across the bedroom alcove to hang her clothes. Richie looked on with bemusement at this advancing domestication, but he let her proceed, knowing it pleased her.

Duke listened and nodded. 'He's good to you, then?'

'He is, Pa.' Sadie's face broke into a radiant smile. You have to know him to see how good. He ain't one for talking, and he don't have much yet in the way of belongings, but he loves me, I know he does.'

'Well then, we'll see.'

'Thanks, Pa.' Sadie sprang from her chair and hugged him once more.

'What for, girl?' He smiled as he patted her shoulder.

'For not staying mad at me. For letting me come home to visit.'

Duke sighed. 'Ah, Sadie, don't you know I miss my little girl? It's lovely to see you looking happy, ain't it, Ett? It's one less thing for us to worry about.'

They settled down to talk in the old, easy way, almost forgetting their pressing troubles as Ernie finished his chores and joined them, and Annie came up the court with fresh scones and strawberry jam.

Sadie was long gone, back to her new home in Mile End, when Rob returned home. The summer evening had turned to soft drizzle as he trod his well-worn path from the depot up Duke Street, but he was oblivious to it. There was something lifeless in his walk, a bleakness in his gaze, an overall impression of defeat in the way he reached the pub and climbed the stairs.

He'd set off that afternoon with Maurice to see the brewers, their hopes high. Maurice had arranged everything; they arrived at four on the dot and were shown into a room whose oak-panelled walls were lined with hunting prints, its leather chairs and polished tables lending an atmosphere of a gentlemen's club. Rob was dressed up smart, according to his brother-in-law's advice, hoping to impress the brewery boss as a likely candidate to take on the problematic tenancy at the Duke. They had to wait ten minutes for the manager called Wakeley to arrive.

He was a tall, thickset man, built in the mould of one of the grey drayhorses that pulled the beer along the cobbled streets. He wore a good tweed suit with a high-buttoning waistcoat. His handshake was firm, his eyes wary.

Maurice opened up the conversation. He spoke well, reminding Mr Wakeley of the good service Duke had done for the brewery over many years. He told him that Duke was well liked and respected in the community, predicting a fall-off in trade if he were to be ousted.

Wakeley listened and nodded. 'But,' he said frankly, 'Mr Parsons seems to have overstepped the mark on this occasion. With the police involved, there isn't much we can do, I'm afraid.'

Maurice leaned across the table. 'We know that, Mr Wakely. And we can see the hole you're in.'

Wakeley nodded. 'It brings us into disrepute, you see. The case will come up in the local paper. It don't look good for the brewery to have its landlords seen to be flouting the law.'

'Right!' Maurice seized his chance. 'So we've come with a proposal that'll help to avoid all that.'

The manager inclined his head. 'Is that so?'

'Yes. Say Duke were to give up the pub without the fuss of going to court? That gets you out of any bad publicity, see. But say then, Duke goes. What happens to trade? It plummets. You lose in the long run.'

Wakeley frowned. 'I don't see where this is leading, Mr Leigh.'

'You see, the Duke of Wellington public house without

158

Duke ain't the answer.' Maurice felt Rob shift uneasily beside him and pushed on. 'So we came up with an alternative.'

Wakeley leaned on the table and pressed his fingertips together. 'Which is?'

'Which is that you hand on the tenancy to someone who keeps the trade rolling in. Someone connected to Duke.' Maurice turned to Rob. 'That's why Robert here came along with me. We talked it over, and Rob would like to take on the tenancy. That way, Duke don't get turfed out, you keep your trade, and everyone's happy!'

The manager seemed to consider the proposal. 'Keep it in the family, eh?' He turned to scrutinize Rob. 'You're fit enough to take on the job?' he inquired.

Rob nodded. 'If you mean the leg, it ain't stopped me so far.'

'And what is your present business, Mr Parsons?'

Rob couldn't tell from the manager's unsmiling face how things were going. He described the taxi firm he'd set up with Walter Davidson. He pointed out how much time he'd put into the pub over the years, organizing the cellar with George Mann, serving behind the bar.

Wakeley listened. 'It might work,' he admitted. He offered them both cigars from a fancy silver box. They refused, but he took one for himself and rolled it between his fingers. 'It's a pity you didn't bring it forward sooner.'

Robert's heart sank. 'How's that?'

'Well, the fact is, Mr Leigh, Mr Parsons, I wanted a chance to meet you in any case. The brewery has its own ideas on Friday's court business, naturally, and we had intended to approach Wilf Parsons to ask him to step down on a voluntary basis.' He was brisk, matter-of-fact.

Maurice leaped in. 'Let us talk to him, then. Rob and me

can get him to listen. I think we can get him to step down as long as Rob can take over.'

'Ah!' Wakeley sat back. 'There's the rub.'

'What? Ain't I good enough?' Rob showed his exasperation.

'Of course. It's not that. Only, our proposal that Mr Parsons should step down of his own accord is based on a different outcome.'

'What's he on about, Maurice?' Rob got to his feet and walked the length of the room. 'Come clean, Mr Wakeley. What is it you're saying?'

Wakeley looked him straight in the eye. 'The fact is, Mr Parsons, we have someone else in mind.'

Maurice tapped the edge of the table with his fingertips. 'A different landlord?'

'Who? Who the bleeding hell can you put in Pa's place?' Rob's control snapped. So much for dressing up and playing the part. 'They got another plan in mind all along,' he said to Maurice in disgust.

'Now, I can't tell you that, Mr Parsons. You wouldn't expect me to. But we want a fresh start; move with the times, that sort of thing.' Wakeley stood up. He clipped the end of his cigar then turned to Maurice. 'No, the best thing you can do, Mr Leigh, is to go back to your father-in-law, explain the brewery's point of view, and advise him to go without a fuss. *Before* Friday, if possible.' He stood firm behind clouds of blue cigar smoke.

Rob took a sharp intake of breath. 'Let's get out of here,' he said to Maurice. He felt stifled. 'Ain't no point hanging round.'

Maurice conceded defeat. They went out of the office, pointedly refusing to shake Wakeley's hand or make any promises on their part.

'We was set up!' Rob said angrily as they found their way

out of the nearest exit, through the stables lined with heavy tack. 'If they want us to do their dirty work, they can think again.'

Two great shire horses stirred restlessly inside their bays. Maurice shook his head. They crossed a wide yard towards the iron gates overlooking a railway siding. 'I gotta go back and tell Jess,' he said, not relishing the task. 'What you gonna do?'

Rob sagged forwards, hands in pockets, shoulders stooped. 'I'll go and tell Pa to expect the worst. There ain't no way he can win now.'

'We done our best.' Maurice turned his starter-handle. The car fired. 'We can say that.'

'And it ain't good enough.' Rob climbed into his taxi.

The two cars slid into the crowd of bicycles and pedestrians filing out of the brewery gates to the sound of the hooter that signalled the end of the working day.

CHAPTER TWELVE

The bad news filtered down Paradise Court that the brewery didn't intend to stick up for Duke when he went to court.

Charlie Ogden met Katie O'Hagan on the market and told her that it was all up; Duke had seen the writing on the wall. He'd admitted defeat. Charlie had got the news from Walter Davidson, who'd got it straight from Rob Parsons.

'He ain't gonna fight?' Katie was devastated. She was a fiery slip of a girl, with a green tinge to her eyes and her father's wide, Irish mouth. Undersized, but making up for her lack of height with non-stop activity and determination, she regarded the Parsons set-up as the ideal home she'd never had. Duke was a rock in the neighbourhood. He ran the pub like clockwork, never took sides in petty quarrels and looked on his family with affectionate pride. And in Katie's eyes, Hettie was an angel of mercy, a saint. 'Does that mean he'll have to pack up and go?'

'Duke's finished,' Charlie told her. 'Ain't nothing he can do.'

She passed on the news to her ma and pa. Joe cursed Wiggin. 'Who they gonna get to fill Duke's shoes? That's what I'd like to know.'

'. . . a new broom?' Dolly Ogden listened to Mary's account with rising scorn. 'Who they trying to kid? Listen, they got the best landlord there is in Duke Parsons.' It was almost unheard of for her not to be first on the scene when a new development occurred. 'And you say Duke ain't gonna fight no more?' she shouted at Mary, as if it were her fault.

'That's according to Katie.' Mary was on her way to deliver a calico sack of clean table linen to Henshaws' when she bumped into Dolly. 'She says they tried talking to the brewery, but they didn't want to know. They got someone else in mind.'

Dolly mouthed Mary's last words to herself, then exploded aloud once more. 'Who the bleeding hell can they get in Duke's place?' she demanded. Then she stormed up to the market to have her say among her women friends. 'The brewery's dropped Duke in it,' she reported. 'They're kicking him out after all these years. It's a bleeding disgrace!' Dolly overlooked the little matter of serving after hours. Who could blame Duke for giving people what they wanted?

Next day, the Thursday, Frances came across to Duke Street to talk things over with Hettie. She still hadn't felt able to broach the important subject with Annie, finding the problem over the licence enough to deal with at any given time. The sisters sat in the living-room together while the business of the pub went on below.

'Is he thinking straight?' Frances asked. They talked in hushed tones, their eyes dark with worry. 'Has he thought what he's gonna do after tomorrow?'

Hettie was dressed in uniform, ready to go out. Her bonnet lay on the table, her Quaker-plain jacket was buttoned to the chin. 'I don't know, Fran, it's like he can't bring himself to think about it. I asked him yesterday after Rob came back from the brewery, should I look round for another place for us? And he just looked up at me with dying eyes. Yes, like he wants to pack up and die.' Hettie's eyes filled with tears. 'I been praying and asking God's help, but I ain't getting no answers.' She sobbed on Frances's shoulder.

'Hush, we'll sort something out, Ett. Just hush, my dear. Don't you cry.' Frances's self-restraint cracked under the strain of comforting Hettie. They sobbed quietly for a few minutes, to the sound of doors swinging, glasses clinking, people drinking in the bar below.

Then Frances blew her nose and went down the court in search of Annie. She needed to tell her that Duke had agreed that she and Hettie should compose a letter to send to the magistrates, admitting his offence of serving after hours and agreeing to give up his licence. Everyone understood, after listening to Rob, that all was lost. Now Frances wanted to spare her father the unnecessary distress of appearing in court.

She didn't find Annie in her own little terraced house, but she was still anxious to explain the latest development to her face to face, before it had time to reach her in a buzz of rumour. So she went on from Annie's house to the tenement, expecting to find her busy tidying up at Wiggin's place.

Frances had never before ventured into number five Eden House, the misnamed tenement where Wiggin had holed up with Annie's support. She disliked the feel of the whole building in fact, objecting to the lack of privacy whenever she came to visit the O'Hagans on the upstairs floor; the dark, bare corridors, the peeling plaster. For the inhabitants it was a poor sort of life, overlooked by the tall walls of a furniture factory at the back, with one toilet shared between all the tenants on each floor. As Frances went under the crumbling stone entrance and down some steps to the semi-basement rooms at the back, she instinctively pulled her cardigan around her and knocked briskly at the shabby door marked number five.

She stood and waited. There was someone in there, she was sure. 'Hello. Annie, is that you?' Frances shivered in the damp, cold corridor. She knocked again.

Inside she heard a shuffling sound of something heavy being dragged across a bare floor.

'Mr Wiggin?' Frances's suspicions were aroused. It seemed he didn't intend to answer the door. 'Is Annie there, please? It's Frances Wray. I need to speak to Annie.'

'I don't know you!' Wiggin's muffled voice came back at last.

Frances heard more grunts and gasps as he shifted the heavy object towards the door. 'I tried Annie's place. She ain't there. I was hoping to catch her. It's very important.'

There was a stream of abuse as Wiggin clattered around inside the room. The message came through loud and clear; he didn't want to be disturbed.

Frances backed off in distaste, then she set her head at a determined angle. 'Ain't no use calling me them names, Mr Wiggin,' she retorted. 'I heard them all before. They don't bother me.'

Wiggin responded by throwing open the door. He clutched on to it to peer out at Frances, a respectable figure in the fawn cardigan and skirt looking him straight in the eye. He swayed unsteadily, growled and spat out phlegm at her neatly shod feet.

Frances stepped quickly back, out of reach. 'I want to know, have you seen Annie?' she persisted. 'Ain't she dropped by with your breakfast today?'

Wiggin's eyes were red, his breath stank of strong drink. He tottered in the doorway, cursing Frances for coming there. 'Annie-this! Annie-that!' he minced, with his top lip curled. 'I ain't seen Annie. Annie don't live here. See for yourself!' He flung open the door, overbalanced and fell against Frances.

She caught him by the shoulders, filled with disgust, but shocked at how little he weighed. He was skin and bone, easy to drag inside the room and pull on to a poor bed in one corner. There were signs of Annie's efforts; clean curtains at the window, a tidy grate. But Wiggin seemed to have been on the rampage, scattering bread and milk across the floor, dragging an old chest out of the alcove by the hearth. As Frances eased the old man on to his bed, the smell coming off him made her feel sick. He collapsed on his back, wheezing and cursing.

'Does Annie know the state you're in?' she said coldly. 'Has she gone for the doctor?'

Wiggin's chest heaved and erupted. Frances realized with horror that he was laughing. His thin lips stretched back, showing ulcerated gums that were red-raw. He clutched his chest, convulsed with unseemly laughter.

'It ain't funny.' Frances made a snap decision to leave him where he was, noticing an empty bottle by the bed and another half-empty one on the mantelpiece. Satisfied that he had left off laughing and subsided into a lethargic stupor, she quickly closed his door and fled.

Now alarm bells rang, not just for Wiggin. Frances had to find out where Annie had got to. Coming up the court, she bumped into Patrick O'Hagan, a boy of about thirteen who played truant and loitered his life away in the alleys and courts. He nodded when Frances rushed by and asked him if he'd seen Annie lately.

'When?' Frances grabbed his arm. 'Which way did she go?'

'Ten minutes since,' Patrick guessed. 'She went home.'

'But I tried her door. Are you sure?'

The boy nodded. 'Sure I'm sure.'

Frances turned on the spot and headed down the street towards Annie's house again. Why hadn't Annie answered her door? Why had Wiggin laughed? She mentioned Annie going to fetch the doctor and he croaked his delight. She knocked hard at Annie's door for a second time. She tried the knob. It turned in her grasp.

'Annie?' Frances hesitated on the doorstep. She called gently, 'It's me, Frances. Are you in?'

'I can't come and see you now, Frances.' Annie's voice drifted down the narrow stairs. 'I'm upstairs having a lie-down.'

This was unheard of. 'I'm coming up.' She mounted the bottom step.

'Leave me alone, there's a good girl. I'm just resting.'

'Ain't you heard me knock before, Annie? I need to talk.' Frances carried on until she came to the landing.

Annie's bedroom door opened. She came out fully dressed, her face averted. She trembled and reached out to the banister for support. 'I didn't want no one to see me,' she whispered.

There was a gash across her left eyebrow, an inch long, just missing the eye. A trickle of blood still ran down her cheek. The eye itself had swollen and begun to bruise. Frances stopped in her tracks. 'Oh, Annie!' she whispered.

'You found me out, Fran.' Annie tried to smile.

'Did Wiggin do this?'

'I slipped. I slipped and fell awkward against the mantelpiece.'

Frances felt herself turn cold with anger against Wiggin.
She went up to her stepmother and led her gently back to
bed. 'Don't stick up for him,' she pleaded. 'Not right
now.'

Annie sighed. 'He had a bottle by the bed. I wanted to
take it away from him. I asked him how he came by it.' Her
account began, slow and flat. She was in a state of shock.
'He got his hand on it first, he held it by the neck and
brought it down on my head, just here.' She pointed with a
trembling finger. 'I must have blacked out for a bit. When
I came to, he was panicking, trying to pull the old chest
across to the door. I got up and out in the nick of time.'

'Just rest, Annie. Don't say no more.' Frances stroked
her forehead. 'I'm so sorry!' She crooned until the trembling stopped and Annie was able to rest her head on the
pillow. 'Shall I go for the doctor, dear?'

'No need for that,' Annie protested. 'But Wiggin might
need him. He's set on drinking himself to death, I think.'

'Leave that for now.' Frances helped Annie to loosen the
neck of her blouse and slip between the sheets. 'Put yourself
first for a change.' She took off her shoes and put them
under the bed. 'I gotta talk to you about Wiggin, Annie.'

'Later,' came the faint plea.

'No, now. You gotta rest and listen to me. I heard a story
about him the other day.'

'Who from?' Annie turned to look at Frances, pain
evident in her tight lips.

'From Dolly.'

'Oh, her.' Annie sighed. 'You don't want to take no
notice of what she says.'

'Maybe not. But I gotta tell you. She went on about how
you two met in the first place.' Frances felt she must go
carefully, but go on she must. She blamed herself for not

trying to get Annie away from Wiggin soon enough. 'It was over in Hoxton, I think?'

Annie closed her eyes. 'I'm tired out, Frances.'

'I know you are. You had a bad shock.'

'He ain't never turned on me before today. Not since he came back. And I don't think he knew me. I could've been anyone getting between him and his next drink.'

'Don't make excuses for him, Annie. I can't bear to hear it.' Frances smoothed down the sheets and patted them. 'About this business in Hoxton. Dolly says Wiggin weren't your first husband after all.'

Tears rolled from the corners of Annie's closed eyes. Frances dabbed them with her handkerchief. 'Don't tell no one, Fran. Don't tell Duke.' She turned her face to the wall, sobbing quietly.

'I won't say nothing if you don't want me to.' Frances took Annie's hand in hers and prepared to listen.

'I was just sixteen, not very old. It's true, I was married then, before I met Wiggin.' She opened her eyes and gave Frances a sharp look. 'Ain't there nothing Dolly Ogden don't know?'

Frances smiled. 'That's more like it. No, there ain't, so you'd best own up.'

'My pa was a cobbler by trade. He mended shoes all his life, and pots and pans when they needed a patch. There was a lot of mouths to feed, and when Michael Kearney came along and offered to take me off their hands, they thought it was a godsend.' Annie paused. 'It weren't, as it turned out, but I couldn't go back and tell my pa that, could I?'

Frances shook her head. 'Did he treat you very bad?'

'He liked a drink, and drink didn't improve his temper. I stuck it out for a year before I left him.'

x

'*You* left him?' Frances asked. 'That ain't what I heard.'

'I was married to Kearney for a year,' Annie insisted. 'Then I was married to Willie Wiggin.'

'But how? That's the real question.' Frances tried to battle a way through Annie's evasiveness. Unless they came to the crux, all these painful reminiscences would be for nothing.

'I think you know the answer to that,' Annie said slowly. 'Let's leave it, Frances. It's hard enough to hold my head up as it is.'

All Frances's notions about women's rights rose to the surface as she considered Annie's injured face and her struggle to come to terms with the past. She felt another surge of anger. 'You ain't done nothing to be ashamed of. Not a single thing. The man who done this to you, that's the one ought to be hanging his head in shame. And Kearney. Two men who put their heads together and make a bargain over a wife! It's disgusting.' Frances couldn't help but show her feelings, though she was trying to keep a level head for Annie's sake. 'Ain't that what they did? You was Kearney's wife, and he went and sold you to Wiggin?'

'They was drunk,' Annie whispered.

'And you was seventeen!' Frances ran out of words to express her disgust.

'It happened in them days. It was the old way of going on.'

'But it weren't the proper way, not even in them days. Ain't you ever thought it weren't right, Annie? Ain't you considered that?'

Annie shook her head. 'Right or wrong, Wiggin struck a bargain and showed me the piece of paper that made everything open and above board. He said he'd got it from

the Register Office and there was no going back on it. Kearney wanted rid of me. Willie took me in. I wore a ring. What could I do?'

'And what happened to Kearney? Didn't he sober up and want you back?'

'Happy ever after? No, he never did get back on his feet. I heard he went on a binge, then he went from bad to worse. He had to go round the builders begging for work, when everyone knew he weren't fit for nothing. One took him on though, and he was still drunk when he went up a ladder one day. They say he just keeled over and that was it. He fell twenty feet to the ground.'

'He died?'

Annie nodded. 'A month after I went with Wiggin. Well, I was in the cart then. Wiggin was no better than Michael Kearney, but I had to stick it out. We got moved on out of Hoxton and we came over to Paradise Court. You know the rest.'

Frances patted her hand. 'I wish you'd told us.'

'And be made a laughing stock?' Annie shook her head. 'Would you own up to being sold on the market like a bolt of cloth? Be honest, what would you have done?'

'The same as you, probably. But let's get one thing straight; you ain't ever been married to Wiggin, no more than I have. Not in the eyes of the law. That marriage certificate Wiggin said he got from the Register Office, it ain't worth the paper it's written on, not without a proper divorce from Kearney.'

Annie considered this, her expression growing agitated. 'And in the eyes of the Lord?' she asked.

Frances paused. 'I ain't no expert, Annie, but I can't see that God would object if you said a prayer or two and told him you done your best for Wiggin, but you can't do no more, and you've decided to follow your heart for once and go back where you know you belong.'

'With Duke?' Annie trembled.

'With Pa. You and him should be together, Annie.'

'He needs me, don't he?'

'He does. He's lost the Duke. That's what I came to tell you. The brewery want him out. He ain't gonna fight it, and he ain't got nowhere to go.'

Annie had her chat with the Almighty, bathed her bruised face in warm water, covered her cut with antiseptic and lint, got dressed and marched with Frances up to the Duke. She spent half an hour with Duke telling him how things stood. First he swore he'd knock Wiggin clean off his feet and got up to do it then and there. Annie restrained him. 'He's already flat on his back. Out cold with drink,' she promised. 'No, you and me gotta talk.'

Duke was ready to believe every word. 'You threw yourself away on Wiggin,' he said. 'We all knew that.'

'And for nothing.' Annie sat in her old fireside chair. 'We was never properly married after all, according to Frances, the law and God Almighty.'

Duke smiled. There was a light in all this. 'Well, if them three agree, it must be right.' He leaned forward to take her hand.

'I never left you for Wiggin, Duke. I left you 'cos I thought we couldn't be married no more.'

'But now we can?'

'I've come round to that way of thinking, Duke. Yes. Thanks to Frances.'

'Thanks to Dolly,' he reminded her. 'It was Dolly tipped Frances off and got things moving.'

Annie sniffed. 'No need to go overboard. We'd never hear the end of it. No, let's move your things down the court here and now. No grand announcements. They can just get used to me and you being back together, and let them say what they want.'

It was agreed. The furniture, Duke and Ernie would move in with Annie. Hettie arranged to live with Jess and her family in Ealing, which would help in running the shop. Rob made a temporary arrangement to share Walter's lodgings. Practically, it all made sense.

'I gotta keep an eye on Willie,' Annie warned them.

They had to let her follow her own charitable course. But Duke insisted on sending Ernie along with her to Eden House, in case Wiggin turned nasty again. Annie gave in to this pressure. She felt safer in Ernie's presence; he was good and strong, and slow to anger. He knew his job was to protect her.

By Friday, 4 July, when Duke should have come before the magistrate, he was ready to leave the pub he'd run for thirty-five years. They crowded out Annie's tiny terraced house with his and Ernie's belongings; the old clock with its quarterly chimes, the two fireside chairs, the old kettle.

The Duke stood empty, cloths covering the pumps, the gauze mantels unlit. No sound came from the pianola, no laughter from the drinkers at the bar. Upstairs in the kitchen, a tap dripped, floorboards eased and creaked in the cool night air. Life that had gone on, year in, year out, voices that had filled the rooms had vanished.

Someone would come and cover the walls with new paper, set different slippers in the hearth. The tap dripped into the stone sink, measuring each empty second. Regulars approached the etched and intricate doors, saw no lights, moved on down Duke Street, grumbling about the changes, blaming the brewery for spoiling their weekend pleasure.

CHAPTER THIRTEEN

If anything brought home to Hettie the fact that she, Rob, Duke and Ernie had left the pub for good, it was a chance encounter with George Mann on the Monday after the move.

Hettie had a night off from Army work, and was hurrying down Duke Street from the tram stop. She was dressed for the summer evening in a light, wrapover dress in pale blue art silk, with a matching cloche hat pulled well down over her forehead. But every few yards, someone would call out to her; Katie O'Hagan from her haberdashery stall, or Bea Henshaw from the eating-house doorway. Then, when she spotted Ernie on his delivery bike, it was she who waved a loud hello. Her brother jammed on his brakes and stuck out his legs to come to a halt, a broad smile breaking out at the sight of Hettie. She hurried across the busy street towards him.

'Hello, Ett. You look nice.' He beamed at her.

Hettie grinned. 'Thanks, Ern. You don't look too bad yourself.' He was dressed up in a smart white collar and tie, in spite of the heat. 'How's things?'

Ernie's smile stayed put. At twenty-eight, he still had the gauche air of a teenaged lad. Sturdily built, with the family's dark brown eyes, his hair brushed carefully to one side, he still took pride in his job as Henshaw's errand boy, never putting a foot wrong in his daily deliveries of fresh bread, butter and eggs. 'Things is fine,' he told her.

'How do you like your new room, Ernie?' Hettie knew that Annie had sorted out a back bedroom for him, arranging his bits and pieces; his photographs of the family and poor Daisy O'Hagan, his collar studs and cufflinks, on an old mahogany dressing-table.

He nodded. 'It's fine, thanks.'

'Good. Well, I'm off to visit Pa,' she told him. 'Will I see you down there?'

'What time is it?'

'Half past five.' She'd left the dress shop early and come over by tube, specially to see how Duke and Ernie were settling in. 'I got some teacakes from the baker's near us. Your favourite.'

He nodded and mounted the saddle once more. 'I'll ask Mrs Henshaw if I can knock off early,' he promised eagerly.

'Watch out!' Hettie warned. Loud trams rattled by, buses lurched from the pavement. 'See you in a tick.'

He nodded and launched his heavy bike into the traffic, weaving skilfully in and out.

Hettie sighed as she lost sight of him amongst the clutter of market stalls, then went on her way. Ernie seemed all right, bless him. Like a child, he was happy if *they* were happy; his pa, Annie, and his brother and sisters. She knew all too well, though, that Duke would hide things from him to spare his feelings.

Intending to ignore the empty pub windows, Hettie ducked her head as she approached the court. She took the corner at a trot, only to come straight up against a ladder, propped over the doorway, jutting out onto the pavement.

Looking up, she spotted George at the top of it, taking down the small sign over the door.

'Wilfred Albert Parsons. Licensed to sell intoxicating liquor from the premises known as the Duke of Wellington public house, Duke Street, Southwark'. She knew that sign; its small, neat, gold lettering on a black background, her father's little-used first names. She stopped, stunned to see George take out the last screw and ease it from the wall.

'Hello, Ett.' George looked down, still holding the sign aloft. Then he swung it sideways, intending to slot it under one arm before he descended the ladder.

'Here, George, I'll take it,' Hettie offered. She held her arms out.

He handed it to her. 'Got it?'

She nodded. Close to, the gold letters had begun to fade and flake. Hettie waited for George to come down. 'The brewery ain't chucked you out then, George?'

'Not yet.' Back on *terra firma*, he took hold of the base of the ladder and swung it level with the pavement. Then he laid it flat, close to the wall.

To her shame, Hettie realized she hadn't given a thought to George's future once the battle to keep the Duke had been lost. Neither had she considered their own future together. Their quiet affair, going along gently through the years, had relied on them both simply being there at the Duke, day in, day out, coming and going. They never made arrangements to see one another; George would simply take it into his head to walk her along to the Mission, or she would come into the bar and chat with him while he worked. Now all that; too, would change. 'They'll have to keep you on as cellarman, don't you worry,' she told him. 'They can't afford to do without you.'

He shrugged. 'Let's wait and see who they put in as landlord. Maybe we won't see eye to eye.' He felt embarrassed at Hettie standing there in her light outfit, holding the old licence board in her gloved hands. 'Here, let me take that.'

But she shook her head. 'Can I have it as a keepsake?'

He nodded, wiping his own hands on his trousers. He edged her on to the doorstep, as a man wearing a sandwich-board over his shoulders sought room to pass. The board was written over in big, neat letters. It read, 'I know 3 trades, I fought for 3 years, I have 3 children, and no work for 3 months. But I only want ONE job.' The man looked respectable in a trilby hat and tweed jacket, but his shoes were worn and he walked with his head hung low.

Hettie followed George's gaze to read the message, then she turned back to him. 'Hang on here as long as you can,' she advised. 'Jobs ain't ten a penny, remember.'

'You won't think badly of me?'

Hettie glanced at the upper storey of the old pub; the rooms where she lived for most of her life. 'Never, George.' She turned to him with a sad smile.

He said he would keep the licence board safe for her while she visited her pa, and Hettie promised to walk out to the park with him later that evening. 'Thanks, that'd be nice,' she agreed, blushing. It was like starting afresh; she felt young and silly over the formal invitation.

Relieved, George took the board from her. 'How long will you be?'

'A couple of hours. I promised Ernie I'd do him toasted teacakes. You could join us,' she suggested suddenly.

It was George's turn to colour up. 'No, I have to finish here. Will you call in on your way back?' A knot of tension dissolved inside his chest: he'd been afraid that Hettie wouldn't care for him if he held on to his job as cellarman under a new boss. And he thought perhaps her affections had faded to the level of friendship only. Undemonstrative himself, with a long sense of being beholden to the Parsons family as a whole, he never pushed himself on Hettie, though he loved her steadily. His strong physique, quiet manner and untalkative nature gave no sign of vulnerability. He was good-tempered, reliable George Mann, steady as a rock.

Hettie nodded. 'About half-seven then?' She put a hand on his arm and reached to kiss his cheek. Then she went on her way past the Ogdens', past the tenement, down to Annie's corner of Paradise Court.

From her own new home in Mile End, Sadie could only keep in touch with her family through phone calls and brief letters. In those early days of living with Richie work took up much of her time, and when she got back at night, traipsing up the stone stairway to the rooms they shared, there was often a feeling in her heart that made her want to hide away and cry.

At first she couldn't tell what this was; after all, she'd got what she wanted by taking a risk over Richie, and the home she was making for him gave her pleasure. Most days on her way home from the office, she would call in at the ironmonger's to buy a new pot or pan, or at a china shop for eggcups decorated with cornflowers or a little glass powder dish for her new dressing-table.

Yet she was sad. She would fuss in the living-room, putting up a picture or introducing lace curtains to stave off this uninvited feeling. She typed all day, cooked, cleaned and sewed in the evenings. One sunny Sunday afternoon, she even made the acquaintance of her neighbour; the woman who'd greeted her decently when she first arrived.

Sarah Morris belonged to the band of now elderly East End women who had dragged up a large brood in the old Board School days, dealing on a daily basis with lice, eye infections, outbreaks of diphtheria and constant hunger. Her husband, Harry Morris, had died in a drunken street fight, leaving her and the four small children only hardship and his ukelele, which Sarah kept hanging to this day on the wall of her miserable front room. She told Sadie she never took it down to play, but she would hum 'Ukelele Lady', remembering how happy she was when Harry was alive. 'Bacon, bread and butter for tea every weekday,' she boasted. 'Harry was a glassmaker. He held down a good job. Only, drink was his downfall, you see.'

Sadie took this to heart. It depressed her to think of families broken up and suffering. And she began to ask Richie not to stay out so late. She'd only come to live with him a few weeks since, yet often he seemed to prefer the company at the pub to being with her. 'Why do you have to stay there till they close?' she asked.

'That's rich,' he said. 'Coming from a landlord's daughter.'

She had the grace to smile, sitting up in bed waiting for him to get undressed. She'd put a glass shade over the gas mantel on the far wall; its light was soft and warm on his strong back. Soon she'd forgotten her lonely, anxious evening.

Richie always undressed as if there was no one else in the room, casting his clothes carelessly on to the floor, whereas she would turn away out of modesty, or if possible slip into bed before he came in. She was still startled by the beginnings of intimacy, willing to let him take the lead, unsure of herself. But when he got into bed and held her close, when he began to kiss her, she would cling to him, arms clasped around his neck, loving his weight and strength.

Richie slid into bed now, resting back on the pillow, staring up at the ceiling. It had been a bad day; they'd laid off the casuals at the docks in large numbers, Richie among them. Tomorrow he would have to scout around for different work. Previously, when he'd lived alone, it wouldn't have worried him. But now there was Sadie. He decided to keep quiet about the job situation until he found himself something else. Not for the first time, he silently cursed Rob Parsons for kicking him out of his steady job at the taxi depot.

'Frances telephoned me at work today,' Sadie said. She curved her body against his side, slipping her slim legs under his. 'She says Pa and Ernie have settled in at Annie's place. Wiggin ain't popular down the court, though.'

Richie turned to look at her through half-closed eyes. 'Ain't the drink finished him off yet, then?'

'No, worse luck. Annie still goes in to look after him, even after what he's done. I wish she wouldn't.' She knew how hard that must be for Duke. Ernie went along to keep an eye on Wiggin these days, in case he turned violent. All this Sadie learned second-hand from Frances or Hettie.

'Someone has to.' Richie slid one hand along the pillow, under Sadie's dark head. Her hair fanned across his arm, he leaned to kiss her mouth.

She put her arms around his neck, gazing at him. 'Richie, what harm is there in you and me going to visit one Sunday?' she said softly. 'Pa would like to see us, I know.' She paused. 'And Rob ain't living with them no more.'

He frowned and pulled away, lying back once more. 'It ain't me they want to see.'

Sadie leaned up on one elbow, letting the sheet fall from her shoulder. Her hair swung across her face. 'Oh, but it is. Pa wants to see us both. And I want you to come!'

'Why?' He turned his head away.

'So they get to know you.'

'They don't want to know me.' He was stubborn. Anyway, there was no other member of the Parsons family he was interested in except Sadie.

'You're wrong there.' Sadie felt the rejection badly, but her tone came out wheedling and high. 'And I don't like to visit without you. Think of me once in a while, why don't you?'

Richie felt they were on the brink of their first quarrel. 'I think of you all the time, Sadie.' He turned to her and gathered her in his arms.

'Do you, Richie?' She stroked his cheek, ran her fingertip across his brow. 'Ain't I being very nice to you?'

He kissed her again. 'It ain't you, Sadie, it's Rob. You know what I think of him.'

'But I don't mean us to visit Rob.' She made one last protest.

'Don't talk about it,' he whispered. 'I ain't going to change.'

Their way out of a quarrel was to make love, swept up in the touch of skin against skin, melted by kisses, so that in the end nothing could matter more.

Only, next morning, as Sadie got ready for the daily grind, she returned to the subject of his staying out late. 'Why don't we go to see a picture tonight?' she suggested. She put on a broad-brimmed straw hat with a deep crown and a green chiffon band. She turned from the mirror, her face eager and fresh. 'I can see if I can get out early and meet you if you like.'

Richie's mind was back on the search for work. He shrugged by way of reply, then took his place in front of the mirror, razor in hand, ready to continue shaving.

Sadie went and picked up her bag from the table. 'Shall we?'

He shook his head. 'I ain't sure what I've got on tonight.'

'Another session down the pub, I shouldn't wonder!' she retorted, suddenly angry. 'Don't mind me. I can always go to the pictures by myself.' She flounced from the room and down the steps.

Richie went on shaving. He wasn't worried by this. As long as Sadie went on wanting to go out with him or take him visiting, that was the main thing. Whether he said yes or no was beside the point. Carefully he wiped the specks of lather from his throat. If she ever stopped wanting that, then he would start to worry. It didn't occur to him that this might be leaving things late. And he didn't recognize the importance of family to Sadie, never having had one himself.

But Sadie sat on the top deck of the bus, eyes smarting. She took deep breaths, hid her face from the gaze of other passengers with the broad brim of her hat. Now she knew what that nagging, aching feeling was, that she staved off with housework and physical arousal. It was loneliness.

Feeling sorry for herself and helpless, she swayed with the motion of the bus, under green trees, past the park. How could she be lonely when she had Richie? she wondered.

*

Pills, ointments, suppositories, powders and plaster. Gripe-water at one and six a bottle, Clarke's Blood Mixture for four shillings. Frances's days were laid end to end, measured out like the medicines she dispensed, the patent remedies she sold over the counter. The only task she disliked was fishing out the leeches from their wide-mouth jar, the black, sluglike creatures that shrivelled into long worms when prodded, which doctors still recommended for sucking out poisons.

Otherwise, skilled and patient as she was, Frances was content with her work, choosing a small bottle of 4711 cologne to take home to Annie, and remembering that Sadie's favourite face powder was Ashes of Roses. She took care of everyone's needs, treating her small nephew and niece to milk chocolate bars whenever she went over to Ealing to visit, taking Duke leaflets and books from the Workers' Educational Institute which she thought might interest him.

'You'll wear yourself to a shadow,' Billy warned. Early August had turned sultry, energy drained from the streets as people stayed indoors or continued to take their annual trips to Kent to combine hop picking with a break from grimy, noisy London. A change was as good as a rest, they said.

'Nonsense.' Frances buttoned her fawn jacket across the hip. 'You're sure you won't come?'

Billy glanced up from his print machine. 'Where is it tonight, Ealing?' He felt uncomfortable visiting Jess's place these days, the house was stuffed with too many gadgets and ornaments for his liking. He stuck to his old nonconformist ways. And though Maurice Leigh still professed to support the ideas of Ramsay MacDonald and the Labour Party, Billy remained doubtful whether a man could live in what he considered to be the lap of luxury and still be a socialist. Frances and he disagreed over it. 'Jess and Maurice deserve to be comfortable,' she would say. 'They work hard for it.'

Frances told him that she was going to Paradise Court to see Annie and Duke. 'There's a book here I want to lend them.' In her considerate way, Frances had realized how heavily time lay on their hands.

'In that case . . .' Billy wiped his hands and switched off the electric light over the machine. He smiled at his wife. 'Give me a minute to go and fetch my jacket. We'll walk over together.'

They took their time, enjoying their quiet walk, noticing a new flower shop open on Union Street, wondering what would eventually happen to Coopers' old drapery store. 'I hear he's left with nothing,' Billy said.

Frances paused to gaze in at the empty shop. Dust and cobwebs; that was all that was left. 'Poor Edith Cooper, I don't know how she'll get on,' she said quietly. Though she didn't say so, she had no sympathy for Jack Cooper, who had brought things on himself. She knew him as a pig-headed, overbearing man who neglected his East End roots after he became a wealthy store owner, treating his women workers abominably. But his wife was altogether a gentler, more charitable sort who'd suffered greatly after Teddy Cooper was killed in the war.

'They say they'll have to sell their big house now.' Billy offered Frances his arm and they set off steadily up the street once more. 'Just to pay off his creditors.'

She shook her head. 'There ain't no one safe these days.'

But as they approached the corner of Paradise Court, their quiet conversation came to an abrupt halt.

Billy stopped short and pointed to the pub. 'Blimey, look at that!'

Frances felt a jolt of anger. Workmen were busy on the building. Scaffolding ran up the front and down the side. Gone was the old green paint, the woodwork stripped bare by blowlamps. All the old green and gold signs were down from the now bare stone frontage. 'What's going on?' Frances gripped Billy's arm.

'Steady on, they're giving the old place a fresh lick of paint, that's all.' But Billy, too, was astonished at the transformation. He took an empty pipe from his pocket and began to suck at it.

Frances couldn't have felt worse if she'd been publicly stripped bare herself. She was scandalized. 'What for? Weren't it good enough?' She recalled how Annie would come out each day, regular as clockwork, carrying her stepladder and a bucket of hot soapy water to wash down the paint around the doorway and windows.

'I expect they want to make a new start,' Billy said quietly. 'When the new landlord comes in.'

'But look at this!' Frances stepped towards smart new signboards propped face down against the door. She caught sight of George Mann working inside the bar and called him out. 'What's going on, George? What are these here?'

George nodded a silent greeting at Billy, wrinkling his eyes against the low sun. 'New signs,' he said, reluctant to have anything to do with them.

'Why do they need them?' She poked at them with her shoe. 'Think of the expense. It's a crying shame!'

'Come on, Frances,' Billy urged. 'Let George carry on here.' He led her to one side, as two men in paint-splashed overalls, carrying a plank between them, made their way into the pub. Inside, they caught a glimpse of walls stripped to the plaster, gas-fittings ripped from the wall, dust-sheets covering all the fixtures.

She dug in her heels. 'Just a second, Billy. I want to take a proper look.' In growing dismay she peeped inside, then as she stepped back, one of the new signs tipped sideways to reveal the words underneath. The blackboard was decorated in modern, straight letters in a style just coming in. Frances read the words out loud. Instead of The Duke of Wellington, it read The Prince of Wales.

'They ain't thinking of renaming the old place?' Billy turned to George. 'That can't be right, surely?'

But George nodded. 'You should hear what they say about it around here.'

'Ain't it going down too well?'

'You could say that.' George turned to Frances. 'I'm sorry,' he said, shaking his head, 'the brewery says it's more up-to-the-minute.'

Frances was stunned. The Duke was to be the Prince of Wales after Prince Edward, the dilettante young heir apparent. She stared at the new signs.

George thought it best to give the full picture. 'They're talking about new windows for downstairs. They ain't sure yet.'

'And does Pa know?'

'He can't hardly help it. Not after Dolly went down earlier and told them the worst. About the name, that is.'

Frances took a deep breath. 'Let's go and see how he's taking it,' she said to Billy, marching in high dudgeon down the court.

George looked at Billy. 'They don't like it, but there ain't a thing they can do about it,' he said sadly.

*

In one way, Duke felt there was nothing more they could do to harm him. If you lost everything, he said, why lose any more sleep over a couple of new signs?

When Frances and Billy showed up, full of fresh indignation, he was sitting in Annie's back kitchen surrounded by family and friends. Rob stood smoking like a chimney by the back door, his face glowering. Dolly made cups of tea. Tommy swore he would never set foot inside the pub again.

'Bleeding stupid.' Dolly frowned. 'What do you think, Frances?' She thrust a full cup and saucer into her hands.

'I know what I think,' France said scornfully. 'How are you, Pa?' She took off her cotton gloves and put them in her bag. She sat down in Annie's empty chair, opposite Duke.

'Bearing up,' he said as always.

'But did you take a look on the inside?' Dolly went over and made a lot of noise at the sink. 'Stripped bare. And God knows what they plan putting up instead. Pictures of young girls half naked with their hair all over the place, I shouldn't wonder.' She grumbled about modern taste.

'Pa?' Frances touched his hand, urging a smile. 'Have you been up to take a look?'

He shook his head. 'It ain't worth making a special trip for.'

'But ain't you been out at all?' Frances frowned. She sipped her tea.

'It's too hot.'

'It ain't that hot, Pa!'

'Leave it, Frances,' Rob said from the doorway. 'If he don't feel like going up on to Duke Street, he don't have to.'

'But a breath of fresh air, Pa. It'd do you good.'

'Annie goes on at me just like you do,' he told her. 'Maybe tomorrow. I'll see how I feel.'

'Where is Annie?'

'She's up the court seeing to Wiggin. She ain't roused him so far today.'

Frances only had time to grumble quietly about Annie doing too much, when heavy steps came running down the passage. Ernie burst in, white in the face. 'Annie says come quick!' he gasped. He seemed to stagger sideways and Tommy had to leap forward to catch him. By now he'd clamped his mouth tight shut, unwilling to say another word. Saying something out loud meant it had happened. If you kept quiet, it would go away. He shut his eyes to block out the misery of what he'd just seen.

'Sit him down here!' Frances sprang up to help Ernie to her seat.

Duke stood up too. 'Look after him, Frances.' He beckoned to his son. 'Rob, you and me will go and take a look.'

'But what is it? What happened?' Dolly insisted. 'What's the matter with him? He ain't going to faint, is he?'

'Help me loosen his tie,' Frances said. 'And Billy, will you make sure Pa and Rob can manage?' She sat Ernie forward in the chair, head between his knees.

Both Billy and Tommy made off after Duke and Rob. The four of them arrived at Eden House together. 'This way!' Tommy yelled. 'Wiggin's in the room under us, down the back.'

They ran down the dark hallway, footsteps ringing in the hollow, tall building. Annie waited for them at the door to Wiggin's room.

Duke pushed his way to the front, relieved that she seemed to be unharmed. 'Is it Wiggin?'

She showed him in. The room was empty and in a dreadful state, the stench of stale alcohol, urine and decay almost unbearable. Wiggin had ripped down Annie's curtains and tried to block the light with old newspapers. His trunk was slewed across the room, the blankets on the bed slashed and torn. Broken bottles had been smashed across the bare floor, and as Duke advanced inside, he saw a dark stain seeping into the boards by the hearth.

'Where is he?' Rob snatched the blanket from the bed and looked wildly round. 'He ain't hit you again?'

Annie shook her head. 'I ain't got a clue where he is,' she admitted. 'I sent Ernie down for help. I think we'll have to set off looking for him.'

Rob relaxed. 'What's Ernie getting so het up over?' As far as he was concerned, if Wiggin had gone missing it was good riddance to bad rubbish.

Duke went over to the hearth. He stared down at the dark patch on the floorboards, still damp. He bent slowly and brushed a fingertip across it. 'This.' His finger was stained rusty red. 'Blood. Ernie can't stand the sight of it.'

'Whose blood?' Rob went to join Duke. 'Wiggin's?'

'Who else do you think?' Tommy kicked around amongst the broken glass. 'There's drops of the stuff over here and all.'

'So where is he?' Billy asked again. He turned to Annie. 'Ain't you seen him at all today?'

She shook her head. 'I ain't got no answer when I came up this morning. So this time I knocked and knocked, and when I got no answer I went to Bertie Hill for the key and let myself in. I thought he was still in here, asleep or dead drunk. I could smell it through the door. But I come in and he ain't nowhere to be seen. I think maybe he's made off up Duke Street on another binge.'

'Maybe he has,' Rob agreed. 'He'll be flat out on the park bench with the other old dossers.'

'Except there's this.' Annie pointed to the bloodstain. 'Ernie spotted it and it gave him a nasty turn. I had to send him down to you, Duke.'

'And it's time to get you back home and all,' he told her, taking her by the arm.

'But we gotta look for Wiggin, remember?'

'Tommy and Billy will take a look, won't you?' Duke agreed to send them off to reassure Annie more than anything else. 'He'll most likely come staggering back of his own accord if we hang on long enough.' He put an arm around her shoulder as they made they way out. 'Rob will see to the mess here. Bring a brush and a bucket of hot water with a scrubbing-brush,' he told him.

Rob went ahead with bad grace. 'Anyone would think I ain't got better things to do,' he grumbled. But he agreed to clean the room, for Annie's sake.

Back home, they calmed her with tea and sympathy. Ernie was upstairs resting, Frances said. 'Billy and Tommy will find Wiggin,' she promised Annie. 'He ain't gone far.'

'It's the blood.' Annie looked up, pale and strained. 'Look, Frances, I know he's a bleeding old nuisance, I don't say he ain't. But he could be out there down some alley, down a siding, he could be dying!'

It was the River Thames that gave up the secret of Wiggin's final journey.

He'd been in the water overnight, the police said. The current had taken him downstream and washed him up against a Norwegian fishing boat unloading for Billingsgate. A fisherman had heard the body knocking against the hull and spotted what he thought was a piece of flotsam. Only when he went for a pole to push it off, it bobbed and turned face up in the water, and he saw what it was. He called in the police. It took several days to track down Annie, Wiggin's only living relative.

Since his disappearance, Annie had been forced to relive the nightmare of his first vanishing act all those years earlier. She went in on herself, refusing to admit that it would be better if he never came back, a constant caller for news at Union Street station. The discovery of the body came as a relief in the end. She and Duke went straight to the morgue and she calmly identified Wiggin, not flinching at the bruised and battered face.

'Was it a drowning?' she asked the attendant, imagining the old man, drunk and weak from loss of blood, toppling over a bridge to his death.

But the man covered the body and shook his head. 'Bled to death. Looks like he was stabbed. Don't ask me. I ain't no expert.'

'Stabbed?' Annie echoed.

Duke and Annie went to the police station to check. 'They're saying Wiggin didn't drown after all?' Duke asked.

The bulky desk sergeant wheezed over to check the file and nodded. 'Vicious attack with sharp implement,' he confirmed. 'Dead before he hit the water.'

Annie's relief turned to distress.

'Weren't hardly nothing to identify him by,' the sergeant continued. He went to a cupboard. 'Just a few old rags. You might as well take them while you're here.' He heaped Wiggin's clothes on to the counter, including the old greatcoat that Annie had rescued from the pawnshop. 'Or you can let us burn them if you like.'

Annie sniffed and nodded, unable to speak.

'Go steady,' Duke warned. 'This ain't easy.'

Ignoring him, the sergeant pushed the heap of clothes to the floor. 'It was the old coat. It had Sally Army tickets in the pocket. We dried them out and went down and checked the numbers with the local spike. They took a look in their registers and came up with his name. They told us about his connection with you. Seems like you was his good Samaritan. Anyhow, that's how we found you.' He sounded proud of the policework behind it. 'At least you can give the poor old blighter a proper funeral.'

Duke took Annie away once more. They stood in a queue for a bus back to Duke Street. Neither felt up to the walk.

'He was stabbed, they say?' Annie puzzled over this all the way home. 'He'd been in the water overnight, but he ain't drowned, he was stabbed?'

'Let the coppers work it out,' Duke advised gently. 'You gotta try and forget it.'

But as they walked down Paradise Court together under a stormy sky, Annie insisted otherwise. 'It ain't right to forget about poor Wiggin,' she said. 'For a start, we gotta give him a send-off, Duke. We gotta put him away splendid, whatever happens.'

CHAPTER FOURTEEN

There was hardly a soul to mourn the violent death of Willie Wiggin. The sailor who'd dragged his battered corpse from the river spent one sleepless night, tossing and turning to rid himself of the old tramp's staring, sightless eyes and the hollow knocking against the boat's empty hull. The police wrote him down as one more dosser destined for a pauper's grave until they turned up an ex-wife to claim his remains and take him off their hands. The unsentimental Tommy O'Hagan told his sister, Katie, that at least they'd get a good night's sleep in future, without the old drunk clattering about below. Dolly Ogden even came out with it straight to Annie's face: she was better off with Wiggin dead and buried, the whole street agreed on that.

Nevertheless, on the morning of 8 August Paradise Court did turn out to 'put him away splendid'. They felt they owed it to Annie and Duke, who laid on a good spread in Annie's front room. Not many bothered with the graveside ceremony, just Annie, Duke and a few family and friends. Mary O'Hagan stood silent in the background as the priest threw soil on the coffin. She said a prayer and remembered the day when the police came knocking on her door with similar news. Daisy too had been stabbed. Mary crossed herself and stood head bowed for Wiggin.

Hettie and Jess had discussed who should stay in charge of the shop, and it was Hettie who came over to the funeral for an hour. She met George on the corner of the court, under the pub's new black and gold sign. He had on a smart jacket and cap, coming along at Hettie's suggestion.

'We're meeting up with the others at the cemetery,' she told him, taking his arm and walking briskly down the noisy street. 'Then Annie's asked us back to her place.' She looked nice in a grey silky dress and a straw hat with a curling brim. George was proud to walk her along to the funeral.

By the graveside, Hettie sang 'The Lord's My Shepherd' in a full, rich voice which soared into the still, blue sky. She sang of quiet waters with such purity that she brought tears to Annie's eyes.

'God rest his soul,' Annie said to Duke as she turned away. Upright and steady in his dark suit, he walked by her side to the cemetery gate. ''Cos he ain't had a happy time this side of the grave.' She dabbed at her eyes with her handkerchief.

Later, back at the house, she told Hettie that today would have been Wiggin's sixty-seventh birthday.

Dolly and Arthur Ogden were among the first to turn out in neighbourly fashion, to go down the bottom of the court and give Annie a boost. It would be a shame if she'd gone to all that trouble over sandwiches and cold pies if no one showed up. Since it was a Friday morning affair, they dragged Charlie out of bed to get dressed and show his face. 'Come and pay your respects,' Dolly said.

'Wiggin ain't worth it,' Charlie complained. He valued his lie-in after working late.

'But Annie and Duke is!' Dolly brooked no argument, as usual. The Ogdens would show up in force.

Rob dropped in, and Katie dragged Tommy off his paint and wallpaper stall to put in an appearance down the court. The hot, sunny day lent an odd festival air to the occasion; Annie's door stood wide open, and mourners brought their food and drink outside on to the pavement to chat.

Billy Wray had come in Frances's place. He talked politics with Joe O'Hagan, predicting more miners' strikes during the coming winter. 'Coal's losing a million pounds a month,' he said. 'Pits are closing all up and down the Welsh valleys, and the owners want to make another cut in wages.' He supported the Federation slogan, 'Not a penny off the pay, not a second on the day'.

Joe wondered where it would all lead. He himself cared less about the miners than the present newspaper outcry against one Patrick Mahon, murderous resident of Crumbles, near Pevensey in Sussex. 'They say he chopped up the body,' he told Billy, having steered the conversation towards the sensational case. Joe's morbid interest in such things no doubt sprang from his own daughter's death, for which Chalky White had eventually got the drop. He followed every detail of the current scandal. 'Her name was Emily Kaye, and she was his mistress.'

'I hope they string him up,' Arthur put in. 'Like they did that Edith Thompson a couple of years back.'

Billy retreated to the safety of Annie's front room for more pork pie and tea from Hettie. 'How's Jess and family?' he asked conversationally.

'They're fine, thanks. Mo and Grace ain't at school for the summer holidays, so Jess is pretty busy.' Hettie told him they were considering taking on help, both in the shop and at home.

He nodded, took his tea out into the court and, spying Joe and Arthur still hard at it, sought out the less lurid company of George Mann. The two men talked of more layoffs on the docks and a threatened strike on public transport. The TUC were heading towards a general strike, Billy felt sure.

'Ramsay MacDonald's against it,' George pointed out.

'But he's sitting on his backside in Westminster, he ain't the one being squeezed by the owners.' Billy felt strongly on the point.

Tommy, pie in hand, had overheard. 'That's why I work from my own stalls,' he put in. 'Ain't no one breathing down my neck.'

'Not till you get yourself hitched, Tommy, no!' George nudged him. 'Ain't it about time you were looking round for a missus?'

But Tommy had no intention, he said. 'Women is a thing I leave alone. It don't pay to get hitched. Look at Annie!'

They spotted her small, slight figure dressed in a long black skirt and high white blouse, bustling around with replenishments.

Tommy struck a serious pose, thumb in waistcoat pocket, chewing as he spoke. 'No, what I mean to say is, women is trouble. I've had my fling, I can tell you, but they always go screeching and carrying on before too long. Then, when they got you well and truly hooked, what do you get? A missus rowing, kids squalling, no coal in the grate and no food on the table. A missus only makes a man miserable. And kids? I won't have them. Look at my ma when we was young, washing and scrubbing till all hours just to keep us fed, and the little ones always crying for bread. No, I'm happy as I am, with my stalls and my mates, and having a beer when I like, and no blessed missus to come home to, ta very much!'

Billy and George applauded Tommy's long and eloquent

speech. 'Blimey!' George winked at Joe. 'I see you brought him up not to fall for the first pair of flashing eyes.'

But Dolly stood prepared to take Tommy on. 'What makes you think any girl would fall for you?' she demanded. 'You ain't exactly no prize catch, Tommy O'Hagan.' She said women liked tall and muscular men like George, not skinny ones like Tommy, or Arthur for that matter. She squared up to him. 'You may be a fast mover and a fast talker, Tommy, but you *h*ain't no *H*adonis. You need beefing up with a bit of muscle, you do. And you won't get far with just them big blue eyes neither!'

'Oh, Dolly, ain't I the one for you?' Tommy cried, as if stricken. 'And here's me thinking I was God's gift.'

'Well, you ain't, Tommy, believe me.' It was her turn to wink at the older men then stroll off.

'Blimey!' Tommy recovered an upright stance, his confidence intact.

The occasion had begun to go with a swing and, by the end of the morning, Dolly was congratulating Annie on a good show. 'Just like the old Coronation days,' she said. 'And we need a good get-together since they closed you down, Duke.' She nudged his arm. 'We miss our Saturday night sing-songs, don't we, Arthur? The Lamb and Flag, it ain't a patch on the Duke.'

'The Prince of Wales,' Annie corrected her with a pinched look. 'You could always try there when they open up them brand-new doors.'

'Ha!' Dolly countered. 'Over my dead body, Annie. Over my dead body.'

At Annie's insistence, the police had begun a desultory investigation into the circumstances behind Wiggin's death.

A few days before the funeral, they'd come down the court, a fresh young constable and the cynical desk sergeant from Union Street. They intended to poke around in Wiggin's old room and to speak to the other inhabitants of Eden House.

'Who cleaned up the mess?' the sergeant asked Bertie Hill, who let them into the room with his key. It was bare except for the bed, the trunk and a hessian sack full of what seemed like rubbish; paper, broken bottles, stale food.

Hill shrugged. He didn't like having police on the property, or having his time wasted. But he knew, as an ex-copper himself, that they had a job to do. 'Maybe it was Annie, the old girl what kept an eye on him.' He thought a bit longer. No, come to think, it was Rob Parsons from the Duke-that-was. The pub on the corner.' He explained to the two policemen the tangled connection between Wiggin, Annie and Rob, taking trouble to point out the things the family would have against the old tramp.

'And Rob Parsons cleared up the evidence?' the sergeant repeated. He paced the room in his shiny boots and came to a standstill by the hearth. 'Looks like he did a proper job.' He looked at the faint stain under his feet and bent to take a closer look.

The enthusiastic constable, whose short blond haircut and smooth face under a too-big helmet gave him the air of a scrubbed schoolboy, surmised that the stain was blood and that a fight must have taken place in the room. 'Broken glass. Blood stains. It could've been the end of a broken bottle what finished him off. Looks like the job was done right here, then they lugged the guts up the Embankment and dropped it off the bridge.'

The sergeant ignored him and turned to Bertie Hill. 'You say you didn't hear nothing?' He knew of the man's reputation. Everyone in the force had heard how, a couple of years before, the whiff of scandal had pushed him back into Civvy Street before a proper investigation could get started. Two or three coppers in Hackney had been taking money from the protection gangs to steer clear of their patches. They'd been dropped in it by a notorious gang member called Gyp the Blood, whom police had hauled in on other, more serious charges. Hill, like his two colleagues, had made a sharp exit from the force.

'Not a dicky bird.' Hill knew the ropes. He didn't want to get involved.

'And when did you last set eyes on him alive?' The sergeant sniffed and stared up at the ceiling.

'I never saw him.'

'Never? How did he pay his rent?'

'He never. The old lady did. She did all his shopping and cooking. He never went out.'

The sergeant sniffed again, as if the smell was bad and it was emanating from Hill. 'You never got on with him, then?'

'I never had the chance. His rent was paid, that's all.' Hill stared steadily back.

'Ain't never had no visitors and such like, I don't suppose?'

'No.'

'Just his old lady?'

'His ex-old lady, like I was saying.'

'And what about this Rob Parsons?'

Hill laughed scornfully. 'No, he ain't no angel of mercy coming to help a poor sinner. That's more his sister, Hettie.'

'So he weren't fond of Wiggin neither?' The sergeant got round to the only line of investigation on offer. After all, Parsons seemed to be the one who'd interfered with the room. If the old woman wanted an investigation, they'd give her one. He liked to inject a touch of irony into life.

Hill frowned, seeing an opportunity to lay it on thick. 'He only said he'd like to do the old bloke in.'

The young constable looked downright eager. 'How's that?' The sergeant turned down the corners of his mouth and poked at the bag of rubbish with his toe.

'In the Duke. I heard Rob Parsons swear he'd cheerfully strangle Wiggin. Him and Tommy O'Hagan from upstairs, they was always on about it. They all think it was Wiggin turned in Rob's old man, see. For serving after hours. The old man lost his licence over it.'

The two policemen considered this. They thanked Hill and set off up the court, noticing the renovations underway at the pub. That part of Hill's account was true, at least. 'No chance of a quick one in there,' the sergeant commented about its locked doors and empty windows. 'How about the Lamb and Flag?'

'Ain't we going to question this Robert Parsons?' The keen young officer was disappointed.

The sergeant looked at him with a sigh. 'Where's the rush? I reckon Annie Whatsername will soon stop bleating about a proper investigation once she hears her stepson's in the frame.' He saw no point in putting much energy into the case; when it came to it, who could care less what had happened to the old tramp? He would go through the motions of an investigation, but that was all.

Sadie Parsons guessed rightly that Rob would take time off to go to Wiggin's funeral. Hearing long-distance of all that was going on, usually through Hettie, she knew they'd all be gathered at Annie's house for the morning of the eighth.

So she applied for a half-day's holiday through her supervisor, Turnbull, and though he frowned and prevaricated, she pleaded compassionate grounds over the funeral, and he was forced to agree. This lie was the first and least obstacle the day held for her, for she had no intention of attending the service to bury Wiggin.

'Ain't you going into work today?' Richie asked from under the sheets. It was eight o'clock on the morning of the funeral.

Sadie was dressing in a V-neck dress without sleeves, part of the cream outfit which Jess and Hettie had made up for her that spring. 'It's Wiggin's funeral, remember.' She offered no further explanation.

'You ain't going to a funeral dressed like that.' He sat up to light a cigarette.

'Says who?' She put on a small cloche hat and pulled it firmly down. 'It ain't nothing formal. Annie don't want it that way.' She smiled briefly. 'How about you?'

He shrugged. 'Ain't no use going down the Labour Exchange and joining the queue again.'

'Well, it's too late for the docks.'

'I know that.' He inhaled deeply. 'Ain't no use going down there neither, not with these lay-offs building up.'

Sadie forced down a bubble of anxiety. 'Never mind.' She went to kiss him before she left. 'Something will turn up.' This morning she was keen not to upset him, so she hid what she wanted to ask; how were they to go on paying the rent, which had just gone up by five shillings a week, or make the place decent and buy food and clothes on her wage only? She knew Richie was trying hard to find work, but wishing and hoping didn't pay the bills.

'When will you be back?' He made much of the kiss, reluctant to let her go.

'Usual time. I'm going on to work after.' She pulled away at last.

He released her and watched her head for the door. She was edgily bright, as if she was hiding something from him. He had an uneasy feeling that the funeral was not where she was headed.

Sadie walked herself into a calmer frame of mind. She timed it to arrive at Meredith Court as the mourners gathered in the next street. She expected to find Walter all alone in the taxi depot.

Her daring deviousness made her heart beat rapidly as she entered the yard. Both cars were parked, and she spotted Walter in his shirt-sleeves, resting against one of the taxis. He was reading a newspaper. She hurried up to him with an awkward admission to make, and a request that would hurt her pride.

Walter looked up as he heard her quick footsteps. She caught him completely off guard. 'Sadie!'

She laughed nervously. 'I ain't a ghost, Walter.' She stood beside him, hands clasped, looking up from under her hat.

'Rob's at the funeral.' He folded his paper, trying to collect his thoughts. In her cream dress she looked slim and girlish.

She nodded. 'I came to see you. I got something to ask, but I've been trying it all ways, and I can't get it right. The words, I mean.'

'What is it?' Her confusion shot down all his defences and made him take her by the arm to lead her into the office. He sat her down and took the phone off its hook. 'Fire away,' he invited, looking intently at her.

'First off, is Rob still mad at me?' she began awkwardly.

'He don't say.' Walter knew better than to upset the applecart by prying into Rob's private affairs.

'Are *you* mad at me?'

He shook his head.

'And are you still upset with Richie?'

'Ah!' He looked down at his desk and spoke softly. 'Ain't Richie got himself fixed up yet?'

Sadie sat opposite him, swallowing her pride, battling to keep both hands and voice steady. 'He ain't, Walter. Things ain't easy.'

'You want us to give Richie his old job back?'

She took a deep breath, pushed on to the offensive by a crowd of uncomfortable feelings. 'He's good at what he does, ain't he? And it weren't fair, what Rob did. I wish you'd talk him round for me.'

'It ain't that easy.' Walter took a few seconds to dampen his own reactions and put them to one side. He tried to look at the problem with clear vision. 'You know what Rob's like as well as I do, Sadie.'

'That's what I'm doing here with you now. Ain't no way I can talk Rob round. But *you* might. You go over it again with him; tell him Richie didn't do nothing wrong, asking me out. Tell him you ain't bothered about me no more.'

'That ain't true,' he said simply.

'Only in the friendly way, then!' Sadie grew desperate. 'You see, Walter, Richie's tried for work, and it's a strain on him. I can't bear to see him low. He needs this job!'

Walter put his head to one side, looking warily at her now. 'Does he know you came here?'

She jumped. 'No. It was my idea. He's not to find out.'

Walter weighed this up. 'That's something, at any rate. Now, the way you see it is, I talk Rob round. I say, "Let's get Richie Palmer back to work on the cars. We need him here." Rob says yes. We go straight to Richie without mentioning your name in all this?'

Sadie nodded. 'It's asking a lot, I know. But you and me are good friends, ain't we? We'll always be that.'

Walter knew Sadie inside out: impetuous, kind, the petted youngest child. She sat there full of torn loyalties, battling with things she couldn't control. 'I'll have a go,' he promised.

Sadie grasped the edge of the desk. 'Thanks, Walter. I knew you'd help.' She stood up, relief flooding her dark eyes. 'You'll telephone me at work?'

'If I get anywhere with Rob, yes. But not today. You gotta give me a couple of days. It ain't likely I'll get the chance to talk to him over the weekend. It's our busy time.'

Sadie nodded and impulsively kissed him on the cheek. Then he watched her rush out across the cinder yard, a sense of loss rekindled in his heart. He put the phone back on its hook, smoothed his newspaper flat on the desk and walked slowly into the yard, where he leaned a forearm against the side of his cab and gave the tyre one hefty, heartfelt kick.

'Temper!' a voice said. It was the cropped constable, hot on Rob's trail. He'd seen a young woman looking hot and bothered dash out of the gates. 'A case of *cherchez la femme*,' he smirked.

Walter stood up straight. 'What's that?'

The policeman strolled across. 'Robert Parsons, is it?' Confidence oozed from him. He stood, feet wide apart, hands behind his back.

'He's out,' Walter said, wary now. 'What's it about?'

The policeman ignored his question. 'You're Walter Davidson, then? The partner.' After the visit to the tenement earlier in the week, the sergeant had more or less dumped the Wiggin murder case in his young colleague's lap. Diligently he set about gathering information on their one and only suspect. Parsons was part-owner of a small taxicab business down Meredith Court. There was a mixture of interesting things in his background. He was sent home wounded from the war with a chip on his shoulder. His brother was had up for murder, but got off. There was a strange coincidence, for a start. He'd been something of a boxer in his day, before the war, and was known for his hot temper.

Slowly Walter nodded. 'Shall I tell Rob you came looking for him?' He glanced over the constable's shoulder. 'No need. Here he comes now.'

Rob had left the funeral and cut along the back way, down a narrow alley running the length of the factory wall from Paradise to Meredith Court. So he came across the yard from an oblique angle and stopped suddenly in mid-stride. The sight of a copper talking to Walter gave him a start. But he soon came forward with a clear conscience. 'There ain't been an accident, I hope?' he asked. He was feeling relaxed. The funeral had gone off better than expected.

'No. I'm looking into the death of William Wiggins. I have to ask you a few questions, sir, if you don't mind.' The policeman drew himself up to full height.

'Cor blimey!' Rob threw down his cigarette butt, amused by the young copper's punctiliousness.

'This is a serious matter.' The policeman recognized the attack on his fragile authority. He'd only been in uniform for six months. 'I have to ask you to think back to where you was on the night of Wiggin's death on the third of August.' He sounded stiff and mechanical, even to himself.

'How the bleeding hell should I know?' Rob hadn't been expecting this. As far as he was concerned, the policeman was taking a liberty.

Walter shot him a look.

There was a short pause, then the policeman cleared his throat. 'That don't sound too good, for a start.'

Rob took a step towards him. 'What the hell's it got to do with you where I was that night?'

'I'd think about it if I was you, never mind why.'

But Rob saw only the absurdity of it all. 'You ain't saying I . . . I ain't one of your suspects?' He laughed at the idea.

'Just answer the question. Where was you on the night of the murder?'

'Not at home, for a start. Ask him.' Rob nodded towards Walter. 'I'm staying at his place. Go on, Walt, tell him I was out. All night! But it ain't against the law, so far as I know.'

The policeman turned to the more respectable-looking partner. Reluctantly Walter had to agree.

'Where then, exactly?'

'I ain't checked my diary, I can't say.' Rob's face set into a sarcastic scowl. This was beginning not to be funny. He dug in his heels. In any case, the coppers twisted everything you told them.

'But you must have some sort of alibi,' the policeman objected.

'Well, I ain't. Sling me in the nick for it if you like.'

Walter walked across the yard to remonstrate with him. 'Give the man an answer, Rob. Just tell him what he wants to hear and then we can get rid of him.'

'Let him find it out,' Rob scoffed. 'Ain't that what he's paid for?' He gave the stiff-looking officer a look loaded with scorn. 'I ain't saying a dicky bird!' He went into the office and slammed the door.

Walter shook his head. The young constable gave in and went off up the court, tight-lipped. He'd been well and truly got at, but that wasn't the end of the matter, as Rob Parsons would soon see.

CHAPTER FIFTEEN

Richie's Friday was spent fruitlessly wandering the streets of
Mile End in search of work. 'No Vacancies' was the word
everywhere he went.

He trudged on in the August heat, hearing children wail
from high in the tenement blocks, and the strains of blues
music issuing through coffee-house doorways in the insalu-
brious back streets. The slow, decadent notes captured his
mood and drew him towards the windows. Inside, there
would be women sitting round tables under a haze of
cigarette smoke, their eyebrows arched, their lips painted
blood-red.

Richie looked, but never entered. Everything cost
money. Charlie Chaplin's white face, with its bowler hat
and black wedge of moustache, stared down from a bill-
board over the entrance to a picture-house. These days he
couldn't afford to take Sadie to see a film, even if he wanted
to. He went home with empty pockets, and was already
there, curtains drawn, stretching his legs out across a chair,
when she came in from work.

'Here I am, I'm back!' She flung down her bag and
whisked back the curtains to let in the sunlight. 'Ain't it
hot? I couldn't half do with a cup of tea.' She waltzed
round the room, picking up his jacket from the floor, lifting

his legs and putting the chair back under the table. 'But first off, what wouldn't I give for a kiss!' She perched on his knee, pecking at his cheeks with friendly little kisses.

'Steady on.' He almost overbalanced backwards in his chair, letting her tip off his knee, then pulling her upright. 'What's got into you all of a sudden?'

She laughed. 'Nothing. The sunshine, that's what. Ain't it a beautiful day?'

'That depends.'

'On what? Oh, I'm sorry, Richie. Ain't you had a good day?' Excitement at what she'd dared to do on his behalf had made her ignore his slog to find work. She kissed him more softly, this time on the mouth.

He let her cuddle up. 'How come?' he asked.

'How come what?'

'How come you ain't miserable? Ain't funerals meant to make you cry?' He stroked his broad thumb against her smooth cheek, his hand cupped around the nape of her neck.

'That was this morning,' she replied, a shade too quick.

'And?'

'And some of us have been to work since then.' His probing made her irritable, but she was straightaway contrite. 'Sorry, I never said that.' She nuzzled up to him, arms slung around his neck.

He sighed and looked directly into her eyes. 'You ain't having me on by any chance?' She was, he was certain. She was too breezy, too determined to cheer him up.

'In what way?' She opened her eyes wide, but couldn't hold his gaze.

'About going to the funeral.' For Richie, there was nothing worse than being made to look a fool.

'I ain't!' she protested faintly.

'I think you are.' He looped his arms around her waist, taking her own hands and pinning them to the small of her back.

She looked up with a half-smile. 'You got a suspicious mind, Richie Palmer.' She was caught between denial and the excitement of her secret.

'Don't. Don't play games.'

His deep, muffled voice swayed things. 'Promise you won't be mad at me,' she said. 'I'll tell you all about it, so long as you see it's all for the best.'

He leaned away. 'How can I, before you tell me what it is?'

She was committed anyway. 'Oh, all right, I ain't been to Wiggin's funeral, you're right about that.' She held a hand to his mouth before he could interrupt. 'I did something for us instead!' She wanted to rush ahead, get into the calm waters without experiencing the storm. 'Just listen. I went to see Walter. He never expected me. I just showed up at the yard. I talked to him, and he promised he'd try to talk Rob round into giving you your job back. What do you think?' She ended up breathless, trying to read his reaction.

Richie broke away from her.

'I said, what do you think, Richie?'

He headed for the bedroom, kicking the door open.

She followed him. 'I asked you nicely, don't be mad,' she pleaded. His silence was like a blow. It knocked her self-control from under her. 'Richie, please don't do this. It ain't fair.'

He turned to yell at her. 'What did you have to go and do that for? You can't push me around! Do this, do that. Work here, work there!'

His savage voice frightened her. 'That ain't fair,' she whispered.

'And it ain't fair of you to go behind my back. You could've asked me first.'

'You'd have said no.'

'Too bleeding right! No, I won't let you go crawling back to that pair! No, I don't want their bleeding job; understand?' He despaired of her naivety and selfishness.

'And where would your "no" leave us?' Sadie found the courage to fight back. '"No" leaves us bleeding well on the breadline, Richie! That's what. If you ain't gonna let Walter give you your old job back, we'll starve to death and you won't lift a finger to stop it!'

They shouted at each other, face to face. His eyes were hooded and averted, hers angry and desperate. Sadie only came to his shoulder, but, slight as she was, she would stand up to him.

'We ain't on the breadline!' he retorted.

'Not yet, we ain't.'

'That's bleeding stupid.'

'It ain't, it ain't! I went to get you work, Richie, that's what. Any work is better than nothing. If you don't start bringing something in soon, we're in the cart!' She began to sob and beat a rhythm on his chest with her fists.

He caught her wrists. 'What are you going on about? They given you the sack? It's that swine, Turnbull, ain't it?'

She shook her head. Her hair fell forward. Wet strands stuck to her cheek. 'No, they ain't given me the sack. Not yet. But they will, soon as they find out.'

'Find out what?' He held her roughly, tempted to shake some sense out of her.

'Will you listen to me, Richie? Swan and Edgar don't keep on women like me!'

'What you on about?' He let her hands drop, stood back. She was trembling and crying.

'Girls who ain't married and go and get themselves pregnant!' She turned to flee from the room.

Richie beat her to the door. He put out his arm to bar her way. 'Say that again!' he whispered.

'I'm pregnant, Richie. I'm gonna have a baby.' She staggered into his arms and buried her head against his shoulder.

Overwhelmed, he stroked her hair. 'You ain't?' He shook his head.

'You can ask the doctor if you don't believe me,' she sobbed. 'What are we gonna do, Richie? What are we gonna do?'

That weekend, as the weather changed from clear blue to grey and thundery, Walter Davidson made sure to drop a word in Duke's ear about the police poking round the yard after Rob. He judged it best to give the old man a chance to look after his headstrong son's interest, since Rob seemed set on a suicide mission all of his own. 'He won't give them what they want,' Walter warned Duke. He'd gone calling to Annie's house on the Sunday morning specially.

'And what's that?' Duke listened, head down, taking it all in. 'What do the police want with him?'

'Where he was the night Wiggin was done in, that's all.' Walter stood in the front room, eyes on the aspidistra, fiddling with his hat. He felt bad about tipping more trouble in the old couple's lap.

Annie drew a sharp breath.

'Why not? Why won't he say?' Duke persisted.

Walter shrugged. 'You know how he is. He don't like coppers.'

Duke stood up and walked to the bay window. 'Ain't he got the sense he was born with?'

'You know he ain't,' Annie put in. She cut a quaint figure; fifteen years out of date with her high bun, her leg-of-mutton sleeves and long skirt. Now what? she wondered. Surely the coppers weren't serious about Rob. She went to the empty grate and rattled away with the poker to no good effect, except to ease her own frustration.

'I thought maybe you'd talk to him.' Walter began to back out of the room. 'Put him straight.'

Duke nodded. 'It's good of you, Walter.'

Walter acknowledged their thanks and left quietly. Annie showed him out. When she closed the front door, she hurried straight back to Duke. 'You ain't to think the worst!' she warned him. 'They ain't about to arrest Rob just 'cos he won't tell them where he was.'

'They will if they want to.' Duke still stared out through the net curtains at the row of narrow, terraced houses opposite. He thought back to Ernie's arrest; how they could snatch someone away and lock them up in the shadow of the hangman's noose for months on end, just for being in the wrong place at the wrong time. If they could do it to poor Ernie, they could certainly do it to Rob.

'Now, I said, get it out of your head that Rob's in for it. We gotta work out a way to make him come clean, that's what we gotta do.'

Duke turned towards her, heavy and slow. The sunlight showed every wrinkle, the unkindness of the years. 'Annie, you don't think Rob done Wiggin in, do you?' There was panic in his eyes.

''Course he ain't. Rob ain't never picked on no one Wiggin's size in his whole life, you know that.' She was full of defiance, standing hands on hips.

213

Duke nodded. 'That's true. Only there's his temper.'

'Never,' Annie repeated. 'So forget it, Duke.'

Duke sighed. 'Right then, I'm off down Meredith Court,' he told her, 'to see if I can catch the blighter in and talk some sense into him.' He went out into the passage and took his cap from the hook.

'You want me to come along?'

'No. Man to man is best,' he told her. 'I ain't gonna pull no punches. The truth ain't that savoury, you can bet. He might not want you to hear.'

Annie tutted. 'He needs a good thrashing, that Rob. At his age and all!'

Duke went over to the taxi depot, but missed his son by a few minutes. Walter had arrived back and let Rob go off for the morning to collect Amy Ogden and take her out for a spin. He told Duke he'd tell Rob to come straight over to Annie's place when he got back.

Meanwhile, Rob and Amy drove out of town in high spirits.

'And I as good as told him he could sling his hook, bleeding nuisance!' Rob was boasting to Amy about the police visit. The car windows were open, the road ahead was clear, and though the day was heavy and grey, threatening rain, they'd both jumped at the chance to drive out into the Kent countryside and breathe some fresh air.

'Bleeding cheek!' Amy agreed jauntily. She flung her hat on the back seat and leaned sideways out of the window. 'What did Annie have to say?'

'I ain't mentioned it to her.' Rob sat in his shirt-sleeves, enjoying the speed on the open downhill stretches.

'The coppers ain't serious, then?' The wind whipped at Amy's hair, tugging it back from her round face. Rob had to veer into the side as a car approached from the opposite direction. 'Watch out!' she cried. A hedge scratched at the side of the car.

Rob swerved into the middle of the road again. 'I don't know if they're serious. I ain't a mind-reader.'

'And did you tell them where you really was that night?' Amy's smile was suggestive. She faced into the wind once more.

'Let them find out for themselves.' There was a patch of woodland ahead. Rob planned a short stop somewhere off the road. He noticed Amy's interest in her surroundings increase as he slowed the car to a steady ten miles per hour.

'Ain't this grand?' She sat up straight and adjusted her tight blue skirt, wriggling to straighten out the creases. 'Nice and shady, nice and quiet.'

'Are you thinking what I'm thinking?' Rob leaned over as he steered the car on to a level verge; an area of grass backed by wild hops, blackberry bushes and hawthorn.

'Oh, so now *I'm* the mind-reader, am I?' Amy liked to catch Rob out. He'd grow touchy and she would cuddle up to him and get the better of him. They would end up kissing and laughing at nothing. He had a handsome smile, and when he laughed, he would throw back his head and she would tickle his neck to make him laugh even more.

'Rightio, then, we won't stop!' He began to edge the car back towards the road.

She flung out her arm and grabbed the steering-wheel, pouting at him. 'Now, don't be like that, Rob. 'Course I want to stop.'

He wrenched at the brake, leaving the car pointing nose

down towards the road. Amy jumped out and stretched her arms above her head. 'We can pick blackberries.' She began to make for them through the long grass.

'They ain't ripe.' Rob strolled behind, hands in pockets. 'Come on, Amy.' He put an arm round her waist to lead her further into the wood. She pretended to resist and he felt he would like to kiss her then and there: she was warm and soft, her skin smelt of sweet, flowery perfume. He put his lips to hers.

After a while Amy pushed him back. 'Not here, Rob. Let's go away from the road a bit.' She knew what the intense look, the close contact would lead to, and she invited it. Rob was a good lover, not too rough, not too gentle. He went directly for what he wanted, but he didn't leave her out of it. He knew she liked soft words, and was neither too shy nor too selfish to deliver them. Lots of men never spoke at all when they made love; it left Amy cold. But not Rob. He was tender, and he made sure she had a nice time. Often, when they made their opportunities and she lay in his arms feeling that nothing in the world was nicer than this, she imagined she might actually be in love with Robert Parsons. But then she would gather her clothes and her thoughts about her and tell herself not to be silly; she'd known him as a pal all her life. Theirs was a pleasant arrangement, that was all.

This particular day ended badly, however. Their open-air love-making had been good, as usual, but heavy raindrops began to splash on to the leaves overhead, and they had to hurry to dress and get back to the car. Amy was still buttoning her white blouse as she ran. She jumped into the car while Rob went to the front to turn the starter-handle. Feeling the rain come down heavier, he wound and swore. The engine stayed dead. He turned again, the rain began to pour. Amy sat safe and dry inside, watching it run down the windscreen. She checked her lip rouge in her hand-mirror. Rob was a blurred shape through the downpour. The engine still refused to start.

For five minutes, Rob struggled on. Cold rain drenched his shirt and trickled down his face. He swore himself blue in the face. In the end, he gave in. He came and stuck his head through the window. 'I have to get to a telephone.'

Amy sighed. 'How long will that take?'

'I don't bleeding know, do I?' He stood in the rain, dripping wet. She looked out and laughed. His dark hair was plastered to his skull. He glared at her, then strode off down the road in the direction they had come. It would take hours to sort this out; Walter would have to come out with a tow-rope. Amy would bleat on about being late back to Dickins and Jones. Before he knew it, the whole of Sunday would be wasted.

Eventually, after tracking down a telephone box and spending a wet afternoon cooped up in the car, alternately bickering and canoodling with the infuriating Amy, Rob spotted Walter's Morris come bowling down the hill towards them. The rain had eased, and it wasn't long before the tow-rope was fixed and Walter had them facing in the direction of home.

'Bleeding car,' Rob muttered. Walter had come up to his driver's window to check that everything was ready for the tow back to town.

Walter looked him in the eye. 'We need a good mechanic, that's what.'

'You can stow that for a start.' Rob picked him up in a flash. 'If you mean Richie bleeding Palmer, I'd rather take a running jump first.'

'Ain't no good *us* trying to tinker with these old engines,

217

though.' Walter sounded as if he was only trying to be realistic. 'Let's face it, Richie knew his way around them.' He seized his opportunity on Sadie's behalf as best he could.

Rob stared back. 'Over my dead body.'

Walter sighed and went ahead to his cab. 'By the way,' he called back, 'your old man wants a word with you. He says it can't wait.'

Rob agreed to be towed through town, straight to Paradise Court. As he'd guessed earlier, the whole day had gone to rack and ruin. 'Might as well get it over with, whatever it is,' he told Amy. They left behind the hedgerows and the woods for the lamp-posts and fire-hydrants of the urban sprawl. 'We'll pop in there first off, then I'll nip you over to Regent Street in Walter's car.'

'But I'll be late,' she complained. 'I only signed out till five. You know how hard they came down on me last time.' She arched her eyebrows.

'That was different,' he pointed out. 'Now, don't go on about it, there's a good girl.' He concentrated on the task of easing the old jalopy on the end of a tow-rope down the narrow streets and byways of Southwark to Paradise Court.

Annie invited Amy to sit in the front room with her as Rob followed Duke down into the back kitchen. 'Duke wants to have a chat,' she explained. She would sit with Amy, asking after her work prospects, reliving the old days on the market stall, while Duke sorted out the problem of the alibi with Rob.

Duke sat his son down at the scrubbed kitchen table, a stern look in his eye. He laid his cards on the table, explaining how Walter had seen fit to tell him the way police thoughts were tending over Wiggin's death. 'And a good thing he did too,' Duke warned him. 'Before you say anything against Walter, I wish to goodness you had a grain of his sense, Rob, I really do.'

Rob frowned and mumbled, 'I don't see it's his business.'

'Where's your common sense, Rob?' Duke pulled him up short. 'Sometimes I think I ain't come down hard enough on you when you was young. Especially when you was sent home wounded, and we all had to pray for you to pull through. After that, I *know* I ain't come down good and proper, 'cos of what you went through.' He paused. 'We was all soft on you then. I was about to say that I let you get away with murder.'

Rob frowned and shifted in his seat. 'Oh, come on, Pa, you ain't saying I had anything to do with Wiggin?'

'What am I supposed to bleeding well think? The coppers come sniffing round and you ain't got the nous to tell them where you was that night. No, you put their backs up good and proper. I call that well done, son. Bleeding well done.' Duke had worked himself into a state. His voice, usually quiet, low and steady, had risen. He slammed the table.

'Pa!'

'Don't "Pa" me! I ain't had my full say. Think about it, the copper goes back to Union Street. He gets the old files down. "Parsons . . . Parsons?" He looks you up. He sees the trouble we had over poor Ernie.'

'That was donkey's years back. Anyhow, he got a not guilty.' Rob found his voice.

'But mud sticks, don't it?' Duke wouldn't be shut up. 'What do you want to do to this family, Rob? Drag us through all that lot again? Ernie can't stand no more, you know that. He had a shock, and he ain't never got over it, not altogether. Annie and me, we got to put him first if the coppers get on our backs. I'm telling you, son, I ain't gonna listen to no excuses, I'm just telling you to get up that station first thing tomorrow morning, and tell them, word for word, what you got up to the night Wiggin copped it!'

Rob stood awkwardly, catching his leg on the table. 'And if I don't?' he challenged.

Duke rose to his feet, looked at him fair and square. 'Then you can say goodbye and we can say good riddance, Rob. 'Cos I ain't never gonna open this door to you no more.' His voice choked, his head dipped and shook sadly.

Stunned, Rob backed off. He mounted the step into the hallway, calling roughly for Amy to come. He was halfway to the door before Annie ran out, followed by a puzzled Amy.

'Just tell him "yes"!' Annie pleaded. She caught Rob's arm from behind. 'It ain't that hard, is it?' She'd guessed from the outcome of Duke's chat, Rob storming off like this, that he'd been stubborn and hot-headed as usual. 'Think before you dash off and do something you might regret.'

Rob shook himself free. 'It ain't me, Annie. I ain't got a word in edgeways.'

'You don't have to. Just tell him the truth. Get yourself off the hook, for God's sake!' Annie felt acutely the pain of the family splintering and breaking up.

'Tell him what?' Amy came slowly down the dark, narrow hall. She glanced back at Duke, standing head bowed in the kitchen.

Annie turned to her. 'Try and talk some sense into him, Amy. Spell it out.'

Amy frowned and patted her hair. 'I would if I could, Annie. You know me, always ready to help. But blow me if I got a clue what's going on round here!' She stood, left out, like an actor who's walked into the middle of the wrong play.

'It's Rob. They're after him. They think he had something to do with Wiggin . . . you know!' Annie couldn't bring herself to say it out loud.

Amy's mouth fell open. She stared at Rob. 'They think you done the old sod in?'

He made a move to grab her arm. She pulled back. 'Amy!' he warned.

'Yes they do!' Annie insisted. 'Look at Duke. Look what it's doing to him. He can't stand it all over again, not after Ernie. It'll break his poor old heart.'

Amy drew herself up and walked slowly down to the kitchen. She saw Duke, the picture of misery. She knew she could sort it all out in a tick. 'Don't take on, Duke.' She put a hand on his arm. 'Ain't no need to worry.'

'Easy to say,' he sighed. He cast a reproachful look at his son.

'No, honest. Rob ain't had nothing to do with Wiggin being done in. It ain't possible.'

'Why not?' Duke glanced up at Amy, his hopes revived.

''Cos he was with me,' she said, keeping her head up, spelling it out loud and clear. 'He was with me all the time it happened. We spent the night together, Rob and me!'

CHAPTER SIXTEEN

'What happens when Dickins and Jones gets to find out?' Annie turned to quiz Amy on their way up to Union Street station that Sunday tea-time. She knew the big West End stores liked to keep a strict eye on their living-in assistants. 'What happens if they catch you hopping the wag?'

'It ain't like school,' Amy retorted. She walked arm-in-arm with Rob up the damp street, following Annie and Duke's steady pace.

'More like a bleeding prison,' Rob grumbled.

'They gonna give you the sack?'

'Yes, and if they do, where does that leave her?' Rob seized on this as the reason why he'd kept quiet about his whereabouts on 3 August. 'On the dole, that's where.' It was partly true; he'd seen himself as doing the decent thing by Amy in refusing to drag her name into the mud. If he upset things for her at work, another new crib would be hard to come by.

'Oh, hush, Rob.' Amy calmed him down. 'I expect they'll land me with a fine, that's all.' She'd got a friend, Ruby Thornton, to forge her signature and sign her back in. Ruby and she would probably both be carpeted and lose half a week's wages. 'Let's get this over with. Ready?' She drew a deep breath as their little group gathered under the blue station lamp. Then they went up the steps together.

Duke pushed open the door and marched up to the desk. He announced their business to a red-haired, freckled youngster in uniform. The constable studied them, head to one side. 'I'll go get the sergeant,' he said.

Soon the old warhorse himself came wheezing out of a back office and ushered them through. He sat them down in a dark green and cream room at a deal table surrounded by six wooden chairs. A dark green metal lampshade hung low over the table. The sergeant slammed down his file and began turning pages until he found his place. 'I hear you want to give a statement?' He looked wearily at Rob. 'You don't half choose your time, pal. I was just about to clock off for the night.' He sat, pen poised.

'Go ahead, Rob.' Annie sat opposite her stepson, upright and stern.

Slowly Rob began. 'I'd like this set on the record. On the night of August the third I took Amy Ogden to the pictures at the Elephant and Castle. And after that, I drove her to my taxi depot in Meredith Court, where we spent the night together.'

Annie frowned and stared at the table. Duke looked up at the ceiling.

'Steady on.' The sergeant's pen scratched slowly over the page. '. . . "Taxi depot in Meredith Court, where we spent the night together,"' he repeated. Finally, he looked up at Rob. 'Anything else?'

'Ain't that enough?' Rob felt he'd been through the mill, with his pa and Annie sitting there and criticizing his every move. 'What do you want, a blow-by-blow account?'

The sergeant didn't blink. 'Times of day might help. When did you end up at the depot, for a start?'

While Rob hesitated, Amy jumped in. 'Half-eleven. We stopped for a drink at the Lamb.'

The sergeant nodded as he wrote it down. 'Decent little pub, that.' Then he glanced at Duke. 'Not a patch on the old Duke, of course. Now, what time was it when you took Miss – er – Ogden here back home?' He turned to Rob and Amy. The girl seemed to be brazening it out nicely. She sat, with her puckered red mouth, her pencilled eyebrows and blonde hair, a free-and-easy sort.

'Half-seven next morning, Sunday that was.' Again Amy supplied the details.

The sergeant wrote it down.

Rob stared at his broad, flat face, the seamed forehead, the thinning grey hair, oiled back and parted down the middle. 'Is that it?' He stood up, ready to go.

'Hold your horses. I ain't up with all the details on the Wiggin case,' he confessed to them all. 'I handed over to Constable Grigg. But he'll want to have this signed by you, Mr Parsons. And Miss Ogden, if you give a statement here and now, it'll save Constable Grigg the bother of coming up Regent Street for it.'

Amy's eyes widened. She hadn't expected they would go to such bother, and to avoid this disastrous possibility, she eagerly gave her own account, corroborating exactly what Rob had said. 'Rob dropped me off at half-seven all right, only you don't need to tell them that at the shop, do you?' She still hoped to salvage her reputation and escape the fine, offering the sergeant, who seemed a man of the world, a sly wink.

The sergeant jumped on this. 'Ain't you told them when you got back?'

Amy's colour rose over her tactical blunder. She sensed Rob's impatience, spotted Duke and Annie's worried glances. 'I had to get someone to sign in for me on the Saturday night,' she confessed. Now Ruby would be in trouble with the bosses for forging her signature.

'So we just got your word to go on that you was down the taxi depot, doing whatever it was you two was doing down there. But according to the book, you was tucked up nice and comfy in your own little bed?' The sergeant shoved the statement book towards her and watched her sign in her childlike hand.

'But they sworn to tell the truth,' Duke put in anxiously. 'Rob's giving it to you straight, I know he is.'

'And Amy,' Annie assured him. 'Else why would she go and ruin her good name, if it weren't the truth?'

The sergeant seemed to agree. 'I'll mention that little fact to Constable Grigg.'

'But this is the end of it, ain't it?' Duke stood up, troubled by the way the interview had turned out.

The sergeant had a soft spot for the ex-publican, who'd had his bellyful of troubles lately, a salt-of-the-earth type, as anyone could tell. 'Well, he ain't off the hook yet,' he explained. 'Sometimes young Grigg's like a rat down a drain; he finds it hard to let go when he thinks he's on to something.'

'But he ain't, is he? Rob ain't mixed up in nothing like this.'

The sergeant nodded. 'From what I hear, he's a bit of a hot-head. And he rubbed my constable up the wrong way all right. That's the thing, you see.' He offered to shake Duke's hand as they all stood up to leave. 'Pity he never came in with his alibi first off, but I'll have a quiet word,' he promised.

As the family left, he closed the file and looked out after them. He decided to keep Grigg off their backs for a bit;

give him the nice little job of going up the Embankment to talk to any of the dossers who might have seen what went on that night. At least it would take the heat off Duke Parsons for a bit. The poor old blighter looked like he couldn't take much more.

August 1924 came to an end, and there was a lull in the police activity over Wiggin's death, as far as Rob, Amy and the residents of Paradise Court were concerned. Street attention focused instead on the shiny new frontage of the Prince of Wales. Workmen came to fix electric lights both inside and out. The smell of fresh paint and varnish, provided by Tommy O'Hagan at special cheap rates, hung heavy in the still, hot air.

'So when do you lot pack in?' Tommy quizzed one of the decorators as he took the money for a tin of brown varnish and a metal comb to pattern the surface. The redecorations seemed to be taking an age.

The young lad, whose own pasty, pliable features seemed to have been pressed on to his face like putty, gave a shrug. 'We've to clear out by the end of September. That's when the new licence comes through.'

'Any word on the new landlord?'

'No, it's all very hush-hush,' the boy replied.

'I expect they're worried in case they have a lynching on their hands if news gets out too soon.' Tommy pushed his cap to the back of his head and settled in for a gossip. The decorator's lad had to stand, varnish pot in hand, and listen to the ins and outs of street politics; everyone was against the brewery and for the old landlord, Duke Parsons. 'What did he do wrong, for God's sake? Put more money in their tills, that's what.' Tommy was gathering an audience in his loud defence of Duke. 'Gave the people round here more of what they wanted, that's what. A nice place to meet your mates and have a quiet drink, that's all.'

'A bit of a sing-song on a Saturday night,' Nora Brady joined in. 'Where's the harm in that?'

'A place to pass the time of day without no one breathing down your bleeding neck,' another, henpecked voice cried.

'A pub that was a cut above some!' The consensus was instantaneous. Feeling came through loud and clear that since the brewery had turfed out Duke Parsons, the heart had gone out of Paradise Court.

Residents moved in and out, as usual. Seamen came and went from Eden House. Willie Wiggin's old room was re-let to a young American fireman from a transatlantic cattle steamer, recognizable by his shiny peaked cap and his disconsolate air. He told Bertie Hill he planned to stay only a few weeks before finding an empty boat to sail back home.

'If he can save his money and stay off the booze,' Joe O'Hagan told Arthur. 'The way I look at it is, he's already been on one binge and drunk away all his wages. Even if he finds work round here, and it don't fall off trees, my bet is that's where his money will end up again, down the bleeding drain.'

But Katie stood up for him. 'He ain't like the men round here, Pa. He don't drink.'

Her father swore she was a fool. Every man worth his salt enjoyed a good pint. 'Hey, you ain't gone and fallen for him, have you?'

She denied it hotly. Which meant she had, her mother realized. The young American's name was Jack. He had wide, grey eyes, a frank expression and a good physique.

Mary noticed he spent much time hanging around the market, looking for the chance to home in on Katie's stall. Her daughter would respond by laughing and looking coy by turns. Mary's heart was squeezed. She remained tight-lipped when Katie came home chattering ten to the dozen about Jack Allenby. 'See!' she reported to her father. 'They ain't allowed a drop to drink in America. Soon as his ship docked and he got paid off, he sent every penny back home to San Francisco, to his mother and his little brothers and sisters!'

'Good for him,' Joe retorted, on his way out to the Lamb and Flag.

But the most significant move into the court was Jack and Edith Cooper's return to one of the terraced houses opposite Annie and Duke.

The house had been rented out for years to immigrant families and transient workers, and was sadly neglected now. It had belonged to Edith Cooper's mother until her death from cancer in 1910. It stood empty for three years, then Jack saw a way to capitalize on Edith's small inheritance by renting it out. Now it was the only thing they could rescue from the bankruptcy courts, since the old East End house was in Edith's name and therefore untouchable. Swallowing their pride, they came back to their roots with worse than nothing. Jack carried a chip on his shoulder so huge that it turned everyone against him. Edith's life of genteel luxury lay in ruins. So they sat in cold and hostile silence in the kitchen of her mother's grimy house, before Frances and Hettie Parsons came calling one Sunday in mid-September, with a polite invitation for tea at Annie's house, which Edith shed a tear over accepting, and at which Jack snorted with bitter contempt.

Annie welcomed Edith to her house, hiding the shock

she felt over her altered appearance. The store-owner's wife's hair had been left to fade from rich autumn brown to its natural grey. She wore it in a plain bun low on her head. Her eyes were red-rimmed and lifeless, her cheeks drawn. Of course, the light cream and fawn coloured clothes were still good, but she wore them without conviction, as if they'd been made for someone else and suited her ill. They'd been tailored in better times for the graceful, confident figure she once possessed. Annie was careful to draw the line between compassion and patronage, offering tea and thin sandwiches, taking care to outline how bad things were in general for the people round here. Still, her sharp eyes picked up the large amber and gold brooch which Edith wore pinned to the high neck of her cream blouse. It seemed that the bailiffs hadn't taken quite all, she remarked to Frances afterwards.

Hettie wished Edith Cooper well and shook her hand before she got up to go and catch her bus to Ealing. 'It's early days for you, I know,' she said, 'and I expect you and Jack will want time to get your feet under the table before you start looking around for the next thing. But it just so happens that me and Jess are looking for help in the shop. Nothing too hard. Just someone to help keep the order book straight and help with appointments and so on. I thought you might like to think about it for yourself.'

Edith considered the sweetly delivered offer.

'Shall I mention your name to Jess?' Hettie urged.

After a long hesitation, Edith agreed. She took Hettie's hand between her own. 'If you think I'd suit. I'll have to ask Jack, of course.'

Hettie nodded. 'No rush. Think about it while I talk to Jess. We've a little place on the High Street, not too grand.'

Edith smiled for the first time since her move. 'Thanks so much, I can't tell you . . .' She struggled for words.

After Hettie and Frances had both gone, Annie let Edith weep on her shoulder. 'Hettie's got a heart of gold,' she told her. 'But she won't offer a person work if she don't think she's up to it.'

At that, Edith cried some more.

'And you tell that old man of yours, you plan to take up Hettie's offer,' Annie insisted. 'Whether he likes it or not.'

'There you go again.' Jess laughed. Hettie had gone into work next day and described the Coopers' plight. She asked her sister to think of having Edith to work in the shop. Jess sat scalloping the hem of a white chiffon dress which hung to a sporty knee length, and was designed to be worn with a jaunty embroidered skull cap set off with a swirling white feather. 'Thinking of others as usual!'

'But Edith could be just what we want.' Hettie pleaded her cause. 'You know how nicely she speaks, a real lady. And she ain't pushy. She knows stock-keeping. It'd leave us free to design and make here in the back room, instead of the "Yes, madam, no, madam" lark out front.'

Jess laughed again. 'I ain't arguing.'

'Does that mean yes?' Sitting at her machine by the window, Hettie paused. She kept her fingers crossed.

'Yes, 'course. I think it's a marvellous idea.'

Hettie's eyes lit up. 'Then I'll go across next weekend and fix it up,' she promised.

For a while the two women worked on in silence, sitting heads bowed, amid yards of clean-smelling new fabrics, surrounded by scissors, pins, measuring-tapes and dressmakers' dummies.

'I been thinking,' Hettie said at last.

'Don't do that. It can lead where you don't want to follow,' Jess joked. 'And then you're in a fine mess.'

'No, honest, Jess. I been thinking about George and me.' For weeks they'd been dancing around one another, unsure of their next move.

'See!' Jess snapped a thread and shook out the skirt of the dress. 'What did I say?' She made it a rule these days to push all worries about herself and Maurice to the back of her mind.

'I mean to say, George and me, we've known each other for years now, but we ain't getting nowhere fast. Not to my mind, we ain't.' Hettie allowed a sigh to escape.

'Don't he make you happy?' Jess took up the subject in earnest; it was rare enough for Hettie to give time to her own concerns.

Hettie thought hard, letting the whir of her machine carry the talk forward. 'Not happy exactly. Contented is more like.'

'And ain't that enough?'

'For me it is.' Hettie's own horizons weren't grand. She'd seen a terrible thing happen to Daisy O'Hagan, and she experienced the effects of raw poverty each time she walked into the Bear Lane Mission. So expectations in this life had to be limited, she knew. It was a subdued life at best, rising to glory at last in Christ's presence. Only, she wasn't so blinded by the light that she didn't notice the hopes and dreams of other, more secular beings. 'I think George wants more,' she admitted.

'Does he want to marry you?'

'He ain't asked me.'

'But does he want to?'

Hettie nodded. 'I think he does.'

231

'And do you want him?'

'I ain't sure, Jess. That's what I been trying to explain. I like George. There ain't no harm in him, and he's good and honest.' She shook her head, annoyed with herself. 'I'm not saying it's him; it's me!'

'Your heart don't race when you see him?' Jess remembered the quick, passionate longing she'd felt for Maurice in their first years together.

'No,' Hettie said quietly. 'I feel warm towards George, but I ain't head over heels and that's a fact.'

For a while silence overtook them again.

'Do you want to break off?' Jess stood up to hang the nearly finished garment around one of the dummies. She stepped back to assess the hang of the skirt from the hip.

'No,' came the quick answer. 'Only I don't know if it's fair on George, the ways things are. Should I tell him I ain't head over heels, Jess?'

Jess considered this. 'He knows you ain't, I expect. And he still sticks with you.' She nodded, satisfied with her work. 'You can stop worrying about George. What about you, Ett? Do you need a bit of mad passion in your life?'

They both laughed, then grew serious again. 'What do *you* think?' Hettie said at last.

Jess smiled. 'I say, passion ain't everything.'

'Meaning?'

'Meaning, I'd take care of what you got, Ett. George is a lovely man and he loves you to bits. Another woman could come up and offer him the whole world, and he'd say no thanks and stick with you. You'd go a long way to find that again in a man,' Jess said sadly. She went across and hugged Hettie's shoulders. 'There, that's what thinking does for you.' She put her cheek against her sister's. 'I'd best be off to collect Mo from school. I'll be back in a few ticks,' she said.

When Maurice got home late that evening, Jess had cause to refer back to her conversation with Hettie. 'Passion ain't everything,' she'd said. It could get you into a marriage, but it didn't make you stick.

Maurice went upstairs for his ritual of looking in on Grace and moving Mo back to his own bed, breathing in the calm of their sleeping bodies. But it wasn't enough to take the edge off a frustrating day. When he went downstairs to greet Jess, he began to relay his trials and tribulations without pausing to ask her how she was.

'We had a projectionist off sick at the Gem, and a reel of film broke down at the Palace. Ten people asked for their money back at the end, and I don't blame them. On top of that, Charlie nearly bit their heads off for asking. I had to step in and keep the peace.' He sighed as he unlaced his shoes and kicked them off under the table. Then he loosened his tie and took out his collar studs. 'I been thinking; Charlie ain't up to it lately.'

Jess picked him up. 'Ain't he allowed one mistake?' She thought Maurice was sometimes hard on his employees, expecting 110 per cent from them all the time.

'I ain't talking about *one* mistake,' he said irritably. 'I'm talking about him going round like it's the end of the bleeding world. People don't go for a night out to look at his miserable face. I have to keep on telling him to cheer up.'

Jess stood in her blue, satiny dressing-gown. 'Is that all he's done wrong?'

'It's enough.' Maurice himself found Charlie's glum face depressing.

'But he ain't never late. He ain't never down on the takings, you said so often enough yourself. He's got a good head for figures, and he ain't never let you down.' She tried to rescue Charlie Ogden's image before Maurice consigned him to the reject pile. He made so few allowances for the differences between people.

'Look, Jess, I ain't asking for your point of view.' He was tired, he had too much on his mind. You had to run just to stand in one place in the cinema business, and Jess didn't appreciate that he needed a bit of care and affection when he came home late at night. Instead, she was forever standing up to him, wanting an argument.

'Shh!' She put a finger to her lips and glanced upwards to the children. 'If you ain't asking for my opinion, why bother telling me all your problems?' she demanded in a whisper.

He flung his loosened collar on to the table and turned away. 'Where's the bleeding milk?'

'Shh! It's in the pantry, the same as always.'

'Don't I even get a decent cup of cocoa made for me when I get in?'

'If you ask nicely, yes.'

They stood face to face, she looking at him in cool disdain, he sulky and spoiling for a fight.

'Anyhow, you helped me make up my mind. I thought about it, and I decided Charlie ain't up to it no more. I used to think he was on the ball, full of ideas and so on. But now he's standing still while things go racing ahead of him. The fact is, I'm gonna have to let him go, ain't no two ways about it.'

Jess stared at him. 'You ain't giving Charlie Ogden the sack? Not after all this time?'

'And what if I am?'

'But what's he done, when all's said and done? You can't sack a bloke just because he don't go round smiling all the bleeding time!' Jess never swore, but she was beside herself. 'What's got into you, Maurice Leigh? I can't believe I've heard this.'

'Well, you wouldn't understand,' he said. To make things worse, he changed tack and tried to belittle her reaction. 'Hold your hat on, I can see you've had a hard day yourself.' He adopted measured tones and waited for her to calm down as he stood over the pan of boiling milk. 'You get yourself off to bed. I'll finish off down here.'

Jess was almost speechless. 'I ain't had a bad day,' she countered, drawn into an irrelevant distraction. 'In fact, I had a very good day. We took orders for over ninety pounds' worth of stuff, and we took on a new assistant to help run the shop.' She gathered her dignity as best she could.

Her success was just the thing to grate on his nerves again. 'Yes, and Mo never sees his own mother.' He flung the worst thing at her; the one he always used when his back was against the wall. She never found a reply to that one.

Jess retired hurt. But tonight she didn't go and cry into her own pillow. She went upstairs and along the landing to the spare back bedroom, took blankets from the chest and curled under them on the bed, praying that Maurice wouldn't soften and come to seek her out. She wanted to be left alone; every nerve ending cried out, every grain of her being detested what was happening between her and Maurice.

*

On the morning of 1 October, the smart black doors of the Prince of Wales were opened for business. George Mann shot the bolts and swung them open, letting the sun shine into the bar with its dainty white window drapes and pale, plain walls. The pub stood ready for business.

George stood on the step, looking up and down the street. A light drizzle dampened enthusiasm, and the crowds weren't exactly flocking.

Arthur Ogden strolled casually down Duke Street, first on the scene. He stood, hands in pockets, his cap pulled well down. 'Lor' lumme!' He glanced inside and whistled in exaggerated surprise. But it wasn't the new decor that had brought him nosing around. He was after the vital piece of information; the one everyone had been seeking. 'You got the new man in there, I take it?' he said, nodding and winking at George. The name of the new landlord had been held back by the brewery like a state secret. Not a soul down the court had been able to winkle it out.

George nodded.

'Come on then, who've we got?' Arthur shoved past and stuck his nose inside the inner door. He caught sight of a stocky, fair-haired figure in waistcoat and shirt-sleeves standing behind the bar. 'Blimey!' Arthur couldn't believe his eyes. He scrambled back on to the street. He blinked in broad daylight. Had his eyes deceived him? He darted back inside for a second look. Then he was out on to Duke Street, bad back forgotten, dancing through the market like a bantamweight, darting into Henshaws', in and out of the market stalls to deliver the news. 'Would you bleeding believe it?' he crowed. 'The blooming brewery, guess who they gone and got for landlord?'

'Who?' came the cry.

Tommy ran out into the middle of the street, Nora Brady

left her fish stall, Bea Henshaw poked her head out at Ernie and told him to go and find out what the fuss was about. Dolly Ogden came trundling up the court.

'Who?' Tommy demanded. 'Spit it out, Arthur!'

'They only gone and got in Bertie Bleeding Hill!' he gasped.

The news dropped into a stunned silence. The doors of the Prince of Wales stood ready to receive customers, and behind the bar stood the ex-copper, owner of Eden House, and now new licensee of the old Duke of Wellington public house: Bertrand Gladstone Hill.

CHAPTER SEVENTEEN

The only person on Duke Street who was pleased with the new situation was Alf Henderson, the landlord at the Lamb and Flag. Trade was booming, with an influx of new regulars since the mass boycott of the Prince of Wales.

Henderson, a whippet-like man in his mid-forties, with wayward grey-brown hair that had the texture of scrubbing-brush bristles, a narrow face and a long nose, couldn't believe his luck. He doubled his orders of beer from the brewery almost overnight, barrels emptied almost as soon as they were tapped. Less meticulous in his methods than Duke Parsons, his cellars were often awash with slops, his spittoons full to overflowing with sawdust and cigarette butts, his glasses ringed with tidemarks from the day before. None of this mattered, however, as the Ogdens, O'Hagans, Walter Davidson, Nora Brady and her market pal, Liz Sargent, Rob Parsons and many others from the Duke crowded through his door, eager to slake their thirst.

'I ain't never gonna set foot inside that horrible new place,' Liz Sargent declared, her hatchet-face stuck glumly over her pint of porter. 'Makes me bleeding sea-sick just to look at it.' She was referring to the new cone-shaped wall lights and streamlined look that gave the Prince of Wales the air of an ocean-going liner.

Nora Brady nodded her agreement. 'Like I says to Annie just the other day, you can see it all now.' The gossip grapevine had turned it all around; Wiggin had been wrongly accused, Bertie Hill had planned every move.

'Yes, you don't have to look far to see who turned old Duke over to the coppers after all.' Liz enjoyed the gloomy talk; it suited the nights that were drawing in and turning cold. Already there was a nip of frost in the air.

'No, and it weren't Willie Wiggin,' Nora said darkly. 'So I hope whoever done him in ain't done it just because of that.' A miscarriage of justice would be a terrible thing; supposing Wiggin had been murdered due to the impression that *he* was the one who'd lost Duke his licence.

Liz reached up to readjust the hatpins in her brown straw hat. She jabbed them into her bun to hold the hat tight in place. 'They ain't still after Rob, are they?'

'They are!' Dolly muscled in, her instinct for gossip undimmed by the change of venue from the Duke to the Flag. 'Ain't you heard? That young copper was down Meredith Court again last week. It seems he ain't happy.'

'Why, what happened?' Nora finished off her drink. She wiped her mouth with her kippery apron and stood up ready to return to her stall.

'Let's just say, Rob weren't too happy neither.'

'Did he clock him one?'

'He would have if Walter hadn't stepped in.' Dolly shook her head. 'They still can't get enough on Rob to arrest him, but they're having a bleeding good try.'

'So, if Wiggin didn't do the business with the licence, who did?' Alf Henderson came round collecting empties, a stained red and white teatowel tucked into the waistband of his trousers. He dropped ash on the table from the cigarette hanging out of the corner of his mouth, and left it there untouched. His motive in finding out the identity of the police informer was clear; he had to be sure he didn't get caught out by the same bloke.

Dolly regarded him with open pity. 'Ain't you put two and two together yet, Alf?'

'And made five, like you, Dolly?' came the quick reply. 'And rob you of the thrill of telling me?' He was a quick-talking, edgy man with a snappy temperament.

'I've a good mind not to let you in on it,' Dolly huffed. 'See how *you* like losing your licence.'

'Come off it, Dolly.' Liz didn't want to run the risk of sacrificing another Duke Street watering-hole. She beckoned Alf across. 'It's obvious, ain't it? Since they opened the old Duke under a new name with Bertie Hill in charge, the whole street's been buzzing with it. Don't you see, it was Hill what dropped Duke in it!'

Alf wasn't slow to see the logic. 'But you can't be sure,' he objected.

Once more, Dolly swept aside doubt. ''Course we're bleeding sure. Think about it, we been pottering along at the Duke nice and quiet, year in, year out, with no one to bother us. Duke opens and closes the doors when it suits his customers. We take no notice of all that after hours lark. Then along comes that snake, Hill. He buys up the old tenement and shoves up the rents, a real old Scrooge. He comes drinking at the Duke, but he ain't welcome. It's never his shout, and he never sticks his hand in his pocket to pay his round. He trots home to bed at half-ten like a good little boy.'

Alf nodded at each emphatic point.

Dolly sailed on. 'And when we come to mention it, we seen him skulking round the place with strangers. They was narks, plain as the nose on your face. He gets Duke in a whole heap of bother with the coppers, then he goes straight down the brewery and sticks his name at the top of the list to be the next landlord, before anyone else gets a look in. The brewery keeps the lid on it; Hill's promised them lots of fancy changes and more money in their tills. He had it all worked out, see.' Dolly had been the very first to spot the conspiracy, forgetting all charges against Wiggin, the moment Arthur had darted on to the street shouting Bertie Hill's name.

'I ain't never taken to him.' Joe O'Hagan, wise after the event, had found his own cramped corner at the over-crowded bar. He rebuffed an approach from a Salvation Army collector, a girl of about eighteen with a mass of wavy, light brown hair tucked under her blue bonnet.

'Just tell your Tommy to give him the cold shoulder, then,' Dolly reminded Joe. 'We don't want no one round here breaking the boycott. We're gonna starve him out, see. If no one buys nothing from the bleeding traitor and the pub stands empty, week in, week out, the brewery will soon get sick of that, and Bertrand Gladstone Hill will be out on his arse!' She grinned in anticipation, ordered Arthur to buy her another drink, and then she settled down at Liz's table for a game of cribbage.

Among the rampant changes and the campaign to freeze Hill out of his new tenancy, George Mann found himself at a loss. He was no more pleased than the next man at discovering the identity of the new landlord, but he decided to hang on as cellarman for a few days, until he'd had a chance to talk things through with Hettie. He went about the business of rolling the empty barrels up the ramp and through the bar, out front on to the pavement, ready for collection. When the drays rolled up to deliver the new ones, he shouldered them from the cart and rolled them on the return journey down into the cellar. There he set them up on the long gantry, tapped the vent holes to allow the keg to breathe and inserted a new tap in one end. No need to worry about giving them a chance to settle before use, however; the barrels stayed full, just as the bar above stayed almost empty of customers.

George quickly learned how to handle his new boss's unsmiling demeanour and lack of experience in the job. He ignored them both, relieved of the necessity of maintaining a false cheerfulness by the former, and simply covering up the latter with his own expertise. George could have run the pub single-handed, with trade the way it now was.

It had one advantage: Bertie Hill's intention of keeping a clean nose with the brewery meant that he stuck to the letter of the licensing laws, so George got off early on the first Saturday night after an evening of desultory passing trade, despite the elegance of the new surroundings.

'Word will soon get round,' Hill assured his trickle of customers, including Jack Cooper. 'Then things will really take off.'

Cooper nodded and knocked back his whisky. He didn't care where he drank, so long as people minded their own business and left him to his. His skin was mottled by years of over-indulgence, and sagged badly around the chin and eyes, which had all but disappeared behind folds of flesh. His appearance was going downhill fast: the good suits to the pawnshop to support his growing drinking habit, the bowler-hat fingermarked and scuffed. These days he neglected to shave and wash. Grime had collected beneath his fingernails, and his shoe leather was grey and cracked. He didn't even care that Edith left him daily to his own devices, setting off at dawn on the bus to Ealing, getting into her stride as the new assistant at Hettie and Jess's dress shop. She took care not to mention it to him, lest his temper flare, when he would snarl abuse about her descent to shop-girl status at the grand old age of fifty-five.

That Saturday, George left the pub at half-ten on the dot. He took his cap from the hook in the hall and collected his old sit-up-and-beg bicycle from the alleyway at the back. Then he shot off in the direction of Bear Lane, to meet Hettie out of the Mission. On his way, he met Rob Parsons, the two men stopped to chat, and George promised Rob that he would see his sister safely home to Ealing.

'Blimey, you ain't gone and got yourself an old jalopy, have you, George?' Rob knew it was too late for the trams and buses.

George grinned. 'No such luck. But a pal of mine's just got hold of an old Matchless motor-bike and side-car. I was planning to ride over and borrow it, then take Hettie home in that.'

'Ett in a side-car, eh?' Rob gave a low whistle. 'Best of luck, mate.' He flicked his cigarette butt into the gutter. 'How's things?' he asked obliquely.

'You mean at the Duke?' George stuck by the old name. 'Slack, Rob. Ain't nothing doing.'

Rob grunted with satisfaction.

'I been thinking of handing in my notice,' George went on. 'I don't sleep easy in my bed no more.'

Rob shook his head. 'Think twice before you jump ship,' he advised. 'No one holds it against you for hanging on to the job.'

George nodded. 'Thanks, Rob. I'd best be off.' He set off again, pedalling hard uphill towards Commercial Street, where his friend, Herbert Burrows, lived. After a rapid bargaining session over the loan of the motor-bike, a gleaming black and silver roadster with a four-cylinder engine, George took the machine out of the back yard on to the road. He kicked the pedal starter and roared the motor into action with a twist of the handlebar throttle. He set off and within minutes was approaching Bear Lane in a cloud of blue smoke and petrol fumes.

Taken aback, Hettie caught sight of him as she came out of the Mission. She accepted the lift and stepped gingerly into the three-wheeled, sporty little side-car. 'Good job I tied my bonnet on,' she joked nervously. It was her first time in such a contraption, which seemed dangerously fast, unstable and close to the ground. She found going round bends too terrifying for words, and the roar of the exhaust as George came down the gears to stop at junctions jarred her nerves.

At last, Ealing Common hove into view, edged by gas-lamps, covered by a fine autumn mist. George slowed to a halt outside Jess's house, jumped off the saddle and ran gallantly to open Hettie's low door. She felt her knees wobble and her hand shake as she stepped out.

'You wasn't scared, was you?' George grinned.

'Not a bit. Just chilly,' she said airily. Then she laughed. 'Scared to death, if you must know.' She invited him in for cocoa, glad to have him there to help break the atmosphere that was bound to develop between Jess and Maurice when he got home from the cinema.

When Maurice did walk in, George was already sitting with his large hand wrapped around a blue and white striped mug. He was there when Maurice told Jess that he'd carried out his threat to sack Charlie Ogden for not pulling his weight. Jess could only sit there in silent, helpless anger. Then George changed the subject by dropping his own bombshell. 'I decided, I'm gonna finish at the Duke tomorrow,' he announced. 'I ain't happy under Bertie Hill. I'm gonna look around for a new place.'

When they got over their surprise, Hettie, Jess and Maurice nodded, understood, showed their appreciation. At just gone midnight, Hettie showed him to the door, waiting for him to fix his cap on his head, back to front, to keep the peak out of the wind. Then she kissed him gently and gratefully.

'I did the right thing, then?' he asked. 'I don't want no one thinking bad of me.'

'No one could,' she whispered. 'Least of all me, George. I think you're a lovely man, and I'm a lucky woman, that's what I think.'

Their embrace, close and warm, sealed his decision. Next day, his day off, he went specially to the Duke and told Hill he could stick his bleeding job on someone else, if he could find anyone in Duke Street low enough to take it on.

In the middle of October, Sadie went back to the doctor to have her pregnancy confirmed. The baby was due in May.

After her row with Richie over going behind his back to see if she could get his old job back, she hadn't dared follow up the possibility, and Richie was still without work. True to his word, Walter had in fact telephoned to say that Rob was fixed as ever against the idea of reinstating Richie. Rob was in a spot of bother himself, and Walter advised her to leave the problem alone for the time being. He was sorry, but try as he might, he hadn't been able to help.

As her troubles mounted, instead of going under as might have been suspected, Sadie's backbone seemed to stiffen. As soon as the baby became definite, the tears and pleas vanished and she became determined to manage. She put it down to an experience she had on coming out of the doctor's surgery with the news that she was indeed pregnant.

She thanked the doctor, a bookish-looking young woman with horn-rimmed glasses, who'd chosen to come and work in London's East End after a medical training in Edinburgh. She was observant enough to notice that Sadie's left hand lacked a wedding ring. 'And you think you'll be able to manage?' Dr McLeod asked, remarking Sadie's slight figure and pale young face.

Sadie nodded. 'Yes, thanks. We'll be fine.'

'We?'

'Me and Richie, the baby's pa.'

Reassured, the doctor smiled. 'And you have family to help?'

'Ain't no need. We'll manage.' Sadie's head went up as she walked from the surgery and headed, only partly consciously, by bus along the leafstrewn and windswept roads to Green Park, where she alighted and gave herself one precious half-hour to absorb the news.

It was five o'clock, the sky already lead-grey and fast losing its light. The leaves of the sycamore trees hung from their branches like so many limp yellow flags. Brown ones, already fallen, crunched underfoot. A cold breeze made her pull her red coat around her, shoulders hunched, cutting across the grass to avoid the paths where tramps slept upright on the benches and stray dogs searched for scraps. No lamps were lit, and it was easy for Sadie to feel herself swallowed by the dusk, to sense a calm beginning to envelop her, here under the trees, among the green and gold and autumnal browns. She stopped to look up through the branches of a great horse-chestnut tree, watching leaves loosen and spiral to the ground. 'Well,' she thought, as clearly, as certainly as she'd ever thought anything, 'I'm gonna have this baby.' Immediately she talked to the child in her womb as if it had life of its own and was capable of hearing. 'Don't you worry, everything's fine now. I'm gonna take care of you and see to you, and you ain't never gonna be left on your own.'

She strode on across the grass. 'We'll have each other, and Richie will grow to love you as much as me. There'll be the three of us, and we don't need no one else. There's gonna be just me and you and Richie. Life's a wonderful thing, I promise. The world's a beautiful place. Look at the trees, them leaves, that sky.'

She walked herself into a trance, only breaking out of it when she reached some far railings, and the sound of trams, buses and other traffic broke into her daydream. Then she caught sight of the clock in the square tower of a church opposite, saw that Richie would be expecting her. She turned to go home to Mile End, and to talk over realities; the fact that she would lose her job as soon as her condition began to show, that they must meanwhile scrape and save every penny, that he must find work at all costs.

For days after Maurice announced that he'd gone ahead and sacked Charlie Ogden, Jess could hardly bring herself to speak to him. His apparent heartlessness frightened her; how could he throw on to the scrapheap someone who'd trusted and relied on him for so long? Charlie had even cut short his school career to go into the cinema business, dreaming the boys' dream of bright lights and success, albeit from the wrong side of the flickering screen. True, his enthusiasm had waned along with those early dreams, but he was reliable, he knew all there was to know about front-of-house, and besides, the Ogdens were close neighbours of the Parsonses, and Jess felt personally responsible for letting them down.

What would Charlie do now? His slight stature and sensitive air made him ill-equipped to vie for work on the docks, or even on the markets, and Jess couldn't see him chained to a factory bench for the rest of his days. These thoughts churned in her head, like a whirring engine that drove her further out of sympathy with her husband's action. Maurice himself, his mouth set firm, his eyes avoiding hers, refused to discuss it.

When she heard of it, Amy sparked like a firework. The idea that Charlie had been badly used lit her anger and sent her running in all directions: to the Gem where she demanded but failed to get a confrontation with Maurice Leigh, down Paradise Court to her own house, where Dolly sat grim-faced, Arthur fumed helplessly, and Charlie himself was nowhere to be seen. Then Amy went down to Annie's house, muffled in her fur collar and black wrapover coat, hammering at their door to see if Duke could be persuaded to reason with Maurice on the phone.

Annie came to the door. 'Duke ain't well,' she reported. 'I sent him to bed with a hot-water bottle and a dose of cough mixture.'

Amy was near the end of her tether. 'I'm sorry he ain't well, Annie. But have you heard what they done to Charlie?' She got rid of some of her frustration by taking Annie through events step by step. 'It ain't right, you gotta admit. Maurice is getting as bad as them bosses in the mines and in the mills up north. He's playing God; ain't nobody gonna stop him?'

Annie shook her head in embarrassment. She'd asked

Amy into the front room. 'I ain't got the full story,' she reminded her. 'I'd have to talk to Maurice.'

Amy seized on this. 'You're a pal, Annie. You do that, and I'll nip across to the depot and see if I can get Rob on our side. I tell you what, by the time we're finished, Maurice will be sorry he started any of this.'

Annie saw her out and watched her go, running up the court between pools of gaslight, disappearing round the strangely quiet corner where the new electric lights glared from the walls of the pub. Quickly she shut her door and went to think over this latest event.

'Rob?' Amy dashed into the taxi depot. He was sitting by the telephone, feet up on the desk, catching forty winks. He awoke with a start.

'Where's the bleeding fire?'

'Ain't no fire, Rob, but I'll light one under Maurice Leigh's backside if he ain't careful!' Once more she recounted the full story. 'You have to tell Maurice to give Charlie his job back, right this minute. Get on the phone to him, why don't you?' She thrust the telephone towards him.

'He'll be at work.' Rob sniffed. 'Anyhow, I can't go barging in. It's his affair, ain't it?'

Amy snorted. 'You bosses, you're all the bleeding same!' She recalled how quick Rob and Walter had been to get rid of Richie Palmer the minute the mechanic crossed them over Sadie.

Rob was stung. 'No, we ain't. Ours was different.' He stared back at her. 'From what you say, Charlie ain't done nothing wrong.'

'Not a blind thing. It's that Maurice. He's too big for his boots these days. Well, if there was a union Charlie could join to look after his rights, he'd sign up like a flash.'

'Steady on, Amy.' Rob stood up. He found himself torn

two ways. His instinctive sympathy in any situation was still for the underdog, even though he respected Maurice's business sense and strong ambition. 'Listen, I'll have a word with Maurice as soon as I can. That'll have to do for the time being.'

Amy subsided into Rob's vacant chair. 'That's something, at any rate.' At last she'd run out of anger over Charlie.

'You're your mother's daughter all right.' Rob perched on the desk and smiled down at her. 'I like it when you get mad,' he said suavely.

'Yes, and you've been watching too many Douglas Fairbanks pictures,' she grumbled, already melting under his flattery.

'Ain't I told you, you're the splitting image of Gloria Swanson?'

'Only when you want something out of me, Robert Parsons.'

Rob's expression was one of pained innocence. 'Me? How could you?' He leaned forward to kiss her on the mouth. 'See, all I wanted was to give you a kiss.'

Amy tilted back her head, closed her eyes and sighed. 'And here I have to go and spoil a good thing.'

'Why, you don't have to get straight off, do you? Can't you stay a bit longer?'

She nodded, opening her eyelids. 'It ain't that. But now I'm here, there's something I gotta tell you.'

Rob leaned back, took out a cigarette and lit it. 'Fire away.' He expected another of the little melodramas that Amy went in for.

She decided not to beat about the bush. 'I ain't sure yet, Rob, but I think I'm having a kid.' She said it straight out.

She'd known for weeks, but only just got around to having it confirmed.

Rob looked as if he'd been shot. He sat rigid, ready to keel over at the news. 'How?' When he did find his voice, out came this childish question.

'How do you think, Rob?' She arched her eyebrows. There: she'd gone and spoiled anything they might have had going for them. She had sense enough to realize that by dropping this hot potato in his lap, Rob would want to run a mile. That was the end of their little jaunts and nights together. 'I thought you ought to know, that's all.' She stood up and gathered her coat about her.

But Rob threw down his cigarette and caught hold of her arm. 'Amy, have I got this right? Are you saying this kid's mine?' He knew he wasn't her only boyfriend, far from it.

Amy, apparently so blasé, seemed wounded by this. 'I wouldn't be telling you if it wasn't yours, now would I? I'd be dropping the bad news on some other poor bleeder.' Her voice was dry, edging towards a break. She tried to pull free and walk away. 'It's all right, Rob. I ain't gonna hold you to nothing. I know we been playing a dangerous game and breaking a few rules here and there if we wanted to stay out of serious trouble. In the end, I only got myself to blame.'

But he stood in her way, still trying to take in the news. 'What you gonna do now?' he whispered.

'Leave it to me,' she sighed. 'A friend of a friend . . . You know the rest.'

'You gonna get rid of it? Is that what you want?' Rob was confused. But he stood in her way, barring her exit.

'Look here, Rob, forget it. Forget I ever said it. I'll deal with it by myself. I won't be the first girl who's had to, and I'm bleeding sure I won't be the last.'

'And you say he's mine?'

'*It*,' she insisted. 'Yes, yes! Got it? Come on, Rob, let go of me. I gotta go.'

Her determination seemed to set him on his own course. Never in his wildest dreams did he think this would happen. At the same time he knew his precautions weren't thorough, but so far they had been without any consequences. Now it had happened, and something told him this wasn't a life you could just throw away. Perhaps he'd seen too much of that in the trenches – human life trampled in the mud and barbed wire – ever to contemplate wasting it himself. But there was a more positive idea too; a flickering notion that he might be a father, a good one at that. No one had planned it this way. He didn't think Amy had trapped him; she was too smart to risk it. No, it was one of those things. Looking at her now, he saw her struggling for control, wanting to walk clean away. 'Don't,' he said, pulling her close. 'I want you to stay.'

'I can't, Rob. I ain't in the mood.' Tears had begun. She was ashamed of her weakness.

'No, I mean I want you to stay with me.' He held her. 'I want us to keep this kid, Amy. And if you like we'll get married beforehand, just to make it all legal and above board for him when he's born.'

CHAPTER EIGHTEEN

Duke was ailing, Annie realized. Bronchitis had settled on to his chest, worsened by thick smog; that combination of wet mist, factory and traffic fumes that they called the London particular. It sank on the lungs like an acrid, cold blanket; filthy, bitter-tasting and thick.

It held up the traffic and clogged up both mind and body. No one felt like venturing out, and if they had to, they muffled up behind thick woollen scarves wrapped two or three times around the face. Other figures would emerge out of the yellow mist, insubstantial as ghosts. Sensible folk stayed in and waited all through late October for the fog to lift.

Duke sat indoors, struggling for breath. Annie tried him with poultices and inhalations to ease the congestion. Frances brought flowers of sulphur, friars' balsam, various pick-me-ups, all to no avail.

'It ain't the same down this end of the court,' he confided to Frances. 'Don't say nothing to Annie, but up at the Duke I could catch my breath, even in the worst of these pea-soupers.' He drew breath through a crackle of congested phlegm and fluid, shaking his head in helpless frustration.

Frances knew it was a state of mind as much as anything. Duke was pining for the beer barrels and pumps, the routine, the company of the old way of life. Down here he felt useless, his life's work valued as nothing by the brewers. It was a bitterness that found no expression, and dragged him into a decline, like the murky fog all around. She patted his hand, shook her head sadly at Annie and trailed off home.

But Annie refused to let Duke sink into apathy. She walked him about the house, wrapped in thick layers of vests, cardigans and scarves folded tight across his chest. She got people to visit and keep him cheerful; he was fond of Walter popping in for a chat, and Arthur Ogden needed no encouragement to come on an evening and put his feet up by their hearth for a game of dominoes and a steady supply of malt whisky. 'Purely medicinal,' he assured Annie, who kept a critical eye on the bottle. 'It helps clear the chest.'

But there was one visit, far from welcome, that occurred as the month drew to a close. There was a knock on the door, and Annie opened it to the uniformed figure of Constable Grigg.

Her smile turned to a frown. 'You come to tell us the name of the one what done Wiggin in?' she barked; a terrier on her home ground.

Grigg stepped over the threshold, shaking out his cape and spying the row of hooks in the hall to hang it from. Reluctantly Annie led him through to the kitchen, where Duke sat, pale and drawn, wheezing heavily. The policeman took in the tidy scene; Annie's copper kettle singing on the old-fashioned hob, the polished steel knobs, the blacked grate. A tub of coloured wooden spills sat on the mantel-piece, next to a fat biscuit barrel and a framed photograph of the whole Parsons clan. Grigg spotted Rob in the back row, recognizable by the black moustache and the jaunty set of his hat. Duke and Annie sat on the front row, bang in the middle, staring proudly out. 'I'm sorry you ain't feeling too good,' he said, thrown off his investigative stride. 'This won't take long, I hope.' He sat on the wooden chair offered by Annie, then cleared his throat.

'It ain't the time it takes I'm worried about.' Duke regarded him with suspicion. 'So long as you get the right man in the end.' It was the first they'd seen of the police since Annie and he had gone up to Union Street with Rob and Amy, and they'd begun to hope that the trail had gone elsewhere. The reappearance of the keen young bobby was by no means good news. 'You seen Rob's statement, I take it?'

The policeman nodded. 'And I went to see him too. There's some things that don't add up, though.' He was feeling increasingly uncomfortable as he pulled out his notebook and pencil. It was his idea alone to pursue the case. His sergeant had put him on to other cases, but at the end of the day he kept coming back to this one, and it was Rob's fault, he told himself. Rob should never have tried to make a fool of him during that first interview at the garage; that's when Grigg had dug in his heels, and never really let go since.

'Like what?' Annie tried to deflect attention from Duke. 'Rob's made it plain where he was, ain't he? What more do you want? It cost Amy Ogden plenty to come clean over that, so I hope you ain't bothered the girl by going up Regent Street and pestering her.'

'No. I've been following other leads. Wiggin knew some of the old dossers and I been asking around, but they ain't giving me nothing new so far. That's why I'm here, see. We're back to square one in some ways.'

Annie sighed and looked at Duke. 'Trust Wiggin.' Even though he was dead, he was still heaping trouble on their heads. 'Look,' she said, 'we already told you all we know. Wiggin went missing more than twenty years since. When he showed up again, I put a roof over his head and I paid his rent. No one knows what he got up to while he was away, except to say he was in prison some of the time, and for the rest he had a bleeding good go at drinking himself to death. By the time he holed up in Bertie Hill's tenement, his mind was unhinged. He weren't easy to look after, I can tell you. All he knew was how to get hold of the next drink.' She told the story quietly, with painful resignation.

Constable Grigg nodded. 'I got all that.' He finished scribbling a few notes. 'Now, what I want to know is exactly what happened when you went and found him missing on the fourth of August.' He sat, pencil poised.

Duke coughed and shifted in his armchair. 'Ain't nothing to tell. She goes in the room with Ernie, finds it turned upside-down, sends for help.'

'Hang on. When did you last see him alive?' Grigg concentrated on Annie.

'Saturday tea-time. I took his tray.'

'How did he seem?'

'Quiet. No trouble.'

'Any drink in the room?'

'Not that I saw. But he'd hide it, see. He was cunning in that direction.' Annie told it without emotion.

'But there *was* drink in the room on Sunday, when you finally got in?'

Annie nodded. 'Broken bottles, spilt liquor; you could smell it from outside the door. No sign of Wiggin, though.'

'So who brought him the drink?' Grigg sucked the end of his pencil. He imagined a session of hard drinking in the fetid cell they called a room, a drunken fight, a lunge with a broken bottle, then the messy business of clearing away the corpse. But how had the murderer got the body up to the river? It was too far to drag it, and too obvious. You'd need a car to hide it in. This brought him back full circle to Rob Parsons. 'Look,' he said, turning to Duke, 'I ain't clear what your son, Rob, was up to. First off, he refuses to give an alibi. Then, when he comes up with one, it's all cobbled together over a girl he's supposed to have spent the night with, only she ain't with him, she's tucked up in her own bed, according to another version. Then there's the business of getting rid of the evidence.'

'How's that?' Duke picked him up sharply.

'Cleaning out the room, removing traces of the victim's blood.' The policeman reverted to official jargon as he saw Duke's colour rise.

'That ain't got nothing to do with removing the evidence,' he protested. 'I told him to do that.' His knuckles gripped the arms of the chair. 'That was me, see. I sent him down here for a scrubbing-brush and bucket to tidy the place up a bit. Rob only did it 'cos I told him to.' A man's every deed could backfire, he realized.

Grigg tapped a loud full stop with his pencil. He flipped his notebook closed and rose to go. 'I see,' he said. It was evident he suspected another cover-up. The family was running round in circles to protect what looked like the black sheep, Robert. He bid the old man and Annie a curt goodbye and went straight back to Union Street to consult with his sergeant.

'Right!' Annie said, as soon as she'd shut the front door on him. 'That bleeding does it! Who's he think he is, bleeding Sherlock Holmes?'

Duke wheezed and coughed. 'Ain't that just our luck

these days? To have some fresh young bobby on the case.' He shook his head, going over what he'd let drop, to see how he might possibly have further incriminated Rob.

'You wait here,' Annie ordered. She went for her hat and coat, then called back in, 'Keep yourself warm, Duke. I'll send Katie to check on you.'

'Where are you off to?'

'To find Rob and sort this lot out once and for all!'

Annie ran through the fog up Duke Street, spotted Rob's parked taxicab and dragged him from his lunch-time break at Henshaws' eating house.

'Hold your horses, Annie, where are we off to?' He managed to gobble his meat pie and swallow a mouthful of tea. Then he followed her small, determined figure out on to the street.

'In the car, Rob. Hop in. We're gonna take a drive, you and me.' She ran to the passenger door and sat in the seat, willing him to hurry and start up the engine.

It fired, he climbed in and leaned forward to wipe the windscreen. Outside, he could see about ten or fifteen yards ahead. 'Where to?'

'Up the river, under the arches, wherever them dossers hang around on a day like this.'

He looked quizzically at her. 'What's this about?'

'Wiggin. We're gonna find who done him in.'

'We are?' Rob pulled away from the kerb, half-amused, half-anxious. 'We ain't gonna do nothing stupid, are we, Annie?'

'Just what the coppers ain't been able to do all these past weeks,' she told him. 'What do you reckon, Rob? Them old tramps, they ain't got nowhere else to go. They hang around the same old places, day in, day out. One of them must have seen or heard something the night Wiggin ended up in the water.'

Rob had to go along with it. There was no stopping Annie in this mood. 'Aye, aye, cap'n,' he said.

'It's getting your pa down.' Annie sat bolt upright as they drove along. 'We still got Wiggin slung round our necks like a bleeding albatross. We gotta get rid of him and give Duke a chance to pick up, otherwise I don't think he can last the winter.' Her voice choked and died, as Rob steered, almost blind, through the swirling fog.

At last, leaving the cab parked under a dripping tree, the two of them walked along the riverside to the sound of foghorns and the muffled chugging of steamboats heading upriver. Annie made Rob accost any bundled-up, stumbling shape who chanced to veer towards them from the wide stone steps leading to the wharves, or sitting silent on wet benches, waiting for the day to end. But her heart sank at each vacant gaze or hostile shove. Rob couldn't even get the tramps to stop and listen.

When they came to Southwark Bridge, they descended to the river bank and approached the stone arches where they knew the men and women slept out in all weathers. Sure enough, the shelter was crowded with misshapen figures, padded with newspaper and wrapped around with blankets, sacking tied around their ankles, half-drunk or crazy, starving, hostile as Rob and Annie went into their midst.

A woman's voice swore at them. Three men huddled over the embers of a fire made from driftwood and foul-smelling refuse. Another man loomed up, hand outstretched and shaking with palsy. Rob refused him and he went off cursing.

'This way.' Rob steered Annie towards the three old tramps crouching over the dying fire.

They were deep in conversation, discussing the means to get themselves a bed for the night.

'I won't stand another night of this,' the first man said. 'I'll go and smash a window, a big one, and get myself run in for a few days. Then I'll have a place to kip, and some grub.'

The two others mumbled on. 'Soaked to the skin,' one complained, his back to Rob and Annie. 'I been out three nights. One more night of this and they'll have to come along and pick me up dead.' He blew on his freezing hands.

The third, a taller, stronger-looking man than his companions, caught sight of their visitors. He turned on Rob fiercely. 'Don't never grow old, lad.'

Rob took a step back and put out an arm to protect his stepmother.

'Die when you're young,' the man went on. 'This is what you get for being old.' He cast a hand towards the huddled, starving shapes. 'We wish we was dead. It can't come too quick.'

In spite of everything, Annie's heart went out to him. He was sober, at least, and with the tough, leathery skin of a seafarer, his eyes wrinkled as if permanently staring across sunlight on the sea. 'It ain't that bad, surely,' she said quietly, still hanging on to Rob's arm for safety. To one side, the sluggish brown water slid by. Overhead, the dirty arch of the mighty bridge rose in the mist.

'Worse.' He shook his head. 'Worn out, I am, and I worked all my life. I ain't never taken charity, but I'm worn out now and on the scrapheap.'

He turned to wander off, but Annie stepped to one side of the fire and followed him, Rob close behind. 'How would you like to earn a bed for the night?' she said, direct as ever. 'Not charity, mind.'

'And pigs might fly.' He shuffled on.

Annie took a florin from her bag. 'There's this for you if you can help us.'

The tramp seized the money and bit at its edge. Rob made as if to snatch it back before he pocketed it without giving them what they wanted in return, but Annie restrained him.

'You got your money, now you gotta help us,' she ordered.

He returned a brief nod.

'Right, did you ever come across a man by the name of Wiggin?' Annie demanded. 'William Wiggin. Smaller than you, thinner, about the same age. Pretty far gone with drink.'

The tramp scratched at his wrinkled, bearded face. He sniffed, caught the phlegm in his throat, spat, then turned to go. 'He ain't here. The coppers already came poking round after him.'

'But you know him?' Annie stepped in quick. 'We know he ain't here. He died, didn't he?'

'Better off dead,' the tramp insisted. 'Yes, I knew a man called Wiggin. Him and me sailed together on more than one crossing. He ended up on the scrapheap, just like me. Only, he found a way out, lucky beggar.'

'How did he die?' Annie asked. 'Did you see?'

This time, Rob had to restrain Annie before she scared off the tramp with her eagerness.

'How?' The old man searched his memory, as unclear as these shapes huddled all around. 'How did old Wiggin die?' he muttered aside to his two companions, still clinging to the last red glow of their fire.

'Bled to death,' came the muffled answer. 'Like a stuck pig.'

The picture came back. 'That's it, Wiggin bled to death.'

'How?'

'He turned up here one night a few weeks back. Came staggering down them steps, blood everywhere. Someone tried to grab the glass in his hand, but not before he gave himself one good cut, right here.' The man pointed to his own chest, then made a stabbing motion.

Annie shuddered and clung to Rob. 'He stabbed himself?' she echoed. 'He done it to himself?'

The tramp nodded. 'He never knew what he was doing, just slashing away with the broken end of the bottle, catching himself here and here, like I said. He never felt nothing, mind, he was too far gone.'

The picture pierced Annie's mind. She put her head into her hands.

'Better off dead,' the tramp insisted. 'That's the one thing he did know. Drunk himself into oblivion, then done himself in with a broken bottle. You should've seen the look on his face when he came down them steps. You could see he was glad. Blood everywhere, and staggering about, and some idiot has to go and try to tear the bottle out of his hand, but he's done enough. He takes his last breath. We stand and watch him keel over the edge. There's a splash. They chuck the bottle in after him. That's it.'

Rob held an arm around Annie's shoulders. 'Why ain't you gone and told the coppers?'

The tramp shook his head. 'They can find out for themselves, I say.' He looked straight at Rob, as if he knew he would understand.

It cost them a couple of half-crown pieces, and took a deal of cajoling to get the tramp into the taxi and up to

Union Street. He'd never set foot inside a police station in the whole of his life, he insisted. But when Annie outlined the situation, what was left of his better nature triumphed. He considered it was a fair bargain; a few shillings for a week's kip in a seaman's hostel in return for the truth, the whole truth, and nothing but the truth.

They buried the mystery surrounding Wiggin's death at last, thanks to Annie. He'd taken his own life and put an end to his misery in the only way he knew. Rob described how Annie had gone down on to the wharf like a little grey pigeon, chest out, shoulders back, narrow boots pit-pattering down the steps, and God help anyone who stood in her way. The dossers had parted for her like the Red Sea. 'I was scared stiff myself, believe me.' Rob held Amy's hand, as they stood side by side in Annie's kitchen, telling Duke, Ernie, Hettie and Frances the full story. 'But I'm off the hook, thanks to Annie.'

Duke growled and smiled. He got up unsteadily from his chair. 'You come up trumps, like always.' He put a fond arm around her shoulder. 'But I don't want you going off no more, see. I was worried sick till you got back.'

Annie tutted. 'It weren't as bad as Rob makes out.' She smiled up at Duke, pleased to see him out of his chair and looking happy.

'Ten times worse,' Rob insisted. 'I thought I'd landed in hell, I can tell you. Them miserable blighters ain't got nowhere to go, asleep on their feet in that horrible fog; women with babes in arms . . .' Suddenly he stopped and turned to Amy. 'Bleeding cheerful charlie, ain't I?'

She squeezed his waist. 'Tell them now,' she whispered. 'Give them our bit of good news to keep them happy.'

'Tell us what?' Annie came up close and studied their secretive faces. Behind her, Duke stood with his thumbs in his waistcoat pocket, looking shrewdly at Rob.

Amy had taken Rob by surprise, as ever. He'd planned to share their news with his pa over a quiet drink, not surrounded by a gang of women who would go and spread it up and down the street. But he couldn't back out. He felt his face redden, began to fiddle with his cuffs, cleared his throat. 'Amy and me is gonna get married,' he said in a flood of embarrassment.

Annie's mouth fell open, then snapped shut. 'About bleeding time,' she said at last.

Duke came forward, wheezing, shaking his head, laughing and saying how glad he was. Frances hugged Ernie. Hettie squeezed Amy. There were smiles all round.

'You mean to say, you don't mind?' Amy was overwhelmed. She thought that, like her, they wouldn't see her as a good match for Rob. Their warmth touched her to the core.

'A wedding!' Even Frances looked genuinely pleased. 'When? When's the big day?' It seemed the news of Rob being in the clear and about to be married had lifted years off her.

'We ain't settled that yet, have we?' Details began to swamp Rob. He hung on to Amy's hand, squeezing it hard.

'Soon,' Amy promised. 'Before Christmas, I hope. We still gotta tell Ma and Pa and make the arrangements. Who's gonna be your best man, Rob?' She looked up at him, rolling her eyes in Ernie's direction.

Rob stepped forward. 'Ern, I want you as best man,' he said awkwardly, with none of his usual slick confidence. 'You gotta be there to help me through this.'

Ernie grinned and nodded. 'Best man!' he said, shaking Rob's hand, smiling at his pa and Annie.

Hettie came up to join in the laughter. 'Me and Jess will make your wedding outfit,' she said to Amy.

'Oh no!' Amy wouldn't dream of it. 'It ain't gonna be nothing posh.'

But Hettie gently insisted. 'Don't go and spoil things. If Jess and me can't make the outfit, how are we gonna feel, watching you go up the aisle in someone else's dress?'

'In that case.' Amy hesitated, Hettie cajoled, Amy accepted. 'A dress made specially!' Her face shone. She threw her arms around Rob. 'Pinch me and tell me I ain't dreaming,' she pleaded.

'You ain't.' He pinched her waist. 'And if I don't bleeding well get back to work, we ain't gonna have nothing to live on once we're hitched.' He hugged her, took his trilby hat from the table and went off whistling. Outside, the fog was thick as ever, and the street-lamps were just being lit. 'Blimey,' he said to himself, turning up his coat collar. 'Look what you just gone and did, you and your big mouth.'

Meanwhile, Amy couldn't wait to release the news to the waiting world. She dashed up the court, cock-a-hoop, to her own house. 'Ma, Rob and me's getting married,' she crowed. For once, Dolly was speechless.

... 'Me and Amy's getting hitched,' Rob told Walter glumly when the latter asked him what was the matter.

'Blimey.' Walter sat down at the desk. 'That's a bit sudden, ain't it?' ...

*

... 'Me and Rob's getting married!' Amy bubbled over with enthusiasm as she delivered the news to Charlie, who she found drowning his own sorrows at the Lamb and Flag.

'Better make it quick,' he commented, staring into his beer.

Amy's heartbeat quickened. Had he got wind of anything he shouldn't? Rob and she had decided to keep the news about the baby secret until the families got used to the idea of them being married. 'How's that, Charlie?'

'If you want me to be there,' he explained. With one dream of success in the cinema game shattered, he was quickly rebuilding another. 'I aim to sail for America as soon as I got the wherewithal.'

Amy gasped. 'Where did you get that idea?'

Charlie jerked his thumb towards a corner of the bar, where the sailor, Jack Allenby, sat deep in conversation with Katie O'Hagan. 'Jack says it's the land of opportunity.'

'What's he doing *here*, then?' Amy asked drily.

'Oh, he ain't gonna be hanging around much longer. Him and Katie are off to San Francisco, soon as ever they can.'

Amy stared. 'They ain't!'

'Ask them.'

'That'll be a bit of a winder for Mary, won't it?' Amy's imagination went full-tilt. She gazed at handsome Jack. 'Mind you, I could see why she'd fall for him.' She paused. 'Only, what's he see in her? She's a little mouse, ain't she?'

'Miaow,' Charlie said, with a gulp of his beer.

'I ain't jealous of Katie O'Hagan.' Amy gave him a shove and waltzed out of the pub, showering congratulations on Katie and Jack, sharing her own good news. 'Me and Rob

Parsons is getting married!' she said to whoever cared to listen . . .

. . . 'Congratulations. Amy's a decent sort.' Walter came to terms with the news and took Rob for a celebratory drink at the Flag. They'd missed Amy by just five minutes, Charlie said.

'Oh, we get on like a house on fire,' Rob assured Walter. He knocked back two quick whiskies.

'So what brought this on?' Walter suspected more. He knew Rob as a footloose, fancy-free sort as far as the girls went. He'd often envied him his flexibility in his choice of girlfriends. There was he, Walter, still stuck on Sadie, all these months after she'd gone off to live with Richie.

Rob fell into confidential mood, the whisky working its way down his gullet. 'Amy's in the cart, you know. I mean, that ain't the only reason, 'course. But I can't drop the girl now, can I? It ain't right.'

Walter drank and nodded. 'You sure, Rob?'

'What?'

'Better think it through now before it's too late. Not that I'm trying to put you off the idea, don't think that. Like I said, I like the girl.'

'But?'

'But do you love her, Rob?' Walter couldn't get it into his head that his friend was serious.

'You make it sound like bleeding prison.' Rob's laugh was shallow. 'I'm only marrying the girl.'

'And how do you know for sure that it's your kid?' Walter pushed the point home.

Rattled, Rob insisted that he was the father. 'Amy says

he's mine, and she ain't a fool. She wouldn't trick me, not over something like this.'

Again, Walter nodded. 'Sorry, Rob. It ain't none of my business.' He extended his hand. 'I hope you'll be very happy, mate.'

Rob accepted the congratulations. It wasn't second thoughts that Walter had just shoved into his head. It was third, fourth or fifth thoughts . . .

. . . 'He ain't getting cold feet?' Jess had invited Amy to the shop to go over some designs for her wedding outfit. She laid out the drawings on the table in the back workroom.

'I think he is,' Amy said, with a bright smile.

'Trust Rob,' Hettie laughed. 'He always knew how to make a girl feel wanted.'

'Anyhow, we already sent out the invites.' Amy studied the styles Jess had come up with. She needed something to disguise her thickening waist; a straight dress with a loose satin jacket and wide revers. Nothing too flimsy or revealing. Luckily Jess had come up with winter designs that would be suitable.

'The thing is, to keep the dress and jacket nice and plain, like this one, cut on the cross so the skirt hangs nice, in a heavy, smooth cream satin for the jacket, and something lighter for the dress.' Jess got caught up in her creation. 'Then we can put all the detail in the head-dress; scalloped lace with a little coronet of seed pearls and lily-of-the-valley. Very up-to-the-minute.'

Amy's eyes glowed. 'It's lovely. That's it. That's the one.'

Then it was Hettie's turn to show her some fabrics,

suggest some shoes from the shop. Edith Cooper was there to offer her congratulations. Amy smiled and said yes to this and that, taking her time to choose. Then she glanced at the time and said she must fly: Rob and she had arranged to look at some rooms to let above Powells' ironmonger's shop on Duke Street. She'd promised to meet him there at half-five.

Hettie and Jess waved her off, then went inside. 'She seems happy,' Jess commented, folding away her drawings.

''Course she's happy. And Rob's a lucky man,' said Hettie, ever generous, ever optimistic . . .

. . . 'I ain't never felt so important in my whole life.' Amy sighed. She sat with Rob in the taxi, parked just off Regent Street. She'd told him about her trip to Ealing to choose her wedding clothes, putting off the moment when she would have to kiss him goodbye and trudge up the metal staircase to the women's dormitory.

Rob caught her enthusiasm. ''Course you're important. Specially now.' He slid a hand around her waist.

'Yes, but Jess and Hettie, they make a girl feel special.' She revelled in it, allowing herself the luxury of believing in what until now had been a dream that happened to other women, not to her. It was a strange process, to strip away layers of worldliness, even cynicism which she'd built up over the years, to dare to be innocent again.

She was hoping for a happy ending with Rob. They'd taken the rooms over the shop, and Rob had told her to hand in her notice at Dickins and Jones. 'Ain't no point in you working after we're hitched,' he told her. 'You'll want to put your feet up.'

269

'I ain't sick,' she protested. 'I'm only having a kid.'

'Bleeding hell!' He stopped her mouth with a kiss. Passers-by might hear.

'They don't care.' Amy laughed. 'But I don't want mollycoddling, Rob. I'll have the rooms to sort out. We'll have to get the stuff from Tommy and paint that ceiling, for a start.'

They argued over who would climb ladders and where the baby would sleep. Nevertheless, Amy knew, as she finally waved Rob on his way round Oxford Circus, that the time would soon be here when they would have their own place, and that this would be one of the last times she would have to watch the taxi disappear into the traffic before she climbed the stairway to her lonely crib.

CHAPTER NINETEEN

St James's, Dolly Ogden's regular church, tucked away behind Marshalsea Road, was the venue for Amy and Rob's wedding on a cold, clear morning in late November 1924. Blackened by soot, its gothic tower a favourite pigeon haunt, nevertheless the bells rang out as the guests arrived spruce and correct in their suits and smart outfits.

Tommy O'Hagan turned up in a new pair of wide trousers and a double-breasted jacket, his mother, Mary, in a decent grey coat and hat. Katie went into the church arm-in-arm with her handsome sailor, the envy of all her friends. Even Joe sloped along to see the couple married. Not so much lapsed from the Church as gone for ever, his memories of the Catholic Mass were uncomfortably revived by the stained-glass angels and brass altar-cross.

Amy had sent out invitations to the whole of Paradise Court, to her pals from Dickins and Jones, and to her old mates on the market. She persuaded Edith Cooper to show up, just for the ceremony, she said. The other older women – Nora, Liz and the rest – had come to accept the ex-storeowner's wife and greeted her cheerfully at the doors of the church. They were all dressed up in Sunday best, with new feathers in their hats from Katie's stall, and fox furs slung around their shoulders.

Jenny Oldfield

Then, once the church was two-thirds full with friends and a gang of children and idlers had gathered at the gate, the families began to arrive.

Frances and Billy, quietly and nicely dressed, slipped in first, followed by a stir when Maurice and his family drew up in their new motor car and stepped out. Grace and Mo walked up to the church hand-in-hand with their mother, the little girl looking lovely in a broad-brimmed emerald velvet hat and matching coat. Mo was buttoned inside his pale camel-hair coat with its brown velvet collar, his black hair brushed across his forehead, looking serious as he held tight to his mother's gloved hand. Jess herself wore a fur-trimmed outfit in autumn gold, plain but beautifully made, with a neat cloche hat to frame her dark features. Maurice followed close behind in his dark suit, the picture of a successful businessman.

Then Hettie came up the path with George, smiling at friends, stopping to wait for Duke and Annie and able to enjoy a few moments of wintry sunshine. Opinion was that although the other sister, Jess, had plenty of style without being showy, Hettie's outfit came off best, with its pearl-grey hip-length jacket trimmed with grey fur, its slim, longer-length skirt and neat kidskin shoes. They thought she suited it and looked more relaxed, whereas Jess was smart but self-conscious. She hadn't quite carried it off, they thought.

But Annie, the stepmother of the groom, looked perfect. Without trying too hard, without being bang up-to-date, she radiated happiness from her little, upright figure. She came only up to Duke's shoulder, and her hat was as wide as she was; a square-crowned blue one with a dipping, broad brim. Her pointed face smiled from under it, she walked tall in her royal blue outfit, her arm in Duke's. The old man wore a white buttonhole in his pinstriped suit. He'd aged, they thought. Still, he looked proud and steady.

Then came the groom and the best man. They drove themselves to church, arriving in good time. Rob stopped in the porch to check details with Ernie: the order of events, the ring. Then they went nervously in.

Just time then for Dolly to arrive all in purple, with Charlie in tow, fussing over her hat, her gloves, her fur stole, Charlie's tie and glum expression. A dozen pigeons perching on a flat black tombstone took flight, clattering into the air as Dolly paused to inspect everyone, took a deep breath and plunged into the church.

On the stroke of midday, Walter drove up with Amy and Arthur, his car decked with white ribbon and gleaming in the sun. He opened the door to let out the bride; a white foot and stocking, a flowing cream skirt to the knee, a silky jacket and cascading veil. Amy clutched her lily-of-the-valley bouquet, steadied herself on her father's arm, and walked the endless path to the church, through the porch, down the aisle.

During the whole ceremony, with half of Southwark gathered behind and lifting the roof of the church with their singing; during the exchange of vows, the fumbling with the ring, the vicar's sing-song blessing and the signing of the book, Amy's terrified fear was that someone would 'find her out'. This was how she put it to herself. Lawful impediments would be produced, something would crash into her happiness and smash her apart from Rob. She trembled with superstition, with the notion that there was still time for him to change his mind, that fierce little Annie would find out about the baby and prevent the match.

Only when the register was signed and witnessed, when they walked clear of the small, fusty vestry to face the congregation and walk down the aisle together to the swelling notes of the organ, did she believe that she, Amy Ogden, was now Amy Parsons, and safely married to Rob.

The groom, still ill at ease, caught sight of Walter in the front pew. He negotiated two shallow steps into the aisle with Amy on his arm. Walter winked and nodded. Rob grinned back. The music pushed the couple down the aisle together, out into the bright sunshine. There was a photographer organizing guests into a horseshoe shape around the happy couple; endless photographs.

Amy's veil was trampled, Arthur fretted for a drink to calm his nerves. The photographer bent over his tripod and ordered them to smile. Dolly reorganized everyone, refused to stay still, insisted on at least two photographs from each angle. The photographer softly blasphemed under cover of his black velvet hood. At last they could disperse.

The wedding party trooped across the streets, down the main thoroughfares, back to Duke Street, where Dolly had got up a reception at Henshaws'.

Then the toasting and the speeches began. Arthur took copious Dutch courage before he stood up. He swayed and thanked everyone for coming. He said how proud he was of Amy, and how lovely she looked. Amy blushed. Dolly sat in her purple finery, challenging anyone to deny it. Arthur said how well matched the couple were, how the Ogdens were proud to have Parsons as in-laws, though at one time they'd hoped for Bishops.

'Pa!' Amy protested.

Arthur laboured the joke. 'One of Amy's young men, his name was Eddie Bishop,' he explained. 'Only, no need to worry, Rob, it never came to nothing.'

By this time, the guests would laugh and caw at anything. Arthur rambled on, people drank up and started to tuck in, lifting their glasses to this toast and that. Rob stood up to sit Arthur down, on Dolly's instructions. He offered more thanks, lost his way, pulled a piece of paper from his pocket. Then he screwed it up and tossed it over his shoulder. 'Ain't no need for that.' He grinned. 'Amy and me, we just want to say thanks to Dolly and Arthur for putting on this do for us, and thanks to Pa and Annie for everything they done.' He smiled broadly to left and right, ran out of people to thank and sat down.

Duke sat at the top table, Annie on one side, Ernie on the other. He brimmed with pride. It was the third wedding in the family, after Jess and Frances, and so far everything had gone smoothly. Rob, whom he never thought would settle down, had met his match in Amy. Duke expected there to be a few fireworks; neither was the placid type, and they'd have struggles over money, like everyone else. But Amy would coax Rob out of his moods when he got down, and if she was a bit loud, like her ma, it was what Rob needed to keep him steady and his nose to the grindstone.

In his turn, Rob had been brought up to take his responsibilities seriously, with a good, strong sense of his roots. And he seemed genuinely fond of the girl. Duke watched them joining hands over the tiered wedding-cake, ready to cut through the white icing. That was the funny thing about weddings, he thought; each one came along coloured by memories. He thought of earlier ones: his daughters', his friends', especially his own. His two marriages, first to Pattie, then to Annie.

Annie leaned over and broke into his reverie. 'There's just one thing I ain't happy with,' she whispered, her dark eyes dancing.

'What's that?' Duke clasped the hand she'd laid on his arm.

'I think that me and Dolly must be related by marriage now.' She pinched her mouth as if tasting a lemon. Dolly was winding up the gramophone, vigorously sending people out on to the dance-floor. Annie shook her head in dismay. 'Who'd have thought it, eh? Me, in-laws with Dolly Bleeding Ogden!'

'I heard about Sadie. Ain't it a shame?' Dolly felt it was time to let her hair down. She'd done the honours and got everyone dancing to gramophone records she'd heard earlier in the year at the Empire Exhibition over in Wembley. The Charleston had really got the young ones going: Katie O'Hagan was teaching the little girls all in a row, hands on knees, pigeon-toed. Now Dolly came and settled on to a chair next to Billy and Frances. 'Word gets round; it can't be helped.'

'She made her own choice.' Frances turned frosty. Dolly was employing her usual crafty tactic of making generalized, sympathetic noises, purely in order to extract more information. The music, breakneck and breathless, clattered on.

Dolly tapped her fingers in her broad lap. 'All the same, she ain't done nothing to deserve this.'

Frances weighed up what Dolly must be getting at. It wasn't Sadie's outright refusal of her invitation to the wedding; this was common knowledge and already discussed to death. Sadie had received the silver-edged card through the post and telephoned Hettie to say she wouldn't be able to come. No reason, no apology. At the same time, she let slip to her sister that she and Richie were expecting a baby. It was due in May, and she asked for it to be kept quiet. Hettie could pass it on to their pa, and he could choose who else to tell within the family. She'd rung off with a brittle cheerfulness. To Frances, the fact of Sadie's illegitimate pregnancy wasn't the stumbling block; it was the way she'd cut herself off from the family that hurt. After all, she could have come to see Annie and Duke to give them the news face to face.

But it was the sort of thing that seeped through the walls of Paradise Court. Not only had Sadie run off with the moody mechanic from the taxi depot, but now she was living in sin with him and having his kid. She would have nothing to do with her family since Rob had sacked her man. She was always spirited and maybe a bit spoiled. A handful at least. The myth grew of Sadie having had too much of her own way, and now she was paying the price.

Frances knew that the gossip about her sister had leaked far and wide. Only the other day, a woman had come into the chemist's shop for Andrews' Liver Salts and asked when the baby was due. She was tired of fobbing people off and telling them to mind their own business.

'I expect she'll have to pack in her job.' Dolly sighed. Her soft, purple, brimless hat had settled into a pork-pie shape on top of her head, in vivid competition with her rosy, round cheeks. The wide sleeves and high collars which still found favour with the older women made her seem trussed up like a leg of lamb, and trapped her body heat. Noisily she fanned her face with a napkin. 'I only hope she knows what she's doing, poor girl!'

'Yes, and I'll pass on your regards, Dolly.' Frances stood up to move away.

Dolly looked startled. 'You ain't never gonna dance the Charleston?' She'd taken offence. Frances was being snootily secretive as usual. Now Dolly got her own back. She glanced at the young girls bending their legs in and out like pieces of elastic, criss-crossing their skinny arms. 'This ain't your type of thing, surely?'

'There's the cake to wrap,' Frances replied. 'Your talking about Sadie just reminded me; I told her I'd take some cake over to her next time I visit. You don't mind, do you?'

Dolly was wrong-footed. 'Go ahead.' She scowled. 'Take her as much as you like. And be sure you tell her I was asking after her.'

It was Dolly's only setback of the afternoon. Straightaway she buttonholed Hettie to hear how Edith Cooper was making out in the shop. 'You've been an angel to that woman, Ett,' she told her. 'With her old man going downhill fast, and everything going to the bailiffs, your little job's just what she needs. I seen her at church, and I says to her she's looking very nice. I can tell she's happy to be there. It's hard on the poor thing, coming down in the world with a bang like that.'

Hettie smiled and nodded until Dolly ran out of steam and moved across to discuss Katie O'Hagan's plans to elope across the Atlantic with Jack Allenby.

'We ain't eloping, Dolly,' Katie laughed. 'Ma and Pa know all about it; it's all above board. We're saving up the passage money. Jack's writing to his ma and pa telling them about me.'

Dolly turned to the open-faced, well-built young sailor. Within five minutes she had his entire life story under her belt; his mother's age, his father's occupation, the jobs on offer in San Francisco for the likes of Katie. 'And what's your ma say?' she asked the girl.

Katie sighed. 'She says "good luck". She wishes she'd had the chance at my age.'

'She'll miss having you round.'

'She will, Dolly. Don't think I don't know.' Katie looked wistfully across the room at her mother, a little one on her knee, Tommy bending over her shoulder to tease the child.

'But good luck to you, I say and all!' Dolly rose, and, letting her purple sail billow in the wind, she drifted across the little square of dance floor to her next port of call.

By late evening, the music had slowed to the veleta and the waltz. The children rested tired heads against adults' shoulders. The feast of cold meats, sandwiches, pickles and pies lay in ruins. The beer barrel was empty, and the wedding cake neatly boxed. Balloons wafted between the feet of close-dancing couples, streamers came unpinned from the walls. Rob had Amy in his arms and they were dancing the last waltz, their hair sprinkled with white confetti, cheek-to-cheek in a world of their own.

'It went off well. It was a nice wedding,' Frances told Sadie. She'd called, desperate to build bridges with her youngest sister. Two small silver cardboard boxes of cake sat on the table between them in the Mile End living-room. 'We all had a good time, considering.'

'Considering what?' Sadie made the effort to be sociable. She'd tidied her hair and put on a touch of make-up for Frances's benefit. Richie had gone out, leaving the place to the two sisters.

'Considering Pa ain't been too well this winter, and we had all that worry over Rob.' She told Sadie about the clumsy police investigation into Wiggin's death. 'Trust them.' She laughed. 'They never get nothing right.'

They shuddered over how history had nearly repeated itself for the family; first Ernie, then Rob.

'But Pa's all right, ain't he?' Sadie knew the strain he'd been under. 'He ain't pining for the pub?'

'Oh, he's pining.' Frances sighed. 'We was worried he'd go under. Then we got the good news about Rob, and the wedding. That picked him up no end.'

Sadie nodded.

'Only, I wish you'd been there.' Frances leaned forward confidentially. 'I don't know, somehow it felt like there was a hole, and we was going round busy mending it all the time, talking ten to the dozen about everything except you, Sadie.'

Sadie tried to laugh it off. 'That's the first time I've ever been called a hole. That's me; a ladder in a stocking!'

'What's wrong, Sadie? Why can't you make it up with Rob? For Pa's sake, at least.' Frances had come as peace-maker. It was early December; Christmas was almost upon them. She wanted the family back together by then.

But Sadie turned serious. 'Rob's gotta make it up with me, Frances. Not the other way round. If Rob admits he was wrong and says sorry to Richie, then maybe I'll consider it.' She half turned away, her shoulders slumped, dark shadows under her eyes. 'But then again, Rob ain't never said sorry to no one.'

'You ain't sleeping well?' Frances changed the intractable subject. 'Are you sick much?'

Sadie nodded. 'Every morning. It ain't too bad though.'

'I'll bring you some herb teas next time. And some Pink Pills. You look a bit anaemic. Are you getting to the doctor?'

Sadie smiled again, and told Frances not to fuss.

'I have to fuss. What else am I for? I'm your big sister, ain't I?' She got up and hugged her tight. 'We miss you down Duke Street. And we wish we could help.'

'Talk to Rob,' Sadie said between her tears.

Frances nodded. 'But from what I heard, Richie won't think of going back in any case. Not after what Rob done. He's proud, ain't he?'

Sadie dried her eyes, settled one hand across her stomach and put on a brave face. 'Everyone's pride has a price,' she pointed out. 'Come spring, when the baby's born and there's no jobs for love nor money, I think even Richie will have to swallow his pride.'

'Don't bank on it.' Frances saw Rob and Richie as two stubborn enemies: one on his high horse about what the mechanic did to his pal, Walter; the other's resentment blinding him to compromise. She asked how Sadie and Richie would manage until spring. Sadie said they had a bit put by from her wages before she had been forced to own up to her condition at the office. Occasionally Richie managed to pick up casual dock work.

'It ain't right,' Frances insisted, getting ready to end her visit. 'You stuck here on your own like this, when you got us ready and willing to help just across the water. You should speak to Richie. One way or another, them two have got to make it up.' She slid her hands into her gloves and took her hat from the table.

'Frances!' Sadie's arms looked as if they would reach out, but she wrapped them around herself instead. 'Nothing.' She hung her head.

'Things is all right between you and Richie?'

'Fine.'

'Well, chin up, then. Give it time. Things usually work out in the end.' Frances tried to end on a cheerful note.

When she said goodbye and went down the stone steps, she looked back at Sadie, still hugging herself, pale and strained, all alone, and her heart turned over with pity.

Sadie herself watched Frances out of sight, then went

inside, quickly tidying away the two boxes containing the pieces of Rob and Amy's wedding-cake. They would only anger Richie, and send him into a black mood. The evening crawled by. Down the landing, a child cried. Sadie put a pan of broth on the stove, turned off the light to economize, tried to read by lamplight. Still no Richie. At eleven o'clock she went to bed, tired and cold, praying that Frances – someone, anyone – would be able to talk Rob round.

CHAPTER TWENTY

Christmas came and went without healing the rift between Sadie and the rest of her family. Neither Rob nor Richie could bear to hear mention of the other's name. Rob swore and struggled with the two unserviced taxicabs, up to his elbows in oil and grease over an undetected knock in the engine, worn-out brakes, a sizzling radiator. Over in Mile End, Richie tried for work as a road digger, or a porter at Liverpool Street Station. He brought home money from this casual work on maybe one or two days each week.

Sadie learned to make a decent meal out of pork rind and bones, a few potatoes. When she heard that a child in the next tenement had died of diphtheria, she sat with her head in her hands. Measles was rife throughout February, so she stopped going down to the public baths for her twice-weekly scrub and soak, for fear of coming into contact with anything infectious.

Her sisters visited her, bringing little nightgowns and socks, in preparation for the baby. She refused all offers of help for herself, would accept neither food nor money. But she took the tiny clothes, white and sweet smelling, wrapped them in tissue paper and put them in the bottom drawer of her dressing-table. Healthwise, the pregnancy was still difficult; her appetite was poor and she didn't gain the expected weight. The baby, due in May, would be undersized, the doctor predicted. As time passed, Jess, Hettie and Frances would choose the time of their visits to avoid Richie, since he made it plain they weren't welcome. They had the idea that he would get at Sadie for letting them come near, so they tried to miss him, letting Sadie keep her own counsel over their regular visits.

Occasionally they would drop Sadie's name in Rob's hearing, telling Amy how her pregnancy was progressing, how Sadie did her best under trying circumstances. 'She keeps the place neat and clean, but it ain't what you'd choose,' Jess reported. In fact, her latest visit to Mile End had shocked her. Sadie tried to keep house in the two rooms, but the floors were bare and there was no easy-chair, let alone a sideboard for her few bits of crockery. As for Sadie herself, she'd lost her quick movement and lively eye. She seemed to have faded, she looked awkward and apathetic.

Amy was quite the opposite, Jess thought. Pregnancy suited her. There was a natural, peachy bloom on her cheeks, even in the dead of winter, a glow of energy and enthusiasm. Her over-neat, regimentally waved blonde hair had been allowed to soften into a longer style that framed her face.

'Poor girl,' Amy commiserated. She sat gratefully in the midst of her own nice things: a tatted rug from Annie, spare pots and pans from Jess, a sturdy table that Frances had passed on from the Institute. She'd hung lace curtains at the big picture window, and she'd got her way over the problem of the dirty green ceiling; it was now a warm cream colour, and Rob had papered the walls to match. Both families had rejoiced when they heard the news that Rob and Amy were expecting a baby, and a tactful veil was drawn over the date of its anticipated arrival.

'Poor girl, nothing,' Rob remonstrated. 'She cooked her own goose, ain't she?' He hid his face behind his newspaper, checking the list of results for Palace's score.

'Still.' Amy sighed. She shook her head at Jess. 'You can't help being sorry.'

Jess said they thought the baby might not be strong. 'It's underweight, see. They say it's to do with how she lives. She don't get much fresh air, and she don't get out much for company, stuck way over there.' She prodded her brother's conscience as far as she safely could.

'Ain't we lucky, though?' Amy said softly. She gazed at the white woollen shawl which Jess had brought as a gift for their baby, so fine it was almost weightless, soft and warm when she held it to her cheek.

'Luck ain't nothing to do with where Sadie's landed herself,' Rob insisted. But he rattled his paper and sounded uncomfortable. 'Palace drew nil–nil,' he said by way of diversion.

Amy gave Jess a lighter glance. He was cracking. On her way out, she predicted that Rob would soon see reason.

Jess went from Amy's back to Annie's house to collect the children. There were signs of spring, even down Paradise Court: a lighter, longer feel to the afternoon, a general lifting of people's spirits. She said hello to Dolly, stopped for a proper word with Charlie, asking after his prospects. She was glad they didn't seem to hold things against her, but was still ashamed of what Maurice had done.

'I ain't sure yet what I'm gonna do,' Charlie told her. 'I've been thinking things through. There's America, the land of opportunity. I've been thinking of that.'

Down the corridor, Dolly dusted door-handles and banged vigorously about.

'Your ma don't sound too happy about that,' Jess said.

'Pie in the sky,' Dolly shouted. 'Pie in the bleeding sky!'

Jess smiled. 'What else, Charlie? If you don't get to America?' She wondered if that was what he was cut out for, the pioneer life, making his way in a foreign country.

'I been thinking of college,' he confided.

'Yes?'

'I only been thinking of it. They say they need teachers. I might go and train as one.' When he put it into words, he thought it sounded foolish; even more far-fetched than the American idea.

'Very good,' Jess nodded. 'I'd say that's more your cup of tea.'

Charlie looked surprised but pleased. 'You on the level?' He stood upright in the doorway, seeking her honest opinion.

'I am. Training as a teacher would be a good thing, I'd say. Shall I ask Frances for you? She'll know how to go about it.'

Gladly Charlie agreed. Here was someone with a bit of faith in him for a change. Both his ma and pa had scoffed at the idea of him going back to school. 'Where's the money in that?' Arthur had been quick to point out. 'Who puts the food in your mouth while you sit with your head stuck in a bleeding book?'

'Maybe there's a scholarship. Frances would know.' Jess promised to find out. She went on down the court, pleased after all to have crossed paths with the Ogdens.

Grace was on the doorstep of Annie's house, playing at marbles with Rosie O'Hagan, the second youngest girl. They rolled the coloured glass balls along the ground and chased after them with squeals and yells, encouraging them into the hole in the pavement which they'd chosen as their target. Jess watched, as a ragged boy appeared from the tenement doorway, ran pell-mell down the street, snatched a handful of the girls' marbles and leaped for the nearby street-lamp. He shinned up it in a flash, and perched on the crossbar out of reach.

Grace, hands on hips, looked at Rosie, then glared up at the boy. Then she hitched her skirt around her waist and promptly shinned up after him.

The boy waited until she grabbed hold of the iron crossbar, then cheekily swung himself down, leaving Grace stranded. But he'd reckoned without Rosie, who came at him like a whirlwind, diving for his pockets and the precious marbles. Grace swung and jumped to the ground. Between them, the two girls recovered their property and boxed the boy's ears. They saw him off, tongues out, calling derisively after him.

When it was over, Jess came quietly by, casting a look of mild disapproval at her daughter. 'That ain't very ladylike.' She frowned.

Grace pulled down her skirt. 'And he weren't no gentleman.'

Rosie giggled. ''Course not. That's my brother, Patrick!'

Jess smiled. 'Grace, don't you go far,' she warned. 'We have to get back home soon.' She knew Grace would pull a face and do her best to squeeze an extra few minutes out of the occasion. Smiling, she went inside to collect Mo and say goodbye to her pa and Annie.

Mo, too, was in seventh heaven. He lay flat on the carpet, face covered in chocolate, chugging his toy train between tracks Annie had sketched out for him on a long length of spare wallpaper. She'd drawn a station, a level-crossing, a signal-box, trees and houses. As Mo chugged the little metal train along, Duke played at station-master, signalman and passenger. He'd found a whistle in the sideboard drawer to add the right flavour to events. Mo blew it loudly while Annie stood by covering her ears.

'Thank God you're here,' she said to Jess. 'I ain't never gonna be able to stop this train otherwise. They been round and round that track till I feel dizzy.'

Mo grinned and leaped up. 'Grandpa's the fireman, I'm the driver!' He jumped clean over the railway track and landed at her feet. She picked him up to wipe his face.

'I hope he ain't been too much for you.' Jess set Mo down and began to gather her things. 'I know what he's like.'

Duke tousled the boy's hair. 'He ain't too much,' he promised.

Jess smiled at him. 'You're looking better, Pa.'

'His chest's clear now the weather's picked up.' Annie gave her bulletin. 'He's eating better, and he can sleep through the night, propped on three pillows.'

'Good, and you're getting out and about?'

Duke shrugged.

'Not enough.' Annie frowned. 'He won't go near the Duke. It's enough to upset anyone, when you see what they've gone and done to it. And, of course, you can't get far without going past the old place, so he stays cooped up here a good deal.'

Jess nodded sadly.

'Memories,' Duke explained. 'Happy memories.' Inside his head, he could play the old pianola tunes, he could hear the warm hum of conversation, the clink of glasses. In his mind, he could still reach for the wooden pump-handle and pull the best pint around.

'No one goes near, now Hill's got the place,' Annie insisted. 'They all swear it was him dropped Duke in it. Arthur and Charlie, Joe, Tommy; they all go up to the Flag.'

'Quite right.' Jess pulled on her gloves and fixed her hair under her hat. Mo made for the front door to go and find his big sister. 'Well, he can't last long, if that's the case.'

'He gets a few in from Union Street and further off. The young ones. They hear the place has been done up and they pop in to take a look. But Hill don't encourage regulars. He ain't got the knack.' Annie picked up the gossip from the market. The boycott of the pub was holding up. George had ditched his job and gone and found cellar work with the stretched landlord at the Flag. None of this did Duke much direct good, but it must hearten him to hear that Hill couldn't make a go of the place.

At last Jess was ready to leave. 'Chin up,' she told her pa. She went and prised the children away from their playmates in the court, told them to wave goodbye, then walked them briskly up Duke Street to catch the tram to the Underground station. On the journey home, Mo sat and chugged his train across his knees, Grace counted and re-counted her pocketful of shiny coloured marbles. Jess stared out of the tram window, swaying to its pitch and jolt, aware of a mounting regret as she left behind the warren of East End streets, burrowed underground, and emerged into her genteel, leafy suburb, and turned the key to her own beautiful, empty house.

Money was tight for Rob and Amy as they struggled through the winter, facing the harsh realities of married life after the artificial excitement of being engaged and married.

Amy had plenty of time to reflect on the loss of her busy daily routine in the company of her department store pals; her naturally sociable nature found it hard to adapt to long days cooking and cleaning inside her own four walls, waiting for Rob to show up at the end of his day's work, waiting for their baby to be born.

She didn't spend much time alone, however. Dolly was forever sailing through the door with news and advice, telling her how Frances Wray had fixed up for Charlie to go and see people at the Workers' Educational Institute. He wanted to apply for something called a Ruskin scholarship to go to college in the autumn. Katie O'Hagan and Jack Allenby had scraped together the money to pay for their tickets on a boat bound for America at the end of May. Bertie Hill was now trying to palm off Eden House on to some poor ignorant buyer, who didn't suspect it was riddled with dry rot from top to bottom. 'The sooner they pull it down the better.' Dolly was sick of living near the place; it harboured rats and dragged down the tone of the whole court.

'Don't let Mary O'Hagan hear you going on like that,' Amy advised. 'Where would they go if they pulled the old place down?'

'They'd get re-housed by the council,' Dolly said, with superior knowledge of the new welfare state. 'Into a brand-new place with their own bath and toilet, instead of the slum they're in now.'

'And who'd pay?' Amy couldn't see it; she'd heard of great new government building plans, but they were far away in Welwyn Garden, and impossible to imagine.

'The penny rate and the council, of course,' Dolly assured her. 'It's the latest thing. A bath of your own. A garden.'

'Hmm.' Amy wasn't immediately taken with the idea.

290

'And bleeding miles from anywhere and all.' She'd read in the newspaper that tenants were being shifted out there against their will, and that they kept coal in their baths, and pigeons too. 'It ain't for me.' She liked being able to walk downstairs on to the street, to the market, the shops, the pub.

Gossip with her ma kept Amy going through the early months of 1925, and the time she spent with Rob more than made up for the loss of her old, more worldly lifestyle. Pregnancy gave her a matronly air and she lost her flirtatious edge, dedicating herself instead to domestic life with a pleasant, humorous optimism that made her laugh at her husband's occasional grumpiness, and bully him into doing something to reinstate his old mechanic, so the whole family could get back into something like their old harmony.

Rob resisted. He swore it was none of her business. Sadie had chosen to slight them over the wedding invitation, and if she was having a hard time now, she had only herself to blame. He got angry. He pointed out how Walter would feel if they brought Richie back to work at the depot. He knew he couldn't find steady work, but he deserved everything he got.

'But Sadie don't,' Amy insisted. She never beat about the bush. 'She only made a mistake, Rob. It makes me miserable to think of her sticking it out without no one to help. I never thought she had it in her.'

Rob looked at his heavily pregnant wife in bed beside him. Their baby, conceived in August, amidst the chaos of Wiggin's murder, was due any day now. 'You know how to get under my skin,' he said, moved to be unusually gentle as he stroked her face and kissed her. He sighed. 'Wait till their kid arrives. Then I might go over and see her.'

Amy settled into a satisfied sleep. At two in the morning,

she woke Rob to tell him to go down and fetch Dolly. Her mother came. At eight she sent for the midwife, and at eleven a healthy baby boy was born.

Four or five weeks went by, but the weather reverted to winter on the day that Sadie's baby, Margaret, was born. A cold, north-eastern wind got up, and brought a flurry of light snow in the middle of May, so that people looked out of their windows and shivered and complained at the dark, unseasonable skies.

It was the middle of the afternoon, a Thursday, when Sadie seized the poker and hammered at the hollow chimney-back to let her neighbour, Sarah Morris, know that she needed help. The baby was early. Richie was out on what had degenerated into a regular, day-long wander through the streets without any real prospect of work. He spent hours hanging about in shop doorways, rolling thin cigarettes and longing for a drink, along with two or three pals in a similar situation. When her labour started, and Sadie hammered for help, Richie couldn't be reached. She would have to manage by herself.

Sarah came running in. She got Sadie to bed and sent for the doctor, at the younger woman's insistence. Sadie was glad of Sarah: a woman who took childbirth like a bad case of measles, a nuisance that disrupted the rhythm of everyday life and meant you got behind with your daily chores, by dint of the fact that you were flat on your back and in agony. 'Time the pains,' she advised. 'When they come bad and often, count your blessings, 'cos it'll soon be over.'

Sadie responded well. She waited for Dr McLeod and measured the pain. It was bearable. The next time, still bearable. She tried to judge how much worse it could get before she was forced to cry out. Quite a bit, she thought. She would grit her teeth and try not to make a fuss.

Sarah boiled water, great pans of it, on her own kitchen range. She asked Sadie for towels and sheets. 'That doctor had best get a move on,' she said, as if doctors were a modern invention, designed to complicate women's ability to give birth. She wiped Sadie's face. 'Else he'll be too late.'

Sadie gripped Sarah's wrist and kept her mouth clamped shut as the contractions tore through her and the groans rose to her throat.

'Her,' she managed to gasp. 'Dr McLeod, it's a woman.'

Sarah's eyes widened. 'That's a step in the right direction, any rate.'

Sadie smiled back.

'Lie with your legs crooked up, like this. Breathe deep.' Sarah was poised, ready for business.

The doctor arrived in the nick of time, with a young district nurse. The baby had presented in an awkward position, and for all Sadie's pushing and Sarah's practical encouragement, it was stuck in the birth canal, with just an ear and the side of its face evident to the doctor's experienced probe. There was the added complication of the cord possibly caught around the infant's neck. The doctor and the nurse prepared Sadie for a difficult delivery with a shot of local anaesthetic. Sarah held her hand tight.

And Sadie did scream as they cut into her and used forceps to deliver the child. They worked quickly, asked her to push, through the pain, through the panic that the baby might not survive. Sadie pushed and cried out.

'Harder,' Sarah urged. She saw the head emerge between the forceps, then the shoulders. The cord was round the neck.

Sadie wished she was dead. Tears streamed down her face, her neck ran with sweat. She pushed harder.

The doctor waited until she could grip the slippery shoulders, laid aside the forceps, and with a little twist and a final pull, the baby was born. 'Good,' she said. 'Very good.' The nurse cut the cord and released the half-strangled infant. She cleared its mouth, willed it to breathe.

'Boy or girl?' Sadie mumbled. The words rolled like heavy pebbles inside her mouth.

The doctor began to stitch. 'A little girl, Sadie. You have a little girl.'

Sadie sobbed. She wanted her baby to live.

The nurse concentrated on the tiny stained shape lying inert in her arms. Gently she tipped the infant upside down and applied the smart slap that was meant to make a child's lungs kick into action. Again; a second slap. The baby's arms shot wide, and in a surprised gasp, she drew her first breath.

The nurse smiled. She reached for a towel and wrapped the baby in it, wiping her face and head, handing her over to her mother. 'A beautiful little girl,' she said. 'And none the worse for wear.'

Sadie held the featherweight of her own child in her shaking arms. She searched her small, creased face, slid her own little finger inside her daughter's curled fist, speechless with joy.

'She's a bit on the small side,' Sarah said, bending forward for a closer look. 'But then, you're on the small side yourself.' She patted Sadie's hand.

'You did very well,' Dr McLeod told her, finishing with the stitching and trying to make her patient as comfortable as possible. She eased her legs straight and the nurse put clean sheets under her.

'Hmm.' Sarah warned them not to make the young mother's head swell. 'Tell her that in twenty years,' she advised. 'Time enough then for compliments.'

Sadie smiled and sighed. She handed the baby back to Sarah. 'There's a crib made up over there.' She pointed to the corner of the room, where she had padded and lined the bottom drawer of her dressing-table with blankets and cut-down sheets. There was a tiny lace pillow, donated by Jess. 'Bring it up close,' she pleaded, 'where I can keep an eye on her.'

Sarah did as she was asked, her heart softening at the feel and sight of the new child. 'She's got your eyes, see. What you gonna call her?'

'Margaret. Richie and me decided on that for a girl.' Sadie turned her head sideways to gaze at her daughter. 'She's beautiful, ain't she?'

'Worth it?' the nurse asked. She bustled to pack away her things.

'Yes,' Sadie sighed. She wanted to sleep. She wanted to wake up and find Richie there by the bedside, holding their litle girl.

Throughout May, Amy was too wrapped up in her baby's feeding and general needs to look outside her own little world. They called the boy Robert, after his father, but this was soon altered to Bobby by all his fond relations, who cooed over his crib and adored his round chubbiness. He had Amy's light colouring and blue eyes. They'd never seen such a bonny baby, such a contented child. Amy walked out with him in his high pram – another contribution from Jess – through the park in the warm spring weather, enjoying the blossom and the birdsong. Rob would worry about taking him out too soon into the traffic and the noise. He worked out the quietest route to the park, and rationed the time Bobby spent in other people's arms. 'He ain't a parcel you're posting.' He told her off for allowing Dolly and Annie too free an access. But Amy wallowed in the grand-mothers' praise, and passed Bobby around as much as she pleased.

Straight away, Rob loved his son with a proud, exclusive fierceness. Though he didn't soften his public face, pretend-ing a disdainful amusement when the womenfolk cooed, he would spend quiet time in the evening by the baby's crib, drinking in his sleeping features, keeping time with his light breathing, planning the very best for his future.

He would work even harder at the taxi business with Walter. They would build up savings until they could afford at least one smart new cab. Setting up a haulage division wasn't entirely out of the question in the long run. Talk of unemployment, strikes and slumps wouldn't deter him. They would undercut their rivals, they would come out on top.

In this mood of determined optimism, he drove across the water one morning in late May. He planned to get to Mile End early, to catch Richie Palmer before he set out on his day's tramp after casual work. There'd be no fuss; he'd offer Richie his old job back, tell him that Walter was behind the move, let Sadie know he was doing it for the sake of the family.

Only, when Sadie came to the door of the tenement rooms, and he saw how pale and thin she looked, how her colour and life had faded, and how she greeted him with a silent, unresponsive gaze, he felt stricken with guilt.

'I come to see the kid,' he stammered. Amy had parcelled up some clothes already too small for Bobby, and some spare blankets. He offered them to Sadie across the threshold.

Sadie motioned him in. 'Don't worry, Richie ain't here,' she said as she noticed him looking around. 'Wait while I go and fetch her.' She didn't show it, but she felt the enormity of the move Rob had made. When she came back from the bedroom with Meggie nestled in her arms, she entrusted her to him; a kind of peace offering.

Rob gazed at the baby. 'Ain't she tiny?'

Sadie nodded. 'Under six pounds when she was first born. She's gaining now, though.' She kept Meggie clean and dry and warm. She fed her on demand. She'd learnt the ropes quickly, with help from Sarah next door, and felt that every day she grew into a better mother; calmer and more confident.

Rob handed her back. 'Our Bobby's twice that size.' He told her all about his son as Sadie made him sit at the table and offered to make him tea.

He shook his head. 'I gotta be off soon. I came over to see Richie, as a matter of fact.' He looked round again, though he knew Sadie had said he wasn't in. 'Where's he got to?'

For a moment Sadie tried to brush it aside. 'He ain't here. Like I said, he's out.' She knew that Rob's unannounced visit could only mean one thing; he wanted to give Richie his job back. She gave a half-angry little laugh. 'You missed him, Rob.'

He took in the drab, bare walls and floor; Sadie's curtains and tablecloth, her early attempts to make a home. He saw how poverty had defeated her. 'When will I catch him in, then?' he asked, doubly stricken by conscience, determined to help set Sadie back up.

'You won't,' she said quietly. She felt she might as well

admit what she'd kept hidden from her sisters when they'd come visiting to see the baby.

After the birth, Sadie had fallen into an exhausted sleep, dreaming of Richie holding the baby in his arms. She'd woken to an empty room. Sarah came in and said she sent word to fetch Richie back home. They'd have to wait and be patient. Daylight faded, the time came when he would trudge up the step and fling down his cap, empty handed. It passed. The slow hours of night ticked by.

Meggie cried to be fed in the dark. Sadie held her close. Morning came, grey and pale. The sun never shone down the side of the tenement. Sarah looked in to report that no one had set eyes on Richie since he'd set off yesterday morning. She warned Sadie to prepare for the worst. 'Waiting's bad,' she said. 'It's the worst bit.'

For two days there was no news. Sadie began to see that Richie wouldn't be there to share their beautiful baby. She was given to understand that it was a deliberate choice on his part. Sarah said there was no point telling the police: she'd heard on the grapevine that Richie had gone off of his own accord. ''Course, he never knew you'd go and have the baby straight off,' she reminded her. 'Maybe he went and got a spell of work on a boat?'

But Sadie had heard that tale too often; men deserted their women and called it taking a job at sea. She remembered Annie and Wiggin. She counted the days.

Now, after she'd covered up to Jess, Hettie and Frances, she admitted the truth to Rob. 'I ain't seen Richie since Meggie was born. He's gone and left us. It's just Meggie and me; we're all on our own.'

PART THREE

The last laugh

CHAPTER TWENTY-ONE

June 1925

The pain of being abandoned by Richie struck deep at Sadie, and stunned her. Although on the surface she coped for little Meggie's sake, and held up her head in the Mile End neighbourhood, inside she felt numb. For him to leave without explanation, for him not to get in touch for news about the baby was something she refused to comprehend. How could he cut off so completely from his own flesh and blood?

'Don't take on,' Sarah Morris advised. She appeared in Sadie's doorway one morning early in June. 'You got your hands full now, girl, without bothering your head about things you can't change.' She'd caught Sadie wiping away the tears.

Sadie looked up and dried her eyes. Her neighbour's down-to-earth approach acted like a tonic. It wasn't as if she was alone in the world, like some women in her situation, she realized. Rob had heard the news about Richie and gone straight home to fetch Annie and Duke. Annie took one look at the room and swore to get her back to Duke Street. She would move heaven and earth to make it happen.

'I ain't got much money put by,' Sadie admitted. 'What I got left won't run to renting nothing posh.'

'But you want to come back?' Annie noticed Duke paying quiet attention to the baby in her makeshift crib.

Sadie nodded, not trusting herself to speak out.

'Yes, and I don't blame you.' Annie hurried on. 'What must it be like, stuck up here with no one on hand? Well, we gotta see what we can do, your pa and me.'

They'd gone off, and the whole family had rallied round with extra clothing, food and money. Her good neighbour, Sarah, kept an eye on her and Meggie, while Annie ran up and down the market on Duke Street, in and out of the shops and eating-houses, to catch word of a good room going at a low rent.

'I brought you a bite to eat.' Sarah came in now and put a bowl of mutton broth on the table. She never changed out of her drab brown dress, roughly pinned and patched. As a concession to summer, she took off the woollen headscarf and replaced it with a faded cotton one. But nothing changed her routine of scraping a living through taking in home work: mending, washing, labelling, picking, and sitting during these long evenings humming her ukelele songs, reminiscing about the days before the war.

Sadie nodded gratefully. As she sat down to eat, she returned to her usual theme. 'You ain't heard nothing?' Sarah was her eyes and ears on the outside world.

'About Richie?'

'Of course about Richie. Ain't nobody heard from him yet?'

Sarah shook her head. 'He don't do nothing by halves, that one. He takes it into his head to do something and he makes a proper job of it.'

Sadie's mind flew back to their courtship; Richie's almost silent, dogged pursuit of her.

'If he wants to drop out of sight, ain't no one better at it than Richie Palmer. Not even Chung Ling Soo, the famous vanishing Chinaman!' She got into her stride. 'That Chung Ling Soo, he came from Lancashire. Ain't no more Chinaman in him than in this little finger! My Harry told me that for a fact.' She rambled back through the years. 'Men like Richie, they don't know they're born, running away at the first sign of trouble. Not that little Meggie's trouble, mind, but men see babies that way. He's young and strong, ain't he? He can lift a shovel and carry a sack, not like some of them poor bleeders, the returnees. You ain't seen nothing like it. They was blinded in them trenches. They was gassed. And what did it leave them fit for, besides selling matches on a street corner?'

At last, Sadie was roused to her lover's defence.

'Richie done his bit, Sarah. He been over the top more times than he could count.'

'And he came back in one piece. He ain't been a mother of one of them kids killed in the schools by the bleeding bombing planes, has he? He ain't had to go down the Underground like a mole, waiting for the bugle all-clear.' Sarah catalogued the miseries of war. 'And you ain't one of them poor young widows sitting at home waiting for the telegram to land on your mat. No, come to think of it, your luck ain't all that bad. What's one little disappointment set alongside all that? Look at you; you're young, and you can make a decent show if you put your mind to it.' She reclaimed the empty bowl and stood up from the table. 'Comb your hair and dig out one of them fancy outfits I first saw you in. Make a bit of effort, for God's sake!'

As Sarah spoke, Sadie ran the gamut of emotions, from aching sadness, through shame, to anger. But as her decent, blunt neighbour stood with her empty dish, nodding encouragement, she laughed. 'You think combing my hair will make all the difference?'

'It's a start.' Sarah smiled back. 'And don't leave it all to that little stepmother of yours,' she warned. 'Ain't nobody going to pull you out of this mess except yourself, Sadie Parsons.'

Sadie nodded. 'Thanks, Sarah.'

'Well, get some fresh air, then. Take Meggie out for a bit.'

'I will, thanks.' Already she felt Sarah's outspoken advice like a breath of new life.

'Ain't nothing to thank me for. What's a drop of soup between us?' she pretended.

Sadie watched the raw-boned, middle-aged woman on her way along the balcony. She went to get Meggie ready for a trek across the river later that morning. She would go and look for work, as well as a better place for them both to live. But first, she wanted to write a letter.

When she left Hope Street, she would leave it with Sarah, addressed to Richie. One day he might come back and be able to read it. She took up pencil and paper.

It read:

Dear Richie,
Our little girl's name is Margaret. Meggie for short. She's got a round mouth and lots of dark hair. Her eyelashes are the longest I ever saw. She don't smile much yet, but she cries plenty, to let me know she's here. Her hands are tiny. Her face is all puckered up when she holds fast to my finger. When she's asleep, you can hardly see her breathing.

I want to tell you she's beautiful. I promise to take good care of her and to do my best not to let her come to harm.

We followed our own hearts, Richie. I ain't sorry. I'll tell

*Meggie all about you, when she grows older. Your loving
Sadie.*

Then she put on her cream jacket and skirt, and dressed
Meggie up in one of the dainty outfits donated by Amy. As
she looked in the mirror, she considered she hadn't done
too badly: with lip-rouge and a touch of powder, she
managed to look decent again. She took the last of her
coins from the dressing-table drawer and stepped outside
with Meggie in her arms.

'Blimey!' Sarah said, sitting in the sun by her door.

'Now, Sarah, don't you say nothing!' She turned the key
in the lock.

'A pair of bobby dazzlers, if you ask me!'

'We ain't.'

'You are too.' She smiled and waved them off. Sadie was
bound to get back on her feet, looking like that. She was
young and pretty. The baby gave her something to live for.
Children did, until they grew up and went away. Then you
sat alone at your doorstep and watched it happen all over
again to the girl next door.

Katie O'Hagan had saved all through the winter. She put
away every penny she could from the takings on her
haberdashery stall. Spring trade in beads and braids, fringes
and feathers was good, as East End girls copied the racy,
slim-hipped styles of the fashion magazines. Lace was
quickly going out of fashion, except on underthings, but
there was a craze for sewing beading on to everything, and
buttons of all shapes and sizes. Katie worked hard and
dreamed of America. Jack Allenby stayed in Eden House
and found work wherever he could. They were both saving

for Katie's passage, planning on a summer departure. Once there, they would save all over again, this time to pay for a wedding, surrounded by Jack's family. Meanwhile, Jack's mother had written to Mary promising to keep a firm eye on the couple until the wedding knot was tied.

These days, Mary hardly recognized her own daughter. She'd grown tall and slender, studied the 'look' and achieved it with considerable success. Her small, lively features were framed by a wavy, dark bob, her eyebrows arched and shaped, her lips painted in a red bow. She wore straight tunics in shiny rayon, over a knee-length, pleated skirt. Her legs looked longer than ever in her dainty, high-heeled shoes.

When the day came to send her and Jack across the Atlantic, Mary had the sensation of saying goodbye to a beautiful stranger. She wondered from where little Katie had got all that determination and spirit of adventure. Not from her father, Joe, who had sunk into his old, moaning ways since Coopers' had closed down. Life for him was sometimes too difficult even to get out of bed.

'You'll write to us?' Mary made Katie promise. 'Rosie will read your letters to me. You'll tell us all about your new life.'

Katie squeezed her mother's hand. They'd decided to say goodbye at Waterloo, to avoid the long drawn-out business of waiting at the embarkation point at the dockside. Jack was working his passage, and Katie had bought a berth in the crowded, third-class section of the same ship. The time had really come. What had seemed like an impossible dream was coming true at last. 'I'll write, Ma, and I'll send money. Don't you worry.'

Mary shook her head. 'So long as you write and tell us you're safe.' She didn't want to let go of Katie's slim hand.

But she relinquished it to Jack as the train doors began to slam shut and the porters heaved the last bags up the steps. Steam hissed and whistles sounded. Everything hurried them towards this last goodbye. 'Good luck,' she whispered.

Katie stepped into the carriage. She turned and leaned out of the window, with Jack at her shoulder. 'Take care of yourself, Ma!' she cried. The train jolted and began to roll away. 'I'll write every week!' She saw her mother's long, pale face fade into the distance, get lost in the crowd. She knew she would stand there until the train drew out from under the giant glass arch, so she waved her handkerchief until the very end. She thought she saw Mary's raised hand still waving them off. Then she hid her face against Jack's shoulder. She was homesick and seasick for the first week, but launching out into a new future.

After Katie left, Annie decided to take on her old stall once more. 'It's not too much for my old bones yet,' she assured Duke. 'Leastways, not now that it's summer.' She convinced him that she was looking forward to getting back to work on the market. 'There's Nora and Liz to keep me company, and Ernie will be there to keep an eye on me, won't you?' She grinned as Ernie replied with a vigorous nod. 'See, it's for the best. I want to see if I can still turn my hand to earning an honest penny.'

And, sure enough, her stall was a lifeline, now that Duke's old trade had been taken away. Not to be outdone by his wife's grit and determination, Duke came to the decision that it wasn't all up with him yet either. On her first day back in business, he took a stroll up the court, 'To see how she's coping', he told Dolly on the way up. He found Annie complaining about the rickety state of her canvas canopy, and went straight back home for hammer and nails. Soon he was deep into repair work on the wooden frame.

'It's all well and good that Katie saving every penny for her new life,' Annie grumbled. 'But these young ones, they let things slip. Another month or two, a good shower of rain, and I'd have the whole bleeding thing down on my head!'

Up the stepladder, Duke hammered happily. 'We could do with sewing a patch or two on this old canvas.' He spotted a weakness and decided to take the whole thing down for repairs.

Annie tutted and shrugged at Liz. 'Bleeding hell; all I ask is for a couple of nails and five minutes of his time. Before you know it, he's stripping the whole lot bare. What am I gonna do if it rains?' she demanded, cocking her head sideways and squinting into the sun at him.

'It ain't gonna rain, Annie. You know very well.'

'Duke, when you've got a minute, you can have a look at this wobbly leg of mine!' Nora Brady called.

Tommy O'Hagan leaned over and leered. 'Now there's an offer for you!' He winked at Duke. 'Nora ain't never asked me to take a look at her wobbly leg.'

'Cheeky monkey!' Nora made as if to box his ears. She shrieked as he ran out from behind his stall and ducked down, promising to examine the offending part of her anatomy. 'Here, get him off me! Stop that!' She beat with the flat of her hands at the side of his head. 'I mean the table leg, you bleeding young idiot!'

'As if he don't know!' Liz said caustically.

'Take no notice, Nora,' Annie said. She served a customer with four yards of blue bias binding. 'Duke will be over to take a proper look just as soon as he finishes here.

He's very handy with his hammer, is Duke.' She made a grimace at Tommy, who had just escaped from Nora and was flitting by the fruit stall run by Queenie Taylor. Tommy picked a choice banana from the top of the pile.

'*Yes, we have no bananas,*' he sang jauntily as he peeled the fruit and bit into it. '*We have no bananas today!*'

'Blow me down, if someone don't clock him one soon!' Annie shook her head, but laughed in spite of herself. It was a lovely day. And to make it perfect, she spotted Sadie all spruced up, with babe-in-arms, coming right down the pavement towards them.

If Sadie was nervous treading back on home turf, she didn't let it show. In fact, she looked more or less her old self, but without the stand-offish edge. Amy leaned out of the window above Powells' to yell out a greeting. 'Sadie, don't you move, I'll be right down!' She came with Bobby straddled on her hip, running to compare offspring with Sadie. Meggie was small and delicate where Bobby was strapping; Meggie dark, Bobby fair-haired. Each admired features of the other's baby.

'He looks like you.' Sadie smiled. A crowd gathered for their first view of Meggie. Annie cut through them like a scythe, claiming grandmother's rights.

'Poor thing!' Amy blushed. 'And little Meggie looks just like you.'

'Do you think so?'

'You Parsons is all the same. It's them big brown eyes.'

Meggie had woken after the tram ride and was gazing round at a sea of faces. Annie offered to take her. 'Your arms must be killing you,' she said to Sadie. 'Here, hand her over. What brings you down here, anyway?'

'You do, Annie. And somewhere to live.'

Annie shook her head. So far, the search for a place for Sadie and Meggie to stay hadn't come up with anything. Duke Street was currently full of families clinging on to their rooms by the skin of their teeth, as landlords cranked up the rents and packed them in like sardines. Few, if any, were interested in taking in a single woman without employment and a child to tie her down. Annie had tried locally, and Frances and Hettie had tried further afield in Union Street and Bear Lane. There was nothing on offer.

'No, I thought it was high time I came looking for myself,' Sadie said. She soaked up the warm atmosphere; the smell of fish and fruit, the sound of taxis and buses, the sight of her old friends. She saw Walter drive by with a fare, glad that he hadn't spotted her. She felt ready to nod and speak with Charlie Ogden, who was filling in time on the market before going off to college in the autumn, but not to Walter. There were still too many recent might-have-beens between them.

'And you reckon you'll like this teaching lark?' Sadie asked. She'd given over Meggie to Annie and strolled into the relative quiet of the court with Charlie. They passed the Prince of Wales, oddly new and shiny, catching up on each other's news.

Charlie put his hands in his pockets and shrugged. 'I don't know about that.'

She smiled at his feigned indifference. 'What are you going into it for, then?'

'Because it's steady. I ain't cut out for the cinema no more. I had a dream once, but I let it slip by me. Maurice was right.'

She listened. 'You don't hold it against him, then?'

'Why should I? He gave me a job and he took it away. No use crying over spilt milk.'

'I wish Richie could hear you say that. It's good of you to see it that way, Charlie.'

They walked on, down the shady side of the street. 'Maurice won't never settle for someone who just wants to be steady,' Charlie pointed out. 'It's got to be bigger, better, newer, faster with him. That's why he's so good.'

Sadie sighed. 'Yes, he is good at his job.'

'I hear he's on to something big?'

'I never heard that, Charlie.' Sadie gave him a worried look. 'Jess ain't mentioned nothing to me.'

'Maybe it won't come off, then.' Charlie stopped outside his own house. 'I never said nothing, right? If it comes off, all well and good.' He looked directly at her. 'It's good to see you again, Sadie. We missed you.'

She smiled back. 'Good to be back, Charlie. Oh, and one other thing.' She had set off, but turned back quickly. She spoke softly. 'I think you'll make a good teacher.'

'How's that?'

''Cos you always had your head stuck in a bleeding book when you and me was walking out together!'

'More fool me.' He smiled, nodded, and went inside. Water under the bridge. He thought of himself as he was then: callow and selfish, too sensitive by half. He thought of Sadie then: careless and fancy-free, with her long plait down her back, her petticoats whirling in the wind as she rode her bike through the bluebell woods.

Sadie's stroll gathered purpose after she left Charlie. An idea entered her head that Eden House would not be the worst solution to her problem of accommodation. It had its drawbacks, it was true. It was old and run down, it held bad memories, and the landlord was Bertie Hill.

But it was on the doorstep to Duke and Annie. It would be cheap. Planning ahead, she thought she could take in typewriting work to pay the rent and make ends meet. She could put up with poky conditions, provided she was standing on her own two feet, taking good care of Meggie and feeling that she belonged. It was a step up from Mile End at least.

Gathering her courage, she entered the central doorway of the old tenement and began to ask around for the landlord.

Duke rolled up the canvas hood from Annie's stall, then went and fixed Nora's gammy leg. He could hear Dolly Ogden holding forth about the relative merits of Bobby and Meggie. She led the healthy, strapping lobby. Annie took the opposite view: round, pink cheeks were fine on a boy, and big, chubby legs, but delicacy was what everyone admired in a girl. 'Meggie will melt a few hearts before too long, you wait and see,' she promised proudly. The grandmothers agreed to differ. Amy invited Annie to bring Meggie up for tea. 'Sadie won't mind, will she?' She stopped for a moment, recalling the feud between Rob and Richie.

'Not a bit,' Annie said firmly. 'Here, Duke, you watch the stall while Amy and me goes for a chat. Tell Sadie to come and fetch Meggie when she comes back.'

Duke looked in bemusement at the hooks and eyes, the press-studs and rolls of elastic set out in neat rows along the stall. He stuck his thumbs in his waistcoat pockets and shuffled into position.

'A pint of the best, Duke!' Tommy yelled.

'And you!' he growled back.

'Tommy!' Liz warned. 'Don't you go pushing your luck,

312

you hear.' Seeing Duke out and about was good news, but seeing him trying to cope behind the stall was like watching a fish out of water.

'You gotta laugh,' Tommy told her. 'Otherwise you'd cry. He took it well, ain't he?'

'Now listen, Tommy.' Liz took him to task. 'You ain't been into Hill's place lately?' Like the other market-stall holders, she stuck rigidly to the boycott of the Prince of Wales. She worked hard to keep the young ones in line.

''Course not. What do you think I am?' Tommy glanced at his watch, wondering whether to nip off and risk a quick one at the Flag. 'Not that it'll do the old man much good in the end.'

'What you on about?' Liz came in quick and sharp.

'The brewery ain't gonna take him back in any case.' Tommy laid things out plain and simple. He kept his voice low. 'Even if Bertie Hill comes a cropper, and I ain't saying he don't deserve to, they ain't gonna give Duke his licence back, are they? He's out on his ear and there ain't nothing we can do.'

Liz shook her head. 'Don't let Annie hear you going on like that,' she warned. 'And don't go thinking of breaking the boycott because of it, you hear?'

The street was determined to force Hill out of business, come what may.

Inside the pub, word came up from the tenement that Mr Hill was wanted down the court. He left the bar to the booze-sodden care of Jack Cooper, to look after the thin trickle of lunch-time custom. It sounded like he could let another room if he went to sort it out on the spot.

But he was in no hurry as he went down. Too thick-skinned to bother about the sour looks that greeted him wherever he went, he sauntered along in the sunshine. He was taken aback, however, as he entered the tenement and found Sadie Parsons waiting for him in the grey inner court. He'd never expected to see another member of the Parsons family come looking for a room.

Sadie asked civilly if he had anything to let. Much as she resented Hill's existence, she must swallow her pride and find somewhere to live. She confined herself to the business in hand. After all, there had been other, more difficult things to swallow recently, and if Rob or anyone got on his high horse about renting a room from the 'enemy', she was prepared to defend her actions. 'I want something close to my pa,' she told Hill with dignity. 'It ain't easy to manage without family close by.' She met his inquisitive stare.

'Miss Parsons,' he began slowly, enjoying the situation. Sadie hadn't lost her looks at any rate, though by all accounts, she'd lost much else, including her reputation, her job and now her man. 'You'll excuse me for asking, but how do you propose to pay the rent? Supposing I have a room, which I don't say I have.'

'I plan to take in typewriting work, Mr Hill, and anything else that comes my way. How much do you charge for a room?'

'That all depends.' He came up, too close. The more civil and distant in manner she grew, the more familiar he became. She could smell the cigarette smoke on his clothes. 'A room at the front costs extra. If I have one available, which I don't say I do, mind.'

Sadie held his gaze. His sandy colouring showed up the redness of his complexion, which was already thickening and coarsening into middle age. His presence was arrogant and insulting, he used his strong physique with overbearing, swaggering pride. 'Do you have a room for me and my daughter, Mr Hill?'

'Well – Sadie, isn't it? – as luck would have it, I think I do.' He liked this idea; one of life's little opportunities to rub salt into the wound. And he liked the look of Sadie Parsons. The shine hadn't quite gone from her. She'd had more than her fair share of it to start with: smooth skin, pretty face, good little figure. In another five years, poverty and disappointment would have rubbed all that off for good. Meanwhile, he would enjoy watching her come and go through the tenement. He offered terms. She showed spirit in haggling him down. They agreed on a price.

She asked to see the room. Even her self-control snapped when he led her to Wiggin's old hole in the semi-basement. It had recently been vacated by the sailor the O'Hagan girl had run off with. 'Number five,' he offered, awaiting her reaction.

'No.' She backed straight out of the room. 'Not this one. If this is all you have, I'll look somewhere else.'

There was number eighteen, he told her. Up on the second storey, opposite the O'Hagans. It would be more expensive.

In the end, the bargain was made. She wanted to move in right away. Hill held out the key. His fingers rested too long in the palm of her hand as he handed it to her.

Annie grumbled, Duke shook his head. Frances admitted it would solve a problem for the time being. No one liked Sadie coming to live in Eden House except Ernie. He could pop in from Annie's house whenever he pleased. In the end, everyone concluded it would have to do as a short term measure.

Rob drove up to Mile End with Sadie to collect her few

possessions, where Sadie bade a tearful farewell to Sarah Morris. She handed over the sealed envelope addressed to Richie. 'If you hear of him, or if he ever comes back, will you give it to him for me?'

'I will,' Sarah promised. 'But don't get your hopes up. Men like Richie, they don't like no responsibility.' She hugged Sadie and wished her well, giving the envelope pride of place on her bare mantelpiece.

'Funny thing, that,' Rob observed, as he strapped the boot lid closed and started up the engine. He climbed into tha driver's seat.

'What's funny about it?' Sadie didn't feel in the mood for jokes.

'Funny peculiar, I mean. What the old girl just said. Richie ain't the kind to take responsibility.'

Sadie glanced back down Hope Street as her brother pulled away from the kerb. 'So?'

'So, that's just what I'd have said about me before now. I don't like to be tied down, you know me. I like to come and go. But look at me now.'

She gave a wan smile. 'Yes, but you're happy, Rob. You found the right person. It's me. I weren't the right one for Richie, that's all.'

'And I got little Bobby.' He headed for the river, threading through the busy streets. 'For God's sake, if you'd told me a year ago that I'd be hitched to Amy, with a kid, I'd have died laughing.'

He helped Sadie with her luggage and left her in Frances's capable hands. Frances was there to help put the room to rights while Annie minded Meggie. Little O'Hagans ran in and out, up and downstairs.

Rob went home to Amy and Bobby. The next day, when he took a break from work and went over to Mile End to collect Sadie's remaining boxes and sticks of furniture, he answered Sarah Morris's beckoning call.

'It ain't taken him long,' she whispered mysteriously from along the balcony.

'Who? Richie?' Rob frowned and went over.

She nodded. 'Who else? He heard she'd flitted and came snooping round late last night. Ain't nothing gets by him, not if he don't want it to.'

'He ain't away at sea, then?'

Sarah snorted. 'Not him. I could hear him knocking things about a bit, so I goes and knocks on the door. I tells him she's gone back to Southwark and I gives him her letter.'

Rob nodded.

'He shoves it straight in his pocket and looks daggers at me. It ain't my fault he's gone and left her in the lurch, is it? Anyhow, he says to me, "Tell her I'm in Hoxton, if she wants to know. She can find me there." But I'm telling you, Sadie would be a fool to go chasing him there.'

'Hoxton? Any address?' Rob got ready to leave.

'Care of the Queen's Head, that's all I know.' Sarah delivered the final scraps of Richie's message. 'He looked in a poor way. I think he's hit the bottle. Like I say, she'd be a fool to chase him.'

'She's a fool all right,' Rob said. 'Look where she landed up.'

'We don't cast the first stone round here,' Sarah replied. 'I thought she was a lovely girl, only a bit soft.' She followed him halfway along the balcony. 'You'll give her the message?'

Rob nodded. He was glad to put a distance between himself and Hope Street. When he got home, he took the boxes out of the taxi and took them upstairs into Eden

House. Sadie looked at him, half-expecting news of Richie, but he shook his head. 'Nothing,' he reported. 'I should forget him, if I was you. He ain't never gonna be no good for you.'

She fought to accept it, sitting over a cup of tea with Frances. She protested that she'd put Richie behind her already. Meggie was all she cared about now. But she lay in bed alone, looking out through the curtainless window at the starlit sky. The street noises died away. Meggie slept soundly.

If Richie walked in now and said he wanted them both, nothing in the world would matter except that. She would sacrifice everything all over again, she knew it for certain. The image of him filled her every waking moment and drifted into her dreams. She longed for him, and wished he would come back. Love was like slavery. It shackled her heart.

CHAPTER TWENTY-TWO

'Ma, spell "Mauretania" for me.' Grace looked up from her homework. She sucked the end of her pencil and stared out of the open french doors, up the long, sloping garden of the house in Ealing.

Jess sat at her sewing. 'M-A-U-R,' she began, then waited for Grace to catch up. '-E-T-A-N-I-A.'

'Miss Shoesmith told us the *Mauretania* was built on the River Tyne by the Swan Hunter shipyard in 1907, since when it has held the Blue Riband for the fastest crossing of the Atlantic at an average speed of 26.06 knots in 4 days, 10 hours and 41 minutes!' Grace recited, word for word.

Jess smiled. Grace liked facts. When she wasn't busy with homework, she was tuned into the wireless, on the 2LO transmitting station, listening to the news broadcasts. She gobbled up information, read every Chalet School book, and shared Maurice's enthusiasm for the latest aviation developments. When she grew up, she wanted to fly a De Havilland Moth at a top speed of ninety miles per hour.

'Rosie says her sister, Katie, sailed the Atlantic even faster than that. But I said, how could it, if the *Mauretania* still holds the Blue Riband?' Grace bent her head and scribbled on.

'And what did Rosie say?'

'She said I shouldn't call her sister a liar, and she'd tell her big brother, Patrick, and I'd better watch out.'

'Hmm. I hope you two didn't have a fight.' Jess took her pointed scissors and snipped into the curved seam. She spread the lilac crêpe-de-Chine fabric flat and took it to the ironing-board to finish. Outside, Mo swung high on the garden swing, slung from a low branch of the apple tree. 'Did she say how Katie was getting on?'

Grace frowned. 'No, she never. She says that in America the tenements are high as the sky. She says you can't walk down the streets in San Francisco 'cos they're too steep. Once, Katie started to run and ended up in the sea.'

Jess laughed. 'And they're paved with gold, I suppose?'

'I don't know about that.' Grace took it seriously. 'Pa says Hollywood is where they make the best cinema films. It's where Charlie Chaplin, the King of Comedy, made *The Kid*, and where Mary Pickford, the World's Sweetheart, lives.' She sighed.

Jess didn't reply. She wasn't sure that Maurice should feed the children so many of these sweet celluloid dreams. Grace knew every sequence in every Douglas Fairbanks film, and Jess wasn't sure that a girl her age could tell the fiction from the reality. If she ever went to Hollywood, she might be surprised to find that the men weren't all dressed in curly wigs and frilled shirts, or that the young women didn't spend all their days tied to railway tracks, awaiting rescue. Still, Maurice took Grace to Saturday matinées to see the latest releases, and she came home thrilled, strutting like Felix and humming his tune.

The evening shadows lengthened in the garden. Mo came in for something to eat, and Hettie came down from upstairs to take him into the kitchen to make him a jam sandwich. She planned a summer evening stroll with George, she told Jess. George had a night off from the Lamb and Flag. He had something he wanted to talk to Hettie about.

Jess raised her eyebrows.

'Now, it ain't nothing like that!' Hettie stood in the doorway, blushing and laughing. She held Mo's sticky hand.

'Nothing like what?'

'Ma means cuddling and stuff, don't you, Ma?' Grace giggled and made a face.

'Now, Grace,' Jess warned.

'It's got to do with work, if you must know,' Hettie protested.

'Is that why you're wearing your best dress, Auntie Ett?'

'She's incorrigible,' Jess sighed.

'In-corri-what?'

'Never mind.' She gave her daughter a firm look and said she hoped that Hettie had a good time. Then she took Mo back into the kitchen to wipe his hands.

When Maurice arrived home late that night, the house was peaceful. He knew Jess would be in the front room, working as usual. The door was open and the light on. He heard the stop-start-stop whir of the sewing-machine, and the even rhythm of the treadle. Instead of going upstairs to Grace and Mo, he went straight in to see her.

She glanced up to receive his kiss on the cheek. 'You look like the cat that got the cream.' She smiled.

Maurice unbuttoned his jacket and flung it on a chair. 'I got some good news.' He rolled up his shirt-sleeves, then came behind her to rest his arms on her shoulders. 'I got us a share in the cinema chain. I'm part-owner now. What do you think of that?'

She stood up, pleased for him, not yet seeing the significance for the family. 'You're very clever, Maurice. And I think you deserve it.'

'Ain't you over the moon?' He embraced her. 'I ain't just a manager no more. I'm a boss.'

'Of the whole thing?' She didn't see how it worked. Maurice hadn't taken her into his confidence over any of this.

'No, not the whole thing.' He smiled. 'I just bought myself into one branch, developing the chain outside London.'

'Meaning what exactly?'

'Meaning, we're branching out, Jess, across the whole country. I'll take on new cinemas, get them on their feet. We're gonna take over the whole country before we're through!' He saw white-stuccoed cinema palaces in every grimy northern town; the clean, modern façades of concrete and steel, the wide open foyers, the raking auditoria, the silver screens.

'You ain't gonna work in London no more?' The picture cleared. It seemed Maurice wanted to uproot them. 'Hold on a minute, Maurice, I ain't exactly sure what this means to us.'

He gave an exasperated sigh. 'Look, if I run new branches, of course it ain't in London. We'll move north, Jess, find a nice new house near Leeds or Manchester. I already telephoned a few people. There's plenty of nice places. It ain't all cotton mills and women in clogs and shawls.'

She shook her head. 'And this is definite?'

'Copper-bottom, all signed, sealed and delivered.' He stepped back from her and began to pace the floor.

'And when would we have to move?'

'It's up to us. Soon. Before Christmas.'

'What about schools?' Objections flooded in. She put to one side for now the overwhelming feeling that he should have discussed it with her first.

'They got schools in Manchester, don't they?'

'And what about the dress shop?' Jess felt strangely calm. Later, she knew, the emotions would rise.

'Let Hettie have it,' he advised. 'She's got Edith Cooper to help her run it now. You're off the hook as far as making dresses goes. No more slaving over a hot sewing-machine.'

'It ain't slaving, Maurice.'

He turned on her. 'Why do you have to go nit-picking, taking me up like that? All I say is, there's plenty of cash now. I'll take a share of the profits, see. It don't make no sense for you to go on working.'

She stared back at him. 'I'm sorry you think I'm nit-picking.'

There was an awkward silence. Then Maurice's temper exploded. 'Go on, poke your spiteful oar in, why don't you? You ain't normal, Jess. A normal woman would be over the moon to be able to take it easy. You can enjoy the good life and I'll take care of everything!' He strode angrily towards her.

She dodged and went to close the door, to contain the noise of raised voices. 'You're saying to me, uproot and go off without a by-your-leave. You never even stopped to think if it suited me!'

He laughed derisively. 'I'm meant to ask if you want to be rich? If you want the kids to have the best of everything? If you want to drive around the posh shops in a big car, instead of being holed up day after day in a back room making things that other women can look down their noses at? I ain't never heard nothing so bleeding stupid!'

'You ain't never heard nothing I said,' she pointed out. 'Not lately.'

'Are you saying you won't move?' He gave a direct challenge, standing over her, demanding an answer.

'I'm saying I ain't made up my mind.'

The answer rocked him. 'Oh, and when do you think you might manage to do that?' He didn't wait for a reply, but went on in a sarcastic tone, 'No, never mind. It don't make no difference to me, see. You take your time. You decide whether or not a wife should be glad for her husband and help him make his way. Ain't no rush. I'll just go ahead and find a place to rent. Manchester ain't that far, not on the train. I'll go by my bleeding self, if that's how you feel!' He slammed the door as he went out.

Jess slumped into her chair, exhausted by the effort of staying calm. In many ways he was right: she should be pleased for him, pure and simple. The family should stick together. She was a bad wife to put obstacles in his way.

Only, Maurice hadn't included her in his plans. *He* would say it was because he knew she'd say no. He wanted to make it a certainty before he gave her chance to object. Looked at in that light, his actions were reasonable.

She began to argue against herself and tear herself in two. All well and good to be ambitious, she thought, but who was Maurice trying to please? Did he imagine the children would be happier taken away from their grandparents, aunts, uncles, cousins? And why didn't he see that her own work was important? He was a man, that's why. He'd struggled out of the gutter with single-minded determination. He didn't understand family. He looked on women as inferior. It was the old way; ingrained and unshakeable.

Jess had never seen herself as forward-looking; not

compared with Frances. She had little social conscience compared with Ett, no training for modern business, like Sadie. But she felt strongly about her own ability to make her way in the world. The success of the shop had allowed her confidence to grow. She knew how to design and make clothes that were a pleasure to wear. She could cut cloth to flatter, her dresses were wearable as well as fashionable. Best of all, she loved the work. The hours spent at the cutting-table with tailor's chalk, paper and pins, were a challenge to both imagination and practical skill. She would work out a design to the last detail, construct her clothes with an architect's precision, an artist's flair. When she went out on to Ealing High Street and saw a smart woman dressed in one of her outfits, she felt a glow of pride.

And Maurice had never once taken this into consideration. As she packed away her sewing things and turned off the light, she felt the grain of stubbornness swell and grow. It wasn't straightforward. A wife need not follow the husband willy-nilly. There might be a compromise. Let Maurice go up north and set himself up in decent lodgings. He could travel south in his time off. This would see them through the first period of time. If he was determined to make big changes to their lives, at least he could let her sort things out at her own pace.

She got no chance to express these things, however. When she went upstairs to bed, she found it empty. This time, Maurice had collected blankets and taken them to the spare room.

In the morning, after a sleepless night, he announced his intention to go up to Manchester before the end of the month. 'No one can afford to hang around in this business,' he explained. 'We gotta get our foot in the door first. I want to show Kinemacolor as well as the old black and whites. I want to take Warner Brothers talkies before Gaumont snaps them up.' He said he planned to find lodgings, give Jess time to sell up and follow with the kids. 'Ain't no rush over that,' he conceded. 'I can see you need time to sort things out.' He felt magnanimous as he kissed her and took the children off to school in the car.

Sadie moved into Eden House, sobered by her bid to follow her own feelings over Richie. She was like a child whose fingers had been burnt, who none the less still finds the flames fascinating and cannot leave the fire alone. Richie cropped up in her thoughts whenever she had a moment to spare from washing, changing and feeding Meggie. Throughout July, in the close heat of the court, she rocked their baby to sleep, humming a lullaby, secretly dreaming that his desertion was temporary and, like a cinema hero, he would gallop over the horizon clutching a fistful of dollars, with a smile on his handsome face.

He would be contrite. He would say he'd come back to be a husband and a father. They would be a family. For Sadie could not believe that she'd fallen for the type of man who would use a girl and ditch her the moment she got pregnant – the old story. She remembered Richie: his hooded, passionate eyes, his unspoken vulnerability, their closeness in bed. He couldn't have pretended then that he loved her without her knowing that he was insincere. She trusted her instinct, a small, dark voice that said Richie was better than he seemed. His love for her and the baby would overcome his doubts. She did expect to see him again, if not with a bagful of money, then at least with his sleeves rolled up, ready to try again.

Work had been the problem. Or lack of it. If Rob hadn't

sacked Richie, Sadie felt that things would have worked out between them. Once out of work, his stride began to falter. He was a proud man, he hadn't liked her being the breadwinner at Swan and Edgar. He felt even worse when she had to leave her job over the pregnancy. He knew he wasn't a real man unless he could provide for her and the baby. Failure had driven him away.

This was not the general opinion on Richie Palmer down Paradise Court. Dolly Ogden denounced him as the ruination of a girl's good name. Long summer evenings gave her the space to proclaim these views among the older women who kept to the custom of sitting at their doorsteps until night fell. These were heatwave days, when dogs kept to the shady alleys, and every rat carried the danger of festering disease. Government promises to keep a hold on prices had been broken. The pound in the pocket didn't go as far. Only gossip was free.

'And you see how the poor girl has to live,' Dolly said. 'In that nasty tenement. It don't matter how many licks of paint she gives it, it won't make no difference. And Frances can bring over all the disinfectant and bleach she likes, it ain't gonna keep them rats away. Not in the long run.'

There was a shaking of heads. Edith Cooper confirmed she'd seen a rat scuttling up a stairway that morning as she set off for work.

'It ain't paint and disinfectant she needs,' Liz Sargent agreed. 'It's a good man.'

'Don't we all?' went up the general murmur.

'But from what I hear, she'd take Palmer back like a shot,' Dolly went on disapprovingly. She brushed biscuit crumbs from her broad lap on to the pavement.

'Never!'

'She wouldn't!'

Jenny Oldfield

'She would.' Dolly leaned confidentially forward. 'She told my Amy as much. Amy wormed it out of her last week. She reckons she still loves him.'

'Hush!' Liz saw Annie strolling up the court, eyes and ears alert. 'And how's the bonny, bouncing baby, Dolly?' She steered the subject on to safe ground.

'Blooming, ta. He's sitting up and taking notice already. We'll have him saying his first word before Christmas at this rate. Won't we, Annie? I was just saying, we got a little prince in young Bobby. He'll soon be toddling around, God bless his cotton socks!'

Annie agreed. 'He's spoilt to death, mind. Amy's gonna have to toughen up on him before too long.'

'And Rob,' Dolly reminded her.

'You'd think no one had ever had babies before.'

'Let them go ahead and spoil him rotten, Annie. It's more than some can do for their littl'uns.' She pushed towards controversy. Life was dull when everyone agreed.

'How's that?' Annie bristled. 'I hope you ain't referring to Sadie?'

Dolly protested innocence. 'I never meant nothing. How *is* Sadie, by the way?'

'Nicely, thanks.' Annie's face stayed stiff and unsmiling.

'Under the circumstances.' Dolly nodded. 'And how's little Meggie?'

'Dancing the tango and doing long multiplication sums,' Annie snapped.

Dolly's eyebrows shot up. 'No need to be like that, Annie. We're all on your side.'

Annie should have known better than to draw Dolly on, but she narrowed her eyes and folded her skinny arms. 'And what side is that, then, Dolly?'

'We all feel sorry for the poor girl. Sadie's been a bit

328

headstrong, we know that. But she ain't done nothing to deserve Richie Palmer. Look how he brought her down, it's a disgrace. I used to look at young Sadie and say to myself, "There's a girl that will go far!"'

Annie growled back. 'Sadie's fine. She ain't feeling sorry for herself and she don't want your pity, Dolly Ogden. She's getting office work and bringing it home. Rob and Walter teamed up and bought her one of them typewriter machines from the pawnshop. She'll soon be on her feet.'

'And she won't hear of taking Palmer back?' Dolly knew she was pushing her luck.

'Don't be bleeding daft,' Annie retorted. 'Where did you hear that?'

'Nowhere.' Dolly pressed her lips together. 'Ain't no one mentioned it to me. I was just asking.'

'And I wonder you don't have nothing better to do, Dolly. Or I would if I didn't know you better, you old windbag.' Before Dolly had chance to reply, Annie nodded at Liz and Edith and marched on her way. She was going over to Ealing to visit Jess and the little ones. She saw trouble brewing in that direction. Maurice had gone and got himself work hundreds of miles away. That would put a strain on any family. Ett had said that Jess wasn't herself lately. Annie wanted to go and see for herself.

August broke with a heavy thunderstorm. Rain hammered on to the grey roofs, single slates slipped and fell. But the air was cleared. A weak sun broke through as Walter Davidson stopped his taxicab outside Eden House and raced up the stone steps in the final splattering drops.

'There's a rainbow,' he told Sadie as she opened the door.

'I ain't got time for no rainbows, Walter.'

'You can't see it from here.' He unbuttoned his jacket and drew out a sheaf of jumbled, dog-eared papers. 'I brought the accounts we want you to type up.'

She nodded. 'Come in. I'm sorry I snapped.'

He took off his cap and followed her inside. 'Ain't nothing wrong, is there?' Meggie was sitting propped in a big, soft chair, wedged around by pillows. Her eyes followed Sadie everywhere.

'No, except it's rent day,' she grumbled. She cleared the table, then offered Walter a seat. Since she'd come back to Paradise Court, he'd taken up their friendship in his old, steady way. He never tried to romance her though, and never referred to what had once been between them. She caught him looking at her with concern and a hand went to her hair to straighten it. 'Thanks for bringing me these.' She put the bundle of papers on to the table.

Walter drew money from his pocket. 'Paid in advance,' he insisted. He noticed how she held her breath, uncertain whether to accept. He placed the coins on the table. 'How about a quick cuppa?'

She smiled and nodded, and set about filling the kettle with water. 'How's things?' Walter often stopped by for a chat like this. It broke the monotony of her days and brought no pressure. He seemed to visit out of sheer kindness. She compared him with Richie, and found no likeness. Walter was patient and steady. His wavy brown hair gave his face an open, friendly look. Though he was tall and upright, his presence felt shy. Ready to smile, slow to take offence, she would even call him handsome. After all, she'd once been attracted to him, before their affair had fallen into its uneventful, companionable pattern.

Sadie listened as Walter ran through the street gossip.

Taxi business was down, as it always was in the summer. Rob and he were still a million miles away from getting their hands on new cars. The old Bullnoses creaked on. The boycott at the Duke was holding up. Rumour had it that Bertie Hill was already feeling the pressure from the brewery. 'I hear he's been forced to serve after hours every now and then, just to boost the takings.'

Sadie laughed. 'Who says so?' She couldn't imagine Hill being so careless of his licence.

'Tommy.'

'Well, then!' She dismissed the rumour. 'Tommy's a dreamer. He says he's moving into Coopers' old shop when he's ready. Swears blind he'll be a millionaire before he's thirty!'

Walter laughed and rose to go. 'I'd best be off.' He took his hat from the table.

'I'll get these accounts typed up and back to Rob or you by the weekend,' she promised.

'No rush.' He nodded and left, passing Bertie Hill on the stairs.

Sadie's door was still open and Hill strolled in without being observed. He stood watching as she worked with her back turned, lifting the sleeping Meggie from the chair and laying her gently in her crib.

When she turned, she started. She felt his eyes devour her, glanced down to straighten her blouse, walked to the far side of the room.

'It's that day already.' Hill strolled to the window and smirked. 'Rent day.' He folded his arms and continued to stare.

Sadie nodded. She had to cross near to him to fetch her purse from the mantelpiece. He stepped after her, trapping her in a small space by the empty hearth. She took out the

331

money and handed it to him. His thick fingers turned the coins in his palm. 'Twelve shillings and sixpence,' she assured him. 'It's what we agreed.'

'You ain't heard the bad news, then?'

His casual manner nettled her further. 'No. What?'

'I put the rent up to thirteen shillings last week. To cover maintenance costs. The roof, it needs mending.'

'You ain't said nothing to me.'

'I am now.' He kept her locked in the corner, studying her figure, noticing the smoothness of her skin.

'But that ain't right.' She fumed against him. Twelve and six was what they'd agreed.

He shrugged. 'Please yourself. There's plenty of others would pay thirteen bob for a nice place like this.' He glanced round at her improvements; clean paintwork, bright tablecloth, a picture or two on the wall.

'It's a crying shame! And you ain't done nothing about the rats, like I asked. It's bad for the baby. Ain't you never heard of the Housing Act? This place ain't fit for nothing!'

Again he shrugged, but didn't move.

She stared back at him, furious.

''Course, we might be able to agree special terms,' he suggested. It seemed to him a reasonable offer he was about to make. 'If you was nice to me, I might see my way to a tidy little rent reduction.' He didn't expect her to turn it down. In his experience, women in Sadie's situation would snap his hand off.

Sadie looked at him with loathing. 'Stay away from me, you hear!' As he advanced, she began to push him off. The offer was meant to operate then and there.

Hill grabbed her by the elbow. 'Ten shillings. How does that sound? Don't that seem fair enough?' He reached to kiss her. She struggled as she felt his lips smear down her cheek on to her neck. She tried to turn away at the last second, and began to yell out. Her fists pummelled ineffectually against him.

He lashed out with his free hand and sent her staggering against the wall. Then he pinned her against it, tearing at the buttons on her white blouse, excited by her resistance. He felt her tug the back of his hair. Her body was soft and slender.

Sadie felt a wave of sick panic. She struggled to break free, but knew at once that he was too brutal and strong. She wouldn't give in, though. She cried out against him.

Walter had seen the landlord going up to Sadie's room and made nothing of it. After all, she'd told him it was rent day. But back in the taxicab, he frowned. Hill had seemed to give him a sneering look of the man-of-the-world type, as if he knew why Walter was a regular visitor to Sadie's room. Walter had shrugged off the implication. Now what he found in the car gave him cause to go back up and check in any case. He took up a loose page which had fallen from the bundle of accounts and grasped it in his hand. Sadie would need it so she could type it up with the rest. He ran back up the stairs, two at a time.

Sadie had almost blacked out from hatred and disgust. Hill had ripped the clothes from her breast and his great hands were mauling her. He held her up to stop her from sinking down, pressing her up against the wall. His mouth worked against her neck. She still fought him off, but was growing feebler.

Walter ran in through the open door. He hurled himself at the landlord, tore him away from Sadie. Then he punched at his body and head, sending him reeling backwards with a bloody nose. Sadie wept and sank to the ground, trying to cover herself.

Crazy with anger, Walter laid into the burly ex-police-man. Hill knew how to handle himself, but Walter was fitter, cleverer. His punch, developed at Milo's gym during his teenaged years, was stronger. There was only so much battering that Hill could take before he slumped to the ground. In the end, Sadie had to drag her defender away, to prevent real damage.

By the time Walter had lugged Hill from the room and watched him stagger away, Sadie too was almost senseless. Walter rushed across the landing to Mary O'Hagan, sent her in to help Sadie, then rushed for Annie. When he brought her back, they found Sadie in tears in Mary's rooms. She was begging for Richie.

Walter stopped short at the door.

Annie shot him a look. 'I'll see to things here. You go get yourself cleaned up.' There was blood trickling from the corner of Walter's mouth. His shirt collar was torn.

In a daze he went down to the taxi and drove himself to the depot. Rob took one look and demanded the full story. Walter spat it out, seeing Rob's own anger boil up. 'A girl ain't safe with Hill around. I hope you gave him a good thrashing, Walt. He bleeding deserved it!'

Walter dabbed at his sore mouth. The cut was swollen and tender. 'If she had someone to look after her, none of this would've gone on. God knows what he'd have done if I hadn't showed up again.'

Rob frowned through his cigarette smoke. 'Ain't you the one to do it, then?'

'What?'

'Look after Sadie, long-term. You know.'

Walter shook his head.

'Why not?'

'It ain't me she wants, Rob. It's Richie Palmer.'

Rob swore and protested, he called Sadie a fool, said Walter was worth ten of Richie. Walter wondered what Sadie would do next. 'She can't stay there no more. Hill will see to that. We gotta do something, Rob. Why can't we find Richie for her?'

'You're stark staring mad.' Rob took a step back and shook his head.

'It's what she wants.'

'Then she *is* a fool.' Rob thought through the new situation. Sadie's position as a single woman with a kid was open to all kinds of abuse. Men like Bertie Hill would crawl out of the woodwork wherever she turned. Driving a taxi round these courts and back streets late at night, Rob knew this all too well. He listened to Walter's account of Sadie sobbing out for Richie to come back. His conscience dug deep. 'We could put out the word.' Still he hesitated before he told Walter the full truth.

'To find Richie?'

Rob nodded. 'It ain't gonna be that hard.'

'You know something?'

'I heard he was in Hoxton,' he admitted. 'I don't know where exactly. And I don't know why I'm telling you this, Walt. We must be bleeding mad.'

Walter pressed him to go on. 'If Sadie wants to see him, you gotta let her.'

Rob gave in. 'Tell her she should try the Queen's Head. Like I say, I must be round the bleeding twist. And you need your head looking at,' he told Walter. 'You wouldn't find me giving up on a girl like that!'

CHAPTER TWENTY-THREE

Walter knew the Shoreditch and Hoxton area well enough to find his way easily to the Queen's Head on the corner of Regent Street and Turner Court. It was an old-style pub where street gangs graduated after a teenage apprenticeship of fights with belts and bottles, where the twentieth century had as yet scarcely impinged, and where assorted carmen, porters, navvies and railway workers gathered until well past midnight.

He had driven through the mean streets, the miles of brick and squalor, the long vistas of bricks and misery, to reach the pub where Richie Palmer was to be contacted. It was a stifling night, yet to his surprise, he found a group of children with enough energy to dance to the music of a barrel organ on the street corner. Two women sat on the pub steps, singing along.

One of them grinned up at him as he stepped by. Her companion jostled her, and their laughter showed their rotten teeth, their crooked smiles. Walter ignored them. He went in and ordered a pint of bitter, served by a small grey Irishman with a long, lined face, whose hangdog expression belied the phrase about the luck of the Irish. 'I'm trying to find Richie Palmer,' he told the man.

'You ain't the only one.' The beer sloshed on to the bar
as he slammed the glass down.

Walter paid up. 'He ain't here, then?'

'I never said that. This is his second home, this is.'

Walter frowned and glanced around the dingy room.
The bar was partitioned by wood and glass panels, giving
drinkers the privacy to play cards or dominoes. Many of the
partitions contained two or three men huddled over their
beer, which he now discovered was flat and lukewarm due
to the heat. 'He *is* here, then?' Walter felt his temper
shorten as he peered round.

'*Was* here. Bought a drink ten minutes since. When I say
"bought", I don't mean to say he had the wherewithal.
What I mean is, he sweet-talked one of the girls into buying
his beer. Richie Palmer ain't had the price of a drink way
back as far as I can remember.'

The Irishman's sad face and tragic tones had a depressing
effect. Realizing that he would never get a straight answer,
Walter wandered away from the bar in search of the
runaway.

He came across him deep in dalliance with a tousle-
haired, pale girl with a shrieking laugh and a pretty, grey-
eyed face. They sat in a dark corner, arms slung around each
other's shoulders, though Walter got the instant impression
that Richie was paying for his drink with a spot of compul-
sory flirting. When he saw his old employer, he leaped to
his feet and pushed the girl away.

'Richie.' Walter gave a peremptory nod. 'I heard I'd find
you here.'

'And what if you did?' He was defensive, resenting
Walter's neatly cut tweed jacket and clean collar and tie.

'I came to ask if you'd come over to see Sadie and the
kid.' Looking at Richie's patched shirt, open at the neck,

his old waistcoat hanging loose, even Walter began to doubt that Sadie knew her own mind. He was unshaven and dirty, and bore all the signs of long-term poverty and unemployment. But if Sadie couldn't get him out of her head, if she was miserable and lonely without him, who was he, Walter Davidson, to stand in her way?

Richie went on viewing him suspiciously. 'What's in it for you? Who sent you? Did she?'

He shook his head. 'But she is asking for you.' He described her new situation and Hill's recent attack. 'She goes on about not wanting to make a fuss, but Annie came in and said it weren't right to leave Sadie in the tenement no more, not after what Hill done to her. She still wants her to go to the police, but Sadie won't.' It was three or four days after the event, and Sadie and Meggie were staying with Annie and Duke. After long family discussion, without Sadie's knowledge, so as not to raise her hopes, it had been decided that Richie should be contacted. 'Rob says you left word at Hope Street about where you was.'

Richie stood silent, avoiding Walter's direct gaze. For almost three months, since he'd left Sadie in the lurch, he'd drifted from one day to the next. He slept on garret floors, on the Embankment, in the parks. He'd left on the spur of the moment, after a build-up of shame about his diminishing prospects that he swiftly turned into resentment against the whole Parsons tribe. He'd even begun to watch Sadie, heavily pregnant, washing dishes or smoothing out the bedclothes, despising her small efforts towards respectability. She'd picked up her finicky ways from her family. Her eyes were the Parsons eyes: deep brown, big and dark.

He'd tried to foresee the future, after the baby was born. There'd have been no money. The sisters would have descended on Hope Street with a vengeance, sweeping him off his own hearth with advice, bits and bobs for the baby, tonics for Sadie. Sadie would have grown homesick, her feeling for him would have waned. She would put all her passion into the baby. Then she would have hankered for them to go back to Duke Street. If he'd given in and they'd gone back, every day he would have seen Rob Parsons in his taxicab, driving by in the car he, Richie, had looked after, and patched, and knew inside-out.

This was the thought that swung things for him. He took off suddenly, without explanation, thinking that Sadie's hurt would soon heal. Abandoned by his own parents, growing up detached from all deep emotion, he saw being let down in life as something to accept and spring back from. Letting people down was likewise nothing serious, not when you saw babies starve, old men drown themselves, girls of twelve walking the streets.

Walter grew uneasy with the awkward silence. 'She had a little girl, did you know?'

Richie nodded. 'She left me a note.' He'd tried through all these weeks to steer his brain away from forming a picture of little Meggie. But Sadie's written words were too graphic. He could see in his mind's eye her long, curling lashes, her rosebud mouth.

'And what shall I tell her when I go back?' He saw how Richie must be going through a silent struggle. Curious faces peered at the two of them, face to face. The pretty, shrieking girl was gossiping with the barman.

'Tell her I'll come and see her when I can,' he mumbled.

Richie came to Southwark a week later, waiting under the railway arch at the top of Duke Street, until he caught sight of Sadie chatting to Amy in the market. Both women wheeled perambulators. As Amy went to talk to Annie on her stall, Sadie turned to make her way up the street towards the park. He waylaid her without warning.

Startled, she stared at him. He was thinner, his expression unreadable as ever. His eyes were half closed, as if to keep his feelings safely dampened down.

Sadie had changed too, he thought. Her movements were slower, more careful. She didn't cry out when she saw him, though he could tell she wanted to. Her light dress, straight and simple, worn with a long row of pearly beads, showed her creamy-brown arms. Her untameable, wavy dark hair framed her face. She clung to the pram handle, but said nothing.

'Can I take a look at Meggie?' Richie took another step forward. People in the street rushed or sauntered by. The traffic roared and a train rumbled overhead.

The baby lay in her little wickerwork carriage, covered by a lacy sheet. He saw the dark hair against the white pillow, the same as Sadie's. He wondered what it was he was feeling. Disbelief. Curiosity. He glanced up at Sadie's proud face. 'Can I walk with you?'

She nodded. They went on past the shops, the chapel, the public baths, through the park gates, wandering like any young couple with their baby.

'I got your letter,' he told her.

She nodded. 'It ain't been easy.'

'I weren't good enough,' he said. The trees spread their leaves in a great, green canopy. They walked slowly through the dappled shadows.

'Don't go on. I ain't listening.' She looked stubbornly away from him, at the pigeons, the children playing. Then she turned back. 'At any rate, that ain't for you to say.'

'It's what they think.'

'Who?'

He pulled at white flowerheads on the rose bushes, crushing petals and scattering them on the grass. 'Frances, your pa, Rob; all of them.'

'They ain't me. Maybe I don't think the same way.' Sadie didn't want to make it too easy. She checked her pleasure in Richie's presence, forcing him to make the running as much as she could.

'I still ain't found no proper work,' he said moodily.

She looked him in the eyes again. 'You could try talking to Walter,' she suggested.

He frowned. 'What about Rob?'

'Rob was the one that told Walter where to find you.' Sadie had learned all this after Walter's successful mission to the Queen's Head. Since then her hopes had been high of bumping into Richie just like this, as if the bitter experience of being deserted had melted away.

Richie considered this. 'Bleeding hell.'

'Right,' she laughed. 'Being a stick-in-the-mud family man himself now, he might see things different, I think, especially with Amy coming down on him like a ton of bricks.'

'Amy's a decent sort,' Richie said. He sat down on a bench and waited for Sadie to put the brake on the pram.

'Who said she weren't?' Sadie and Amy were firm friends now. It was Amy's persuasive tongue that had laid the ground for offering Richie his old job back once he finally showed up to see Sadie and the baby.

'What's the use of him coming back to play the pa if he don't have no work?' she'd demanded. She'd recognized Rob's stubborn use of his newspaper as a shield. She went and tore it away. 'Now you listen to me, Rob Parsons!

When Richie Palmer shows his face down Paradise Court again, you gotta be man enough to let bygones be bygones, you hear?'

This was just after Walter had returned from the Queen's Head. She pinched and teased her husband until he yelled out and woke the baby. 'Get the gripewater,' she ordered, withdrawing her labour until he gave in.

Rob went and settled Bobby and fussed him back to sleep. When he got to bed, he found she'd withdrawn conjugal rights too. 'Bleeding hell,' he moaned. 'I'm married to a right bleeding battleaxe!'

'You are,' she warned. 'Until you learn how to behave.' She preached charity and forgiveness until well past midnight.

In a mixture of exhaustion and desire, he gave in. 'All right, he can have his bleeding job back, then.' He sighed, taking Amy in his arms. 'If it means I can get a bit of peace and quiet.'

'There ain't nothing peaceful about what you got in mind, Rob Parsons,' she challenged, kissing him all over his face, tickling herself with his moustache. 'I can see it in your eyes!'

So, by the end of August, Sadie's life had turned around once more. She was out of the crumbling tenement, and had converted her temporary stay at Annie's house into permanent lodgings at Edith and Jack Cooper's; an idea mooted by clear-thinking Frances. Since his meeting up with Sadie under the railway arch, Richie had scarcely been able to keep away from her and Meggie. He'd been humble to Annie and Duke, sincere in his desire to do better from now on. The final hurdle had been cleared when Rob came specially to find him at Annie's house. Keeping things formal and stiff, he offered him his old position at the depot.

They shook hands on it. Richie was due to start back on the first of next month. Sadie's cup was overflowing, but still she wouldn't be the one to suggest a full reconciliation with Richie. She would hold out until he asked.

'Happy now?' he said, after accepting Rob's offer. They took a stroll up the court, before he walked back over the river to Hoxton.

She nodded.

'And will you take me back?' He looked down at the pavement, up at the roofs, anywhere but at her.

'I thought you'd never ask!'

Her sharp answer drew his gaze. He grinned and kissed her. 'Ain't I the worst devil in Duke Street no more?' He'd caught sight of Dolly Ogden's lace curtain twitching.

'You never were.' Sadie linked arms and walked on with him. 'No, the worst devil by far is Bertie Hill.' She glanced at the open door of the Prince of Wales. 'So you can move back in with me whenever you like, never mind what Dolly says.' She had to check with Edith, smooth the way in that direction. 'She'll be glad of the extra rent, and the company.' She would talk her new landlady round by explaining that Richie was now all set to become the respectable family man. Sadie noticed Jack Cooper shambling up the street, and across into the Prince of Wales.

Richie said nothing, but he'd seen Tommy O'Hagan slip in just ahead. He asked Sadie about the boycott, and for five more minutes they stood by the pillar-box discussing Bertie Hill's worsening situation. 'George is sure the brewery won't stand the losses much longer.'

'How long will they give him?'

She shrugged. 'That depends. Tommy says he's up to Pa's old tricks, serving after hours.'

Richie laughed. 'That's why I just seen him heading in there, then?'

Sadie was incensed. 'Tommy? Bleeding traitor. I'll box his bleeding ears!' she promised.

All was back to normal. They parted, lovers once more. The next day, Richie moved into Edith Cooper's with Sadie, ready to start work at the depot on the Monday.

George Mann's courtship of Hettie went along on an altogether more sedate basis. For months since he went to work at the Flag, they'd been meeting quietly, watching family developments and worrying about the welfare of others. Hettie's work at the Salvation Army Mission and at the Ealing shop took her away from Duke Street a good deal, but she was satisfied that things were as good as they could be for Duke and Annie, now that Wiggin's influence was past. She scarcely forgave herself for her lack of charity towards the poor old drunk, however, and she redoubled her energies in the Christian hostel, soldiering for Jesus and putting her own needs way down the line. It didn't occur to her that sacrifice also affects those close to the martyr for the cause; her family lacked her gentle, affectionate presence, and George had to make do with fleeting conversations between shop and hostel, or fitted into one of Hettie's rare free days.

One Saturday in early September, he succeeded in persuading her to take time off to go and queue with him to take a boat out on to the Serpentine. The warm day made it a popular pastime with the young girls and their beaus, few things were as romantic and accessible as sculling across the flat surface in the mellow light. At last, George and Hettie came to the front of the queue, stepped into their slim wooden boat and headed into the stillness, away from the crowds.

George rowed for a while in silence. Hettie trailed her fingers in the cool water and took in the scene, guessing that he might have something special to say. She even had some warning of what it might be. He had been keeping her up-to-date on Bertie Hill's declining popularity with Mr Wakeley, the brewery manager – information gleaned from Alf Henderson, the landlord at the Flag. She waited patiently for George to speak.

'I'm in a spot of bother,' he began, lifting the oars and letting the boat drift.

'Oh?' This was unusual, not what she'd expected. She studied his broad, tanned face. 'How can I help?'

'That's just it, Ett. *You*'re the problem.'

'Oh,' she said again. The pleasantness of the day threatened to fall flat. 'What did I do?'

'Well, no, you didn't do nothing. You're not the problem; I said it wrong. Only, I got a problem over you, that's what I mean to say. I got myself tied up in knots.' He sighed.

Hettie let her hand continue to float on the water. In fact, she didn't feel George's problem, whatever it was, as such a threat after all. 'Spit it out, why don't you?' She held on to her wide-brimmed, light straw hat and smiled.

'First off,' he began again, 'you know Wakeley has got his beady eye on Hill. According to Alf, he only has to wait for him to make one false move before he gives him his marching orders.'

Hettie's eyes widened. 'Ain't that something? God forgive me, but I hope and pray they don't take too long

345

about it. The sooner Duke Street sees the back of that man, the better.'

George nodded. 'So you see, Wakeley must be on the lookout for someone to step into his shoes.'

Hettie spied another rowing-boat cutting swiftly across their bows. She shouted, George seized the oars and swung away. 'And that someone could be you, is that it?'

'Could be.' He rowed for a while. The soft sun glinted on millions of ripples, the oars dipped and cleared the water in a steady, even rhythm. 'But here's where I get tied up. See, I could go right up and put my name down for Wakeley to keep in mind. Alf says he'd back me. I already know the old Duke like the back of my hand. I stand a good chance of being first in line for the licence.'

Hettie's smile broadened. 'It'd be a dream come true. It'd make Pa very happy.' She hardly dared to think about it: Duke free to come and go on his old stamping-ground.

'I know it would. Now, Ett, *there's* my problem. If I get the licence, how can I ask you to marry me? If you said yes, I'd be the happiest man alive, but I'd be thinking you only said yes for your pa's sake, to get him back where he belongs through the back door, so to speak. And I'd never know if you'd said yes because you wanted me!' He blushed and let the oars rest again. 'There ain't no way round it as far as I can see.'

During the speech, one of the longest of his life, the smile faded from Hettie's face. She lifted her hand clear of the water and let it drip on to her dark green skirt. 'Hold on, George, let me get this straight. Is what I just heard a proposal of marriage?'

George looked alarmed. One oar slipped and the boat tipped sideways. 'That's the knot I can't undo, see. Now I can't never ask you to marry me, can I? Not if I go and put my name down with the brewery.'

At last Hettie broke into a laugh. 'Try me, George.'

'And you'll give a straight answer? Never mind Duke and the pub?'

'Hand across my heart and hope to die!'

He took a deep breath and steadied the boat. 'Here goes. Hettie Parsons, will you marry me?'

'Yes,' she said. 'Yes, yes, yes.'

'Blimey.' They were behaving like a couple of kids, out in the middle of the lake, with people in the distance beginning to look their way.

Hettie laughed and cried. 'I love you, George Mann. And I don't think there's a girl in the whole world could have had a nicer proposal!'

'And here's me thinking I'd messed it up good and proper.'

'Well, you ain't. And you know that problem you was on about, about you not being sure why I'd said yes? It's simple as pie!'

'It is?'

'Yes. George, watch out!' she cried, too late to stop them from careering into the willow overhanging the bank. The boat lurched to a halt. She stepped forward and put both arms around his neck. 'Simple. All we gotta do is get married straight off, with Hill still dug in there at the Duke. That way, ain't no one can think I'm doing it just for Pa!'

'Straight off? Now?' He fended her off. 'Get hitched now? You sure it ain't a bit sudden?'

Her eyes sparkled as she looked at him. 'George Mann, I'm thirty-six years old. What's sudden about that?' She lost him among the silvery leaves, her hat fell off into the water.

'If we don't hurry up and get cracking, we'll be drawing our old age pension!'

He leaned forward to hold her steady, then kissed her as she fell into his arms.

They married at Southwark Register Office on 21 September 1925. The family radiated happiness and even warmed the heart of the registrar, who'd tied the knot with less than obvious enthusiasm for most of his thirty-year-long career.

The next day, George and Hettie went along together to see Mr Wakeley. The manager saw them in a small downstairs office, amid the smell of fermenting hops and the sound of horses' hoofs stamping on the cobbled yard. As a hard-headed businessman, he gave nothing away about the present state of affairs at the Prince of Wales, but he noted with approval George's work as cellarman and said he would certainly keep him in mind. He made no connection between Hettie and the previous, unsuccessful interview with Maurice and Rob, on Duke's behalf. To him, she was Mrs Mann, a quiet, good-looking woman who seemed likely to do good service with her husband behind a respectable bar.

'Good job you ain't mentioned you're with the Army,' George joked. He tucked her hand inside his arm as they walked out through the yard.

'I know.' Hettie's pledge wasn't the ideal qualification for publican's wife. She included this dilemma in her prayers, and sought time to consult with the Mission commandant over it. She felt it was a problem they would have to solve when and if the time ever came.

*

Maurice used the occasion of Hettie's marriage to travel south and talk things over with Jess. They met up, for the first time in a month, almost as strangers, outside the Register Office, just in time for the short ceremony. He saw her from a distance, dressed in an elegant grey and silver outfit, with a neat brimmed hat tilted forward in the style of a man's trilby. Mo and Grace were kitted out for the wedding in new fawn coats and shiny black shoes. He felt proud and lonely. Jess came forward to embrace him and they went in together.

'I miss you,' he told her, short and sweet. It was later that day, after they'd toasted the bride and groom, and Annie had shed tears of happiness. George had stood up and thanked them, and promised them he would move mountains to oust Bertie Hill and get Duke back where he belonged. Jess and Maurice had finally driven home to Ealing and got the two over-excited children to bed. Now he sat on the edge of their own bed, watching Jess unpin her hair.

She went and sat down beside him. 'Yes, and the house ain't the same without you coming home at night,' she confessed. The rhythm of her day had changed, shifted out of balance. She missed the slow, unperceived build-up of expectation in the evening when she used to sit at her work, waiting for Maurice to arrive.

'You mean that?' He looked at her, his face drawn and miserable. His dark, strong features matched Jess's own rich colouring.

She stroked his cheek and nodded, 'Anyhow, you ain't got time to miss us that much. You're too busy building your blessed picture palaces.'

'Not twenty-four hours a day, I ain't.' He described his lodgings in a respectable Manchester suburb, which he shared with his landlady, Mrs Walters, her two Pekinese dogs, and her three other 'gentlemen'.

Jess frowned. Her initial anger against him for re-ordering their universe without consultation hadn't stood the test of separation. Already she was beginning to work around the obstacles, trying to talk the problem through with Hettie. But she often turned in ever-decreasing circles instead of coming up with any answers. 'Ett says I gotta make up my own mind,' she dropped into the conversation. 'Only, with her being married to George now, I don't reckon she'd want to take on the shop all by herself.'

'But you'd give it up?' he asked in surprise. He felt a surge of hope. During the lonely hours in his single bed, Maurice had convinced himself that Jess was more married to the shop than she was to him. He veered from sadness to bitterness, especially over his enforced separation from Grace and Mo. Being apart from them felt like an amputation, and he blamed Jess's selfishness. But now he began to regret his own high-handedness, as he saw her struggling to come to a decision. 'Come and live up north with me, and let's be a family again!'

'I can't, Maurice. I just can't!'

He gathered her to him and comforted her. 'This is bleeding stupid,' he whispered. He kissed her tears.

'And you don't hate me?' she implored.

'I love you, Jess. We can work this out. By Christmas, we'll have come up with something, don't you worry.'

The separation that had softened their anger sharpened their passion. They made love with uninhibited eagerness, rediscovering each intimacy afresh. He loved her softly curved breasts and hips. She clung to his broad, smooth shoulders, stroking the heel of her hand down his long, straight back.

Autumn loosened the leaves from the tree in the park and carpeted the grass golden-brown. A co-operative food and household goods department store opened on Coopers' old premises. Tommy O'Hagan fulfilled his boast by opening a paint and wallpaper section in the basement. He soon began to walk out with one of the pretty new shop girls, Moira Blackstone, attracted by her dark auburn hair and quick smile.

Dolly offered firm advice. 'Don't have nothing to do with that bleeding traitor,' she told a bewildered Moira, accosting her on the street outside the Prince of Wales. Moira stood waiting for Tommy, dressed in a soft-brimmed velvet hat and a matching dark blue coat. 'They should lock Tommy O'Hagan up and throw away the key for what he's done.'

Moira was startled. She'd only started work on the co-op cheese counter that Monday, and was immediately swept off her feet by Tommy's lively flattery. 'Why, what's he gone and done?' She clutched her coat tight to her throat and looked the length of the street for a means of escape.

Dolly got into her full stride. 'It ain't just me that says so. Annie thinks the same. He ain't fit to speak to. We all give him the cold shoulder these days; ain't no decent, self-respecting body will give him the time of day!' Her chin disappeared into folds of indignant flesh.

'He ain't gone and robbed a bank, has he?' Moira's imagination ran wild. Tommy didn't look like a bank robber, with his ready grin and sparkling grey eyes. But there must be something behind Dolly's account.

She snorted. 'Worse. He good as killed Duke Parsons!'

Moira gasped. 'Oh, my!'

'Yes. Might as well stick the knife straight in his back and get it over with.' She looked daggers at the sign over the pub door. 'I expect he'll take you in here for a quick drink before he takes you to the pictures?'

The girl shook her head. 'I ain't gonna go with him, after all. You say he as good as killed someone?' She backed away, stepping down into the gutter and searching in her bag for coins for the tram home. She feared she'd spotted Tommy leaving the co-op and heading up the street.

'That's what I call it. Helping to fill Bertie Hill's till is the same as signing Duke's death warrant. If he takes you in here for a drink, he's a dirty, rotten traitor, tell him.' Dolly seized Moira's arm and drew her on to the pavement. 'Tell him from me, if we don't get Hill out by Christmas, the old man won't make it through another winter. Just you tell him that!' She, too had spied Tommy, who whistled as he approached.

She left a breathless Moira to convey the message, refusing to lower herself to speak to him in person.

'Fancy a drop of something before we see the flick?' he suggested cheerily.

Moira stared at him. 'Here?' She pointed over her shoulder at the shiny new doors.

'No. Up at the Flag.' He linked arms, surprised by her stiffness. 'Ain't nothing wrong, is there?'

She took a deep breath. 'No. The Lamb and Flag, you say?' From what she could work out from Dolly's garbled story, visiting the Lamb and Flag didn't amount to a crime against the realm. For the minute, Tommy's treachery seemed to have receded. 'Right you are,' she agreed, relaxing into things.

But he'd lulled her suspicions with a decoy. After a drink at the Flag, they went down to the Gem to see the new Chaplin film, then Tommy brought her back up Duke Street and waltzed her straight through the doors of the Prince of Wales.

'A pint of best and a glass of port,' he ordered. He stood chatting at the bar with Jack Cooper, while Moira shrank into a corner.

There was only a handful of customers in the pub, two young lads from the tea and coffee counter at the co-op, new to the area like her, and an older, red-faced man with a stained waistcoat and a battered trilby hat. Much later a young man came in. Tommy was already on to his third drink. The young man scowled at her and went and slammed his money on to the bar. 'Give me a pint, Bert,' he ordered, without lifting his head in greeting.

She saw Tommy frown. Then he went up to the new-comer. 'How's tricks, Richie?' she heard him say.

The reply was mumbled. Soon Tommy left the bar and came to rejoin Moira. 'Bleeding cheerful charlie, he is.' He took a gulp from his glass. 'I bet he ain't mentioned to Sadie that he uses this as his watering-hole neither!'

'I don't like this place,' Moira whispered. 'It ain't friendly. Can't we go?'

Tommy ignored her. 'From what I hear, Richie and Rob still don't get on like a house on fire down at the depot. Walter's had to break up more than one row already.' He shook his head. 'Even I wouldn't have the brass neck to turn up here, not after what Hill done to Sadie, see. It don't seem right.'

'Let's go, Tommy.' Her evening was turning sour. She didn't understand what everyone had against the place: it was lovely and new, with posh electric lights and a brand-new, patterned carpet.

Tommy glanced at his watch. 'We can't. Not yet,' he replied. 'We gotta hang on a bit longer.'

Moira sat in the silent, almost empty bar, miserably sipping her port wine. This would be the last time she came out with Tommy O'Hagan, she decided. He ignored a girl's wishes, and he drank too much. She sulked as she watched him go unsteadily to the bar for his fifth pint of beer.

CHAPTER TWENTY-FOUR

Tommy's turncoat activities, relayed loud and clear to Annie by Dolly, were out of character. 'What's he up to?' Annie frowned and slapped her bread dough on to a floured board. 'It ain't like young Tommy to let the street down.'

Duke had heard the rumours too: Tommy was turning into a regular at the Prince of Wales. He seemed to prefer late-night drinking sessions there to keeping in with his old pals. But Duke didn't want to get involved. The days were drawing in, there was another long, idle winter ahead. He would fashion wooden toys for his new grandchildren and potter about the house as general handyman, while Annie braved the weather out on the market stall. 'Mr Baldwin's warning against an all-out strike.' He read the headline news in the evening paper. 'He wants to set up a royal commission on the miners, and much good may it do them.' He sniffed.

Annie thumped and pummelled her dough. The sweet, yeasty smell filled the kitchen. 'You ain't listening to a word I say. I'm telling you, Tommy O'Hagan's up to something. He's a cheeky little bleeder, always has been, but there ain't a bad bone in his body. No, if he's taken to lining Bertie Hill's pockets, it's gotta be for a good reason.' She scooped the dough back into the earthenware bowl, covered it with a linen cloth and set it by the range to rise a second time.

Still Duke ignored her. 'Here's an advertisement for an electric ignition set for motor cars. I'll let Rob know about that. Maybe he can get Richie to fit it to the old Bullnoses. And listen, if there's a general strike over the miners, what's the betting they just bring in the troops to keep things moving? The miners ain't got a chance, poor bleeders.' He grumbled on as he took a small pair of scissors and cut out the clipping to show his son.

Annie lost patience and began to clatter about at the sink. You ain't gonna make things no better by hiding your head in the sand,' she warned. 'I think you should pay some mind to what people round here do for you, trying to get shut of that nasty piece of work at the pub.'

He sighed. 'You think I ain't grateful?'

'No, I know you are.' Annie softened her tone and turned to face him. She dried her hands on a towel. 'I'm sorry for going on about it, Duke. Only, young Tommy's gone and got my goat, unless he *is* hiding something up his sleeve.'

He nodded. They were friends again, when they heard the latch of the front door open.

'That'll be Ernie calling in for his tea,' Annie said. She had the first batch of loaves in the oven, and there was a calm, warm feel to the room.

Ernie came in, his face red with cycling, the feeling of autumn wind about him, as he stuffed his cap into his pocket and came to sit by the fire. Annie swung the kettle on to the hob, cheered by Ernie's smiles.

Then there was a knock. Duke went and answered the door to George. 'You're just in time for a cuppa.' He led him into the kitchen. 'I think Annie's knocking together some scones. Come in, come in.'

The tall cellarman stooped his head as he went down into the kitchen and squeezed his large frame into a seat at the table, opposite Duke.

Annie made a great fuss of her new son-in-law. He and Hettie were just setting up nicely in rooms down Meredith Court. Because of his size and occupation, she made frequent comparisons between him and Duke at a young age; both built on a large scale, both correct in manner, but with hearts of gold. She made sure he had plenty of melting butter on his warm, home-made scones. They discussed the price of cheese at the new co-op. George told Ernie to look out for the forthcoming match between Palace and Bury. He sat there, passing the time of day, without a sign of there being anything unusual in his visit.

But, just as he picked up his cap to go, he cleared his throat and made an announcement. 'I came to give you a bit of good news,' he said quietly.

Annie, who was tapping out loaves on to a cooling tray, looked up sharply. 'Hettie ain't expecting already?'

George blushed. 'Give us a chance, Annie. No, it ain't that.' He turned to Duke, reluctant as ever to make long speeches, unsure how to deliver the news. 'We thought you'd like to know. Tommy O'Hagan brought in the coppers to the Prince of Wales last night. They caught Bertie Hill serving after hours.'

The news sank in. Ernie caught the word 'coppers' and assumed something bad had happened. He looked at Annie, who was standing face flushed, open-mouthed and speechless. Duke sat still as a statue.

'It seems Tommy reckoned the old boycott was getting

357

a bit long-winded. It was only grinding Hill down slowly, and Tommy wanted action. You know how he is.'

'I'll bleeding kill him!' Annie found her tongue at last. 'Leading us up the garden path, and all along he was working to get Hill out. Dolly will go spare with him.'

George was puzzled. 'You don't reckon she'll be glad to see the back of Hill?'

Annie tutted. ''Course she bleeding well will. We all will. But she'll skin him alive for not letting on. You know Dolly, she likes to be in the thick of things.' She went over to Duke and put an arm around his shoulder. 'You hear that? Tommy's a bleeding hero!'

George filled the silence by explaining in detail to Ernie, 'Everything worked out fine. The police will get Hill into court for breaking the law over hours, see. Hill will be out on his ear, thanks to Tommy. He didn't let anyone in on his little plan because he didn't want the word to get back to Hill. Once he got the evidence that he was serving after hours regular, he got the coppers in. They came last night and closed the place down, no messing. And you know something? Tommy ain't breathed a word to no one about the part he played. It was Dolly. She saw the pub locked up and set about finding out from the brewery what was up. Word leaked out about an hour ago.'

Ernie nodded. His face lit up. 'Does this mean we can all go home, then?'

Annie quickly came and gave him a hug. 'No, I'm afraid it don't, Ern. It's good news to get Hill out. But it don't mean we can all go back.'

Again George cleared his throat. 'Now, don't go raising your hopes too high,' he warned. 'But Hettie and me, we got our name down with the brewery. And if we get the licence, we want you and Annie and Ernie to move right back in with us. Ett said to come over and tell you straight away. I telephoned her at the shop when I heard Hill was out. She said to tell you we was in with a chance.'

'And you let us sit here drinking tea and talking about football as if nothing had happened?' Annie advanced on George in mock outrage. 'Why, you and Tommy O'Hagan, the pair of you, I could . . . why, I don't know what I could do!' Speechless, she flung her arms around George's neck.

Slowly Duke stood up and walked to the door. He shook his head. 'Thanks, son.' There was a catch in his voice as he turned away.

George shot a look at Annie. 'I ain't upset him, have I?'

'No, you just made his dream come alive again.' Her own voice choked. 'Go and see him, George. I'll wait here with Ernie.' She blew her nose and set to, refilling the kettle at the tap. 'Come on, Ern, wash these few pots before you get back to work. Look lively.'

George followed Duke into the front parlour. Annie's aspidistra stood in its round, glazed pot in the window. The cream lace curtains hung in neat folds. A marble-cased clock ticked on the mantelpiece. Duke sat himself in an upright chair beside the polished, empty grate.

'We ain't got the place, not yet.' George stood awkwardly at the door, holding the peak of his cap in both hands. 'But we gotta be high on their list. I got experience, and I know my way around the old place. With Hill out of the way, Ett thought I should let you know how things stood.'

Duke looked across the room at him. He tried to clear his throat. 'You're a good lad, George. Thanks.'

He nodded. 'I'd best be on my way then.' He was

uncomfortable for the old man. Sometimes hope was harder to bear than defeat. 'Ett says she'll come over after she finishes at work.'

At first, Duke didn't answer. Then he made an effort to get to his feet. He came to shake hands. 'Let me tell you something, George. I don't mind telling you, there ain't much left in life for an old man like me. But if there's one thing that would make everything right before I die, it's to end my days in the old Duke of Wellington.' He clasped the younger man's hand between his own and shook it. 'Now, if it don't turn out that way, it ain't for the want of trying, and I'll die thankful for all you done. You and the whole family. The whole street.' His eyes filled up as he released George's hand.

Grudgingly Dolly had to admit that Tommy was the hero of the hour. Not a soul spared an ounce of pity for Bertie Hill, who took to his room in the tenement, having failed to persuade his ex-colleagues in the police force to let him stay open at the Prince of Wales until the case came to court. The brewery moved in quickly to sack him, and let it be known that the pub would re-open under new management just as soon as possible. They wanted to settle things quickly, before lucrative Christmas trade was lost. Now the whole of Paradise Court had to keep their fingers crossed for George Mann.

October winds tore the leaves from the trees. Yellow chrysanthemums appeared on the flower stalls in the street markets. The government awaited the commission's report on the miners. Trade was slow in the docks as winter crept in.

Perhaps it was general gloom in the country and scant

business for the taxi firm that put Rob's temper on a short fuse throughout October. Contented with family life, he tried not to present a worried face to Amy, and he doted on his son, Bobby, now six months old and thriving.

But at work it was a different story. He and Walter fought to keep trade buoyant by fixing their fares low. But it meant they had to be on call when sensible men were at home with their families, and Richie's wage, which they'd been spared throughout the summer, was hard to find.

Walter worked through thick and thin. Decent to the core, he didn't resent Richie's return. Seeing Sadie recover her old sparkling eye was enough, knowing that he, Walter, had played some part in bringing her back together with the man she loved. Every baby should have a father, he reasoned. God knew, too many didn't these days. He thought of the families torn apart by war, and the millions who never returned. When he looked at things on this big scale, he saw his own sacrifice as small.

But he worried about the grating, tense relationship between Rob and Richie. Rob's worry about business translated into a bullying attitude: he was always picking on Richie for slow or shoddy work, expecting him to put in unreasonable hours for what, after all, was a poor wage for a trained mechanic. Walter knew that it was only Sadie's continued part-time work as a typist that kept the wolf from their door. 'Leave him be,' Walter advised. 'He's a good mechanic, when all's said and done.'

But Rob was irritated by Richie's very presence. There was something about his look: the eyes, the slightly slouching posture that seemed to challenge, a take-it-or-leave-it attitude that was insulting, once picked up and taken personally. Whenever he came out of the office into the workshop, Rob would have to hold back what amounted to a loathing of Richie. Instead, he would niggle and argue over the best way of carrying out a repair, nit-picking over Richie's slapdash timekeeping, making it plain who was the boss.

For his part, Richie enjoyed getting under Rob's skin without making the slightest effort. He'd taken up the job again under sufferance, as part of the deal for getting back with Sadie. He had no regrets there: Sadie was loving, and seemingly contented with the way things had worked out. They both cared for Meggie with blind devotion. Only, Richie could not swallow his resentment against Rob, who had always held something against him and had sacked him for no good cause. He'd taken to drinking at the Prince of Wales, knowing that Rob would find out and hate him more bitterly. He admitted as much to Sadie, when, hurt and tearful, she had objected to his use of the place.

'Ain't there nowhere else you can go for your pint?' she cried.

He'd shrugged.

'Yes, and even if you're doing it to get back at Rob, can't you see what it's doing to me?'

'It's only a bleeding pub, for God's sake.'

'So why does it have to be *that* pub, then? Don't it make no difference what Hill tried to do to me?'

He felt low and sneaking, but he wouldn't back down. 'Listen,' he said. 'I'm with you now, ain't I? If Hill tried something again, I'd kill him with my bare hands. But it ain't gonna stop me drinking where I want.'

Sadie had to admit defeat, and accept that Richie was set on a course that didn't include finer feelings such as family loyalty.

*

They got through most of October, on tenterhooks for news from the brewery, sitting on the keg of gunpowder that was the relationship between the taxi boss and his mechanic.

After school on Hallowe'en, Jess brought Grace and Mo to Paradise Court with turnip lanterns, to meet up in the street with the O'Hagans. Jess herself planned a chat with Annie and Duke. Frances was to come over, with home-made toffee for the children. Hettie, Sadie and Amy were all due for tea; it was to be a great gathering of the women. By six o'clock Annie's little house was bursting at the seams, while down the next court, Richie was still hard at work fixing the brake rods on Rob's Morris.

'Ain't you finished yet?' Rob looked at his watch. He had to pick up a fare in ten minutes.

Richie, stretched full-length under the car, said it was a job that couldn't be rushed. 'These rods are rusted pretty bad,' he advised. 'And the split pin through this one is snapped clean in two, see.' He flung two pieces of metal sideways. They landed at Rob's feet.

Rob bent to pick them up. 'How long will you be?' Walter was out on another fare. 'Can't you get a move on?'

Richie eased himself clear of the car and hauled himself to his feet. 'I need the right size pin to fit back in,' he muttered. He went to search in a metal box sitting on the oily workbench.

'And a lot you bleeding care, by the look of things.' Rob was beginning to fume. 'I suppose you think tomorrow morning's soon enough?'

Richie found a pin that would do, and slid back under the car. He worked silently, watching Rob's legs and feet stalk the length of the workshop with their characteristic, heavy limp.

'Bleeding hell!' Rob threw a cigarette butt to the ground. After five more minutes, his patience was exhausted. He watched as Richie slid out from under the car for a second time. 'What now?'

Richie wiped his forehead with the back of his hand, smearing oil on to his face. 'I gotta test the brakes, don't I?' He reached for the door-handle, as if to climb in.

Exasperated, Rob caught hold of his arm. 'No time for that!'

Richie reacted as if he'd been burnt. He jerked his arm free and rounded on Rob.

Rob stepped quickly back. 'Touchy all of a sudden, ain't we?'

'Look who's talking.' Deliberately, with his face set in a sneer, Richie brushed off his sleeve where Rob had caught it.

The action felt like a slap in the face. 'You keep a civil tongue in your head,' he warned, stabbing his finger at the mechanic. 'Or you'll find yourself short of a job again.'

Richie drew air through his nostrils. 'And what'll you tell Sadie this time? That you gave me the sack 'cos I wanted to check the brakes?'

The comment rubbed salt in Rob's wound. He knew all too well that Sadie and Meggie's future rested on Richie keeping his job at the depot. He was trapped good and proper, and his reaction was to get deeper into the argument. 'You're too big for your bleeding boots!' he accused, forgetting the waiting passenger, forgetting his promises to Amy to stay calm when Richie riled him.

'And what'll you tell your lovely missus, eh?' Richie eyed him with contempt. 'Ain't many men tied to two sets of apron strings, like you, Mister Parsons.'

Rob launched himself at Richie and grabbed his open

shirt collar. His face came within inches of Richie's, saliva gathered at the corners of his mouth. 'You take that back, you hear?'

Richie would rather have died. 'I expect you think you've got it all worked out,' he sneered. 'Nice little business, nice wife, nice kid.' He outstared his opponent, gripping his wrists and wrenching Rob's hands from his collar. He pushed him back and turned away.

'What's that supposed to mean?' Rob felt his blood run cold. Richie meant something by that remark; something that Rob knew nothing about, that was going to make him look a fool in the eyes of the world.

'Nothing.'

'Yes, bleeding something!' He ran at Richie. Richie shoved him to one side, overbalancing Rob and sending the metal box clattering from the bench.

'You don't want to hear.'

'I'll break your bleeding neck.' Rob gasped with rage.

'I'm telling you, you don't want to hear.' Richie was so confident that he stuck his hands in his pockets. His desire to damage Rob went deep, but he didn't intend to do it with his fists. 'Why don't you ask your wife what I'm on about?'

Rob shook his head. 'What's Amy got to do with this?'

'Ain't she put you up to giving me my job back?' Richie's grin was insolent. He watched Rob's outrage swell and explode.

'So bleeding what?'

'So, she thought she'd better keep me sweet. She knew I knew. Stupid cow, she thought if she made up to me, I'd keep my mouth shut!'

'Knew what, for God's sake?' Beside himself, Rob grabbed a heavy spanner from the workbench and lunged again at Richie. He pinned him against the wall. 'You spit it out,' he demanded, like a man who knows he's just signed his own death warrant. He levered the spanner against Richie's throat, as if to throttle him.

Eye to eye, in bare hatred, Richie delivered the sentence. 'Amy ain't been a very good girl before she married you, Rob. She tells you you're the kid's pa, but you ain't. It's Eddie Bishop. We all enjoyed the laugh being on you. Bishop made himself scarce over the water, see. He weren't keen on being a pa, it seems. So Amy comes to you, and you fall for it!' He laughed.

Rob felt the strength drain from his body. He dropped the spanner and bent forward, leaning one hand against the wall. All the colour left his face. The pain was in his chest, his guts, from head to toe. With a yell he launched himself from the wall, pounding at Richie, feeling his fists make contact with muscles, skin and bone.

Richie defended himself. He ducked and grabbed Rob's waist, dragged him to the floor. The two men rolled and kicked. Rob lashed out with his fists: nothing mattered except to grind Richie's face to a pulp. He saw the blood, felt his own mouth begin to bleed.

CHAPTER TWENTY-FIVE

As Walter drove down Meredith Court towards the depot, he was in time to see the two men on the ground, still struggling. He ran in to separate them. Not caring who got in the way, Rob hit out in all directions, but at last Walter forced them apart and dragged them to their feet.

Rob's breath came in short, harsh gasps. Richie wiped his nose and mouth, head down, refusing to meet Walter's gaze.

'Get him out of here!' Rob yelled. 'Get him out before I do him in!' He seized a heavy pair of pliers from the bench and aimed them, ready to throw in Richie's face. 'And don't never set foot in here again, or I'll fix your dirty mouth for good I'll swing for you, Richie Palmer, I mean it! Get him out,' he gasped at Walter.

But there was no need. Wiping the blood from his face, Richie looked at them from under hooded eyes. 'Stick your bleeding job,' he told them. He left without his coat and cap, limping up Meredith Court towards the Flag.

Once he was gone, Rob collapsed forward, bent double, holding his arms tight around his stomach.

'Are you hurt?' Walter grabbed hold of him to stop him from falling.

Rob struggled for breath. 'No.' With an effort, he

straightened up. 'Collect this next fare for me, will you, Walt? I gotta go up home and have a word with Amy.'

He didn't wait for a reply, but set off, running as best he could up on to Duke Street, to catch her before she set off for tea at Annie's.

Amy had just wiped Bobby's face clean and put him into the perambulator in the downstairs hallway. She stepped out on to Duke Street, tucking the blankets well up under the baby's chin and heading briskly across the street to Paradise Court. She was already late, having waited for Bobby to finish his nap before she got him ready to go out. She was passing her mother's house when Rob headed her off.

'Oh no you don't!' He swerved the pram in towards the doorstep and hammered on the door. They heard someone come running.

'What is it, Rob? Oh my God, you look terrible.' She saw that his eyes were cut and puffy, his nose bleeding.

Charlie flung open the door and called straight away for Dolly, who ran to investigate. Rob thrust the pram handle towards her. 'Look after the kid. Amy's coming home with me!'

Amy felt herself dragged by the arm, back up the street. She ran to keep up, losing her hat, as Rob took her blindly through the traffic and back up their own stairs. He slammed the door behind them and stood facing her.

'You hurt my wrist,' she cried, sobbing from fear and frustration. 'What the bleeding hell got into you?'

'You tell me, Amy. You tell me God's honest truth. Have you lied to me about Bobby? Is Eddie Bishop his real pa? Is he?'

Amy backed off against the far wall. For a moment she struggled to make sense of what he was saying. The name,

Eddie Bishop, flew at her from nowhere. She put a hand to her mouth and sobbed.

'Tell me. Cry all you like, it don't make no difference. You gotta tell me the truth.' He stood in agony, as if his life depended on it. If it turned out to be true, that he wasn't Bobby's father after all, and that Amy had tricked him into marriage, he felt he would wreak a terrible revenge.

Amy saw what it meant. She knew in a flash what this would do to her and Rob, and quelled a rising panic. She must stay calm. As a great force swept through her, threatening to blow her apart, she held fast to the one fact that he wanted to hear. Holding her hurt wrist in the palm of her other hand, she stopped sobbing and looked him straight in the eye. 'I ain't lied to you, Rob. I don't know who's put you up to this, but there ain't a grain of truth in it.' She spoke calmly, willing him to believe.

'Sure?' Rob closed his eyes. He was shaking. 'You sure Bobby's mine?' Flesh of his flesh. His own son.

'I'm sure.' By her own calculations, it had been the night of Wiggin's disappearance. She explained it now to Rob, pinning down the time and place. 'What more can I say?' She bit her lip, waiting for him to open his eyes.

His head went down, he took a huge sigh. 'I'm his pa?' he repeated.

Amy went and took him in her arms. 'As sure as I'm standing here, Rob.' She rocked him to and fro. 'It's Richie what done this, ain't it? He's got his knife into you again. Well, don't take no notice. Bobby's your baby.'

They cried together, until Rob came round and swore to knock Richie's block off for trying to ruin Amy's name. She grinned. 'Looks like you already done that.' She went for warm water and cotton-wool to bathe his face.

A few minutes later, they recognized Dolly's knock. She

entered in full war cry, demanding to know what Rob had done to her girl, swearing that if he so much as laid a finger on her she'd see him sent down for good. She'd rushed out of the house in her carpet-slippers and apron, armed with a poker; a formidable sight.

Amy dried her eyes. She explained the whole thing. 'Ain't no real harm done,' she finished. 'Rob believes me, don't you, Rob? And he stuck up for me, see, Ma. Now put that poker down and don't take on.'

'No harm done! Don't take on!' Dolly spluttered. 'He only set out to ruin a girl's good name, that's all.'

'Well, Rob's given him the sack.' Amy led her mother to a chair.

'Wait till I tell your pa!' She was unstoppable now. 'Wait till I tell Charlie and Annie and Duke! Richie Palmer ain't gonna get away with this.' She was up and out of the room and down the stairs before they could stop her.

'Me and my big mouth.' Amy sighed. 'Now the whole bleeding street will know.' Her ma didn't recognize the word discretion.

Rob, still recovering from the battering around his heart, found it was his turn to comfort her. Amy began sobbing for the loss of her reputation. 'Mud sticks,' she cried. 'Sling it in my direction, and there's plenty round here that'll believe it.'

'And they'll answer to me if they do,' he promised. He felt strong again. Amy couldn't be lying now. The worm of doubt lay still.

By the time they went down to collect Bobby from Dolly's, the street was already awash with rumour. Liz and Nora got it straight from the horse's mouth: Dolly told them that Richie Palmer had tried to drag her girl's name into the mud, but Rob stuck up for her and gave him a good hiding. Richie was a nasty piece of work. Charlie confirmed to Tommy that Rob had a pair of black eyes, but he'd heard Richie Palmer was in an even worse state. Arthur joined the fray. If anyone dragged down the Ogden name, he said, standing at the bar of the Flag with his fist around the handle of a pint glass later that evening, they'd have him to answer to.

The episode had broken up the Hallowe'en gathering at Annie's house. When they heard, via Grace and Rosie, that the street was in uproar, Frances straight away volunteered to go up to Powells' to see if Rob's injuries needed any further attention. Hettie promised to take Sadie and Meggie home.

'She's had a shock,' Annie whispered. 'Not that we couldn't see it coming a mile off.' They'd all known how unhealthy it was for Rob and Richie to be working together, but they'd hoped it would work out, for Sadie's sake. 'Look after her. God knows when Richie will show up. I can't see no light in Edith's house, can you?' She went up and hugged an unresponsive Sadie. 'You're sure you won't stay here?'

Sadie shook her head. 'No, I'd best get back home with Meggie.' Her voice was hollow and flat. She wanted to talk to Richie before she jumped to any conclusions, but the shock of what he'd just done cut deep.

It dug beneath the false gloss she'd tried to put on her present situation, to those layers of uncertainty over Richie's treatment of her and her family. If he truly loved her, how could he carry on the feud with Rob, for a start? If he wanted to give Meggie a home and family, how could he spend so much of what he earned at the Prince of Wales? This latest row over Amy was scarcely a surprise, even to her. It seemed that Richie had a mission to destroy Rob in whatever way he could, and it didn't matter that in the process he would destroy her love for him.

Sadie stood outside Edith's house and insisted to Hettie that she would go in by herself. 'It looks like he's gone and done it this time,' she said with an empty smile. 'But don't you worry about me; Ett. I can manage.'

Hettie kissed her cold cheek. 'Annie says remember she's just across the street if you need her.'

Sadie nodded and carried a sleeping Meggie up the stairs.

She found Richie sitting alone in the dark. She started, then she went quietly next door to put Meggie into her crib. She turned on a small paraffin lamp on the living-room table and sat down, waiting for an explanation.

'I ain't gonna say I'm sorry,' he began, his voice more slurred than ever. He'd drunk himself calm at the Flag, but his mind was fuddled. He'd stumbled home to wait for Sadie.

'I never thought you would.' Sadie sat upright; staring straight ahead. Her face was lit down one side by the yellow flame. Inside she felt numb.

'That brother of yours deserves everything he gets, always picking on me, never leaving me be.'

'I expect he does.'

'What are you so bleeding cool about?' Richie turned his frustration against her. 'You heard I got the sack?'

'Yes,' she said. 'Again.' She folded her hands in her lap. 'I heard all about it from Dolly.'

'Snooty bleeding cow.'

'Keep your voice down, Richie. You'll wake Meggie.'

He took no notice. 'On your high horse. Miss High and Bleeding Mighty!'

She sighed. 'Ain't you done enough for one day?' She glanced at his swollen face, his cut hands.

'Oh yes, take *their* side, why don't you?' Incoherent guilt gnawed at him. He knew that everything lay in ruins, but he wouldn't take responsibility for it. 'Well, I'm sick up to here with you and your bleeding family!'

'So I see.' In turn, Sadie couldn't refrain from her snide little remarks. It was either this or break down in tears at the impending disaster.

'"So I see!"' he mimicked. 'Well, let them pick up the pieces, if they're so good and bleeding holy.'

'I never said they was. I never said nothing, Richie.' Slowly she looked at him. The angry, battered man sitting there in the dark was not the person she thought she loved. His sullen silences were no longer romantic, but destructive. His physical strength conveyed moral clumsiness; she thought him dishonourable. All this she realized in a single, icy moment.

Richie sprang from his chair. Instantly she cowered back. 'Oh,' he sneered, 'so now I batter my girl?'

She sat up straight again, avoiding his eyes. 'What will you do?' She knew they'd reached the point of no return.

'Go.' He was cruel, careless.

'Well, before you do, I want to say something.' She stood, only shoulder level to him, looking up at him. 'I want to say I don't believe a word of what you said against Amy, and it was a nasty thing to do.' Richie sneered again, about to interrupt, but she held up her hand. 'No, I don't want to hear no more. I think you're a fool, Richie, to throw all this away. Yes, like a spoilt child. You turn your back on Meggie and me now, you run away again and I never want to speak to you no more.

'We're better off managing by ourselves, just the two of us, and I won't stick up for you no more. Rob's worth ten of you for being man enough to give you your job back, and Walter's worth more than the pair of you put together, only I was too slow and blind to see it. Go on, Richie, hit me, why don't you?'

This time she didn't shrink as he raised his hand. Her stare beat it down. 'I done all I can, Richie, to give little Meggie a good start. But I don't call it fair when you pick rows with my family and drag Amy's name down.'

Sadie ran out of breath. She couldn't find the strength to say any more. She turned and went quietly into the bedroom. Richie was a big man, but he had no real courage. He was small in mind and deed. Quickly her contempt rose, allowing her to steel herself to the sound of the door slamming, and Richie's footsteps disappearing down the stairs. The front door banged. She sat a long time in silence.

Three boys sat on the step of the Lamb and Flag, their stuffed Guy sprawled across the pavement, a cap upturned ready to receive pennies, when Arthur Ogden stumbled out late that same night. George Mann, just going off-duty, helped him negotiate the exit and threw a halfpenny into the kids' cap.

'Watch it, Arthur,' he said cheerfully, as the older man swayed and set his own cap askew on his head. 'And mind how you go!'

The kids called after him. 'Wotch it, Arfer! Moind 'ow y'gow!'

'Cheeky monkeys!' He turned and hit out at them. They ducked and rolled away laughing. Arthur steered his own unsteady course up on to Duke Street.

George turned up his jacket collar and headed for home. Meredith Court was lit by gas-lamps. His own new lodgings were halfway down, midway between two pools of light. As he set off, he saw a shadowy figure moving ahead of him, towards the bottom of the court. He frowned as he identified it. Still unsure as he climbed his own stairs, he greeted Hettie with a preoccupied kiss. 'I think I just seen Richie Palmer heading down to the depot,' he reported.

Hettie's heart sank. 'What's he want there at this time of night?' She went to the window, parted the curtains and peered down into the dark street. 'Are you sure it was him, George?'

'I couldn't swear. I only caught a glimpse. I'm only saying it looked like him, that's all.' Uneasily he took off his jacket and warmed himself at the fire.

'Maybe he went back to get his coat,' Hettie suggested. She herself had just arrived back from Annie's house, having learnt all the details of the row between Rob and Richie from Walter Davidson.

'And pigs might fly,' he said dubiously.

She looked at him. 'That ain't like you, George. What's wrong? You think he's up to no good?'

George felt the warmth of the fire penetrate his face and hands. He sighed. Hettie came up to him and put her arms around him. They swayed in a long embrace.

'No,' he said, tempted to dismiss the shadowy figure. 'Maybe I was imagining things.' He held Hettie and kissed her. The novelty of being married, of having her to come home to, after all the years of respectable walking out, made him feel like a kid. He wrapped his arms around her and made a show of his feeling, kissing her softly and leading her towards their bedroom.

Hettie smiled, then sighed.

'What is it?' He cupped her cheek in the palm of his hand, murmuring against her.

'Sadie.' She thought of her youngest sister, and what the future held for her now. She looked up at George. 'What if Richie ain't just gone back for his belongings?' she asked uneasily.

Meanwhile, Richie hoped that he'd slipped down Meredith Court unseen. He kept to the shadowy parts of the street, using his own key to open up the outer gates of the depot, and leaving the padlock off as he stole across the yard to the workshop. What he planned to do would be the work of five minutes.

He switched on the electric light over the workbench and took hold of the heavy pair of pliers that Rob had threatened him with, then he eased himself under Rob's stationary car. No one had moved it since earlier that evening, when the final row had brewed.

Richie knew exactly what he was doing as he examined the underside of the old car. There, where the brake rods led up to the pedal, was the crucial main joint; a yoke which connected the rods to the pedal. It was held in place by a clevis pin. He got into position, then used the pliers to wrench the new split-pin from the clevis pin. It looked like a long, steel tooth with a forked root. He grunted, pocketed the pin, and edged out from under the car. The yoke wouldn't immediately fall apart. But some day soon, Rob would be driving along, he would hit a bump, the yoke would work loose. Then the brake rods would disconnect, he would put his foot on the pedal, and nothing would happen . . .

Richie slithered out. He caught sight of his own reflection, cut and bruised, in the windscreen. His rage wasn't spent yet. Taking his jacket from its hook on the workshop wall, he wrapped its thickness around his forearm and bludgeoned at the small pane of glass above the handle on the door into the tiny office. Then he freed his hand, shook out the shattered glass and reached through to take a spare key hanging inside. He used this to open the office door, then he went and took up a long screwdriver and used it to prise open the cash drawer. Inside was a handful of coins. He snatched them all.

By the time George had responded to Hettie's unease, had put on his jacket and braved the cold night air to go quietly down the court to investigate, Richie had stolen the petty cash and fled. He left the light on and the outer doors unlocked, careless about who discovered the break-in. Realizing that something was amiss, George stepped inside to survey the scene. There was a pane of broken glass in the office door, and the cash drawer had been forced open. He ran up to Powells'. He had to get Rob out of bed to bring him down to the depot to see what Richie had done.

'It's my fault,' he said, shaking his head at the missing money. 'I should've followed him down straight away.'

Rob stepped on to the glass and wrenched the empty drawer out of the desk. 'Bleeding bastard!' he swore, flinging the drawer against the wall. 'He's gone and done it this time, at any rate!'

'How much is missing?'

Rob shrugged. 'A few shillings. A couple of quid at the most.'

'Will you call the coppers?' George was worried as he studied Rob's pale, bitter face.

He shook his head. 'Good riddance,' he snapped. 'What I say is, it's cheap at the price!'

*

Sadie didn't think so. Losing Richie had cost her dearly. All her hopes of sharing the pleasure of Meggie with him, of planning for the future and feeling his love as the mainstay of her existence lay smashed. Only the necessity of feeding and caring for the baby held her together. In her despair she blamed herself. It was her fault entirely that Richie had fought with Rob and broken into the depot in his final spiteful act. It was her fault that Amy had been dragged down, her fault that she'd fallen for Richie in the first place and misread his character. She was unable to rouse herself from this self-pitying guilt, even when visitors came to the house; Frances, Walter, her pa and Annie.

'I been a fool,' she said over and over, sitting pale and drawn by the empty grate.

Annie took the poker and rattled the ashes into the pan. 'You can say that again.' She frowned at Duke and gestured for him to go and leave the two of them alone together.

'Right, I'll take Meggie out for a stroll,' he suggested, rising stiffly to his feet. 'It ain't too cold, is it?' It was four days after Richie's disappearance, and Sadie showed no sign of rallying. In fact, she seemed to be fading, day by day. She took no interest in anything, not even in the brewery's decision over the licence, which was due to be announced any day now.

'Good idea.' Annie nodded her approval. 'Give you both a bit of fresh air. Don't be long, mind. I left Nora to keep an eye on my stall, said I'd be back in half an hour.' She bustled into the bedroom and brought Meggie out, well wrapped up, looking sleepily around. She went down and laid her in the pram in the hall, then she stood in the doorway, waving Duke off up the court. She went back up to Sadie.

'Pleased as punch,' she commented. 'There he goes,

378

head up, chest out, strutting along. He was just the same with Grace when she was little. And Mo, when he came along.'

Sadie's face broke into a faint smile.

'That's more like it.' Annie went back to scooping the ashes from the hearth and brushing it clean. Then she rolled sheets of old newspaper and bent the tubes into a loose knot, laid several of these, stacked kindling against them and put a match to it all. Soon she was placing coal on to the growing flames. 'Ain't it time you tried to pull yourself together?' she said at last, looking shrewdly at Sadie from her kneeling position by the fire.

Sadie shook her head. 'I'm sorry, Annie.'

Her stepmother rose to her feet, frowning. 'Don't be. Don't be sorry. Get mad, girl. Take a swipe at something. Swear your bleeding head off. Being sorry never did no one no good. Being sorry will eat you away inside. Who are you sorry for, when all's said and done?' She pummelled at the cushion behind Sadie's back and made her sit up straight.

'Myself,' came the small reply.

'Exactly. And what for? So, Richie went and left you. Well, I ain't no Gypsy Rose Lee, but I could've told you he weren't the type to stick.'

'He said he loved me.'

'And most likely he did.' Annie refused to relent at Sadie's pitiful tone. 'Or what he called "love". With men like him, what's it mean? Wiggin said he loved me, once.'

Sadie stared. 'Richie ain't like Wiggin.'

'Not yet, he ain't,' came the firm reply. 'Look, if you have to feel sorry for someone, feel sorry for him. What's he got? He ain't got a job no more, he ain't got a baby to care for, he ain't got you to love him. And what have you got? You got Meggie and you got us.' She shook her head, stooping to look Sadie full in the face. 'It ain't nice to be left in the cart, I know that. But life ain't a bottomless pit, and sooner or later you're gonna stop falling and come to your senses. Only, let's make it sooner, eh?' She stroked Sadie's white cheek, saw her listless eyes fill with tears. 'Go ahead, you have a good cry,' she whispered.

Sadie let the tears fall. She put her head into her hands and sobbed, while Annie held her shoulders. Eventually she stopped.

'Good. Now, dry them eyes. Don't let your pa come back and catch you crying. That's right.' Annie kissed her cheek. 'That's the girl I know!'

Sadie took a deep breath and stood up to comb her hair. She washed her face in cold water. 'Right,' she said, 'what's the word from the brewery?' She began to make tea, looking out of the window for Duke and Meggie.

'Nothing yet,' Annie replied, satisfied that Sadie was over the worst. It was a long journey back to feeling she could face the world again, but she'd made a start. 'Poor George and Ett, they're on tenterhooks. And as for your pa, he can't hardly sleep nor eat for fretting about it.'

'Penny for the Guy!' The cry went up along the dark, damp streets. Bonfires took shape on patches of waste ground and in the parks all through the East End. On the morning of 5 November the rain came down relentlessly.

'Bleeding lovely,' Rob said. He peered miserably out on to the depot yard at the dancing puddles. He stepped to one side as Walter turned up his collar and pulled his woollen scarf high under his chin.

The rain dripped from the brim of his hat the moment Walter stepped out. 'I'll be back by eleven,' he called as he bent to turn the starter-handle. 'Look, Rob, I gotta take your cab while the sparking plugs on mine dry out. All right? I gotta pick up a fare from Waterloo and take it over the water.' He jumped in and slammed the car door.

Standing in the shelter of the garage arch, Rob nodded and swore that one day soon they would fit those electric ignition sets his pa went on about. No more starting up in the rain.

Inside the cab, Walter flung his sodden hat down on the passenger seat and drove out through the puddles, up Meredith Court.

There was nothing in his mind, except rain, as he negotiated Duke Street. This was the scene – the market stalls, the shops, trams rattling by, errand boys leaning their bikes against lamp-posts – that he'd known all his life. He waved at Tommy O'Hagan, stopped by Powells' and went down Paradise Court to see if there was anything Sadie wanted from the shops.

She looked up from the sink in Edith's back kitchen at the dark splashes of rain on his jacket. She gave a grateful smile. 'Ain't nothing I want that money can buy,' she said sadly.

He shrugged and promised to call in later with a treat for her tea.

'I don't deserve a treat.' She sighed, overcome by his kindness. Walter didn't know what it meant to bear a grudge. He was always steady, always kind.

'And I got a fare waiting at Waterloo.' He backed off before she got herself visibly upset. 'See you later?'

She nodded and took a deep breath. 'Thanks, Walter. For everything.'

He grinned awkwardly and went out. The rain had eased, but the pavement and gutter stood in huge, grey puddles.

Walter stepped into Rob's cab and set off, noticing the boys wheeling out their sodden Guys on home-made carts knocked up out of orange boxes and old pram wheels. He drove on in a good mood.

Sadie and he had slipped back into their old friendship since Richie had gone off for good. Apart from a few odd bruises under Rob's eyes, the whole street had managed to put the whole affair out of mind.

Though Amy lamented her 'ruined' reputation, they all knew she was tough as old boots in that respect. If anything, poor Sadie was the one who had lost most face. But even she was back on her feet, as Walter made it his business to check. He whistled as he drove, cursing the omnibuses that lurched from the kerb into the middle of the road without warning.

By the railway arch at the top of the street he turned left, nipping down side streets to miss the main traffic. He was late. When he came out on to a fairly empty stretch of Bear Lane, he put his foot down.

It happened every day; he was rushing to collect a fare, taking a few short cuts. There was nothing unusual, except perhaps the stiffer steering on Rob's car and the greasy surface of the road after rain.

A boy ran out from an alleyway. Walter saw him cut in front of a stationary taxi, and out on to the street. He wore grey braces and black, knee-length trousers. His head was shaved almost bare, and his thick boots were tied with pieces of string. He glanced sideways at Walter from under lowered brows. He was in a hurry, and no approaching taxicab would stop him from darting into the street, straight through a puddle, straight into the path of the car.

Walter slammed on the brake. Nothing happened. He pressed again. The rods flew apart and clattered to the cobbled ground. Sparks flew. The car kept on. Walter saw the boy's face, saw his hand go up to protect himself.

He swerved. The brake was useless. He tore at the handbrake, too late. He missed the boy, but the swerve took the taxi on to its two offside wheels, at a wild angle across the street. A tram rattled towards it, a steel giant, thundering along its track. Walter wrenched at the wheel, righted the car, too late to avoid the tram.

There was a crunch of metal, crumpling like paper. A moment's silence, before a woman screamed, the tram driver jumped to the ground and ran to the car. It lay upside-down, its wheels still spinning, the cab section invisible under the front end of the tram.

CHAPTER TWENTY-SIX

Doctors and nurses kept visitors at bay. The corridors of the infirmary were crowded with stretchers and wheelchairs, with silent, upright young women in starched uniforms and important-looking men with a dozen jobs to do.

They told Rob and Sadie that Walter had been badly injured in a traffic accident, that his case was an emergency, that they would have to sit quiet and wait for news.

Sadie sat with a tight band of fear around her heart as the inexorable hospital machine wheeled an invisible Walter into the operating theatre. His ribs were crushed, there were internal injuries. He had been unconscious when they pulled him from the wreck, and so far no one had been able to establish the cause of the accident.

Rob sat holding Sadie's hand. Annie had come along with Duke, to help keep an eye on Sadie, who was the most shocked of them all. They all held their silent vigil.

Outside, rain fell once more, and the wind battered against the long windows of the infirmary waiting-room. Duke recalled the time, eleven years earlier, when Rob had been sent home from the front, badly wounded. History had almost repeated itself again, except for the freak chance of it being Walter who had taken Rob's cab out in the rain.

384

'They say he swerved out of the path of a young lad to save his life,' Sadie told Annie more than once.

She nodded and slipped her hand into Sadie's. They must be patient and keep hoping. The afternoon ticked by, daylight faded. There was still no news.

'Mr Parsons?' A nurse came through, looking for Rob.

He got up.

'The doctor says you can see Mr Davidson now.'

Instinctively, Sadie jumped to her feet. 'Can I come?' she asked Rob, clinging to his hand. Rob glanced at the nurse.

'Just the two of you, then,' she argued with a curt nod, imagining perhaps that Sadie was the injured man's girl.

Mechanically, Rob and Sadie followed her through double doors, down a long, polished corridor. The pervading smell of disinfectant momentarily distracted Rob's attention, brought him out of his state of bewilderment. 'How is he?' he asked, walking quickly to keep up with the nurse.

'Comfortable.'

'Meaning what? Is he awake?'

'Not yet, Mr Parsons.'

'What's wrong with him, do they know?'

'You'll have to ask the doctor. I only know they've sent him on to the ward and made him comfortable.'

The nurse paused to swing to the left into a cream room with twenty or so iron beds, a central aisle, and a high ceiling, arched and raftered like a chapel. 'This way.' She did her duty coolly, efficiently, in her quaint, nun-like uniform with the starched collar and stiff head-dress. She led them to a bed at the far end of the ward and quietly left them alone with Walter.

Sadie approached the bed while Rob hung back. A wire

cage lifted the bedclothes clear of Walter's injured ribs, obscuring his face. She went down between his bed and the empty neighbouring one, saw his eyes closed, unprepared for stitches in his forehead, the deathly pallor of his skin. She caught her breath.

A doctor approached on the far side of the bed, standing over his patient. He was a stern, sturdy man with slicked, grey hair, immaculately parted, and a dark moustache, and was dressed in an everyday suit, a watch-chain slung neatly across his chest. He studied the wound on Walter's forehead, lifted the bedclothes to check a catheter tube directly into the chest cavity, which drained fluid from the lungs. He seemed satisfied, and stood back, hands clasped behind his back, rocking on to his heels.

'He's gonna be all right, ain't he?' Sadie pleaded for the right answer.

'It's too soon to say. We'll do all we can.' Another cool, professional voice refused to get involved.

'Why, what's the matter with him?'

'Crushed ribs, punctured left lung. Perhaps abdominal injuries. We don't know yet.'

'What's that mean?' She wanted a plain answer. 'He ain't gonna die, is he?'

There was no eye contact with the reply. 'As I said, it's too soon to tell. First of all, we must drain the fluid from his lungs, wait for him to regain consciousness, before we can really assesss the damage.'

The answer crushed her. Her head went down, tears came.

The doctor went and called the nurse, who drew up a chair for Sadie at the bedside, told her she could sit for ten minutes and advised Rob to take a seat beside her. Then she went off.

Sadie gazed at Walter through her tears. Only the scar across his forehead, the pale skin made him look different. He could be sleeping, one brown lock of hair falling forwards over his brow, dark lashes fringing his eyes, a small pulse flickering at the corner of his jaw. Soon he would open his eyes and smile to see her there.

'Walter,' Sadie whispered. Gently she pushed the stray lock back into place. 'Don't leave us, Walt.' She wanted him back down the court, bringing home the treat for her tea.

She watched the shallow, difficult breaths, glanced with horror at the tube feeding under the bedclothes, between the ribs of the wire cage.

'Time to go.' The nurse came back at last. 'You can come and see him again tomorrow, if you like. But there's no more you can do here now.' She took Sadie by the elbow and led her and Rob away, out of the ward, up the long corridor. Without the nurse's support, Sadie felt she would swoon away into nothingness.

'Take her home, look after her,' the nurse told Rob. 'It's hit her pretty hard. I wouldn't leave her by herself tonight if I was you. You can come again tomorrow.'

They left the hospital; Duke and Annie, Rob and Sadie. News went up and down Paradise Court: Walter Davidson was in a bad way. His brakes had failed and he hit a tram. He was unconscious in the infirmary. They reckoned his chances were fifty-fifty.

'He's strong and he's a fighter. He'll pull through,' some said.

Others shook their heads. 'You never saw the cab when they pulled it clear. Crushed like a matchbox, it was.'

Bonfires were lit for Guy Fawkes, the night sky exploded with firecrackers. In the morning, the smell of spent fireworks hung in the damp air. The police called early on Rob Parsons at the depot in Meredith Court.

Rob had spent the night in fitful dozes and sudden, chilly starts into consciousness. Unable to face breakfast, and keen to be on the spot for any news, he kissed Amy an early goodbye, went to work and sat through the grey hour of dawn on 6 November reliving Walter's parting words, 'Back by eleven ... Waterloo.' It could so easily have been him, he thought. It *should* have been him; *his* cab, *his* accident.

When the police knocked on the yard gates at seven in the morning, he went to greet them with shaking hands.

'Any news from the hospital?' He broke the silence, turned on a few lights, invited the two bobbies into the office.

'Not that we heard.' It was Grigg, the eager constable from the Wiggin investigation, in charge now of an even younger raw recruit. 'No, we came to find out if by any chance Richie Palmer's shown his face.'

'No, why?' Rob was surprised they thought he might. Everyone was convinced they'd seen the last of him after the spiteful break-in at the depot. The coppers had all the evidence: Richie's missing cap and coat, the fact that the thief knew his way around, the clincher of George Mann seeing him sneak down the court. 'Does that mean you ain't seen hide nor hair of him neither?'

Constable Grigg shook his head. 'Bleeding Houdini. Vanished into thin air.'

'So what brings you down here, if you ain't got no news?' Rob lit up a cigarette to steady his nerves.

'We never said that.' The copper sat self-importantly in the spare office chair; Walter's chair.

Rob shot him a glance. 'What's going on?'

After much throat-clearing and settling of his helmet on

the desk, Grigg went on, 'We think there may be a link between the burglary and yesterday's accident,' he claimed. 'According to witnesses, the cab swerved into the path of the oncoming tramcar to avoid a pedestrian, a young lad called Dixie Smethurst. They couldn't understand why the cab never braked, see. They said his speed never altered. Some of them said they seen sparks fly, and when we took a look, we found loose brake rods lying in the road, some distance from the collison. Then we got an expert in to look at the cab, and he's sure the brakes had been tampered with.'

Rob sat stunned. 'You think Richie done that? Is that what you're saying?'

'We want you to help us out, sir. According to our bloke, there's meant to be a pin through a bolt that yokes all the rods together. If the pin comes loose and falls out, sooner or later that bolt, the clevis pin, comes apart, and Bob's your uncle!'

He nodded. 'That's right. And Richie just put a new split-pin in, the afternoon I went and gave him the sack.' Rob tailed off as he realized the implications. 'Oh, my God!'

The constable nodded. 'As far as we can tell, there was no split-pin holding the whole thing in place. What we're saying is, that cab was a death-trap.'

Rob stared in disbelief. 'That's *my* cab you're on about!'

'It seems like your days should've been numbered, the minute you gave Richie Palmer his marching orders. Only the plan backfired.'

'He done it on purpose?'

'You say he'd worked on the brakes?' The policeman stood up. As it happened, he didn't feel as good about delivering the result of the investigation as he expected. There was nothing wrong with the detective work: it was the effect it had on those who were innocent. He watched Rob struggling to hold himself together. 'So it looks like he made a proper job of getting his own back: breaking in here to nick the cash, *and* making a little adjustment to the brakes. That's how it looks. Only, he never guessed Mr Davidson would take the cab out that one time. He got the wrong man, as it turns out.'

Rob nodded. 'Thanks. I'll think this through.'

'We ain't got no hard and fast evidence, mind. Not till we get our hands on the suspect.' He put his hat on and pulled the strap under his chin.

Rob showed them out. 'No evidence. I got that.' He watched them up the street, two caped, uniformed figures, thinking he would have to go and tell Sadie the latest development. If she felt anything like he did, she'd straight-away see Walt's blood on her own hands for taking Richie back.

Sadie herself had been up since dawn. She tended to Meggie and left her in Edith's care for five minutes while she popped up the street to see Amy. Rob had already gone to work, Amy said. There was no news from the hospital.

Sadie nodded and returned home. Curtains were still drawn. A lad came down the court delivering milk. Safely upstairs in her own room, she checked the baby and started work on a typing task. When Rob came up and knocked on the door, she answered it quietly.

'Come in, Rob.' She was surprised, uneasy. She thought he was busy at work. 'What is it?'

'Can I sit down?' He avoided looking at her and sat at the table. He noticed she had the room tidy. A fire was already lit, small articles of clothing hung to air around the wire-mesh fire-guard.

She steeled herself, drew her own chair towards him. 'It must be something bad. You look done in.'

He nodded. 'It's Richie.'

'They ain't found him, have they?'

'No. There's no sign. But they think he's gone and done something terrible.'

'It couldn't be worse, surely.' Presentiments crowded in. She remembered sending him away with scornful, stinging words ringing in his ears.

Rob made a tight fist and thumped the table. 'Don't I wish I never told Walter he was in Hoxton!' he repented bitterly.

Sadie closed her hand over his. 'You done it for the best. I know that.'

'I should've known better.'

'So what's he done now?' She felt stretched to breaking-point, unless Rob told her soon.

'They think the accident was his fault. The brakes on my cab; they think he had a go at them. A death-trap, that's what they said it was. Richie wanted me dead, and that's a fact.'

Sadie shuddered. 'You saying he tried to do you in?' Was Richie capable of this, she wondered. Would he go so far? He was drunk. He hated Rob like poison. He deliberately smashed all he had to smithereens and left her and Meggie in a desperate state. 'Yes,' she said slowly. 'I believe he did.'

'But poor old Walter got it in the neck instead. I hope he ain't gonna die,' Rob pleaded. 'He's gonna pull through, ain't he, Sadie?'

'He is,' she breathed.

Rob got shakily to his feet. 'I wanted to come and tell you for myself, before word got round.'

She nodded. 'Thanks, Rob.'

'You'll be all right?'

Sadie stared back at him, her dark eyes blank. 'Me? Yes, I'm fine.' But she was racked by a spasm of bleak, bitter guilt. She put a hand to her mouth, turned deathly pale.

Rob caught her before she could fall. He sat her down, heard her begin to cry. She leaned against the chair. 'I'm sorry, I'm sorry!' She wept for every one of her mistakes, for Rob's narrow escape, for Walter. 'I been as bad as I could be to him, Rob! I ditched him, then I played on his good nature. Why doesn't he hate me for it?'

'He loves you,' Rob said quietly. 'He always has.'

'And I treated him rotten.' She sobbed, as if her heart would finally break. Then she looked up through her tears. 'I want him to live, Rob. Make him live!'

'He's gonna be all right, you see. Walt's like a brother to me.'

'Oh, yes,' she cried, and held on to him. 'We can't lose him, not like this, please God!'

On the afternoon of the accident Jess telephoned Maurice in Manchester, and, leaving everything under the charge of his deputy, he took the evening train down.

In spite of his reason for being there, his spirits rose as he stepped off at King's Cross, glad to be back on home turf. Grey stone instead of red brick, plain classical lines instead of the Victorian scrolls and furbelows of Manchester's master brickies. Even the Underground seemed familiar and welcoming, inviting cosy purchases of Quaker Oats, Nestlé's chocolate and Player's Navy Cut.

At home in Ealing, Jess told him the latest news on Walter. They were to visit the hospital next day, slotting in after Annie and Duke, if all went well. In his own mind, Maurice readily believed that Walter's toughness of character would see him through; a view which would hold good only until the first hospital visit brought home the frailty of the human condition.

Talking in bed together, after a gentle and loving reunion, Maurice admitted to Jess that he was feeling homesick. 'It ain't just you and Mo and Grace,' he confessed. 'It's the whole place I miss. The smell and the feel of it.'

She smiled, luxuriating in the warmth of his body. 'You ain't going soft on us, are you?' She'd never thought of him as nostalgic; only as forward-looking, thrusting into the future, feeding people their impossible celluloid dreams.

He grinned back. 'A tiny little bit maybe.'

'You ain't serious?' She put her arms around his neck, wondering where this would lead.

'Why?' Absence had worked its miracle: to him Jess seemed lovelier than ever. She'd softened into her old ways, and that evening as he'd watched her putting the children to bed, he'd realized what a good mother she was; practical and calm, ready to smile and praise, full of cuddles and goodnight promises.

''Cos I been thinking about us, Maurice.'

He unwrapped her arms from around his neck. 'Am I gonna like this?'

'I don't know. Are you?' She took a deep breath and lay back on her pillow. 'I've been thinking, the family needs to be together. I been over and over it: how can I make it happen withouut giving up the things that mean something to me; the shop, designing, taking a pride in all of that.'

393

He nodded, leaning on one elbow and jutting out his chin. 'Go on, hit me as hard as you like,' he invited. 'I deserve it for dropping the choice in your lap. It weren't fair.'

'Is that you saying sorry, Maurice Leigh?' She turned towards him, a smile playing around her lips. 'Well, it was a hard decision, I don't mind telling you. But I finally talked it through with Ett earlier this week, and we think we come up with the answer.' Pulling the sheets around her, she sat up and hugged her knees.

'Come on then. Spit it out.'

'Who says Ett and me only have to design and sell clothes here in London? When you think about it, why can't I do the same thing anywhere I like?'

He caught on. 'In Manchester, even?'

'Yes, or in Leeds, or Bradford. The women up there like to dress up in nice things, don't they?'

'I should say so,' he said slowly.

'Well, then, that's the idea. I'll move up to Manchester and open a new branch. Hettie will work from here, but we'll get together on the designing. We'll sell up here and buy a house in Manchester if you like, and find Mo and Grace good schools. What do you say?'

'Is that what you want?' He held his breath. No more Mrs Walters. Farewell to her travelling gentlemen and her snuffling Pekineses.

Jess smiled at him. 'You won't go on at me for opening another shop? We're not asking you for money, mind. This is something we want to do for ourselves. But I won't have no time to go to the library for you, or nothing like that. I'm gonna be busy, Maurice, I give you fair warning.'

He put up his hands in surrender. 'Anything you say, Jess.'

'Don't look so gormless, for God's sake. I ain't said we'll fly to the moon together!' She gave him a gentle push. He toppled sideways, clean out of bed. 'Maurice!' She scrambled after him towards the edge.

He pulled her down on top of him, and they lay on the floor, tangled in sheets and eiderdown.

'It's settled, then?'

'What about your pa?'

'He's got Annie and Ernie, and there's Ett and Sadie and Frances. And Rob,' she added.

That night they slept peacefully, their big decision made. They'd move north. London would be all the nicer to come home to: Duke Street and Paradise Court, with Duke in the old pub, God willing, and Walter on the mend, everything as it was, nicely in place.

Next morning Sadie had her heart set on finding Walter fully conscious and sitting up in bed. Annie, recognizing her change of heart towards her old flame, warned her not to hope for too much. Rob drove her to the hospital to keep an eye on her if Walter turned out not to be as well as she expected. He couldn't help but feel proud of his sister, walking with her head up, her wavy hair hidden under a cream cloche hat, her pretty dark face set in determined lines. They parted in the waiting-room and Sadie went on ahead, down the already familiar corridor to Walter's ward.

There were old men in here, mere skeletons, hanging on to life by a thread. There were men with mottled faces and high fevers, men with hoarse, rattling coughs and hollow eyes. Walter was not as sick as any of these, she told herself. He was ten times as strong, with everything to live for.

She approached his bed. 'He's awake,' the nurse whispered. 'And asking for Sadie.'

'That's me.' Sadie nodded and went forward. The wire cage lay in place. Walter was flat on his back, still connected to tubes.

The only piece of him that seemed alive was his face. With the rest of his body deathly still, his dark eyes slid sideways at her approach. She saw the click of recognition, checked her own distress and broke out in pleased tones, 'Walter, what have you been up to, you bleeding idiot? Giving us heart failure like this.' She bustled up and took off her hat, sat down, bent to put one hand against his pillow. 'What happened? No, don't try to talk. Tell me later. God, you ain't half given us all a shock.' She chattered on, trying to breathe life back into him. 'What have they told you, Walt? How long are you gonna have to lie there with them tube things sticking in you?'

'Sadie,' he whispered.

She put a hand on his shoulder.

'Sadie.'

'I'm here. Don't cry, Walt. I can't bear it. Listen, Annie and Duke and everyone send their love. Rob's outside waiting. He says, how's he supposed to get by without you?' Gradually her voice broke down. 'Oh, Walt, what is it? What do you want?'

'Sadie?' His eyes beseeched her. The word rolled around his mouth and seemed to fall from his lips like a heavy stone.

'I'm here, Walt. I'm here for as long as you want me to stay.'

He closed his eyes.

'Walt!' She could see he was tired, but it seemed more

than that. She was afraid he was going to slip away from her for good.

His eyes opened.

'You're gonna be all right, Walt.'

He shook his head and sighed. 'I want you to stay, you hear? Don't leave me now.' He tried to free a hand from under the bedclothes, but the vigilant nurse came and told him to lie still. 'Don't send her away,' he whispered.

Sadie looked up through her tears at the nurse.

'I don't know about that.' She looked doubtfully down the ward. 'I'll have to ask Dr Matthews.'

'Please.' Walter managed another faint sound.

The nurse nodded and went off.

It would have taken an army of doctors to shift Sadie from Walter's bedside. 'I'm still here, Walt. You sleep. I'll be here when you wake up.' She stroked his cold, clammy face, she listened to his breathing, scarcely moving a muscle in all the hours she sat there.

Matthews, the thickset doctor in the good City suit, with the gold watch-chain and the look of a prosperous merchant, reported instead to Rob. 'Your sister's still with him, Mr Parsons. He's very poorly, I'm afraid. The fluid has seeped into the chest cavity. We're doing our best to clear it, but our guess is that it's gathered around the heart and that will affect the rhythm of the heartbeat. He's a strong young man, granted, and the heart muscle's good, but it's a matter of draining off the fluid before it affects things too badly. There may be an infection too, and that can inflame the heart.' He shrugged. 'You understand what I'm saying?'

Rob nodded. 'But he ain't gonna die?'

'Touch and go, Mr Parsons. Touch and go. Try to

persuade your sister to have a rest. There's no point her wearing herself out, you know.'

'You won't prise her away from there,' Rob warned, as dogged as Sadie herself. 'Ain't no point even trying.'

During the course of the day all the Parsons family filtered in to sit for a few minutes with Sadie by Walter's bedside. No one spoke much. Sadie stroked his face and whispered to him. He woke in the early hours of next morning to find her still sitting there. 'See,' she said. 'I knew you'd wake in your own good time.'

He smiled weakly. She slipped her hand between the sheets and held on to his.

'Anyhow, Walter Davidson, just hurry up and get better and let's get you out of here. I can't stand hospitals, they make me come over all shaky.'

He gripped her hand. 'You and me, Sadie. You and me both.'

'Well, that's a good enough reason to get you out,' she promised with a brave smile.

If her willpower could do it, combined with Walter's strength and courage, they would get him home. Between them they'd pull him through, for all the doctors' shaking heads and the nice, neat nurses' cold sympathy.

CHAPTER TWENTY-SEVEN

Fever set in. The infection that the doctor had feared took hold and racked Walter's weakened frame. For days he was delirious on a nightmare sea, dredging past horrors to the surface; the whine of bullets, the stinging stench of mustard gas, the unburied dead.

He saw the faces of his young pals, smoking cigarettes, hunched up in the trenches over letters from homes that they would never see again. He stepped over them, face-down in the mud, praying that the whine of the shell with his own name written on it would never reach his terrified ears and send him reeling down into the chambers of darkest hell.

They fought to keep down the fever, tried to persuade Sadie to get some rest.

'He won't know you, even if he does come round,' they told her. 'Not at present.'

'I said I'd be here,' she said stubbornly. She turned to Walter's unconscious form. 'I will be, Walter. There ain't nothing or no one can take me away from you, never again.' She would only agree at last to give up her place at the bedside to Rob, who volunteered to sit with his friend on the third night after the accident. 'You send for me the minute he wakes up,' she made him promise.

Annie took her home to see Meggie and to persuade her to sleep.

Rob took up the vigil. A strange calm came over him as he sat at the bedside in the quiet ward. Walter's face was thin and pale but not much marked, except for the livid scar on his forehead. There was no sign of struggle; only sharp, shallow breaths and beads of sweat on his brow, which Rob sponged with a cold cloth. The night nurse passed occasionally. Far off down the ward, a man coughed and turned in his sleep.

At three o'clock, Walter opened his eyes. He turned his head towards Rob. 'Where's Sadie?' He sounded peaceful and rational.

'At home, having a rest.' Rob leaned forward so that Walter could have a clear view of him. Walter nodded and sighed. 'Know something? I think things is gonna be fine between us from now on.' He had a misty memory of Sadie leaning over him and whispering that nothing would take her away ever again.

Rob nodded. 'I said I'd sit with you for a while.'

Walter hovered on the edge of consciousness, lured by the warm, drifting haziness of sleep, alarmed by his crisp, clinical surroundings. He focused on Rob. 'What time is it?'

'Three in the morning. Don't you worry, Walt, they're taking good care of you.'

Walter sighed. 'How's Sadie?'

'Worried sick, if you must know. She don't let on though.' He thought she'd been a marvel of toughness and loyalty. It had taken the accident to do it, but her feelings for Walter were shining out strong and true.

'And little Meggie?'

'Happy as Larry.' Rob kept his voice to a whisper. He

knew the nurse was keeping an eye on them. 'What about you, pal?'

'Not so good, Rob. I'm weak as a bleeding kitten.'

'I ain't surprised.' Rob whispered an account of the accident and Walter's injuries. He took care not to upset him by mentioning Richie Palmer's probable part in the whole ugly business. 'We all knew you'd give it your best shot, though. Sadie, she won't listen to no Jeremiahs. She says you're tougher than any bleeding tramcar!'

Walter smiled.

Rob leaned forward to speak in his ear. 'I reckon she might be right. We're proud of you, Walt, for doing what you did. The kid got off without a scratch, thanks to you.' He watched his friend give a faint nod.

'I ain't done nothing special.'

'We think you have, and you gotta keep that in mind. It's a hero's welcome for you, Walt, when we get you out of here, back to the old Duke.' Rob's voice trembled.

'How's that?' Walt stared at him. Had he heard right?

'I said, back to the old Duke. That's where we'll be celebrating when you get back. Pa just got the word from Wakeley at the brewery. The licence came through for George this morning. He's taking over. It's all signed and sealed.'

Walter grasped his hand.

Rob nodded. 'We're all thrilled to bits. Ett says she'll finish with the Sally Army. Her major says it's the right thing. She says Ett's given the Army more than most already, and God won't mind her helping to run a decent, honest pub. You know Ett, she'd give her last farthing away. She's a saint.' He chatted on, knowing that the good news would help raise Walter's spirits.

'Whoa!' he protested. 'You say it's all settled?'

'Signed, sealed and delivered.'

'Blimey.'

The nurse came up at last and warned Rob not to overtire her patient. She checked his temperature. 'Going down nicely,' she reported.

When Sadie came in early the following morning, Walter was sleeping peacefully. Dr Matthews came and studied his charts, sounded his chest without waking him. He nodded briefly.

'What's he say?' Sadie demanded of another brisk, pretty nurse, as soon as the doctor had passed by.

'He says things look a lot brighter than they did this time yesterday,' she reported.

Sadie held her breath. She thought she saw the colour creep back into Walter's cheeks as he slept.

So far, since she'd realized the depth of her feelings for Walt, she'd merely managed to outstare despair, convincing herself with blind faith that he would pull through. Now she relaxed as she looked at him. His breathing was deeper, he slept soundly, without the haunted, tormented look. They said he was over the worst.

He would come back to Duke Street. She thanked God and the doctors and nurses. For the first time since the accident, she was able to think beyond Walter lying in danger on his hospital bed, to having him home safe and well.

There was a collective deep breath down Duke Street as Walter Davidson turned the corner on the road to recovery. His survival raised spirits and was seen as the triumph of courage over adversity. It made a change from short-time working, rising prices and dire warnings on the radio against the depraved new craze for Dixieland jazz. This, and the prospect of Duke returning to his pub, under the auspices of George and Hettie Mann, brought the year of 1925 to a happy close.

They likened Richie Palmer's disappearance to the famous music hall illusionist, Lafayette. He'd vanished in a puff of smoke. It was just as well: a lynching mood overtook the men of the area whenever they thought of him tampering with the brakes on Rob's car; an ugly, riotous intention which the police were glad to see dissolve, as Christmas approached. There was no trace of Palmer, either in Mile End or in Hoxton, and they made no great effort to bring him to book. People said he'd joined the restless, unhoused tramps whose shadowy figures drifted under the railway arches and along the Embankment: anonymous, faceless, hopeless men who shrugged off another layer of their humanity with each cold and bitter night they spent, numbed by drink, drifting into oblivion.

Sadie shivered when she thought of him. Richie and Wiggin began to mingle in her mind. She cried when she thought of what he might have been, decently set up in the motor trade, with a loving family. She forced her mind over what had sent him downhill on his destructive path. In the end, she saw that forces of degradation were too strong for some; for every Maurice who rose out of the bleak misery of East End poverty there were ten thousand Richies. She felt that in her own distress she had judged him too harshly. 'Poor Richie,' she thought now. 'I read him wrong, right from the start.'

As usual, Annie was the one to pull Sadie out of the past. 'Ain't no use moping, not when you've got more than enough to do already.'

'I ain't moping, Annie.' Sadie folded freshly laundered clothes for Meggie.

'You been over to see Walter lately?'

'This morning. I took Meggie along. He's nicely on the mend, he says.'

'And what about you and him?' Annie's inquisition was less sharp than it sounded. She wanted to heal the wounds for good, now that Walter had been given a date for coming home. 'We don't want no more rows over you-know-who!'

Sadie sighed. 'Over Richie. No, I ain't gonna think no more about him. Walter says I weren't the one to blame.' She ran her fingertips along her forehead. 'It's good of him, Annie, but it ain't all that easy to forgive myself.'

Annie took her up sharply. 'Oh, so you *meant* Richie to go and take them bleeding brakes to bits, did you? You meant Walter to jump right into Rob's car and have his accident? On top of getting yourself dumped with a kid and no job? It was part of your plan? Oh, very clever, I must say!'

Sadie felt her eyes smart. ''Course not.'

'Well, then.' Annie's fierce gaze drew a smile from her stepdaughter. 'Listen, girl, if Walt's forgiven you, I should say you're duty bound to let yourself off the hook, otherwise we'll all end up in the cart!'

'You're a hard-hearted woman, Annie Parsons. Can't a girl have no guilty feelings?'

Annie shook her head. 'Who did you intend to harm? That's the test.'

'No one.'

'Well, then.'

'But it ain't just the accident. I treated Walter rotten from the start.'

'Bleeding hell, if they handed out medals for feeling bad,

you'd be the first in line. Like I said before, did you plan it so that Walter Davidson would mope after you for the rest of his life? Or did he choose that for himself?'

Sadie shrugged. 'I never meant to hurt him, you know that. And so does he. I told him that in the hospital this morning. He's been very good.'

'More fool him, then.'

'Annie! Whose side are you on?'

'You just mind how you go, and don't go leading him on, not unless you made up your mind this time.'

Sadie was exasperated. She went through to the other room to lift Meggie and get her ready for a trip to the market. 'I thought you said not to feel bad.' Now she couldn't make head nor tail of Annie's inconsistent advice.

'Just don't take him for granted, that's all.' Annie took Meggie into her arms and smiled down at her. 'Dress up nice for his homecoming. He'd like that.'

Sadie grinned. She saw that Annie wasn't beyond a spot of matchmaking. They went downstairs together and walked up the court, Annie still carrying Meggie. They paused on the corner to watch the workmen restore the old pub name. Down came the Prince of Wales, up went the Duke of Wellington, in traditional gold letters against a beautiful green background. Annie beamed and nodded. 'Prince of Bleeding Wales!' she chuntered, handing Meggie over to Sadie, shaking her head and trudging back up to her haberdashery stall.

Walter came home from hospital on 12 December. Rob drove him down an empty Duke Street. It was half past five. The traders had packed up their market stalls and the street-lamps were already lit. Walter noticed the lights on in

Jenny Oldfield

Cooper's old place. The co-op was already well stocked for Christmas, with game-birds hanging in windows piled high with cheeses, tins, pies, cakes, nuts and dates. There was a buzz of activity. Shop boys mopped the floors and shook out the doormats. Girls wiped down the counters. Blinds came down and lights went off as they closed up for the day.

'Good to be back?' Rob grinned. He held open the door for Walt to step on to the pavement outside the Duke.

Walter stared up at the old building. The name felt right. He wasn't so sure about the electric lights as he stepped inside. Gas ones had been good enough before Bertie Hill came and upset the applecart.

Sadie came out on to the front step to greet him, dressed in a lovely, soft dress of pale blue wool. She held out both arms. For a moment he clasped her to him.

'Come on, you two love birds, get a move on!' Rob stood on the pavement in the icy wind.

Sadie ignored him. 'I love you, Walter Davidson,' she said. 'And I don't care who knows it.'

'At this rate, that's the whole bleeding world,' Rob grumbled. He pushed past the embracing couple and swung open the doors into the crowded bar.

Inside, Tommy led the rousing cheer of greeting. He stood there grinning like a Cheshire cat, a pint in his hand. Walter released Sadie at last and went up to shake his free hand warmly. He let the noise die down before he walked across to the bar, leaned both elbows on the copper top and waited for Duke to come up and serve him.

Duke slung a teatowel over one shoulder. He stuck his thumbs in his waistcoat pockets and took his time. He winked at Annie. 'What'll it be?' he inquired.

'A pint of best, please, Duke.' Walter enjoyed every

406

syllable. He watched the action of the pump handle as the old man drew the clear, amber liquid from the barrel.

'It's on the house,' Duke said, 'and a Happy Christmas to you.'

'Down the hatch.' Walter grinned.

There was another cheer. Grace darted out of the crowd and began to dance around the guest of honour. Soon Rosie O'Hagan followed, and the formality of the welcoming group broke up. Walter found his hand shaken right, left and centre. All the regulars were there: Joe and Arthur, Tommy with another new girl, Charlie talking ten to the dozen about his college course. There were newcomers from the co-op swelling the crowd, and ever more customers walked in off the street at the sound of cheerful celebration.

George and Duke worked as a team, serving pint after pint. Ernie put in a marathon washing-up stint, while Annie and Hettie went round clearing empties. Dolly insisted on music.

'Scott Joplin!' one of the girls from Dickins and Jones cried out.

'Scott who?' Dolly dug deep into the box of pianola rolls.

'No, the hokey-cokey!'

'Ta-ra-ra-boom-de-ay!'

'Give a girl a chance,' Dolly muttered. 'How about this one, "Abide With Me"?'

'God save us!' Annie came and turfed her to one side. She delved into the box. '"Tipperary", "Sister Susie".' One by one, the wartime favourites were discarded.

'"Ragtime Infantry"!' Tommy leaned across and pulled out the roll he wanted. Before anyone could stop him, he slotted it into position and set the pianola playing. He began to march in and out of the tables, followed by Mo, Grace and Rosie, leading them in a raucous chorus, with the pianola thumping out the tune in the background.

'We are Fred Karno's Army, the ragtime infantry,
We cannot fight, we cannot march, what bleeding good
    are we?'

'Tommy!' Jess stood up to protest, but Maurice grinned and held her back.

'And when we get to Berlin, the Kaiser he will say,
Hoch, hoch, mein Gott, what a bloody rotten lot
Are the ragtime infantry!'

'That ain't nice, Tommy!' Dolly pretended to be shocked. 'You little ones, you cover up your ears, you hear!'

Mo clapped both hands to his head and marched on. '*Hoch, hoch, mein Gott,*' he chanted, while Grace and Mo filled in the rest.

New music soon took over. Sadie, Amy and Frances brought down food on large wooden trays: cheese-straws, sandwiches, pies. The party was in full swing. Soon Walter drifted across to chat to Sadie. She slid her arm around his waist and gave his cheek a kiss, bold as anything. Walter blushed, but he looked like a man whose dreams had come true.

Looking on from across the room, Rob thought that Sadie seemed different; less cocksure somehow, and more gentle. She was still pretty enough to turn heads, though.

He turned to Amy. 'Is Bobby asleep?'

She nodded. 'In Sadie's old room, with Meggie. They've

got their heads on the pillow like two little angels. Come up and take a look.' She could tell he wanted to.

They crept upstairs hand-in-hand to view the sleeping children, and afterwards stayed in the old living-room, listening to the laughter and music rise.

Duke had taken his eyes off Walter and Sadie for a moment to watch Rob and Amy go upstairs. He glanced round the bar at the joking, laughing crowd, caught sight of Frances and Billy sitting talking to Edith Cooper. He spotted Jess, and remembered the family would soon have to bear another split when Maurice took them off to Manchester, and good luck to them. Sadie caught his eye and smiled. She passed more empty glasses to Ernie. 'Here,' Annie said, shoving Ernie along. 'Let a dog see the rabbit.' Soon she was up to her elbows in soap suds, helping him get through the work.

George went down and tapped two new barrels. He rolled the old ones off the gantry and stood them on end. At this rate they'd need to re-order before the end of the week. He came up from the cellar and grinned at Duke.

'You seen the time, Duke?' Annie finished at the sink and glanced at the clock above the till. 'Time for last orders.'

'Let's give them just a few more minutes,' he suggested, reluctant to break things up. The music was still in full swing, the party at its height.

'Duke Parsons!' Annie gave him the full force of her most severe stare. 'If you don't go and put them towels over them pumps, I'll do it myself!'

He grumbled, but he knew she was right. 'Time, gentlemen, please!' he called in his gravelly voice.

Slowly they drank up and wished Duke and George goodnight. 'Never thought we'd live to see the day.' Arthur shook Duke's hand and slapped his shoulder.

'O ye of little faith!' Dolly quoted. She pulled him from the bar. 'Bleeding limpet,' she complained. Then she hooked her arm through Arthur's and turned for a final say. 'We all knew you'd get back where you belong, Duke!'

He turned and thanked them. 'Come along now. Time, gents!'

The noise died. The doors swung and closed until the pub stood empty. The family left Duke to lock up and went upstairs. He slotted the bolts into position, taking a moment to look around the old place, hearing last orders echo down the years.